Nicola Thorne is the author of a number of well-known novels which include *Champagne Gold*, *Pride of Place*, *Where the Rivers Meet*, *Bird of Passage* and The Askham Chronicles (*Never Such Innocence*, *Yesterday's Promises*, *Bright Morning* and *A Place in the Sun*). Born in South Africa, she was educated at the LSE. She lived for many years in London, but has now made her home in Dorset.

By the same author

The Girls
In Love
Bridie Climbing
A Woman Like Us
The Perfect Wife and Mother
The Daughters of the House
Where the Rivers Meet
Affairs of Love
The Enchantress Saga
Champagne
Pride of Place
Bird of Passage
The Rector's Daughter
Champagne Gold

The Askham Chronicles:
Never Such Innocence
Yesterday's Promises
Bright Morning
A Place in the Sun

NICOLA THORNE

A Wind in Summer

This edition published by Diamond Books, 2000

Diamond Books is an imprint of
HarperCollins*Publishers*
77-85 Fulham Palace Road,
Hammersmith, London W6 8JB

First published by Grafton 1993
9 8 7 6 5 4 3 2 1

A catalogue record for this book
is available from the British Library

ISBN 0 26 167397 1

Set in Meridien

Printed and bound in Great Britain by
Caledonian International Book Manufacturing Ltd, Glasgow

Contents

What is more gentle than a wind in summer?
John Keats, *Sleep and Poetry*

PART ONE

Father and Sons

1932–1944

Chapter 1

Doctor Geoffrey Blair sat bowed over his desk writing busily, while, on the other side, his patient waited humbly.

'There,' Doctor Blair said, handing the woman opposite him a script. 'Three spoonfuls a day until the pain subsides. If it doesn't, come and see me again in a week.'

'Thank you, Doctor,' the woman said submissively, taking the piece of paper and rising. 'How much do I owe you, Doctor?' She fumbled awkwardly in the shabby handbag that hung from her wrist.

'See how you feel next week,' the doctor said with a kindly smile. 'We can talk about money then.'

The woman mumbled something, turned her back and walked rather slowly to the door as if she had more on her mind than the state of her health. Doctor Blair rose and, swiftly overtaking her, stood in front of the door before opening it.

'I shan't charge you, Minnie, you know that,' he said. 'There's no need to pay me until Jim gets work again.'

'It's worry that's making him ill.'

'And you too, Minnie.' Geoffrey Blair bent and looked into her faded, once undoubtedly pretty eyes. 'You won't get better if you worry too much about Jim, or the children. You must think of yourself as well.'

Minnie Parsons put out her hand and he pressed it. Her eyes filled with tears. 'You're a very good man, Doctor Blair,' she said rather tersely and brushed past him through the door.

Sitting at her own desk in the reception area outside the surgery, Catherine Wills looked up with an air of resignation as Mrs Parsons walked straight past her and went through the outside door.

She glanced at Geoffrey Blair who still stood with his hand on the knob of the door leading to his surgery. The reception area was now empty and, rising slowly from her desk, Catherine crossed the room and locked the outside door. Then she turned towards the doctor, the expression on her face changing to one of reproach.

'You can't go *on* like that, not charging your patients, Doctor Blair. You'll be in the dole queue yourself.'

It was 1932 and the Depression had affected Netherwick as much as any other area of England. In the north it was particularly severe. Maybe Netherwick was protected by the fact that it was a prosperous market town on the edge of the Yorkshire Dales, but it was a centre of the woollen industry too and some of its mills had laid off workers; others had closed down for good. Jim Parsons was one of the unlucky ones who had been affected by the closure of a long-established family business and had been on the dole for months.

Doctor Blair hadn't replied to his receptionist's reproaches but, instead, wandered back into his surgery, drawing the curtains against the cold and the encroaching dark outside. In the grate a fire burned brightly, and an oil burner in the corner protected those of his patients who had to remove items of clothing for medical examination.

It was a warm, friendly room lacking the usual austerity of a doctor's surgery. Doctor Blair returned to his desk and went through the cards of the patients he had seen that evening, making notes on their conditions, the treatment prescribed and, in the space provided for a fee, invariably leaving a blank.

When he had finished his notes he gathered up his cards and returned to the reception area where Catherine sat frowning at the paper in her typewriter before glancing at a card beside her on her desk.

'Do you actually *want* to refer Mrs Longridge to Mr Banks privately, or to the hospital, Doctor Blair?'

Even with a scowl on her brow she looked so appealing, Geoffrey Blair thought, standing by the side of her desk, scarcely paying any attention to what she was saying. She had pale golden hair and a peculiarly white translucent skin; her eyebrows swept upwards tapering to a point which focused the gaze of the onlooker on the deep recesses of her eyes. Conscious of his expression she averted her eyes, concentrating on the task before her.

'Er . . .' Geoffrey Blair leaned over the desk so that he could read the document in question and, at the same time, inhale the very faint perfume which was part of her freshness and naturalness.

'It's really a question of money,' Catherine said.

'Oh, she can afford private fees,' Doctor Blair said, aware that the moment of intimacy had passed. 'And,' he stared at her over his half-moon glasses, 'so can Mr Binns. Now, Mrs Hapgood . . .' He took another card from her desk and looked at it, scratching the side of his face. 'No, I'm afraid she'll have to go to the clinic at the hospital.' Suddenly he slumped in the chair beside her desk and let the card dangle between his hands. 'It is a terrible business you know, Catherine, when people can't afford medical treatment. Some perfectly respectable people are now forced to beg for charity.'

'Not here,' Catherine said, again pursing her lips. 'Do you know, I reckon that about half the people you see don't pay you . . .'

'Don't pay me *now*, Catherine,' Doctor Blair chided her

gently, 'but they will. When times improve they will.'

'Yes, but when *will* they improve?' Catherine sharply drew the paper from her typewriter and screwed it into a ball before committing it to the wastepaper basket. 'Everyone says the Depression shows no signs of lifting.' But her question seemed a rhetorical one and she proceeded with the typing while Geoffrey, conscious of her proximity, continued to sort through his patients' cards, reluctant to leave her side.

He well understood Catherine's worry. Her family were millworkers, ordinary townsfolk of Netherwick but, as yet, unaffected by the Depression. Her father and mother worked in the mill together with a brother and two sisters; but, so far, it had been one of the successful ones, relatively unaffected by the times.

It was a life that had never appealed to Catherine. She was pretty and she was ambitious, and after working for some time in a baker's shop, she decided to go to one of the new secretarial colleges that were springing up for the women newly emancipated by the challenge of war work, the promise of the vote and the whole host of opportunities that had opened up for women ever since.

But Catherine, who had been born the year before Geoffrey Blair qualified as a doctor, had little recollection of those times. She was a modern woman, a woman of the post-war world and twenty-three years younger than the employer she had worked for for two years.

She was much, much too young for him.

The doctor cleared his throat and suddenly stood up, his expression business-like. 'Now, have you any letters for me to sign before you go?'

It was true they were worrying times, but when hadn't they been since the end of the war? Geoffrey Blair had qualified in 1912, but poor sight had kept him out of the army and, with a few doctors, mostly of retirement age, he had helped to look after the population of Netherwick then as he had done ever since.

Netherwick had been scarcely touched by the war except in the number of men who had lost their lives fighting in the trenches, particularly on the Somme, where the enthusiastic 'pals' brigades had been decimated. Netherwick had its share of memorials of the dead as much as any other town in England. It had been the doctors' task to care for the mourners as well as those who eventually returned home.

Geoffrey William Blair was now the senior partner in a practice he had joined in 1914, the year he was rejected for service in the army. In the same year he married Claire Ransom who had been a nurse at the General Hospital in Leeds. In 1915 they had a son, Edward, and in 1917 another son, Jeremy. Claire had died of tuberculosis in 1920 and since then Geoffrey had remained a widower devoted to his practice and his children, mainly in that order. His sons he had sent to boarding school as soon as they were old enough, and he lived alone in the large house of which the surgery formed a part and which had belonged to the former senior partner, Doctor Darrell, who retired in 1919.

After Catherine had left for the night Geoffrey Blair went through the door which led directly from his surgery into the house, the large cold house which seemed permanently inhabited by ghosts of the past. Geoffrey cared little for his creature comforts, and would eat without enthusiasm the meal left for him in the oven of the large stove in the kitchen by his housekeeper who came at eight in the morning and left promptly at four-thirty when evening surgery began. There were also two daily women and a gardener; but, from the close of surgery until eight the next morning, Geoffrey Blair, unless he was called out in the night, remained alone. He never entertained and seldom these days received private invitations because he had hardly ever been known to accept any. At first people attributed this desire for solitude to grief at the death of his young wife; but then they came to realize that he liked solitude for solitude's sake. He was a solitary, and cared little for companionship. But he was a good, conscientious doctor, much respected; otherwise he left others alone and was left alone himself.

When the Blair boys came home for the school holidays they never stayed long. Claire had come from a large family and Geoffrey planned well in advance for his sons to spend time with their cousins, uncles, aunts and grandparents on his wife's side. He himself had been an only child and his parents died when he was relatively young.

Maybe it was from that state of early bereavement that he became someone perfectly satisfied with his own company, uneasy in social gatherings.

Uneasy, that is, until his life was invaded by the life-enhancing presence of Catherine Wills. The shadows began to fall away from his existence and life slowly, very slowly assumed a new meaning.

But was it fair to her? Sitting over his solitary supper that night, a dull fire flickering in the grate, Doctor Blair glanced round a room which, like the rest of the house, bore traces of considerable neglect. It was not damp, it was not dirty or badly furnished but it had that unlived-in, unloved air of a house that has seen little laughter, little noise and bustle of children or animals, little love.

Geoffrey Blair had been aware of a quickening of the pulse almost from the day his new receptionist arrived; but he dismissed it as the folly of an ageing and disappointed man. Besides, she was only a few years older than his eldest son, young enough to be his daughter. Somehow, in his mind, the feelings he had for her appeared obscene and he felt that anyone else would be shocked by them.

As the months had gone by he had taken care never to let her have any indication of his interest which, he soon knew, was not paternal. She was a young, beautiful, vibrant woman and he wanted to make love to her. In time he found the temptation to touch her almost overwhelming and at one time he considered dismissing her, selling his practice to his partner and moving away, out of temptation.

Yet there were times, and more of them recently, when he had a feeling that she was aware of what went on in his mind as he sat by her: the stirrings of the flesh, the overwhelming sense of desire. He sensed no revulsion on her part, no abrupt movement of her chair away from his.

Could she . . . ? But what would people say? Geoffrey Blair vigorously shook salt on his stew as though to punish himself for the carnal nature of the thoughts that increasingly tormented him.

After dinner he usually read medical magazines, case papers and letters from specialists about his patients. He listened to the news on the wireless and went to bed at about ten o'clock, a practice that he had started as a house doctor when he had been summoned to the wards at any hour of the night.

He never worked in his consulting room but in his study in the house which was a large room, gloomy like the rest but perhaps a little more lived-in with faded leather chairs, pipe racks, books, papers, the paraphernalia of a bachelor existence.

Last thing at night the doctor smoked a pipe and had a cup of Ovaltine – never whisky, in case he was called out – and then he went to bed, checking the clocks in each room and carefully putting out the lights as he went upstairs to the solitary bed where he had slept alone for so many years.

Geoffrey Blair was on the point of going to the kitchen to boil the milk for his drink when the telephone rang. He checked his watch, shrugged his shoulders and answered it in the terse, crisp manner that, intentionally or not, invariably had the effect of putting people off.

'Yes? Doctor Blair speaking.'

'Oh, Doctor,' a voice said that made his heart lurch immediately. 'Do you think you could come? It's my dad.'

'What is it, Catherine?' The doctor kept his voice as steady as he could.

'I think he's had a stroke, Doctor Blair.'

Thus did the mills of God begin to work; mysteriously to bring about, through the misfortune of one, happiness, fulfilment and blessing to others.

When Geoffrey Blair arrived at the small terraced house in Castle Street, the opposite side of the town from his own, it was a little after ten o'clock. All the lights in the house were on, whereas those in the rest of the street were in darkness as the working day in the mill began early.

At the bottom of the cobbled street rose the mill on which the welfare of so many families depended. Its huge chimney stack dominated the town, and alongside it ran the canal which linked Liverpool in the west to the port of Hull in the east. This canal served as a lifeline, a kind of artery carrying the huge, ponderous, laden barges through the Pennines from one side of the country to the other, stopping at the small towns through which they passed to unload or take on goods; balls of raw unbleached wool, straight from the body of the sheep, machinery for the cotton mills and sacks of shoddy to be turned into carpets and various kinds of cloth.

As soon as the doctor stopped outside the house the front door opened to reveal the anxious faces of Catherine, her mother, her brother and the two sisters who all stood close behind her.

Doctor Blair smiled reassuringly as if to assert his professional competence and, without waiting to be introduced, was led into the small front parlour of the house where George Wills still lay on his back, snoring – his head propped up on a cushion but, otherwise, in the position in which he had fallen.

'I thought it best to leave him,' Catherine said, looking anxiously from father to doctor.

'You did quite right,' Geoffrey said approvingly, kneeling down and unfastening the collar of the unconscious man so that he could listen to his heartbeat. Then he lifted the man's eyelids to examine his pupils and sat back on his heels staring thoughtfully at his patient for a few moments.

'Your father is in coma,' he said at last, getting up and removing his stethoscope from his ears. 'I think this is a diabetic coma. Does your father suffer from diabetes?'

'Not that *I* know of, Doctor.' Mrs Wills stepped nervously forward, her hands kneading her apron, sometimes bringing the corners up to her mouth. 'But then he would never see the doctor, either you or Doctor Thackery. He's that sort of person.'

'I did try and call Doctor Thackery,' Catherine said, referring to Doctor Blair's partner, a much younger man, 'but he was out. His wife didn't know . . .'

'Don't apologize.' Geoffrey smiled again at her. 'You

did the right thing.' He rummaged in his black bag and, producing a syringe, began to fill it from a phial which he turned upside down. 'I'm going to give him a shot of insulin. We must then get him to hospital. Call the County General will you, Catherine, and ask them to send an ambulance?'

'Yes, Doctor,' Catherine said, as she did a hundred times a day at the surgery, in a voice that managed to combine competence with a hint of deference. She felt worried but at the same time important, a key person, next to the doctor, in the drama being played out. As she looked around at the faces of her family she had a strange feeling of exhilaration, peace and happiness.

Doctor Blair, her admired, revered Doctor Blair, had finally come to her house.

Doctor Blair's diagnosis had proved correct and, after treatment, George Wills returned home to resume a life governed now by the fact that, from now on, he would need medication.

Doctor Blair continued to keep his eye on his patient and, of course, refused to accept payment.

'It isn't as though we can't afford it,' Catherine exclaimed one day as she showed him to the door after a home visit to her father.

'I know that,' Geoffrey Blair said. 'But how can I charge the father of someone who works for me? I assure you I regard it as a privilege to do something for your family, after all you've done for me.'

And, with that, as though confused by the vehemence of his feelings, he gave a nervous bow, smiled at Catherine's mother standing beside her and, putting on his hat, went swiftly out to his car which stood by the side of the pavement.

Jean Wills watched him thoughtfully as he got into his car, and then turned and waved; but not at her, at her daughter who was standing by her mother's side silently watching him. Slowly Catherine raised her hand and waved until the car was out of sight. Then just as thoughtfully she followed her mother back into the house and closed the door behind her. Still without speaking the two women went into the kitchen and began clearing up the breakfast things. Upstairs George Wills, well on the way to recovery, read the morning paper. The three other children were at work, Jean having taken unpaid holiday until her husband could be left alone.

Jean stood by the sink in the kitchen letting the boiling water run over the dishes which she stirred absent-mindedly with a mop. Catherine carried the rest of the plates from the table, dropped them into the sink and shook the tablecloth out of the back door before carefully folding it and popping it into a drawer. Then she stood by her mother, a tea-towel in her hand waiting for the first of the scalding dishes to appear on the draining board.

But instead of handing her a plate, her mother, head on one side, turned and stared straight into her daughter's eyes. 'If you ask *me*, Doctor Blair likes you. You know what I mean?'

Swiftly Catherine averted her eyes, her hands nervously playing with the tea-towel, knotting and unknotting it. Then her eyes met those of her mother. 'I know he does, and I like him.'

'Oh.' Now her mother, appearing nonplussed, dropped her gaze to the floor. 'Has he ever *said* anything?'

'No. He's very reticent. I think he's afraid.'

'Afraid?' Her mother looked at her in some surprise. 'How do you mean *afraid*, love?'

'Well, he's afraid, Mother. And so am I.'

'You're afraid of . . .' Her mother left the word unsaid. Perhaps she didn't know how to finish the sentence.

'He's that much older than me, Mother. He could be my father.'

'Does *that* worry you so much, dear?' her mother said gently, abandoning the washing-up and drawing her daughter to a chair by the table.

'Oh no. I think Doctor Blair is a very fine man. I can't help admiring him. He's nice looking too . . . don't you think, Mother?' She seemed anxious to have her mother's reassurance.

'Oh, he's very nice, dear. He's a gentleman, but . . .' her mother shook her head. 'I don't think you should allow yourself to raise your hopes too much.'

'I haven't any *hopes*, Mother,' Catherine said with a sad smile on her face.

'Oh dear, I do hope . . .' Jean Wills put both hands against her cheeks to hide the sudden flush that had come to them. 'He's never taken advantage . . .'

'Doctor Blair is *not* that sort of man,' Catherine replied severely. 'He would *never* take advantage, or do anything improper, I can assure you, Mother. But socially we are very far apart. He likes me . . . but . . . would he marry the daughter of a millworker?'

'Well . . .' now her mother began to clasp and unclasp her own fingers, red with the suds, upon which her gold wedding ring gleamed in the pale morning light. 'Is it *really* marriage you're thinking of?'

'*I'm* not thinking of marriage. I wouldn't presume to think about it, unless it was what Doctor Blair wanted. It's not up to me is it, Mother?'

'Not really,' her mother said, shaking her head. 'Though you're every bit as good as any girl in this town. What worries me is that if Doctor Blair . . . well if he did

. . . he has a son nearly as old as you. *What* would people say?'

'Would it matter what they said?' Catherine glanced wryly at her mother. 'It would be different if we were . . . living together. *Then* people would have something to say.'

'Oh don't even *suggest* such a thing!' her mother said with a look of alarm on her face. 'I can recall when a woman who shall be nameless . . . well don't let's go into that, but,' she leaned forwards and shook her finger at her daughter, '*all* the town knew.'

'Knew what?'

'That she was doing something she shouldn't. I won't say with whom because it's past history now and not for the ears of a respectable girl like you. But *no one* had much respect either for *her* or her family again, not for a long time. I assure you that if your father so much as entertained the idea that you would *do* such a thing with Doctor Blair, he would not have you in the house. He would put you out in the street. He would.' Jean shook her head so vigorously that it made her daughter smile.

'And would you let him, Mother?'

'I'd have to,' her mother said, getting up and returning to the sink. 'But just you be careful. You mark my words. You be careful.'

Catherine Wills knew, indeed, that she had to be very careful. She knew quite well how Doctor Blair felt about her; but she did not feel quite the same way about him. He was nearly as old as her father who had had his forty-sixth birthday the month before. She could really only think of him like she thought of her father: an old man with old skin, with an old man's ways and an old man's smell.

Although she knew how old Doctor Blair was – she

had once had to fill in an insurance form for him on which his date of birth was given as 1888 – in fact he seemed much older. His hair was greying at the temples and he walked slowly like a man advanced in years. Everyone said that the death of his young wife twelve years before had aged him overnight.

But, counteracting these obvious disadvantages was the fact that Doctor Blair was a man of position; position and some wealth, despite the fact that he wouldn't take money from many of his patients. Most of those in his care were the better-off members of the population, because Doctor Blair was considered the best doctor in Netherwick, and some of them were very wealthy indeed. Also, Doctor Blair had inherited wealth, and she knew that he owned some property in the West Country and had investments in the City.

If one were to set these advantages against his, to her, obvious lack of physical appeal, the prospect offered was an attractive one for a girl whose parents were mill-workers like their parents before them; for a girl who had looks but no money, no social position and not much hope of marrying beyond her class. This was an unappealing prospect for someone of her ambition that went beyond most of her contemporaries in Netherwick.

For Catherine Wills had ambition that overrode class and fortune, and what better way of achieving this than to be the wife of Netherwick's most prominent, most respected physician: a man of education, position and substance? The wife? Was it really possible? Sometimes she thought it was.

By the summer George Wills was ready to return to work and Doctor Blair gave him a certificate to say so. But he warned him that he had to be careful for the rest of his life: care, medication and rest.

'Your father is not really an ill man,' the doctor explained carefully to Catherine one day as she was typing up the notes on his case. 'Diabetes can now be treated; but its implications are serious if it is ignored. And . . .'

'I can't tell you how grateful we all are, Doctor,' Catherine said, sitting back in her chair, long fingers just brushing the keys of the typewriter, eyes shining. He closed his eyes and gulped.

'Is there something *wrong*, Doctor Blair?' Catherine enquired anxiously. 'Shall I open a window? Oh dear, I hope *you* aren't ill too.'

'Not ill at all, my dear,' the doctor said, but he realized he was trembling. If he allowed this situation, these thoughts, to continue much longer he might indeed become very ill indeed. If love were a sickness, and a lot of people thought it was, then he was sick. Sick, sick, sick. He was a sick man and he needed a cure.

'I wondered if you'd like to come out on Sunday for a run to Whitby?' he enquired almost casually, getting up and standing beside her by the window which she had hurried to open. 'I dare say the sea . . .'

'Oh that *would* be lovely, Doctor Blair,' Catherine cried, hands clasped.

'Would your family mind?'

'Oh no . . .' for a moment she looked doubtful, thinking of her father.

'Because my intentions *are* honourable.'

'Oh!' Catherine, hands still clasped, looked on in amazement as the doctor sank rather unsteadily onto one knee and looked so earnestly up at her that his expression was comical.

'I don't suppose you could consider, could *ever* consider being my wife, Catherine?' he blurted out, exhibiting an enthusiasm, a lack of control such as she had never seen in the two, nearly three, years since she had worked for him. 'I know I am much, much older than you. I dare say it's something you never thought about. Maybe the idea revolts you. If so, please . . .'

He shut his eyes and rocked backwards and forwards on one knee, hands tightly joined as if he were earnestly in prayer. When he opened them again he saw that she was smiling, leaning towards him, so seraphic, so beautiful she resembled a pre-Raphaelite portrait of an angel. He even imagined he saw the suggestion of a halo round her head. Could it be possible? He reached for her hands. Willingly she clasped his.

'Oh, Doctor *Blair*,' she gasped.

'Geoffrey,' he said, feeling rather weak. 'Call me Geoffrey.'

'Oh, Geoffrey.' Her firm young hands tightened over his. And he knew the answer without being told.

The marriage of Doctor Geoffrey Blair to his receptionist, who was not only young enough to be his daughter but whose family were millworkers, rocked the small town of Netherwick. Ideas change little from generation to generation; indeed, Doctor Blair's infatuation was seen as a sexual aberration, the attraction for a much older man of a young and nubile woman. Some of his patients left him, even those who had liked Catherine Wills and considered her a cut above her station.

The marriage took place in Leeds rather than Netherwick because of the mixed reactions of the population. The last thing either Geoffrey Blair or his fiancée's family wished to do was to cause offence to the heightened sensibilities of the easily shocked. Furthermore, as his own two sons had expressed their preference to stay away from their father's marriage to the woman who had succeeded their mother, the couple decided on a quiet register office marriage with only family present and a luncheon at the Grand Hotel afterwards.

It was not the sort of ceremony, the sort of occasion that Catherine Wills had wished for or, indeed, expected. She was a normal young girl and had been brought up in the anticipation that her wedding day would be the happiest, as well as the greatest occasion of her life. She had not seen it in the prurient way of so many of the townspeople, and she was hurt. But Jean Wills, who was her friend as well as her mother, counselled her to obey the wishes of a man so much older. It was natural, inevitable, that he would expect a certain submissiveness on her part; he would expect her to do as he wished and much of what he wished, her mother implied with a look in her eye, might not be especially pleasant. Catherine had little doubt as to her meaning.

But Catherine had not spent nearly three years as a medical receptionist for nothing. Unlike a good many girls she knew the facts of life, and what her husband would expect of her and how. She didn't enter her marriage in ignorance about either its physical or social implications. She knew quite well what she was doing and she expected to succeed at it. The transformation from Miss Catherine Wills to Mrs Geoffrey Blair would surprise everybody. It would be smooth, assured and lacking in awkwardness, she was quite sure about that.

All her life Catherine had succeeded in what she set out to do. She had risen above her class, above family, above a small terraced dwelling in a back street of Netherwick and now, as the wife of the doctor, transformed by a few words exchanged in front of a Registrar into a woman of means, of respectability, she was determined to be successful too.

*   *   *

For a long time Catherine lay on her back staring through the darkness at the ceiling. Beside her she had a feeling Geoffrey was awake too. Her whole body was shaking from the experience during which she had thought she would be torn asunder, split from her crotch to her head and Geoffrey would be charged with her murder. His lovemaking had been clumsy, rough, inexperienced, as if what was happening between them was happening to him, too, for the first time. And yet he had two sons, as proof that he had done it at least twice before.

Of course they had never discussed it. In the six months of their engagement they had talked about everything: the future of the practice, her replacement as receptionist, the redecoration of the house, the purchase of a new car, of clothes suitable for the doctor's wife, of planning the honeymoon, of fun, of business, in particular the settlement he would be making on her. But they had never talked about that, the physical side of their marriage and its possible, perhaps inevitable, consequences: children. He had always managed to skirt round the subject and she, trusting him implicitly because he was a doctor, was sure that with him she was in safe hands. That when the time came it would be all right.

He had been too long a widower. She knew that now and, if he had ever had any deftness or skill in lovemaking, he had, perhaps, forgotten it. Maybe the next time it would be better. She knew that men were hungry for sex and a number of them went to any lengths to get it. At least she'd known that Geoffrey had never had a mistress, would never have done anything underhand or despicable in *that* way. He had only kissed her twice before their marriage and neither time was it very passionate. Although she was twenty-two she was relatively innocent and had little idea of the practicalities, of what to expect.

Well, now she knew. This was what wives went through. They went through it and it was over; or was it like this every time? She touched the soft, sore spot between her legs. She was sure she was bleeding and she was ashamed of it. The sheets would be soiled and what would the chambermaid in the hotel think? What would Geoffrey think? She was even ashamed that her husband should see the consequences of his own behaviour. Somehow she blamed herself.

If only sex could be clean, and not like this. But it was the lot of women. It was also the price for achieving respectability, wealth and a certain station above one's fellows.

It was the price of becoming the wife of the doctor: Mrs Geoffrey William Blair.

In every other respect, however, and certainly as far as appearances went, the honeymoon was a success, the newly married couple ostensibly contented and blissfully happy, particularly the bridegroom. For if Geoffrey lacked finesse in the marriage bed he made up for it in his considerate manner towards his wife: the many little courtesies and acts of tenderness and regard with which he treated her.

For he did love her, there was no doubt about that. He loved her so much that he felt there was nothing he wouldn't do for her. He was charming, civilized and gallant and he made the former Catherine Wills feel not merely like a doctor's wife; she felt like a queen. The queen of Paris, gracious and elegant in their promenades along the Champs-Elysées, along the Avenue Montaigne to gaze at the august portals of the great fashion houses;

across the Place de la Concorde and along the Rue de Rivoli, stopping, perhaps, to take coffee or a cup of chocolate, pausing in their apparent endless quest for enlightenment, for the sights, sounds and, above all, the spectacle that Paris had to offer: Les Invalides, the exterior of Notre Dame, the extraordinary glass of the Sainte Chapelle, the grim interior of the Conciergerie, the majestic rooms of the Louvre, its windows overlooking the Seine, the trips to Versailles, to Fontainebleau; and then the nightlife . . . A change of clothes and they were off to dine: a restaurant in Montmartre, Les Halles or the Left Bank with its narrow winding streets, its mysterious corners, its *hôtels particuliers*, their secrets and, sometimes, their splendours, hidden behind high walls and locked gates. Or, occasionally, they were glimpsed through railings, the sumptuousness of their interiors, their salons and halls illuminated by massive chandeliers that hung from the ceilings, sparkling and twinkling like the myriads of diamonds that graced the elegant necks of the beautiful fur-clad women who sometimes emerged, escorted by men in evening dress, to step into limousines drawn up by the side.

It was a life very far from Netherwick and one that Catherine would never forget and which, in a way, compensated for the darker side of the honeymoon that she would never forget either.

Geoffrey was a knowledgeable man whose studies and interests had not just been confined to medicine, and which he had been able to extend in the long years of his widowerhood during which he had read omnivorously. He was able to teach his young bride a lot, especially about art and, in particular, the works of the great masters which lined the walls of the Louvre. He was interested in architecture and explained the development of the clear, beautiful lines of the Gothic from the ideas which burst forth at the Renaissance. Geoffrey also knew a lot about the kings and queens of France and not just Louis XIV or the unfortunate Queen Marie Antoinette; but about the wise and enlightened Henri IV, and the accomplished François I who met the English King Henry VIII on the field of the Cloth of Gold.

It was doubtful if the people, the tourists and others, in Paris that autumn of 1933 who thronged the galleries and the places of historical interest as the Blairs did, would have looked twice at the couple who gazed with such earnestness at the Mona Lisa or the huge marble tomb of Napoleon that rose beneath the cupola of the dome of Les Invalides. If they had they might have thought they were father and daughter rather than husband and wife. For Geoffrey, although his appearance was distinguished, had always looked older than his years. His marriage might have helped to restore his youth physically as well as emotionally; but it didn't yet show or maybe it was too late and never would. He was a tall, aesthetic-looking man with a walrus moustache and a military bearing. He could have been a senior member of the armed forces approaching retirement. The young woman on his arm, though pretty, was not outstanding enough in that city of beautiful women to attract more than a few passing glances but, yes, father and daughter, people would have said; not husband and wife. Yes, father and daughter, or, perhaps, a married man taking a risk being seen abroad with his young mistress.

Not that any of this conjecture would have mattered to the Blairs for, increasingly, they became more and more absorbed in each other, too much to care whether people stared at them or not. Geoffrey loved explaining things to this young, nubile woman rather as Professor Higgins had to Eliza Doolittle or Svengali to Trilby. He was proud to be seen with her, by her side, Catherine gazing earnestly and trustfully into his eyes as she searched for enlightenment and instruction.

For a young girl whose education, whose knowledge of the world was very limited, it opened the gates to a life of enchantment, to prospects undreamed of and gradually, almost hesitantly, she fell in love not only with Paris, but with her husband too.

Geoffrey sensed this change in his wife, for he was a perceptive man who knew that she had not loved him when she agreed to marry him. He had felt that, for a time, his love was enough for both of them and that by cocooning his darling, treasuring her, delighting her with flowers and buying her beautiful clothes, she would realize that he was as indispensable to her as she had become to him.

Soon, too soon, the honeymoon was over. The day for the return came and, sadly, Catherine stood at the window of the little hotel room in the Rue de l'Université that had been home for nearly three weeks.

The suitcases were on the bed ready for that final push that would enable the lids to be fastened and secured, and she could hear Geoffrey in the bathroom attached to the bedroom, washing his hands. It reminded her of the sounds of the surgery, of life in Netherwick, of the doctor emerging from the surgery drying his hands after examining a patient, smiling and looking at her and now . . .

'Penny for your thoughts?' Geoffrey murmured in her ear as an arm encircled her waist.

'I was thinking about Netherwick.' Catherine tried to turn to face him but was unable to because his clasp was so firm.

'Looking forward to going back, my darling?' His face nuzzled her, the bristles of his moustache like a soft brush against the back of her neck.

'No.'

'Nor I. It has been a lovely time together hasn't it, my darling Catherine?'

'Lovely,' Catherine said, 'really lovely.'

Chapter 2

Geoffrey Blair paced anxiously up and down in the waiting room of the hospital, occasionally pausing to tap his wrist-watch to ensure it was still working, then comparing it with the time on the clock on the wall. It was a situation, to say the least, that was unusual for him and, momentarily, it gave him a brief sympathy with his patients who, all too often, stood or sat as he did this day, waiting for news.

Doctor Blair was not a man given to anxiety. If he were it would have been unwise for him to have answered the call to practise medicine. A doctor had to take care not to transfer any sense of apprehension to his patients. If the news was not good it was important to try and conceal it with a reassuring expression, a tone of hope and encouragement to his voice. Now to be at the other end, the receiving end of news good or bad . . .

He stopped and checked his watch again with the clock on the wall. Surely by this time something . . . Suddenly he was overwhelmed by a sensation he had seldom known in his life. It seemed to travel up his legs, along his spine around his neck and to descend via his chest to his legs again. It was fear: pure, unadulterated fear. Fear of the unknown, fear of the unexpected, fear of loss, fear that all was not well, fear of fear itself, fear . . .

'Doctor Blair,' the nurse said with a bright practised smile as she flung open the swing doors of the waiting room. 'I am delighted to tell you your wife has given birth to twins.'

Doctor Blair closed his eyes, opened them again and

then looked at the nurse. The routine smile vanished from her face. 'Twins, Doctor Blair, a boy and a girl. They both weigh over six pounds. No wonder she was so large. Doctor Blair . . .' the nurse leaned forwards, 'are you all right?'

'Twins,' Geoffrey said repeating it again to himself. 'Twins, a boy and a girl.' Then he stared fixedly at the nurse, aware that the fear had not left him.

'Is my wife all right? You said "was" so large. Is she . . . ?'

'Mrs Blair is as well as can be expected, Doctor,' the nurse said with a note of caution in her voice. 'After all, you can hardly expect, after fourteen hours' labour . . .'

'I *must* see her,' Geoffrey cried, giving vent to his desperation, his foreboding that things had gone wrong. As he hurried to the door the nurse reached out an arm and firmly restrained him.

'Mrs Blair is *perfectly* all right, Doctor. She is a healthy young woman; but she is tired and she is sleeping. Afterwards . . .'

'Oh thank God,' Geoffrey Blair said, a tremor in his voice. 'Oh thank God, Nurse. If you knew . . .'

The nurse was to tell her companions round the dinner table that night in the Nurses' Home about the doctor's reaction. It caused a great deal of mirth.

The twins were christened Gilbert Wills and Tansy Jennifer Blair at the parish church. Unlike their parents' rather surreptitious wedding, this time there was a good deal of celebration and rejoicing both at the parish church and afterwards at the Blair home. There seemed nothing shameful now about a union between a young woman and a much older man once it had been blessed with offspring. The enhanced status of the new Mrs Blair was quickly assimilated by a town that, despite its snobbish side, was on the whole full of citizens who were both charitable and well intentioned.

The doctor was of the community yet he was also apart from it. He was a person to whom people deferred, whose opinion was respected, whose advice was sought and whose calling was deeply honoured: a doctor, by his power, was a man above men and inevitably the same aura attached itself to his wife rather as nobility is conferred on the spouse, however humble her origins, of a member of the aristocracy. Miss X became Lady Y simply through the honour that Lord Y had conferred on her by making her his wife: in all things they were equal, and so it was with the Blairs.

When the twins were born some townspeople had even forgotten that a little over a year before Miss Catherine Wills had emerged from the ranks of the working classes to assume a status of pre-eminence in the community.

It was noted by those attending the ceremony, and the party at the house afterwards, how proud Geoffrey Blair was, not only of the twins but of the wife who had produced them. It seemed to those present that he was, indeed, a man transformed from the dour, remote person who had lived a solitary widowed existence until his unexpected marriage to Catherine. The years appeared to have slipped away from the careworn Doctor Blair and now he looked as he felt, rejuvenated.

Also at the christening were the offspring of his first marriage who were now young men. Edward, the elder, was nineteen, a medical student in London and there strictly by the wishes of his father. Jeremy was seventeen and in his last year at school.

Little had been seen since the second marriage of the progeny of the first. It was thought that Edward, at least, did not approve of his father's marriage and had stayed away from home. Jeremy was the sort of carefree, good-locking young man who got around a lot, who was invited to summer parties and winter sports festivities and who would probably have spent little time at home anyway.

During the ceremony Edward Blair stood at the back of the throng gathered round the baptismal font, as though to distance himself from the proceedings. He was tall and grave, bearing a strong resemblance to his father. His hair was cropped close to his head and he had a thin pencil moustache on the upper lip of a mouth that seldom seemed to smile.

At the party Edward again hung back, talking to some old acquaintances who remembered his mother, people who, because of their superior social position, would have had very little to do in the past or, even perhaps in the present, with the new Mrs Blair.

Catherine, busy supervising the maids who served the tea, dainty sandwiches and christening cake to the throng gathered in the Blair drawing room, with its view over the town, kept glancing anxiously at her stepsons, neither of whom had done much to endear themselves to her.

It was true that it was a very difficult situation. She was only four years older than Edward and sometimes his presence made her feel younger because he was such a solemn, stern, unsmiling young man. What terror, she thought, he would strike into his patients when the time came, but, of course, he would be good at what he did because he was clever and capable, like his father.

But at the christening party which spilled out into the garden on that happy afternoon in midsummer of the year 1934, even Catherine would not allow Edward's air of detachment to spoil her enjoyment, her pride as people gathered round the prams in which the six-month-old

A Wind in Summer

twins lay, presided over by a nanny and a nursery nurse. Little Tansy was wide awake, smiling and gurgling, kicking her legs with joy now that she was out of the stifling christening robe. Her brother Gilbert, on the other hand, as though worn out by all the fuss, was fast asleep, his tiny arms raised above his head, his chubby fists tightly clasped on the pillow behind him.

Looking at her, Catherine hoped Tansy would always have the joy in life that she seemed to have now, blue eyes alert, her golden downy-hair like a halo on the pillow, her cheeks pink with the exertion of kicking. And Gilbert . . . Catherine's eyes momentarily clouded over as she gazed at him. She did so hope that Gilbert would not be like Edward.

'So adorable,' Mary Wentworth said, bending over the babies and smiling into Catherine's eyes as she straightened up.

The Wentworths were prosperous millowners, prominent citizens of Netherwick who had a large house on the far side of the town. In age Mary and Peter Wentworth were somewhere between Geoffrey and Catherine Blair and they had young children who would, in time, be playfriends of the newly christened twins.

Despite their friendship Catherine always felt a little awkward with Mary Wentworth because it was her husband's family who owned the mill where the Willses had worked for so many years. Peter Wentworth hardly spoke to her at all but addressed himself to her husband, though Geoffrey denied it was because he thought there was a social difference between them.

But Mary Wentworth, too, was a wife a few years younger than her husband, though she had come from a wealthy family who owned mills in Lancashire. She was extremely friendly towards Catherine and had been among the first to make her feel welcome, inviting her to those coffee mornings where the young wives and mothers of Netherwick gathered to exchange gossip and information, mostly about their children, but also about any other interesting titbit of the day.

Catherine now stood beside her friend who was making baby noises at Tansy and getting an enthusiastic response. Mary held out a finger and looked delightedly at Catherine as Tansy seized it in a firm grip, seeming intent on hanging on to it.

'Why does Edward look so *fierce*?' she enquired sotto voce to Catherine, but keeping her eyes on the face of the gurgling baby.

'He didn't like me marrying his father,' Catherine murmured back, her eyes also on those of her daughter.

'Did he want him to remain a crusty old widower?' Mary whispered.

'I think he thought his father was too old.'

'Forty-five is not *old*.'

'Too old for Edward, anyway. Or maybe he thought that I was not good enough for his father.' Catherine cast her a quizzical glance. 'Who knows?'

She sighed deeply and was about to turn when Mary caught her by the arm.

'Don't let it upset you. We *all* like you very much and are happy for Geoffrey. Don't let Edward destroy this happiness. It is such a precious thing.' And she looked rather wistfully, Catherine thought, at her own husband.

At this point Geoffrey came over, kissed Mary on the cheek and surreptitiously slipped his arm round Catherine's waist. His face was glowing with a happiness which even the grey shadow of Edward hovering at the back of the room seemed unable to dispel.

'Nearly time for my surgery, dear,' he said. 'I'll just slip away.'

'Oh, Geoffrey,' Mary exclaimed. 'Surely *not* on a day

like this. Couldn't your partner . . .'

'I couldn't let something like this interfere with our arrangements, Mary.' Geoffrey looked across the garden to where his partner, Tom Thackery, stood with a group of friends. 'Besides, Tom is a guest. Why shouldn't *he* enjoy himself as much as me?'

Geoffrey stooped to kiss Tansy on the cheek, stroked Gilbert's fair head without disturbing him and then, with a fond gaze at his wife, crossed the lawn towards the house.

'He still puts his patients first,' Catherine said with a resigned smile. 'No reason why he shouldn't. He was their doctor long before I came along.' Mary seemed on the verge of replying when her husband appeared with Councillor Todd, the mayor, who shook Catherine warmly by the hand to congratulate her, and then bent to inspect the twins more closely. In the background his wife was talking to a group of people, none of whom Catherine had known socially until now.

She stood awkwardly to one side while her twins were fussed over by these important people, while her own family gathered closely together on the lawn like a cluster of frightened sheep, isolated, clearly nervous and very shy. She excused herself to the Wentworths and the Todds and walked through the throng to her father who was sitting down, his hand resting on the top of his stick, his eyes restlessly wandering over the lawn as if he couldn't quite understand what he was doing there.

'How are you, Dad?' Catherine swiftly bent to kiss him. 'Feeling tired?'

'Your father feels awkward with all these big-wigs,' Jean Wills said, eyeing her daughter frankly. 'To be chit-chatting with the mayor! Your dad feels out of place and so do I. Think we best be going, love.'

'Oh, *Mum*.' Catherine impulsively threw an arm round

her. 'You mustn't think that.'

'We can't help it, Cath. They don't know what to say
to us and we don't know what to say to them. I think in
future we'll stay away from "do's" like this.'

'But that's absurd,' Catherine said heatedly, 'I want
you here. Apart from me and Geoffrey you're the most
important people to our children, their grandparents.'

'It's not that the doctor makes us feel awkward, love,'
Jean protested – she always referred to him as 'the
doctor'. 'He is kindness itself.'

'Nobody actually *does* anything,' her father grumbled.
'Folk go out of their way to be nice. It's that we feel we
don't belong.'

'Well you do . . .'

'And that lad of your husband's,' her father cast a
glance across the lawn and shook his head, 'how *you* get
along with him I don't know.'

'Oh Edward,' Catherine said off-handedly. 'He's all
right.' But a blight seemed to have overshadowed her
happiness and she knew the cause of it was Edward.

Geoffrey Blair was still in his surgery when there was a
tap on the door. His new receptionist, Sally, had gone
home and, with a frown, he called: 'Who is it?'

'It's Edward, Father,' a voice replied and Geoffrey told
him to come in. He went on writing without looking up
as his son slowly crossed the room and sat opposite him,
politely waiting for him to finish.

'Shan't be a moment.' Geoffrey looked up with a
smile.

'Take your time, Father.' Edward sat casually in the
chair flinging one leg over the other and joining his
fingers so that they formed a church steeple.

'Know the symptoms of appendicitis, Edward?'
Geoffrey enquired, his eyes still on his paper.

'Sickness, acute pain in lower abdomen . . .'

'Not always.' Geoffrey looked up and was surprised at the lack of interest on his son's face. 'Sometimes there is . . .'

'I didn't really come to talk to you about medicine, Father.' Edward uncrossed his legs and then crossed them again. He seemed ill at ease.

'Do you wish to consult me about something?' His father leaned forwards anxiously. 'Is something wrong?'

'I hope you're not going to continue making a spectacle of yourself by having babies, Father. In my opinion it's not suitable, or dignified,' Edward said abruptly.

'Oh dear.' Geoffrey put down his pen and went to the window where, hands in pockets, he remained staring towards the lawn where some remnants of the party still lingered. 'That's what you think, is it?'

'Yes it is, and a lot of other people think so too. When the twins are twenty you will be in your sixties. You are old enough to be their *grandfather*.'

'You never approved of this marriage, did you, Edward?' Abruptly Geoffrey turned round.

'I didn't think Catherine was very suitable for you, Father, either in age or social class to be quite honest. People think you married her for, well . . .' Edward studied the tips of his well-polished shoes.

'Reasons of concupiscence?' his father suggested.

'To put it mildly, yes. What else had you in common with her?'

'I loved her. I loved her and I still do. I love her more than ever.' Slowly his father crossed the room until he stood by the side of his desk, facing his son. 'I hope it is the sort of love that one day *you* will be lucky enough to know, Edward.'

'I very much hope not, Father.' Edward gazed at him stubbornly. 'I hope I shall marry a woman of my class *and* of a suitable age. I hope people will not consider *me* a laughing stock.'

'You think the people of Netherwick consider me a laughing stock?' Anger entered Geoffrey's voice.

'I know they do.'

'Then why do they come to see us in such numbers?'

'People always like a spectacle, didn't you know?' Edward's expression as he gazed at his father was laconic, almost impertinent. 'They come out of curiosity. How many dinner invitations have *you* had since you and Catherine were married?'

'A number.'

'From people you consider real friends?'

'No, actually none of them, since you ask. But Eric Todd *is* a very busy man and his wife is on any number of committees. The Wentworths now . . .'

'Maybe they want their marriage to be accepted too. Peter Wentworth is almost as old as you, Father.'

Geoffrey felt himself whiten and a faint pain gripped his heart. A touch of indigestion; he had it quite frequently. 'I really have had enough of this conversation, Edward. I find it extremely distasteful; distasteful *and* disloyal. I can't believe it is my own son talking to me. You would have thought that you, of all people, would be happy for me. You were very young when your mother died and I have been a very lonely man. Did you ever think of *me*, Edward?'

'Did you ever think of *us*, Father?' Edward's expression was angry as he leaned forwards, one hand clutching the side of his leg. 'Did you ever consider our feelings? Did you ever think of marrying again after Mother died, but sooner and to someone more suitable? We missed the love of a mother, just as you missed the comfort of a wife. We knew we were not wanted here. Every holiday we were farmed off to different relations, seeing little of you, knowing little of you except that we weren't wanted.'

'That's *not* true, Edward.' Indignantly Geoffrey thumped the desk. 'I wanted you to be happy.'

'You wanted us to be out of the way, Father. It wasn't very convenient really, to have two little boys you didn't know what to do with, how to manage. I think you were very selfish, Father, and I still do. You were selfish because you have only thought of yourself, your own pleasure. It must be very flattering for you now to have the attentions of a young woman who is only a little older than your son. It must be very satisfying.' Slowly Edward rose, hands in pockets, and leaning against his father's desk met his eyes. 'Satisfying and rather disgusting, in my opinion. If I were you I'd feel ashamed of myself for having such base and degrading desires.'

Edward then rose and swiftly left the room, not seeing that behind him his father had doubled up in pain, clutching his heart.

'If they make you ill they can't come here,' Catherine said, leaning over the bed as her husband, propped against the pillow, sipped at his customary cup of Ovaltine, a night-time habit from the days of his widowerhood that he was reluctant to abandon.

'It is only indigestion.'

'I still think Tom should run you over. As for Edward . . .' Catherine sat on the side of the bed, arms folded, an expression on her face that seemed to suggest that words, momentarily, had failed her.

'Edward is a good boy, he means well,' Geoffrey said hurriedly. He hadn't told Catherine the whole truth about his talk with his eldest son. He had told her it was something personal that had upset him; but Catherine had a pretty shrewd idea what that was.

'I suppose he told you he didn't approve of me,' Catherine said at last. 'That I was the wrong class . . . Also too young,' she added as her husband didn't reply.

'Edward disapproves of me being a father again at my age,' Geoffrey said at last, shrugging his shoulders as he carefully placed his cup on the bedside table beside him.

Catherine thought with a pang of alarm how thin and emaciated his shoulders looked, bent like an old man; and the pallor of his face worried her.

'I suppose he's right,' he murmured with a wry smile and settled back against the pillow, sighing deeply.

'He's *not* right,' Catherine said sharply, unfolding her arms and standing up. 'There is nothing disgraceful in a man fathering a child by a woman who is his wife.'

Geoffrey reached out and drew Catherine down beside him. 'I think his feeling is natural. It's not only jealousy . . . or, rather, it's not *merely* jealousy. There is some natural aversion to the thought of one's father, well,' he looked up at her and smiled, 'I needn't tell you what I'm trying to say, even if it is difficult to find the words to say it.'

Catherine squeezed his hand, smoothed the coverlet on the bed and rose, conscious of a constraint between them. If Geoffrey found it difficult to talk to his sons about the intimate side of marriage it was even more so with his wife. It was easier for him to do it rather than discuss it.

Thankfully their lovemaking now seemed confined to Sundays, Geoffrey's day off: no patients, no rounds, no calls, unless there was an emergency, and he shared these with his partner. It was the day Geoffrey relaxed and enjoyed himself and it began in the morning when he took his pleasure from his wife. From, but not with.

Catherine was quite accustomed now to this demand

which, of course, was her marital duty. She even tried to relax and enjoy it; but Geoffrey made it hard for her because his only consideration seemed to be his pleasure, not hers. Yet, despite his roughness, he began and ended the act with words of love, passionate and tender. These embraces she sometimes enjoyed, together with the knowledge of his affection, his desire for her, his undoubted love; but little else. She guessed it was the lot of women.

And yet she loved Geoffrey in a way she never imagined she would when she married him. It was very strange; a difficult emotion to put into words, even if she could, for she would never have dreamt of discussing it with anyone, even her mother, her sister or her new friend Mary Wentworth. People just didn't.

By the time Catherine had undressed, washed, done her hair and climbed into bed beside him, Geoffrey was lying on his side, his tiny snores indicative of the fact that he was fast asleep. She put her arm around his waist and leaned her head against his back, conscious of a wave of tenderness and gratitude that he was hers and would, she knew, remain so, whatever his sons said about her.

Breakfast the next morning, always taken early in the Blair household because the first surgery was at nine, was attended by Edward but not by Jeremy who liked to sleep late. Geoffrey was turning over the pages of *The Times* when Edward entered the dining room and Dorothy the maid came out from the kitchen to see what he wanted to eat. Catherine sat at her side of the table surreptitiously eyeing Edward as he gave his order and then took his place at the table between his father and stepmother.

'Morning, Edward,' Geoffrey said affably, putting aside the paper. 'Sleep well?'

'Yes thank you, Father. And you?'

'Very well.'

'Your father actually *wasn't* very well,' Catherine said with a sharp note in her voice.

'Oh?' Edward looked at him and shook out the *Morning Post* which lay by his plate.

'Just a bit of indigestion.' Geoffrey gave Catherine a warning look. 'Nothing to worry about.'

'Following his talk with *you*,' Catherine went on, whereupon Geoffrey put the paper aside completely and looked angrily at her.

'*Please*, Catherine. What goes on between me and my son . . .' he stopped as if groping for the right words.

'Is none of my business?' Catherine's mouth tightened as she carefully buttered the toast which was all she took with tea for breakfast.

'I didn't say that, my dear.'

'I think you meant it,' Catherine acknowledged with a pleasant smile that included Edward. 'And it's under-standable. Edward is not my son and you have a perfect right to have a life with him apart from me. However, what is my concern is your health and after your talk with Edward you were very upset indeed. You were so upset that you had acute pain and had to go to bed.'

'Father . . .' Edward looked up in dismay but Catherine went on rapidly:

'I know you'll say, Geoffrey, that you had a busy day: the christening of the twins, normal surgery and so on; but you did look extremely ill and I was worried about you. That's all I said. I don't want your sons to make you ill. It is my task to make your life easy and this I will do to the best of my ability. If I have to protect you from them then I shall. Now,' Catherine got up and rang the bell for the maid who came scurrying in with a tray on which lay bacon and eggs and fresh, hot buttered toast, 'I have a lot to do. Please excuse me.' She turned to the maid who was carefully putting the plate in front of Edward. 'Dorothy, I would like a word with you in my sitting room when you have done the washing-up. We have to talk about the dinner for Mr and Mrs Wentworth and Mr and Mrs Garrett tomorrow night.'

'Yes, mum,' Dorothy said with a little bob and began to clear away the plates left by the doctor.

When they were alone together Edward swept a lock of hair back from his forehead.

'I'm sorry about yesterday, Father. I said things I shouldn't have said. I'm sorry it made you ill. I was a bit out of sorts, that's all.'

'Put it out of your mind,' Geoffrey said with a fatherly pat as he got up. He let his hand linger for a moment and then he said almost casually: 'Do you know there is nothing better I would like than to take a walking holiday with you boys. What do you say to our taking a week or two together walking in the Lakes; or how about somewhere further afield, say Switzerland?'

'No thank you,' Edward said politely, gently but firmly removing his father's hand from his shoulder.

Geoffrey looked more hurt than surprised. 'But why not? You have a long vacation. We can relax, unwind. I could do with a holiday, I can tell you. Say a few weeks by Lake Geneva in Switzerland?' He looked closely at Edward. 'I mean just the three of us: you, me and Jeremy.'

'The *three* of us?' Edward's expression underwent a complete transformation. 'What about Catherine and the twins?'

'Oh, I shan't take them with us,' Geoffrey said with a smile. 'Just you, me and Jeremy together. Just us three; the family.'

And Geoffrey gave his son the kind of secret smile that seemed to draw him into a conspiracy, excluding his wife and tiny twins.

Chapter 3

Tom Thackery had been Geoffrey Blair's partner for five years when Geoffrey married his second wife Catherine. As Geoffrey had been when he joined the practice in 1914, Tom was then a newly qualified doctor, having missed the years of carnage which had decimated so many of his contemporaries.

Like Geoffrey, Tom married a local girl, a nurse at the General Hospital, but he went on to have four children, two boys and two girls. The eldest was now eight and the youngest three.

Tom was a quiet man, rather like Geoffrey in temperament and the two, despite the difference in their ages, got on well. Yet Tom had watched with concern the development of Geoffrey's hermit-like existence and no one was more pleased than he when the senior partner began to show an interest in the new young receptionist, Catherine Wills.

Tom was one of the godfathers to Tansy and his wife was godmother to Gilbert. The families were close but not intimate, largely because Helen Thackery was not the kind of woman who liked to congregate with other mothers. Maybe it was because she had trained as a nurse that she liked to keep herself apart. She was rather a brusque, practical woman, whose sole devotion and interest were her husband and family.

A few weeks after the christening Tom Thackery came out of the surgery, locked the door behind him and was on his way to his car when he saw Catherine in the distance sitting under a tree, the two babies crawling on a rug beside her. The nanny was throwing a ball to the Yorkshire terrier, who was a new family acquisition, and the scene was one of such domestic peace and happiness that Tom put his car keys in his pocket and strolled across the asphalt stretch, which divided the surgery from the house, onto the lawn. He was almost on top of the small group when Grace, the nanny, looked up and, seeing him, rose to her feet, wiping her hands on her apron.

Catherine who had appeared lost in reverie started as she heard the footfalls behind her and turned, her face lighting into a smile when she saw Tom. She raised a hand in greeting and, as he clasped it, she said: 'I hope you don't mind if I don't get up. I feel terribly lazy.'

'It's that kind of day,' Tom agreed, squatting on his haunches so that he was nearly on the same level as the babies who stared at him with interest. Tansy, as usual, was smiling while Gilbert remained solemn-faced.

'How's life without Geoffrey?' Tom said, straightening up. 'Helen was asking if you'd like to come over to dinner?'

'Well, that is kind of her.' Catherine paused, as any kind of invitation from Helen Thackery was unusual. 'I . . .'

'I'd fetch you and bring you back of course.'

'Then tell her I'd love to.'

'Good.' Tom rolled up his jacket and stretched out on the grass beside her, making the folded coat into a pillow. 'I'll tell her to telephone you. Have you heard from Geoffrey?'

'Oh yes.' Tom noticed Catherine glance quickly at Grace who, however, had resumed her game with the dog and was some way off. 'He telephones me every night. It's hot in Switzerland too.'

'Lucky things. I wish I could be in Switzerland,' Tom said without thinking.

'So do I.' The bitterness in Catherine's voice was unmistakable. Tom felt uncomfortable and wished he'd gone straight home; but the picture of mother and children on the lawn had been somehow irresistible.

'Well, I should be getting back,' he said, sitting up and glancing at his watch. 'I'll tell Helen . . .'

'Tom,' Catherine said sharply, putting a hand on his arm as though to restrain him. 'Do you think I'm unreasonable?'

'I gather you wanted to go on the holiday?' Tom said in a low voice. 'I did wonder.'

'*Of course* I wanted to go on holiday! Fancy going off with the two boys and leaving *me* and the twins behind! Do you call *that* fair or reasonable?'

'I really don't know the circumstances,' Tom said cautiously. 'You know Geoffrey and I never discuss personal matters. He just said he was going on holiday with Edward and Jeremy, and that was that.'

'Has he ever confided in you? Ever?' Catherine's eyes had a curious expression as she looked at him.

Tom sat back on the grass and crossed his legs. He liked Catherine, but since she had been Geoffrey's wife he was very careful about what he said to her. Like everybody else he had, at the time, been very surprised by Geoffrey's decision to marry her. Even more, because he knew her, he was puzzled by Catherine's acceptance. Pleased, but still puzzled.

'No, Geoffrey has never confided in me. He has always been reserved, a person who kept himself to himself. I used to worry about him at one time, but I respected his privacy. Of course Claire had been dead some years when I joined the practice. Geoffrey was quite set in his ways, stoical and unwilling to unburden himself. He never seemed to want to. He was always meticulous and careful with his patients and would freely discuss cases, especially difficult ones, with me; but he never talked about his personal life. Before he met you he would come and dine with us about once a year; but we were never invited back. He never entertained, and I don't honestly think he enjoyed life. I'm afraid this lack of joy was passed on to the boys. In reality they had rather an unhappy childhood which I suppose is why he is trying to make up for it now.'

'But why *now*?' Catherine stamped her foot. 'Why does he take them on holiday now when he didn't before? Do you think I'm unreasonable to mind? Do you?'

Tom found the question embarrassing. 'I expect he'll go on holiday with you and the twins later somewhere else. I think he talked about the Lakes.'

'The *Lakes*!' Catherine said derisively. 'Forty miles away. I would like to have gone to Switzerland too.'

'Without the twins?' Tom looked surprised. 'They are very young to travel.'

'Well, somewhere by the seaside.' Catherine tossed her head. 'Somewhere where we could *all* have enjoyed ourselves, as a family. That is,' she added thoughtfully, 'if we *could* enjoy ourselves as a family with Edward and Jeremy.'

And then, to Tom's discomfiture, tears trickled down her cheeks despite her obvious attempt to keep her predicament both from him and Grace.

'I say!' Tom said, getting up. 'Would you like to take a little walk around the lawn?' and, with a courtly gesture, he held out his arm.

The Blairs' house, Glenhadden, was set well back from the road and apart from the other houses in the street, as though to emphasize the fact that, although part of the community, the doctor was separate from it. The house was larger than all the others, being a double-fronted building built of grey Yorkshire stone. It was quite a large house with six bedrooms, two reception rooms, a dining room, study and servants' quarters. The surgery had been specially built onto it by the doctor who started the practice at the beginning of the century. It was linked to the house by a short passage, like an umbilicus, and there were two separate entrances, one into the house and one to the drive.

It was thus possible for patients and doctors to be kept entirely separate from the house so that, sometimes, Tom didn't see Catherine for weeks, even months.

As she took his arm and they began to walk towards the house he realized she was trembling and he pressed her arm, at the same time slipping her a large white handkerchief from his pocket.

'It's clean,' he said.

Catherine took it without a word and, after dabbing at her eyes, gave her nose a good long blow. Then she crushed the handkerchief and tucked it up her sleeve.

'I'll be all right in a moment,' she said. 'I don't know what got into me.'

'Don't think about it,' Tom said. 'Don't be embarrassed because it's me. I shan't say a word to Geoffrey.'

'It's not only that. It's something else.' Catherine rubbed her eyes hard. 'I realize I am jealous of Geoffrey's boys and I always have been. I have tried since our marriage to exclude them from our life, and I know they hate me. They hated me to start with anyway so I hadn't got much of a chance; and I suppose I never tried to woo their affections. I thought "they are quite old they will soon be grown up," and that it wouldn't matter. But it does. I thought when I was pregnant that at last I would have my own child and then, perhaps, another and another, and Geoffrey would forget about Edward and Jeremy altogether. But, instead, he seems to have come closer to them because he feels guilty about them, and now he has gone on holiday with them! He is closer to them and more distant from me, and you've no idea how lonely and isolated it makes me feel.'

'I can imagine,' Tom said avoiding her eyes and gazing at the ground.

Jeremy Blair, unlike Edward, was a mountain enthusiast. The two brothers were very distinctive, individualistic characters and had little in common. Jeremy had no pretensions to scholarship, and had resisted his father's efforts to get him to go to university. He would like to have played cricket for England but, as that seemed an impossible dream, he was going to get a job like any other young man when he left school. As yet he didn't know what; but it would have to include time for a great deal of sport, dancing, seeing girls and enjoying the good things in life.

There was one way, however, in which Jeremy and Edward Blair were united: they did not like their step-mother and they did not like their father having a young family at his age. They thought it dishonoured their mother's memory and they were ashamed of him. They'd even kept the birth of the twins from a number of their friends.

Sex and fatherhood seemed to go with youth, not age. In a few years Geoffrey Blair could expect to be a grandfather and here he was with a new young family. In the eyes of both his sons Geoffrey Blair had demeaned himself; he had made himself ridiculous.

They had agreed, with some reluctance, to go on holiday to Switzerland. The only real pleasure it gave

them was to know that Catherine was left behind and
that she minded. They knew about the row their father
and stepmother had had the night before they departed
for Switzerland and how morose and angry their father
was for days. Yet every night he made a dutiful call back
to their stepmother, but he never reported on the
conversation or gave them any message.

Geoffrey Blair did his best during the holiday to endear
himself to the sons he had never really known. Yet, to
him, they were rather strange young men and he found
he had little in common with either. They were young
and yet they were old; they were both grown up and
mature, fine specimens of emerging manhood who could
quite do without him now. He soon realized he had
made a mistake coming with them to Switzerland. So far
he had failed in his belated mission to engage their
affections, and he had alienated and hurt his young wife
as he could tell from her voice on the phone.

Yet every day the men walked; they walked off all
their energy so that they had little opportunity for
conversation, and at night they ate a hearty meal and
went early to bed. Some days Jeremy joined a local team
of mountain climbers and got up at five to go scaling
neighbouring peaks and on those days Geoffrey and
Edward walked alone and usually in silence, pausing to
have a beer and a sandwich at some hostelry on the way.

On days like this Geoffrey knew that Edward was
trying to tell him something and, as he thought it would
only be more criticism about his marriage to Catherine,
he did nothing to encourage him, or to make the
awkward silences any easier.

There were too many things he would rather not hear
his son talk about.

But one day, as they sat in the bright sun outside a
hostelry gazing at the magnificent peaks around them,

up one of which Jeremy would now be climbing, a tiny ant among so many on the sides of the mountains, Edward began to talk about his mother, to ask his father questions in a gentle, conciliatory way to which Geoffrey, even though he sensed a trap, could only reply politely.

He told him how they met, and how they married in haste because of the war, thinking that he would be sent to France. But he was turned down because of bad eyesight and then Edward was born a year after war was declared.

Edward had never really asked about his mother and Geoffrey found himself suffused with memories, memories that he had tried to obliterate because the pain of Claire's death had been so sharp.

'Was she what you would call beautiful, Father?'

'Not exactly beautiful,' Geoffrey said, blinking his eyes against the brilliance of the sun which now, at noon, was high overhead.

It was really quite hard to remember now, if one were honest and, inevitably, the passage of time had obliterated the sharpness of Claire's features in his memory. At times he knew they were confused with those of Catherine.

Had he been very disloyal? Yet, after all, it was fifteen years. He had a photograph of Claire in his surgery which Catherine had never objected to; but he knew she wouldn't have a photograph in the house, she would certainly not approve of that.

'It's very difficult to remember your mother, to be honest with you, Edward,' Geoffrey said sadly, avoiding his son's eyes. 'It may sound an awful thing to say . . . and I know how you feel about Catherine, but that is not the reason I can't recall your mother's features very well. It is simply the passage of time.'

To his surprise Geoffrey felt his son's hand steal over his very briefly, and then being hastily withdrawn because, presumably, it was an unmanly thing to do.

'I shouldn't have spoken to you the way I did that night, Father. I was very ashamed of myself afterwards.'

'That's all right. We've never found it easy to talk,' Geoffrey said gruffly. 'I think it's my fault rather than yours. I should have told you more about Catherine before I married her. I know it was sudden, a shock.' Geoffrey rubbed his hand over his face and looked towards the snow-capped peaks of the Alps. 'I've been very bad at communicating with people all my life. Not my patients. I think I can communicate with them, explain things to them, help and sympathize with them. But my own family have always been a different matter. Even your mother and I didn't talk a lot about intimate things. She never even told me when she began to feel ill. There was a natural reticence between us and there is . . . between Catherine and me, even though I love her so much. I wish it wasn't so, but it is. Now with you boys . . .'

'We're men now, Father.' Edward made the gesture towards him with his hand again but without touching him. 'The fact is I've been wanting to talk to you for some time and haven't known how to begin. When I came to see you the day of the christening I didn't mean to say what I said, I meant to say something else; but I didn't have the nerve. Now . . .'

'For God's sake I hope *you* aren't ill,' Geoffrey said in alarm, remembering how advanced Claire's TB was before she even mentioned her tiredness, the pains in her chest. What was it about him that inspired confidences from patients but not his immediate family?

'No, I'm not ill, Father,' Edward said reassuringly. 'But I know what I'm going to say will upset you. Believe me

I don't want to because I know how much it means to you. But the fact is, Father . . .' Edward stood up as though his height would give him advantage. 'I'm not very happy in what I am doing.'

'Not happy?' Geoffrey said, reaching for his pipe as he always did in an emergency, as though it were a baby's comforter. 'Not happy doing what?'

'Medicine.'

'You're not happy doing medicine? I don't understand.'

'I don't want to be a doctor, Father. That's what I wanted to tell you before, only I couldn't bring myself to say it. My emotions became confused by the natural resentment I do feel about Catherine. I am just muddled and very disturbed at the moment, Father; but I don't feel the least calling to be a doctor and I want to leave medical school.'

'Well, you can't,' Geoffrey said bluntly, beginning to fill his pipe.

'Why not?'

'Because I don't think it's the right thing to do. I think you'll regret it.'

'But you can't *force* me to stay there if I don't want to.'

'Naturally I can't; but I think it is in your best interests, and I hope you will be guided by me.'

'But, Father, how can it be in my best interests if I don't like it?'

'Because you haven't been there long enough. You are only in your second year of medical school. You haven't even *begun* clinical medicine. You've no idea what it's like. I think, personally, you will make a very fine doctor.'

'Well, I don't.'

'Why don't you?' Geoffrey glared at him and stuck his cold, unlit pipe in his mouth.

'I don't like people very much. I'm not terribly interested in them.'

'You don't have to like people to be a good doctor. Better in a way if you don't. Then you won't get involved.'

'That seems to me a very cynical thing to say, Father.'

'Nevertheless it's true. Some of the best doctors I have known have been indifferent to their fellow men. To be a good clinician you need to have knowledge and good judgement. It is also a very fine profession and, incidently, not without its financial rewards.'

'You don't become a doctor, surely, just to make money!'

'Nevertheless,' Geoffrey began to fiddle with his tobacco pouch again, 'you do. A good doctor attracts rich patients. I am quite able to manage without half of Netherwick paying me fees in these hard times, and yet earn a good living.' Geoffrey paused to chuckle. 'Catherine was quite upset about it at one time; but I am not a greedy man, and if people can't afford to pay then I will not take their money. Yet still we have sufficient means to enjoy a good life, Edward.' Abruptly Geoffrey rose and put his arm around his son's shoulders. 'Come on, let's forget all this nonsense about giving up medicine. We've had a good talk today haven't we? We understand each other better already? My one wish for you is to come into practice with me when you've qualified. I've always set my heart on it. Doctor G. Blair and Doctor E. Blair. You don't know how much it means to me.' He left his hand where he had placed it and remained looking wistfully at his son.

'I'm sorry, Father, but I can't,' Edward said, moving reluctantly away, conscious that this precious, this unusual moment of togetherness would be gone for ever. 'I've already applied for a transfer.'

'A transfer to where?' Geoffrey said sharply, letting his hand fall.

'To another department. I'm going to read philosophy and history.'

'Philosophy and *what*?' Geoffrey said as though hearing a sacrilegious announcement.

'History.'

'But that's got nothing at all to do with medicine.'

'I know; but that's what I want to do. I think I'd quite like to teach.'

'Then it's a *fait accompli*,' Geoffrey murmured, turning once more towards the mountain peaks as though for solace.

'I'm afraid so, Father,' Edward said gently. 'I can't tell you how sorry I am.'

But Geoffrey continued walking slowly away from the inn and along the road they had been following, as though intent on obliterating his son and his words from his mind.

Catherine noticed the difference in Geoffrey as soon as he returned from holiday. He came back alone, as both of the boys had stopped off in London where they intended to spend the rest of the vacation.

He had been in the house almost an hour before she knew he was back, having gone straight to his surgery though it was out of surgery hours.

The gardener had seen his baggage in the hall and brought it up to his room where Catherine had been tidying some drawers. She looked up in surprise as the luggage arrived but said nothing, getting on quietly with her task. Only when the gardener had gone did she quickly descend the staircase, running through the passage that connected Geoffrey's surgery with the house. She stopped for a moment rather fearfully outside the door before knocking timidly and waiting for a reply. When there was none she turned the handle and opened the door, walking slowly into the room.

Geoffrey was not at his desk, but sat in a chair facing the window that overlooked a pleasant view of the garden. For a moment she thought he was asleep.

'Geoffrey,' she whispered, creeping up to him, 'are you all right?'

'Ah, Catherine,' Geoffrey said, stirring himself. 'Just very tired, my dear; a long, long journey. Too many people travelling; far, far too many. Many, they say, on the move from Germany.'

'I wasn't expecting you until the end of the week.' She felt strangely timorous, like a schoolgirl, perched on the edge of his desk, not sitting or standing. There was still something about Geoffrey that made her in awe of him.

'Well, the holiday wasn't a great success, to be frank.' Geoffrey passed his hand over his brow and groped with the other for his pipe. 'I've left it too late. My sons don't know me and I don't know or understand them. Edward wants to give up medicine.'

'*What*?' Catherine felt a spasm of horror because she knew how much it meant to Geoffrey to have a son following in his footsteps. He had always told her that he'd set his heart on it.

'Exactly,' he grimaced at her. 'You can imagine how much it upset me when he first told me. He chose to do it on top of a mountain, in the middle of a long walk. He'd had it on his mind for ages. It was only a few days ago, but that was it. I'd had enough, and so had they. It wasn't an enjoyable holiday. It was a mistake. You can't undo the past, you know; you can't undo the mistakes you once made.'

'I'm awfully sorry, Geoffrey.' Catherine wanted to kiss him, but his attitude seemed to forbid such a gesture.

She thought of their stilted, almost monosyllabic conversations on the phone at night. Suddenly she felt an overwhelming sense of pity for her husband: a man who failed to please either his wife or his sons. No wonder he had gone straight to his surgery, from which his only satisfaction in life seemed to come. It was Geoffrey's way of returning to the comfort of the womb.

'What's the use?' he said looking at her with eyes that were clouded with pain. 'What's the use of anything? I told them we had to come straight back. I think they wanted to anyway, though Jeremy got in a few days good climbing. Jeremy enjoyed it more than Edward or me because, most days, he was away from us. I think he would have liked to stay, but the atmosphere on the continent is too unsettled, you know. That chap Hitler means trouble for Germany. There's even talk of war.'

'Oh no, don't say that!' Catherine put a hand to her face.

'People are already streaming out of Germany,' Geoffrey continued. 'They say that Hitler is building concentration camps and herding all his enemies into them: communists and Jews mostly. I've said all the time that the fellow should be stopped but how, is the question. How does one stop a steamroller?'

Impulsively Catherine bent to kiss him, a chaste kiss on the brow. He put up his arms and returned her kiss, but chastely, too, on each cheek. It was though all the vitality, all the spirit had been drained from him and, once again, she feared for his health.

'Come and have a drink,' she said. 'A stiff whisky is what you need.'

'Thank you, my dear.' Geoffrey smiled for the first time since she had come into the room, and put out his hand. 'You've no idea how good it is to see you again. How much I need you. Being away from you made me realize that all too well; made me value how much I rely on you. You're essential to me, Catherine. Do you know that? And you don't even reproach me for going off without you.'

'Too late for that now,' Catherine replied softly, stroking his hair away from his brow. 'No point now that it is done. Maybe later in the year we'll go to Keswick.'

Geoffrey appeared to be not really listening to her, but was still ruminating on the lost chances of the ruined holiday.

'My children have disappointed me,' he muttered, half to himself. 'I have failed them. As if it weren't bad enough Edward giving up medicine, Jeremy wants to go into a bank! A *bank*, I ask you!'

'What's wrong with a bank?' Catherine said with a smile, picking up his pipe and pouch and taking them with her as she linked an arm through his.

'A bank, I should think, is about one of the most boring places on this earth,' Geoffrey said fiercely.

'But secure, and very necessary. *If* there is a war . . .'

'*If* there is a war both my boys will be in it,' Geoffrey whispered sadly. 'And I can't bear to think what will happen then.'

'Come and see the twins,' Catherine tugged at his hand. 'They at any rate will be very pleased to see *you*.'

At eight months Tansy Blair was trying her hardest to walk. Her progress was astonishing, her intelligence palpable, even at her age. Gilbert was much slower. He was a lazy baby who didn't crawl much, never mind attempt to walk. There was nothing wrong with Gilbert: his reactions were all in order; he was a perfectly normal baby; but even at eight months he had a rather slow, meditative manner that would be one of his characteristics all his life, whereas Tansy would be quick and alert, vivacious as she was now.

They were on the floor of their nursery when their father came in and Tansy, as if to impress him, tried to get up on her little legs and come towards him; but instead she fell flat on her face and her father and mother burst out laughing. Even Gilbert joined in. His sister's predicament seemed to amuse him a good deal and he remained where he was on his back, kicking his legs in the air with mirth in a rare display of high spirits.

At that moment Geoffrey was seized by such a feeling of gratitude and joy that he swept Tansy into his arms swinging her high towards the ceiling.

'My beautiful little girl,' he cried. 'My baby daughter.' Then he hugged her tight and his eyes were so bright that Catherine thought he would burst into tears but, instead, he rubbed his face on Tansy's shoulder and when he looked up again the brightness had gone. Tenderly he put Tansy down, then he knelt and tickled Gilbert, who had grown solemn again, in the ribs.

'And how is my little boy?' Geoffrey said in a grown-up voice as though expecting his infant son would answer. But Gilbert stared at his father with an air of bewilderment as though he wondered who he was.

'My little doctor,' Geoffrey said, lovingly, tickling his ribs again. 'You're the one who will succeed me, Gilbert Blair. I can see it in your eyes. Twenty years hence, just you wait!'

Geoffrey rose from his knees with a smile of satisfaction, and he looked at Catherine as though in one fell swoop all his troubles had been resolved, all his disappointment dissipated. 'Twenty years hence, you mark my words!'

'I do love you,' Geoffrey said, clinging to Catherine as they lay in bed that night. 'I may not show it very well, but I do. For a time in Switzerland I was afraid of losing you too.'

'Oh no, never.'

'That's why I hurried back because I wanted you. You were always so cold to me on the phone.'

'You sounded angry with me.'

'I was.'

'I wasn't very nice to you, before you went away,' she said.

'But you had a good reason,' Geoffrey protested. 'You wanted a holiday and you needed one. *I* was selfish not to see it. But I was very hurt by my boys. Hurt and humiliated. I wanted them to love you too.'

'I never expected *them* to love me,' Catherine said, conscious of the fact that a Sunday morning situation was developing. 'I should have set out to befriend them, but I didn't. My attitude to them was all wrong. I was jealous of them, childish really. But what I said to *you* wasn't very nice. I was ashamed of myself afterwards.'

'You called me a dirty old man,' Geoffrey said with a smile in the dark, though she couldn't see it.

'I did, and I'm sorry.'

'I may not be the best lover in the world, but nevertheless I do love you.'

'You *could* be a little gentler,' Catherine whispered, 'then I wouldn't dread it so much.'

'Dread?'

He pondered the word 'dread', finding it a shocking thing for her to say, and at that moment, all desire, the pent up emotion of weeks, went from him and, out of sheer exhaustion, he fell asleep.

Chapter 4

On 30 September 1938 the Prime Minister, Neville Chamberlain, flew home from a meeting with Hitler in Germany with a scrap of paper in his hand. 'I believe it is peace in our time,' he said, waving the paper above his head. It was an image that was to remain in the memories of most people for a very long time.

By the time this momentous event took place Edward Blair had begun as an assistant master at a grammar school in Finchley teaching history. It was a well run, well disciplined school and it suited that curiously orderly and determined kind of temperament that Edward seemed to have inherited from his father. Edward rented two furnished rooms in Finchley, sharing a kitchen and bathroom, in a Victorian terraced house not far from the school. He moved into it the few possessions he had had in his father's house, and he now thought of it as home.

One of the first visitors to his flat was his brother Jeremy who worked in a bank in Swiss Cottage. He also had a two-room flat which he shared with a fellow employee, a handsome and genial young Jewish man called Derek Lester who was taking banking seriously and, unlike Jeremy, doing all the exams.

By coincidence Derek Lester's sister was also a school-teacher at the girls' school in Finchley that complemented the boys'. The grounds practically touched, and the schools shared certain facilities including the gym and the playing fields.

One evening Jeremy arrived for dinner with his friend

Derek and his own recently acquired girlfriend, Barbara Chance, who worked at the bank. Barbara was one of the new generation of emancipated females who enjoyed the independence that work gave her; but she still lived with her parents in Muswell Hill and travelled daily to the bank by bus and tube.

Jeremy Blair had just celebrated his twenty-first birthday. He was a tall, engaging young man; dark haired, slim, athletic-looking, vibrant with youth and with a distinctive charm, a sexual allure, that neither his father or his brother had. Jeremy looked roguish, almost devilish, and women liked that. He was a great success with them and changed partners very often. They seldom lasted for more than a month or two, although Barbara Chance seemed to be in with more hopes than most. She was not only compellingly attractive, but resembled Jeremy in temperament and enjoyed the things Jeremy liked: dancing, all kinds of sports, amateur dramatics and visits to the theatre.

Barbara had never met Jeremy's brother, but she had heard a lot about the family, about the crisis after the twins had been born and their father's anger when Edward decided not to pursue his medical studies.

Since then Edward had made only cursory visits to his father's home, token gestures of filial devotion that never lasted more than a few days.

Jeremy went home even less frequently. His job at the bank kept him tied to London and he only had short holidays. These he preferred to spend with the parents of the current girlfriend who were always delighted to welcome him in their home in the hope that, one day, he might become a more permanent fixture in the family. Jeremy had a way of getting on with the mothers of his girlfriends as well as the girls themselves. In fact older women, in particular, seemed to adore him. Jeremy not only had striking good looks; but he was the sort of personable young man from a good family, and with a steady job, that every mother hoped for for her daughter's lasting happiness. Consequently he was never short of invitations.

Edward was not good at entertaining. He had never learned to cook because it was not expected of men, and he used to eat out with his unmarried friends or at the homes of the married ones. Not as entertaining or attractive as Jeremy, he nevertheless did not lack friends, especially the serious-minded masters and the older and less decorative women teachers at the girls' school, who regarded him, and whom he regarded, as 'safe'.

Consequently, on the night of Jeremy's visit to Edward's flat with his girlfriend Barbara and fellow workmate Derek, they all ate at a nearby Chinese restaurant. Edward insisted on paying because he said it was instead of a housewarming party.

'But you *must* have a housewarming party,' Barbara cried. 'No home is complete without one,' and she turned to Jeremy who casually put an arm round her waist.

'No home,' he said solemnly and impulsively kissed her on the cheek before bursting into laughter.

'All right then, a housewarming party,' Edward said with little enthusiasm. 'Just a small one. A few people from the school.' He had little liking for parties and, as he took his work very seriously, he had a lot of preparation to do. Edward had not taken the usual teachers' training course following his degree because the school was short of a history teacher when he applied. Also the international situation was threatening and, in their minds if not their hearts, many people were preparing for war.

'My sister is a first-class party giver; she'll give you a

few tips,' Derek said, glancing at his watch. 'Incidentally she's a colleague of yours at the girls' school.'

'Oh really?' Edward said with little interest. He had formed a poor, and typically prejudiced, view of women teachers.

'She teaches classics at the Girls' Grammar.'

'Oh really?' Edward said again. He had absolutely no expectations of a girl who taught classics. The image of a female teacher of clasics was of a bun, tortoiseshell spectacles and no bosom.

'She might be home now.' Derek warmed to the idea. 'I told her we might pop in.'

'I think I should be getting back.' Edward glanced at his watch. 'Henry II is not a monarch with whose politics I am particularly familiar and I have to give a class to the upper fifth about him tomorrow.'

'It will only take a few minutes,' Derek said.

'Yes, come on.' Jeremy looked impatiently at his brother. 'Don't be such a spoil-sport.'

'I'm *not* a spoil-sport,' Edward said crossly. 'I simply have too much to do.'

'Another time, then,' Jeremy said, adding, 'she's quite pretty, actually.'

'Oh.' Edward seemed to hesitate. 'Then I hope I run into her some day. I mean I hope I run into her in any case.' He glanced apologetically at Derek.

'You really *are* a misery,' Jeremy said to Edward as they waited outside on the pavement for Derek who had gone to fetch his car.

'Just because I want to get home and do my work.'

'But it's only *nine o'clock*!'

'Yes and I have two or three hours of work to do.'

'All we want to do is have a coffee and say "hello". It's a bit embarrassing really.' Jeremy shifted from one foot to the other blowing into his hands because of the cold.

'Derek has told her about you and I think she is rather looking forward to meeting you. As a colleague, I mean. Nothing else.'

'Oh all right, then,' Edward said crossly, also stamping his feet. 'I'm sure I shan't like her and I'm not going to stay long. But I don't want to embarrass your friend, that's all. In future, Jeremy, please don't undertake engagements on my behalf without consulting me.'

Jeremy murmured something derogatory under his breath, but Barbara gave a loud cough and slapped Jeremy on the arm, whispering into his ear.

Edward sat in the back of Derek's car feeling bad-tempered and disgruntled because of his ruined evening. He knew he would be very late to bed and, as he didn't always sleep well, he would feel tired. He vowed that never again would he allow himself to be talked by his brother into doing something he didn't want to do.

But this was not the first time and he had reluctantly to concede that, in all probability, it wouldn't be the last. Jeremy had a way with him, a charm that carried even his sceptical sibling along, one who was used to his wiles. Jeremy led and he followed, even though he was two years older than his brother.

Edward's ruminations were brought abruptly to an end as the car stopped outside a semi-detached house in Finchley not far from the school, in one of the many anonymous little streets that surrounded it. It had white stucco walls, a porch and a neat little garden, and had been built, along with most of the houses on either side of it and, indeed, stretching for streets behind, at the beginning of the thirties.

Derek had a key to the house which seemed to be in darkness and, as he sat at the back of the car waiting, Edward hoped no one would be in. But he saw a light go on in the hall and heard Derek talking to someone.

Then Derek turned and beckoned and Edward, Jeremy and Barbara got out and walked towards the house and into the hall where Derek was standing talking to a dainty, rather spinsterish-looking girl, just as Edward had thought she would be. She wore gold-rimmed glasses and her hair was in a roll around her head; her arms were folded against her chest, and she wore a twin-set and tweed skirt with sensible shoes, which also conformed to his stereotype of a teacher of classics.

'God,' he mumbled under his breath but, as he was the last to go in, no one heard him except his brother who immediately preceded him. 'I thought you said she was *pretty*,' he murmured in Jeremy's ear and nudging him in the back.

'Wait until you see her with no clothes on,' Jeremy said with a smile which enraged Edward who hated smutty talk of any kind. Smutty and untrue. Jeremy, as usual, was just trying to shock him.

'How do you do?' he said politely when his turn came to be introduced to Emily Lester. 'I hear you teach at the Girls'!' he added politely.

'Yes I do,' she replied, just as politely, 'and you're the new history master. I've heard about you.' Her smile was friendly, but the main impression she made on Edward was that her voice was low and melodic. She seemed quite at ease in strange company and led them into the sitting room, apologizing for the lack of heat, but as her parents were out she had been working in her bedroom which was at the back.

'I had a lot of preparation to do,' she added.

'Oh dear, I am *sorry*,' Barbara looked reproachfully at Derek. 'Your brother said you were expecting us.'

'I was,' Emily assured her, taking off her glasses. 'I have practically finished as my last lesson today was a free period, and I came straight home.'

She smiled suddenly at Edward and he realized that, indeed, she was pretty. Her hair was mouse-coloured, but she had a good clear skin, which was slightly tanned from a summer spent abroad. She had large brown intelligent eyes and a firm mouth; she was a strong, determined-looking girl.

Edward immediately forgot about his preparation for the next day. His social life had, on the whole, been very bleak and here was a chance to do something about it. He knew himself to be rather a withdrawn man who, unlike Jeremy, did not immediately charm. To a certain extent he was a little jealous of his brother and the success he had with women.

Edward had never had a steady girlfriend in his life. He had never properly kissed a woman and he certainly had never made love to one. He blamed his father for his inability either to inspire or form affection. He thought it was the cold, dark side of the Blair family, his father's side, coming out, whereas Jeremy had inherited the genes of his mother whom he knew was beautiful, whatever his father said, because he had seen her photograph. The years had simply made his father forget just how beautiful.

Edward observed, with approval, that Emily was a practical girl as well as a clever one. She prepared the coffee tray in the kitchen whence she was followed by Barbara with whom, it appeared, she was on good terms. As Derek rekindled the fire in the grate Edward stood in front of it and, as his father would have done in a similar circumstance, produced his tobacco pouch and began to fill his pipe.

Derek began to look through the records stacked by the gramophone and, as Emily came in with the tray,

followed by Barbara carrying a plate of cakes, he began
to wind up the gramophone and put on 'The Way You
Look Tonight'.

Edward continued to stand by the fire, slowly, methodically filling his pipe, following Emily's movements as
she poured the coffee, added milk and handed the cups
around while Barbara stood at her elbow ready with the
sugar bowl and a plate of cakes. As she came to Edward
he smiled, tucked his still cold, unlit pipe into his pocket
and accepted the cup.

'Thank you very much,' he said politely.

'I see you're a pipe smoker like your father,' Emily
remarked conversationally.

'Do you *know* my father?' Edward looked at her in
surprise, but she laughed and shook her head.

'No, but every time I am with Jeremy, he talks about
him a lot. He says you're very like him.'

'I'm afraid that's true.' Edward carefully inspected the
cakes held out on a plate by a smiling Barbara who was
swaying in time to the music. 'Here, why don't I take
that?' Edward said, reaching for the plate of cakes, and
then he looked for somewhere to put it while Emily
returned for her cup, the last to be served, and then
rejoined him.

'I don't suppose you'd met my brother Derek before,
had you?' she remarked with a naturalness that Edward
found very pleasing.

'I met him briefly at Jeremy's. But I was away all the
summer.'

'So was I,' Emily said. 'Where were you?'

'I went to Italy and Germany, not a very good choice,
particularly the latter.'

'Do you *really* think there'll be a war?' Emily had a
note of incredulity in her voice. 'Aren't *you* convinced by
Mr Chamberlain?'

'I think he's sincere, and that he does want peace,' Edward replied, 'but I don't think Herr Hitler does. I think he wants to pay the Allies back for the Treaty of Versailles and nothing will stop him. No one *wants* to stop him. What we let happen in Czechoslovakia was disgraceful.'

'I think it was too,' Emily said with a decisiveness which Edward liked. 'It seems that we will do anything for peace.' She remained silent for a moment then burst out suddenly: 'I suppose you know we're Jewish?'

'Oh yes,' Edward seemed surprised by the remark. 'Not that you look it. Oh pardon!' his hand flew to his mouth. 'I didn't mean at all . . .' Edward knew he was blushing.

Emily smiled and put a hand reassuringly, naturally on his arm. 'Don't let it worry you,' she said. 'We're not kosher either, but we don't like Hitler. There are too many nasty stories coming out of Germany.'

'You can say that again.' Edward selected another cake and began to peel the greaseproof paper away from it. 'Did you make these?' he enquired as though anxious to change the subject.

'Oh no. I'm not a *bit* domestic, I'm afraid. My mother's the cook.'

'Well, you'll have to do something about that before you get married,' Edward said, also smiling, then he realized he'd been too familiar and putting a hand up to stroke his moustache murmured: 'I'm very sorry. I had no right to say that.'

'That's quite all right,' Emily replied cheerfully. 'It's what men expect, isn't it?'

'It seems to be.'

'Do you?' He was aware that she was looking searchingly into his eyes.

'Yes, I suppose I do, to be honest,' he said after a few

moments' thought. 'It seems to me the natural order of things.'

Briefly, he thought he saw disappointment in her face; but just then Jeremy came over, his hand reaching for Emily's.

'Would you have this dance with me, Miss?'

Edward noticed the way that Emily got up, quickly and with obvious pleasure and he thought that, yet again, he'd fluffed his chances.

But at least he was honest. He *did* expect a woman to be domesticated, even if she were clever and he felt in a way that his brother did too but, unlike him, he wouldn't be honest enough to say so. He'd go along with a girl and then he'd change when he was sure of her. This was always why his relationships ended. It had happened with others and, in time, it would happen with Barbara. He began by wooing them and ended up by using them.

'My brother's watching you,' Jeremy murmured into Emily's ear. 'I think he likes you.'

'What a silly thing to say!' Emily said, but softly so that her voice didn't carry. 'I've only just met him!'

'Yes, but I can tell by the way he's looking at you. I thought you two would have a lot in common, which was why I wanted you to meet.'

'That's not very nice is it?' Emily said coldly, and he could feel her body drawing away from his.

'I don't know what you mean.' Jeremy, by the pressure of his hands, tried to draw her closer. By this time Derek and Barbara had found a new record they liked, and the dancing continued uninterrupted while, in the corner, Edward sat reflectively, no longer watching the dancers but staring into the fire.

'What do you mean, "it's not very nice"?' Jeremy asked her again.

'Trying to throw me and your brother together,' she answered defensively.

'I'm not trying to "throw" anybody together.' By this time Jeremy was so close to Emily that Barbara was staring at them, dancing apathetically with Derek.

'When two people seem alike you'd like them to meet,' he continued. 'Edward is rather lonely here. He doesn't know many people. I thought . . .'

'I've *quite* enough to occupy me, thank you,' Emily said as the record finished and the dancing stopped. Then she left Jeremy abruptly and went back to the coffee table to pour another cup.

Soon after that it was time to go. Emily said that her parents would soon be home and Edward that he had his preparation to do. There were 'goodbyes' at the door and then the small party went out to Derek's car while Emily stood in the doorway waving.

'I'll drop you off first,' Derek said to Barbara who was sitting in the back with Jeremy. 'If that's OK.'

'That's perfectly OK,' Barbara replied, and Jeremy put his mouth to her ear and whispered, 'Come back to my place.'

'You know I can't,' she whispered back, even though the sound of their voices was drowned by the rasping of the old Ford engine. 'My parents would have a fit.'

'You could say you stayed with Emily.'

'I couldn't!' she protested with a giggle. 'Anyway,' she went on trying to edge away from him, 'I didn't care for the way you danced with Emily. You were much too close to her. How do you think *I* felt?'

'A little jealous perhaps?' Jeremy said with a pleased smile.

'If you behave like that, Jeremy Blair,' Barbara continued in an aggrieved voice, 'I shan't want to see you again.'

'Oh, don't be so silly, I'm just having you on.' He tried to tuck his hand in hers and whispered so that the front passengers couldn't hear. 'That kind of bluestocking doesn't attract me at all, but I thought she might appeal to Edward.'

'Funny way you had of showing it.' Barbara shook her head sulkily.

'I even told her I thought Edward fancied her. She didn't seem to like it much.'

Barbara put her finger to her mouth as if to warn him that Edward, sitting in front with Derek, might be able to hear; but Edward was gazing in front of him, his eyes on the road, as though quite oblivious to what was going on in the back seat of the car.

1938 merged into 1939 and the international news got worse. In Berlin Hitler opened the Reichstag building which had been gutted in the fire of 1933, an event which had ultimately helped to bring the Nazis to power. Jews were being banned from all the professions yet Neville Chamberlain, still in search of peace, visited Mussolini in Rome.

In Netherwick in January the Blair twins celebrated their fifth birthday, and in London it was the start of their half-brother Edward's second term at the grammar school.

1939, which was to be such a momentous year for so many people, thus began quietly on the domestic front as far as the Blairs, and so many families like them, were concerned. But the air of restlessness that pervaded the country pervaded them too, and Jeremy Blair began to tire of his clerical work at the bank.

He felt that he needed more than the sedentary life to satisfy him, and he began to toy with the idea of joining one of the armed forces if Britain was soon to be engulfed in war.

On the last Saturday in January a football match was taking place in the field between the Boys' and the Girls' Grammar in Finchley. It was between staff and senior students and Edward had been due to play centre-forward for the staff. But the day before he had fallen down some steps leading to the staff room and sprained his ankle, not badly, but badly enough to make him unfit to play. No substitute could be found at the last moment, so Edward rang Jeremy and asked him to play in his place.

It was a cold day with frost on the ground and there were few spectators except a sprinkling of supporters from both schools who had friends or relations playing for one of the teams.

Edward, feeling honour-bound to support his brother despite his mounds of preparation, was among the staff from the boys' school standing on the touchline, his arms folded against his chest, a muffler bound round his neck against the cold.

It was not until the game was well advanced that he saw Derek Lester on the other side of the field and, at half-time, he walked round to greet him while the members of the team went into the pavilion to drink warm drinks and be lectured to by their respective coaches.

As Edward got nearer he realized that Derek was with his sister who was so muffled against the cold that at first he didn't recognize her.

'I'm awfully sorry,' he said apologetically, 'I thought you were someone else. How have you been?'

'Fine,' Emily said, clapping her hands against her side. 'And you?'

'Fine. I've just about settled down. Are you keen on football?'

'Not very. But Derek said he was going, so I thought I'd go with him. One or two of the members of our staff and several of the girls have friends in the boys' school as you can see.' She gestured about with her gloved hands. 'Quite a crowd.'

'I told her Jeremy was playing,' Derek said with a smile. 'I think that's the attraction.'

'Oh Derek, don't be so *stupid*,' Emily said angrily, and Edward noticed the hot flush that had immediately stung her face. 'What an *idiotic* thing to say.'

'I'm sorry,' Derek said contritely, but he gave Edward a knowing smile.

'Anyway he's got a girlfriend,' Emily said in a detached tone of voice, as though she felt she'd been rather childish. 'That very nice girl we met before Christmas.'

'Oh, that was Barbara,' Edward said dismissively. 'There have been two or three since Barbara.'

'Your brother *is* a lad, isn't he?' Emily said, and Edward thought there was a trace of admiration in her voice.

'He's certainly that,' Edward turned thoughtfully towards the field, 'and now he's thinking of joining up.'

'Joining up?' Emily sounded as if she didn't know what he meant.

'The forces. He's keen on the RAF.'

'Did *you* know that, Derek?' Emily turned to her brother who nodded his head.

'He's given notice to the bank. I don't blame him. It's an awfully dull job.'

'Well, don't *you* go joining up.' Emily tucked a hand firmly in his arm. 'I'd rather have you safe at the bank, even if it is dull.'

'If we do have a war,' Derek said solemnly, 'none of

us will be very safe. If there's a war here it will be like Spain.'

'How do you mean?' Emily's apprehension seemed to be growing.

'Bombing.'

'But not on civilians, surely?'

'Oh, yes, on civilians.' Edward's voice was grave. 'What they've done in Spain they will do elsewhere. If we have war with Germany they will bomb us and we shall bomb them.'

'Oh, don't *talk* about it,' Emily said as the teams emerged from the pavilion, and she hugged her brother very close.

That evening Edward, Jeremy, Derek and Emily again ate at the Chinese restaurant in Finchley. It was like a repeat of the meal they'd had there before only this time the girl was Emily.

Barbara had been followed by a Jane, and then a Primrose and currently Jeremy had no girlfriend at all which was a most unusual state of affairs. However, he was in a good mood as, largely thanks to him, the older side had won, regaining a trophy from the youngsters who had had it for some years.

'I hear you're joining up,' Emily said, smiling at him across the table as the waiter bore down on them with a tray containing several bowls of Chinese delicacies.

'I'm hoping the RAF will have me. It's a grand career,' Jeremy said with an enthusiasm that contained no trace of doubt at all. 'They teach you to fly so that if there isn't a war I'll be able to be a civilian pilot. The aeroplane, you know, is the machine of the future. I don't think any of us realize what its implications can be, not only for war but in civilian use. I intend to be in there at the beginning.'

'I can't honestly believe there'll be a war.' Emily shook her head and Edward, watching her across the table, thought that she was really pretty without her glasses, with her hair worn loose and not tucked severely into a ribbon around her head, and a pretty woollen dress with a high, sculpted collar. Her face had clear, clean, classical lines and her gravity was belied by the sudden spontaneous burst of laughter, by her vivacity which transformed her features and gave her a softer, more feminine look.

Yet he knew that she was watching Jeremy. She was aware of Jeremy. Maybe she was laughing *for* Jeremy, and that all the little feminine wiles and gestures she employed throughout the night were for him.

Edward shuddered at the idea of Emily being just another in Jeremy's assembly line of women friends and suddenly he realized that he wanted her for himself and, if necessary, he would fight for her.

Emily said: 'It's awfully nice of you to call, Edward. But I've loads of prep for tomorrow.'

'It was just a thought,' Edward said on the other end of the line. It was a few days after the meeting on the football field. 'It seems a nice evening,' he went on, 'not too cold, and I thought a meal at the Chinese maybe . . .'

'I really can't. Not tonight.' Her voice sounded polite but apathetic and he knew that she was wishing he was his brother. In fact he knew for sure that she would have downed prep for the sake of Jeremy.

Edward Blair loved his brother but, at that moment, he was overwhelmed by a feeling of malice towards him: malice and envy too.

'How about *Saturday*?' he said in a firm voice. 'Say Saturday and I'll try and ask my brother to join us.'

'Oh, Saturday would be fine,' Emily said in a different voice altogether. 'There's no prep to do on Saturday.'

The following Saturday Edward dressed in a new suit he had bought in Oxford Street for the occasion. With it he wore a woollen shirt and a knitted tie and he thought he looked the epitome of the country gentleman. He groomed himself very carefully for the occasion, putting Brylcreem on his hair and carefully combing his moustache, which was now as thick and heavy as his father's. He knew he looked old for his years, but he didn't mind that.

Promptly at seven he left in his new Ford Popular to pick up the first girl he had ever dated.

He knew at once that she was disappointed as she looked past him at the door. 'Isn't your brother with you?' she said immediately, peering anxiously towards the car.

'He couldn't make it,' Edward lied. 'He sends his regards. I thought we'd go somewhere different from the Chinese.' He boldly dismissed any further talk of Jeremy as of no consequence. 'There's a very nice new French restaurant in Brent.'

'That sounds lovely,' Emily said with a smile of resignation and, as she closed the door behind her, he knew that she was a well brought-up, good-mannered girl who would accept the inevitable. She was just the sort for him.

Emily paused to admire his new green car which, he explained, was the first motor vehicle he had ever owned. 'Your brother would have a sports car I expect,' she said lightly, but there was nothing insinuating in her voice.

'I expect he would if he could afford it,' Edward said

in a voice which suggested that Jeremy was a bit of a joke. 'He goes into the RAF next week.'

'My, that's quick.'

But now her voice was perfectly controlled as though Jeremy and his fate were of little interest to her too.

Edward closed the door carefully on her side and strode confidently round to the driving seat.

This time, he, Edward Blair, knew what he wanted and he would win.

In fact they had a great deal in common, as the dinner revealed. They both loved history and travel; Emily spent each summer in Italy or Greece and had a profound knowledge of antiquities. She had got a first-class degree from Bedford College of the University of London, and Edward remarked on the fact that they must both have been at the university at the same time yet, because they had belonged to different colleges, they had never met.

'Except, of course,' he said tasting the wine the waiter poured for them, 'I'm probably a year or two older than you, although I graduated at the same time.'

'Why was that?' Emily gazed at him curiously. He thought, or imagined, he saw a new expression of interest in her eyes. 'Did you do something else first?'

'My father wanted me to be a doctor so I started studying medicine. I hated it.'

Edward gave a sudden disarming smile and, for the first time, Emily who, when she looked at him saw only his brother, saw him as he was. She realized that he was not only educated, entertaining and knowledgeable, but he wasn't bad looking either.

Jeremy was a completely different kind of person from his brother Edward — instantly attractive, engaging and good-looking. But, she thought, with the benefit of hindsight, certainly not as clever as Edward.

Maybe, after all, there was something in the man sitting opposite her that made him even more interesting than his brother. He was open and honest, and didn't try to defend his decision to drop medicine or reproach his father for trying unduly to influence him. Moreover he most certainly was not a womanizer which Jeremy undoubtedly was – a man who, all her instincts told her, would never make one happy.

Emily was not consciously looking for a husband, but she was twenty-three. She knew that sometimes she looked and behaved like an old maid, and that her mother worried that she would be. She was too serious, her mother told her. Men weren't interested in intellectual women; they didn't want a challenge but a helpmeet, a companion.

It was true that her mother belonged to a much older generation; but Emily was influenced by her all the same. She loved her work but she didn't want to be a school mistress all the time; she didn't want it to mean she would be left on the shelf.

She looked up at Edward and gave him a warm, intimate smile. He was twenty-four, yet he looked thirty; but there was something solid and reliable about him – adjectives one could never use about his brother. Jeremy was unattainable anyway and had never shown any interest in her. She wasn't his sort and, in her heart, she knew he wasn't hers.

'This is very good,' she said, tucking into her food with enthusiasm.

The *filet mignon* was tender, perfectly cooked with a pink centre and the narrow French *pommes frites* and green salad the perfect accompaniment.

'My father took my decision not to do medicine very badly,' Edward said, acknowledging the compliment with a smile as he went on. 'He is a man who likes to impose his wishes on others and I had defied him.' Emily could tell that Edward was anxious to talk about himself. She gave an encouraging nod.

'What does he think about Jeremy joining up?' she asked.

'I don't think Jeremy's told him yet.' Edward reached over to pour her more wine. 'Maybe he won't announce it until he's in uniform.'

Now he felt able to mention Jeremy's name quite naturally. In the few hours they had been together he knew that he had established dominance and captured her interest.

'Your father sounds rather frightening,' Emily said over the *crème brulée* which followed the main course.

'Why do you say that?' Edward looked at her curiously.

'It's the way your tone changes when you mention him. I'm sorry, but I couldn't help noticing.'

'We have always had a difficult relationship with our father.' Edward leaned confidentially towards her across the table. 'Frankly, I don't mind mentioning it now. Our mother died when we were very young and my father withdrew into himself, not having much time for us.'

'How awful,' Emily exclaimed sympathetically. She was a modern woman and she smoked and now she vigorously stubbed out her cigarette in the ashtray in front of her. Edward didn't mind. He liked a woman to be feminine, it was true; but also to have a viewpoint, to have character and personality as well as looks. Emily had all of these.

'When I was eighteen my father married again,' he went on, 'to a much younger woman. Neither my brother nor I liked her very much. Or she us. She did very little to make us welcome and we resented it.'

'Did they have children?' Emily enquired, leaning

forward, her interest well and truly aroused. Their heads almost touched across the table.

'Twins, a boy and a girl. They're only just five. I'm twenty years older than they are. It's a very big gap.'

'I should think it is,' Emily said, and her tone of voice was now warm and sympathetic. 'Not very nice for you at all, really.'

'How kind of you to think of me, I mean us.' Edward wanted to reach for her hand but didn't dare. Yet he was clearly overwhelmed by her kindness, her sympathy and her gentle, almost maternal beauty. Emily was able to read his intentions, his feelings towards her, from the expression on his face:

'Well, you'll be forty, when they're twenty. One has to think of that. It's a wonder your father didn't think of it. But I expect he was a very lonely man,' she added hastily. 'Do you like your stepmother any better now?'

'Some people like her very much,' Edward answered cautiously. 'We never really grew to care for her, Jeremy and I. Now that I'm a bit older I realize it wasn't all her fault; she was young and so were we. But she loved my father and she has had her work cut out since the twins were born. He has become very morose at times and depressed, and we all worry about him.

'You see,' Edward looked at her earnestly, 'unless he gets his own way he can very quickly become ill and make everyone feel guilty; it's been that way ever since I can remember.'

Chapter 5

'You look perfectly ghastly in that outfit.' Geoffrey Blair stared belligerently at his younger son. 'I can't think what got into you.'

As Edward had prophesied he would, Jeremy had, indeed, lacked the nerve to announce his enlistment to his father until he was in the blue uniform of a trainee pilot officer.

'It's not the uniform, Father,' Jeremy said politely but with an edge to his voice. 'It's the fact that, without any doubt, this country will soon be at war. You know that and I know that.'

'Well, what made you enlist in such a hurry?' Geoffrey said querulously. 'Can't you wait? Wasn't the bank good enough for you? Why do you have to rush into things?'

Geoffrey reached irritably for his pipe and Jeremy, sighing, sat down without being invited to, unfastening the buttons of his jacket as he did.

'Banking I found profoundly boring, Father. I would have left anyway. After the rape of Czechoslovakia I knew there would be a war. I just wanted to be in there first.'

'Get yourself killed,' Geoffrey said, rolling up his pouch and attempting to light his pipe with a hand that trembled slightly. Jeremy didn't know whether it was due to nerves, anger or old age. Though his father was only just past fifty, he looked sixty.

Jeremy felt a sudden wave of pity for his parent upon whom the years seemed to sit so heavily. Here was a man who had never, in fact, recovered from that single disaster in 1920: the death of their mother, his first wife. Yet people said that melancholia had its beginnings in infancy and, certainly, his father had got worse. Every time he saw him he was more grumpy, more morose. Was it always going to be like this?

By now Doctor Blair had lit his pipe and looked up as there was a knock on the door of his study and Catherine came in carrying a tray on which there were two cups.

'Coffee?' she said with forced brightness, dreading the effect of a fresh confrontation between father and son.

'That's very good of you.' Jeremy got up to take the tray. 'Aren't you joining us, Catherine?'

'Oh, would you like me to?' Catherine looked at him with an air of surprise; a surprise that had a hint of diffidence about it. 'Well, I was going to have mine in the kitchen with my daily, but if you like . . .'

'Bring it in, bring it in,' Geoffrey cried waving his hand. 'Jeremy is going to tell us about his views on the forthcoming war and how to win it.'

Neither Jeremy nor Catherine made any comment, and Catherine left the room for a few moments to fetch her coffee while Jeremy and his father sat silently waiting for her, each staring out of the window, the new silence an awkward one.

Netherwick, Jeremy thought, was a place he had never really known nor ever liked, though it was where he had been born. Some people called it a dead place, or a place partly dead and partly alive, where people lived out their lives in anonymous conformity. The very thought of Netherwick sometimes made him shudder, with its claustrophobic hills, its tall, smoke-laden mill chimneys. No one from Netherwick had ever made much of an impact on the world at large and yet, within its confines, enough worthy personalities had emerged over the years, each making his or her contribution to the community; people like his father, for example. His father was widely respected as a medical man, and patients came from all over the Dales to consult him. Yet here he was sucking at his pipe, invariably cold, as though it were a dummy; a choleric man, prematurely old, or so it seemed to his family.

No, Netherwick was no place for the young.

At that moment, ahead of their mother, Tansy scampered into the study clutching in her arms a small kitten who was wailing pitifully. Immediately her father put down his pipe and jumped up with surprising agility, gently detaching the squalling cat from Tansy's clasp. Equally gently he put it on his desk where it continued to protest as if unaware of, or at least ungrateful for, its deliverance.

'There, darling,' Geoffrey said tenderly, bending towards his daughter. 'That is not the way to carry a small kitten. They have such little tummies that you will crush all the stuffing out of it.'

'*Stuffing*,' Tansy said, looking up at her father with wonder. 'Is that what kittens have in their tummies, Daddy?'

'A sort of stuffing, darling,' the doctor said again in a tone of voice that was completely new to Jeremy, who looked at the source with some amazement. Geoffrey took Tansy onto his lap while, with the other hand, he continued gently to stroke and pacify the frightened kitten.

The scene caused Jeremy to adjust his image of a man he had always instinctively feared. This was a stranger to him, a character of compassion and tenderness towards the young, human or animal. Even the tone of voice Jeremy had not heard before. Maybe it was because Tansy was a girl.

Tansy had clambered willingly onto her father's lap

and now she imperiously stretched out her arms for the kitten which he was still stroking.

It was a scene of such beauty and domestic charm that it revealed to Jeremy his father in a new dimension; and he had to admit to himself a pang of envy that was mixed with nostalgia for a parent he had never known.

To Catherine, however, this was obviously nothing unusual because, as she came in with her cup of coffee in her hand, she commented rather brusquely in her soft northern-accented voice: 'Been at that cat again have you, Tansy? One day you'll hug it so tight it will die.'

'Oh, Daddy!' Tansy knew where to go for sympathy and buried her face in his warm tweed jacket, while her father put both arms around her, casting a reproachful glance at her mother.

'There, there,' he said, patting her back. 'Mummy didn't mean that.'

'Mummy *did*,' Catherine said firmly. 'One day . . .'

'*Please* don't go *on* about it, dear,' Geoffrey pleaded in a reproving voice, his expression subtly changing as he looked from daughter to mother. 'I've told her and she knows and that is all there is to it. Now,' he raised Tansy's face tenderly with his hand and gazed into her blue eyes, his own clearly alight with love, 'what do you think of your brother here in this fine uniform? He's going to fly aeroplanes.'

Tansy looked shyly at Jeremy and, when he returned her gaze, he felt rather shy himself. It was true he hardly knew her, had had little chance to follow her progress from baby to toddler and, now, little girl. She was an extraordinarily pretty child with golden hair that seemed to float around her head in little wisps and tendrils. Her large blue eyes were knowing, almost like those of an adult but having, withal, a hint of childlike curiosity. She wore a pink muslin dress tied at the waist by a dark blue ribbon which matched one that ran through her hair to keep its errant curls in order. She had long white socks up to her knee and patent black leather shoes fastened with a strap.

Unlike other small girls Tansy always seemed dressed as though for an outing: an important encounter with grown-ups. He never saw her dirty or dishevelled but, perhaps, Catherine so kept her daughter, of whom she was so proud, in order to impress her stepbrother. It was obvious to Jeremy that Catherine had the film star Shirley Temple in mind when she dressed her daughter, though Tansy was about half the age of the child star. There was, however, a definite resemblance; an air of bubbling, perky good nature, teeth perpetually gleaming in an open, friendly smile.

The inspection over, Tansy impulsively climbed down from her father's knee and, crossing to Jeremy, stood in front of him, hands clasped behind her back.

'Aren't aeroplanes very big and dangerous things?' she asked. Certainly they were hardly ever seen in the skies over Netherwick.

'They're very big,' Jeremy acknowledged, smiling down at her. 'But they're not dangerous. They're great fun to fly. You whizz away in the sky.' He made a soaring motion with his hand.

'Have you been in one?' she asked with an air of wonder.

'I certainly have.' Jeremy patted his lap invitingly, but she backed away. Maybe, but not just yet, she seemed to be saying; not this time.

Catherine, stirring her coffee, looked obliquely at Jeremy. 'Aren't you proud of your son, then, Geoffrey? In uniform!'

'No I am not,' Geoffrey said in a completely different tone of voice from the one with which he addressed his small daughter. 'I told him I thought he was precipitous and foolish. No one wants war, Hitler doesn't want war . . .'

'Well he has a very funny way of showing it,' Jeremy said. 'He has occupied Austria and Czechoslovakia and no European country has done a thing to stop him.'

'What can they do?' Geoffrey shrugged his shoulders. 'Countries have territorial rights, you know. The Austrian people voted for the Nazis, and part of Czechoslovakia belonged to Germany anyway. The Sudetan Germans . . .'

'Really, Father,' Jeremy said with irritation, getting up and rebuttoning his jacket. 'You sound like an apologist for the Nazis. I can't understand . . .'

'I sound like *what*?' his father thundered, banging his fist on the desk behind him with such force that the kitten who had just settled down, purring contentedly, gave another shriek and shot off the desk, rushing across the room and through the door which was half open.

Tansy looked first amazed and then put her hands to her face and began to squeal with laughter. 'Daddy, you terrified poor pussy. After what you said to me . . .'

'I'm sorry,' Geoffrey said, gesturing awkwardly towards his small daughter. 'I didn't mean to upset the pussy, darling, or you. Will you go after her?' He put both hands on her shoulders and gave her a gentle push while her mother nodded encouragingly.

'Go after her, Tansy, and pick her up in your arms. Do it gently though and tell her Daddy didn't mean to frighten her.'

She then rose and steered her daughter to the door, closing it firmly behind her.

'Really, Geoffrey,' Catherine said angrily, 'your sudden tempers will be the death of you if you don't control them. No wonder you have pains in your chest . . .'

'Father has pains?' Jeremy, his own temper suddenly cooled, anxiously looked at him.

'Indigestion,' Geoffrey replied brusquely. 'I have absolutely nothing wrong with my heart or my lungs; but I must say I have quite a lot of provocation in this household. Yet I am expected at all times to control *myself*.'

'Not *control*, Geoffrey.' Catherine looked at him reprovingly. 'You are not expected to control yourself all the time; just not let fly so much. That's all I ask.'

'He called *me* a Nazi.' Geoffrey pointed a finger at his son. 'Here, in my own house; and *you* expect me not to lose *control*?'

'I did not call you a Nazi, Father,' Jeremy said heatedly. 'I merely said you were making excuses for them.'

'Look,' his father rose to his feet and crossed the room until he stood a few feet away from his son, 'I am *not* making excuses for the Nazis. I merely said that the Austrian and Czechoslovakian people, to say nothing of about ninety per cent of the population of Germany, seem to want Hitler as their leader. I'm not concerned with what goes on in Europe, I'm concerned what happens *here* in *England*. And let me tell you that we have had one war this century and we don't want another. No thank you. If you knew as much about the carnage in the last war as I do you would never have volunteered for the RAF.'

Jeremy gazed at his father for a moment as though trying to stem the rising tide of his own temper. Then he spun round on his heels and went over towards the window, jingling the loose change in his pocket.

'If I recall correctly you didn't even serve in the last war, Father, but stayed home here in Netherwick in comparative peace and safety. I would have thought . . .'

Jeremy felt the presence of his father a split second

before the blow struck the side of his head and Catherine with a loud gasp cried out: 'Geoffrey, *no*! Please!'

The blow neither hurt nor toppled Jeremy, but it stung him to an anger as violent as his father's and he turned suddenly, his fist raised in the air.

'Please, Jeremy, Geoffrey, control yourselves at once!' Catherine said. Then she raised her own hand in the air and shook a finger at Jeremy.

'Don't you *dare* touch your father, young man. If you do you will never put a foot inside this house again.'

She continued to wag her finger at him as though to emphasize her warning and then she returned to Geoffrey who sat in his chair looking very pale, trying to take deep breaths.

'Are you all right?' she asked.

'Perfectly all right if you can call the anger I feel for my son being "all right". That he had the *nerve* to suggest I didn't *want* to fight in the last war . . .'

'I didn't say that, Father.' Jeremy, also pale and, to his surprise, trembling, leaned against the wall. He produced a handkerchief from his breast pocket with which he mopped his face. 'I know that you were rejected on the grounds of poor eyesight. I'm just saying you weren't there. I didn't mean to be rude.'

'What about all the casualties I saw when they got back?' Geoffrey said in a menacing tone. 'The hundreds of blighted lives, mentally and physically that were in my care? Do you think, do you dare tell *me* I don't know about the war, young man? Get out of here.' He pointed towards the door in an unmistakable gesture of dismissal.

'Please, Geoffrey.' Catherine put a restraining hand on his arm.

'I said "get out of here",' Geoffrey said again, only this time louder and more forcefully, 'and don't come back.'

'You don't *mean* that, Geoffrey,' Catherine said in a

wheedling tone, 'you know you don't.'

'I do. Neither Jeremy nor his brother Edward has ever done anything to make me proud of them, or even like them particularly. I'm sorry to have to say this but I must. They have thwarted me from boyhood. They have been selfish, wilful and thoughtless from their youth. They gave no thought to me, a man stricken with grief at the death of a young wife, but only to themselves; and even when I tried to make up to them for the loss of their mother they rejected me. I made many attempts but they came to nothing. I . . .'

'I'll go, Father,' Jeremy said, fastening the belt round his waist. 'I'll go and, don't worry, I shan't come back. I'm not going to argue with you because I feel sorry for you. I really do. As for the love you say you tried to show us . . .'

'Please, Jeremy,' Catherine gently pushed him towards the door, 'wait for me in the lounge while I attend to your father.'

After Jeremy had left the room without another word Catherine turned to her husband, whose pallor worried her. 'Well, you brought that on yourself, Geoffrey Blair,' she said shortly, and without much sympathy in her voice. 'You had better go upstairs and rest or you won't be ready for your Mothers' and Babies' Clinic at two.'

'There's nothing wrong with *me*,' Geoffrey began, but his brow was damp with perspiration and he was panting as though he found breathing difficult. 'As for my son calling *me* a Nazi.'

'He did no such thing.' Catherine took hold of his arm and began to pull him from his chair. 'But I'm not going to go back over what was said or not said except that that young man came all the way up here to tell you about his intentions . . .'

'*Intentions*,' Geoffrey began to bluster again. '*Intentions*.

Deeds you mean. Not intentions, my dear. He has left the bank where, despite my initial doubts, they were very good to him and where he had prospects of a career, for what? What sort of expectation of life do you think he'll have as a pilot? Nil. Germany has been re-arming for most of this decade and if there is a war it will crush us in no time. We're ill-prepared, my dear, ill-prepared, you mark my words. I read the papers. Do you think I want to see my son's life snuffed out like a candle? No I tell you, no.'

'Well you have a very funny way of showing affection if that's what you feel,' Catherine said quietly, tucking her arm through his and leading him to the door. 'You have got across each other so much this afternoon that I doubt whether you will ever see him again. If he takes you at your word he will leave and not come back. Is that what you *really* want?'

Geoffrey stopped their slow progress across the floor and shook his head. 'You know it isn't. You know I love my boys.'

'But neither you nor the boys understand one another,' Catherine said. 'If you are ever going to do it, now is the time to start. You are going to go up and rest and I am going to go in and talk to Jeremy and try and persuade him to stay, if I can. Then, this evening, we are going to have a very happy and civilized meal together. Now that, Geoffrey, is your last chance of holding on to a son whom I believe you *do* love, don't you?'

'I love him,' Geoffrey said in a voice that was scarcely audible and, slowly, tears, the size of small pearls, welled from his eyes and trickled down his face.

When Catherine returned after pacifying her husband – escorting him up to their bedroom and making him lie down – she went quickly to the lounge expecting to find that, perhaps, the volatile Jeremy had already left. She was relieved, therefore, to see him standing by the window smoking and, as she softly closed the door, he turned.

'How is he?' he asked, crossing the room towards her.

'Oh I'm so glad you're still here,' Catherine said impulsively clasping his arm. 'I thought you'd leave in a huff.'

Jeremy was aware of the pressure of her hand and, for a moment, it was very sweet, as though it were his own mother who touched him. Impulsively his hand closed over hers. 'Of course I wouldn't have left,' he said. 'Also, I shouldn't have spoken to my father as I did. But that's it, you see, Dad and I never get on.'

'Your father gets on with very few people,' Catherine said, aware of the clasp of his hand, and grateful for it. It seemed to show her that, rather late in the day, Jeremy had accepted her. 'He is an irritable and cantankerous man; but he loves his family and he loves his patients. That I do know. He loves you, whatever you think.'

'Why is it, then, that he doesn't show it?' Jeremy sadly flicked his cigarette ash into the empty hearth.

'He finds it hard to express emotion. I know he always has. And he *is* easily hurt. He is hurt by the fact you and Edward come here so seldom. He would like to see more of you. I wish you would too, Jeremy.' She looked at him anxiously. 'We didn't start off too well, but we're wiser now. And, if there is a war . . .'

'There is going to be a war, Catherine,' Jeremy said gravely. 'Nothing can stop it now. I'm not telling you any secrets by saying we are all prepared for it. I know what you're trying to say: if there is a war I may not come back. Edward may go to war and not come back. We don't want any bad memories, do we?'

'No.' Catherine let go his hand and tucked away a lock of hair that fell over her brow.

'Besides,' Jeremy continued, 'I think you're very good for Father. Maybe when I was younger I was jealous. But no more. You're good for him and with him. You do marvels for him, actually. Neither Edward nor I have been very nice to you, and yet you have always been very nice to us. Today I think you literally saved the relationship between Dad and me. I *was* sorely tempted to walk out of here.'

'I knew you were,' Catherine took a seat by the fireplace, 'and I was pleased you didn't. I *had* to see to your father first. I had to make him rest before his afternoon surgery.'

'Is Dad really ill?' Jeremy asked, sitting opposite her. His tone was one of enquiry rather than anxiety. She knew that, like many people, Jeremy probably thought his father's troubles were self-inflicted.

'I'm always trying to get him to let Tom Thackery check him over, but he won't. I think he's afraid of what he may find.'

'Really?' Jeremy's expression changed to one of concern. 'Is it as bad as that?'

'I think there is something wrong with him. I wouldn't be surprised if he has a mild heart condition. I mean, he has had these turns ever since I've known him, but the shortness of breath . . . well, that's pretty recent.'

'Well, something must be done,' Jeremy said getting up again. 'If *you* think it's bad it must be.'

'Oh no, I don't say it's *bad*,' Catherine said hastily. 'Some sort of warning that he must take care. I try and keep him as peaceful as possible, and he *does* love the children,' she went on quickly. 'I mean the twins. Maybe I shouldn't have said that.'

'Not at all.' Jeremy's smile, though polite, was strained. 'I'm glad to see Dad so happy with Tansy. Is he the same with Gilbert?'

'Gilbert hasn't Tansy's charm,' his mother said cautiously. 'But, oh yes, he loves Gilbert. He teaches him a lot. He wants him to be a doctor.'

'Oh gosh!' Jeremy raised his eyes to the ceiling. 'Here we go, Edward all over again.'

'Oh, I shan't let him force Gilbert to be a doctor if he doesn't want to, don't you worry about that!'

Jeremy instinctively admired the determination in her voice. In fact he began to have a regard for his stepmother that he had not felt before, a regard that was also admiration, perhaps the beginning of affection.

'Gilbert has a natural curiosity for things that might one day *possibly* interest him if he were to think of becoming a doctor,' Catherine went on cautiously. 'He loves nature, and your father takes him into the garden, and they walk around the pond and your father chatters about tadpoles and the fish that swim there and the wonders of pond and animal life. Gilbert is very absorbed by it all, whereas Tansy is not a bit interested.'

'Well I'm sure you have things under control – there was no one to stop Father when he pushed Edward into medicine.'

'Only me and I was too young to,' Catherine said in a small voice. 'I was a bit afraid of your father, as well. Afraid and in love, all at the same time. Rather odd.'

'I understand, though.' Jeremy got up and strolled over to the window looking out at the hills across the town.

'I have never really liked Netherwick. I never felt at home here.'

'I'm very sorry to hear that. I love it,' Catherine said from behind him.

'I know you do.' Jeremy continued to gaze broodingly

out of the window. 'I was born here, like you; but our upbringing . . .'

Catherine rose and came over to him. 'You have no need to explain, Jeremy. Maybe, from now on, it will all be different.'

Slowly Jeremy turned round and faced her. 'It's too late,' he said with a note of melancholy in his voice that reminded her of Geoffrey. 'Don't you realize, Catherine, that I can't help wondering whether, in case of war, I will ever see Netherwick, or you and Dad again?'

Dinner that night was a subdued meal in which the issues of the day were gravely discussed. The King and Queen had just arrived in America for the first visit of a reigning British monarch to that country since the War of Independence. But Jeremy rejected the idea they wouldn't have gone if they'd thought war to be imminent.

'The visit was arranged ages ago, Dad, and they had to behave normally. I'm not saying war will break out tomorrow.'

'When, then?' his father urged, leaning across the table. Jeremy rubbed his chin and looked ruminatively at the ceiling. 'September,' he said. 'By September or October I think we'll be at war.'

Catherine looked anxiously at Geoffrey but he showed no signs of the choleric temper of the morning. After his short rest he had attended his surgery and then gone on a couple of medical visits to villages on the outskirts of Netherwick. When he had returned just before dinner he seemed surprised, but happy, to find that his son was still in residence. Without referring to their argument that morning he had offered him a drink, and the two had started to discuss the prospects for Yorkshire in the county cricket league that summer.

'Being born in Yorkshire I could still play for my county,' Jeremy had said with a smile, and his father, his mood completely changed, had thumped him lightly in the chest and said that it would be the age of miracles all over again if Jeremy were ever to be chosen for the side, although he had played in the first eleven in the team fielded by the bank. This was a long-standing joke between them; a forced, if still welcome, sign of a return to good relationships.

This good-humoured camaraderie had been interrupted by Catherine to announce dinner and, after the maid had served the main course, the conversation had returned to the so-called Pact of Steel recently signed between Hitler and Mussolini, and the threat posed by the alliance of these two aggressive powers to world peace.

'I think we've said enough about the war,' Catherine said suddenly. 'Let's talk about something pleasant and happy.'

'Does anyone know anything pleasant and happy?' Geoffrey looked round with a smile.

'I do,' Jeremy announced, 'and what's more it will please *you*, Father.'

'Oh, what's that?' Geoffrey enquired with an air of jocularity.

'I think Edward is seriously interested in a girl.'

'A girl?' Catherine exclaimed. 'Good heavens.'

'Didn't you think he liked girls, dear?' Geoffrey said in a tone of mild reproof as though some slur were being cast against his son's masculinity.

'Well, he's never showed much interest . . . as far as I know,' Catherine concluded cautiously.

'My elder son is too shy,' Geoffrey said firmly, looking across at Jeremy. 'Not like *you*. You're too forward, broken the heart of many a young woman, I'll be bound.'

'Oh *Dad*, at the moment I have no girlfriend at all.' Jeremy looked virtuously at his father. 'I'm keepng myself pure to serve our nation.'

'That *does* sound like Nazism,' Geoffrey said, but Catherine hastily intervened.

'Please, Geoffrey, dear, not *again*. What's she like, Jeremy?'

'She's rather nice,' Jeremy said with a frown as though he were trying to recall her. 'The family's Jewish but they're not orthodox.'

'Oh, Jewish,' Geoffrey said frowning.

'*Dad*,' Jeremy stared at him.

'Nothing against them. Nothing at all,' Geoffrey said hastily. 'Don't misunderstand me. It's simply that in Netherwick there are not many Jewish families.'

'Her name's Emily and she teaches classics at the girls' school which is the counterpart to the one where Edward teaches.'

'Sounds very suitable,' Catherine said gravely.

'I'm not saying they're going to *marry*,' Jeremy went on, 'but she is nice, and I think he's quite smitten and, if there's a war . . . who knows?'

He left the words unspoken as he looked around the table at the expression of wonderment on the faces of his father and stepmother.

'Quite,' he said, smiling meaningfully at Geoffrey. 'You may soon be a grandpappy.'

Tentatively Edward's hand crept over the table towards Emily's.

'I realize we don't know each other very well,' Edward said, and as his hand reached hers, it stopped just before touching it. 'But I think we like each other. In fact . . .' he gulped and, knowing what was coming, Emily endeavoured to make herself relax.

Army uniform suited Edward. With the single pip of a second lieutenant on his shoulder he even looked distinguished. His moustache no longer hung over his lip, like a walrus's, but was clipped close to his face and his hair was cut short back and sides, in true army fashion. Yes, he looked distinguished, even handsome; but he was not Jeremy.

Edward was gazing at her as if for help and suddenly she put her hand over his, a touch as light as thistledown alighting on grass.

'Yes,' she said.

'Yes what?' Edward gulped again and a blush crept up from his neck across his cheeks.

'Yes, we do like each other. Very much.'

'I love you, I think,' Edward blurted out and, compulsively, he clasped her hand. His palm was clammy with sweat. 'I want to marry you, Emily. I know we haven't been out together much. But . . . there's so little time,' he added awkwardly.

She allowed his hand to remain on hers until the back of her hand felt as hot and sticky as his.

'The war is not going to go on for ever, Edward,' she said gently. 'When we get to know each other better *then* we can decide.'

'Yes but it's the *time*,' Edward said, leaning forwards with an air of urgency. 'The *time*, don't you see? I can't say much. I don't *know* much; but I may be sent abroad. I may not see you again . . . well, until it's over.'

His forehead was covered with perspiration and she could see the pulse pounding in his neck just above his collar. She liked him, but she did not love him. Now, if it were his brother she would be feeling very different. How unfair it seemed, to be loved by the man she did not love, while the other . . .

'I couldn't *possibly*,' she said with a kindly smile. 'I

can't marry you just because you may go abroad. It wouldn't be right.'

'Don't you like me a little?' he whispered in a pleading voice. Then he suddenly became aware that one or two people in the pub near them were looking at him curiously. He seemed to see derision in their eyes, or imagined he did. He took his hand off Emily's and drank his beer. It was cool and it quenched his thirst, and the swift beat of his heart slowed down. He felt like a schoolboy, not an officer in His Majesty's army. 'Is it anything to do with me not being Jewish?' he asked after a while.

'Of course it's not!' she said indignantly. 'I told you we were not orthodox or even practising Jews. Apart from Yom Kippur we never go near the synagogue. I suppose Mum and Dad would *prefer* me to marry a Jewish boy, but they would never insist on it. Besides,' she pursed her lips mulishly, 'when I marry religion will have nothing to do with it. Edward, I like you a lot,' Emily's voice throbbed with sincerity, 'but I don't want to marry you. I don't like you in that way, yet . . .' now she began to feel awkward and embarrassed. Apart from a few feeble fumblings in the car when he had brought her home he had made no attempt to make love to her, or even to kiss her properly. Unlike his brother she knew instinctively that Edward was inadequate in that respect. He was nice; he was civilized, cultured and able; but he lacked passion. She doubted if he'd ever been to bed with a woman.

Edward got up and went to the bar. She thought he was ordering more drinks but he was simply taking the glasses back. The bar was short of staff. Everyone was being called up, quickly, to fight the escalating war.

For the first three months after war was declared the opposing sides had sniffed round one another, like dogs.

Everyone said it would be over by Christmas, that the British Expeditionary Force which had gone to France had nothing to do except enjoy the culinary delights of our allies across the Channel and, of course, its women.

But in January and February of 1940 the tide seemed to turn and events became altogether more sinister. Food rationing was introduced for the first time since 1918, and Hitler declared war on all neutral ships which entered allied ports.

Emily, feeling embarrassed at the sudden and unwished-for intimacy introduced by Edward, got up too and stood at the door of the pub with her handbag clasped under her arm.

Edward had disappeared and when he joined her he apologized. 'Sorry, call of nature.'

'That's OK,' she said, smiling, as they stepped out into the Charing Cross Road which, like the rest of London, was in darkness. A pall of gloom seemed to hang over the metropolis as though in anxious anticipation of a messenger of doom who would descend from the skies.

Edward had left his car in Covent Garden, parked in a side street which was virtually empty of vehicles. Yet the pub had been full and the crowds thronged down the Charing Cross Road towards Trafalgar Square as though it were the spiritual home of the nation. In a sense it was, the place where the common people collected within sight of the Mother of Parliaments and the home of the Monarch: twin rocks amid shifting sands.

Edward and Emily slipped out of the Charing Cross Road through a side alley into St Martin's Lane and then through another into Covent Garden itself where, already, lorries filled with goods for the market were arriving stealthily, like ghosts in the night, lights dipped.

'I shan't have this for much longer,' Edward said as he

helped her into the seat beside him. 'Shan't have the petrol.'

'What will you do with it?' Emily tucked the rug he handed to her round her knees.

'I thought I'd drive it up to my parents' and leave it there.' He paused for a moment. 'I wondered if you'd like to come too and meet them?'

'I don't think so, Edward, not just now,' she said, knowing nevertheless that she was hurting him. 'What's the point?'

'I see. Yes.' He released the handbrake and let out the clutch, his heart feeling very heavy and cold.

Emily's mother said: 'I can't understand what's the *matter* with you lately, Emily. I've never known you so nervous and fidgety. Is it the war, or are you in love?'

Emily smiled and, sitting back from her desk, removed her glasses as she reached up for the cup her mother had brought her. 'It's neither, Mum.'

'It's that Edward, I think,' her mother said, sitting on the bed. 'You see an awful lot of him.'

'I like him.'

'Dad and I like him too,' her mother said, crossing her legs and folding her hands over her knees. 'Of course he's not Jewish, but your father and I would raise no objection. He's a real gentleman.'

'Well, it's not just being a *gentleman* that counts, Mum,' Emily said, stirring her coffee before bringing the cup to her lips.

'Oh, Emily, that's a very silly view to take,' her mother said crossly. 'It counts for a lot. You can be sure he would stand by you when others might not. He's the solid, faithful type. They may not be so glamorous or romantic, but, believe me, my girl, they're the best.'

'Maybe you're right, Mum,' Emily said, briefly closing her eyes and visualizing the face of the one who wore air-force blue. How many women had *he* got through, in the past year alone? Whereas poor Edward . . . he really was so inexperienced.

'You're getting on you know, Emily,' the anxiety in her mother's voice increased. 'I mean, you're not old but, if you're not careful, you will share the fate of a lot of women after the last war, like your Aunt Frances.'

'What about Aunt Frances, Mum?' Emily looked at her sceptically but already she knew the answer. Aunt Frances had never married because, it was said, there had not been enough men after the last war, Jew or non-Jew. There simply hadn't been enough of a suitable age left alive.

'All the men were killed,' her mother said, as if reading Emily's mind. 'A whole generation, your aunt's generation, was wiped out. There were not enough of them left and women like your Aunt Frances, who was a pretty girl in her day, never knew the joys of marriage and having children.'

'Or the sorrows, Mum,' Emily said, as she finished her coffee and put the empty cup down in its saucer.

'I *beg* your pardon?' her mother said.

'Marriage has sorrows as well as joys.'

'You'd soon know which you preferred if you didn't have a husband, my girl,' her mother said, rising and taking her daughter's cup, lips pursed. 'Far better to marry a man you don't love but respect, whatever religion he is, than spend the rest of your life as a spinster . . . teaching classics!'

Jennifer Lester almost spat the words at her as she took the cup and marched through the open door, kicking it closed behind her. She had made her meaning clear.

* * *

In the end it was Dunkirk that decided Emily. It was a set-back for England on a gigantic scale and, for a time, it seemed that an air of defeatism loomed over a country that had not known occupation by a conqueror for nearly a thousand years.

With astonishing rapidity Hitler's troops had overrun first the low countries and then, with an ease that took everyone by surprise, France had fallen. The scattered remnants of the allied forces and the BEF which only a few weeks before had been enjoying wine, women and song, took to the beaches around the French port of Dunkirk, in a desperate fight for their lives.

The casualty figures began to be reported in the newspapers and, as Nazi troops made their insulting march through the Arc de Triomphe and down the Champs-Elysées, those who had so far been excused military service in England received their call-up papers.

It was nearly the end of term and Emily felt she must make a decision not only about her life but her career as well.

The summer of 1940 was to be remembered for many years to come. It seemed, in retrospect, to mark the end of a golden age and the beginning of a more sombre, more frightening future. It was after Dunkirk that enemy aircraft began to appear in the skies over Britain, and the battle for survival had begun.

Naturally, among the first of the pilots sent aloft to repel the enemy was Jeremy Blair, now a Flight-Lieutenant after rapid promotion. The expectation of life among young pilots was about three weeks but, in the glamour of combat, he never counted the cost. Nor did he expect to die. He had acquired an attractive new girlfriend called Jill who was in the WAAF and, as September came, Emily Lester promised to marry his brother Edward Blair, more as a gesture of pity than

anything else. Pity and a desire to banish once and for all
the threat of spinsterhood that had tainted the lives of
her Aunt Frances, and so many like her.

There was no time for a proper wedding, or to meet his
parents. A special licence, forty-eight hours' embarkation
leave and he was gone.

But he left her with a wedding ring and an experience
of the wedding night that would be deeply imprinted on
her memory for ever.

Edward Blair, like his father, was no great lover.

Chapter 6

Catherine Blair was a spirited, active woman, always on the go. The war seemed to bring out the best in her and, if she were truthful, she would have to admit that she rather enjoyed it.

Netherwick was well away from the bombing. It was too insignificant, tucked in the heart of the Yorkshire Dales between the massive ports of Hull and Liverpool, which were heavily raided. But 1941, as a whole, was a year of unmitigated disaster for England and her allies. The war news was bad and every day it got worse.

But Catherine was the kind of person who thrives on disaster. The worse the news the better she felt. She was one of those buoyant, effervescent people to whom others naturally turned for comfort and reassurance. There seemed to be no limit to her endurance. She helped to run the WVS with Mrs Todd, wife of the mayor, assisted by the ladies of the town. Her whole day was full and it was with difficulty she found the time to join her husband who enjoyed a glance at the evening paper and a glass of sherry after evening surgery.

'Busy?' Geoffrey enquired.

'Very.' She brushed a lock of hair away from her head.

'You mustn't overdo it, you know.' He looked at her severely over the rims of his spectacles. 'Your first duty is to your family.

'*You* in particular, I suppose.' Catherine impulsively put her arms round his neck and nuzzled her cheek against his. 'Don't worry, I shan't neglect you. I *do* love you, Geoffrey Blair,' she said. 'I don't know why but I do.'

He reached up and stroked the side of her face, but his mind was on the headlines in the paper and the war news. 'It's a terrible time for the country,' he murmured, putting the paper on his lap. 'I wish to God I knew what has happened to Jeremy and Edward.'

Catherine dropped to her knees and took his hand. 'They'll be all right, dear. We know Jeremy is somewhere in the Far East. At least he's out of the Battle of Britain. You should feel grateful for that.'

'Who says the Far East is any better?' Geoffrey observed gloomily. 'If Singapore falls . . .'

'Don't *think* of it, Geoffrey,' Catherine said briskly, getting to her feet and putting a hand on his shoulder. 'Don't torment yourself. Your sons are doing their bit, and you should be proud of them.'

'I am.' Geoffrey held out his glass for another drink. 'That day we went to Buckingham Palace when Jeremy got his medal will be one of the proudest of my life.'

It was shortly after his award of the DFC that Jeremy got his own squadron and was sent to the Far East. Those were days of swift promotion to take the place of the mounting toll of the dead.

It was also the day, the first and only occasion so far, when they had met Edward's hastily married wife, Emily. She was introduced to them afterwards at Lyons Corner House in Piccadilly where Jeremy had organized a lunch. His latest girlfriend, Jill, was now his fiancée and the family meeting, despite the gravity of the war news, was a happy, light-hearted affair.

They had liked Emily; she was the sort of sensible, solid girl that they had hoped Edward would marry. No fuss, no frills and she wore glasses. They made her look decidedly plain; but, maybe, her condition didn't make her appearance any better, and her pallor was remarked on. She had then been three months pregnant.

'Emily's baby will be due any day now.' Catherine handed Geoffrey his second glass of sherry. 'That will be exciting.' She stretched her arms in the air and sighed. 'I do *wish* we knew her better. She must be so lonely with Edward gone.'

'Plenty of time to get to know her after the war,' Geoffrey said. 'When Edward comes back.'

'The war won't be over so soon, you know, Geoffrey.' Catherine thought she should strike a note of warning. 'And if it is, we may not be the victors.'

'Do you know, I think you can be put in prison for saying something like that.' Her husband again looked at her gravely through his glasses; but this time he had a smile on his face. 'It shows a lack of patriotism. Of *course* we shall win the war. It's just a matter of time.'

Catherine swiftly bent down and planted a kiss on the top of his head. She wished, oh how she wished, she shared his optimism.

'He's a gorgeous little boy.' Jennifer Lester pushed back the white shawl to gaze at her grandson. 'He's the spitting image of his father.'

'Oh, I don't think so,' Ted Lester put his head on one side, 'I think he takes after his mother. What are you going to call him, Emily?'

'Mark,' Emily replied, gently rocking her baby in her arms.

'Why Mark, dear?'

'Why not?' Emily asked.

After that her parents said nothing. Their daughter, as they knew only too well, had a will of her own. The birth had been like the honeymoon: difficult. Yet, as the honeymoon had had the unexpected reward of conception, the birth had produced a living, healthy, beautiful child and, from that moment, Emily Blair felt her life transformed. It was immediately given a new meaning and purpose and she was glad she had accepted Edward Blair as her husband, or, for that matter, anyone as a husband. To have a baby like the one she carried in her arms was the best reward of all.

Emily now felt that she had something to hang on to; someone to hope for, whatever the outcome of the war, whatever the fate of the baby's father.

Mark Blair was born in Edgware General Hospital because Emily had moved into a flat nearby after Edward was sent overseas. It was not too far from the school where she continued to teach until a month before her baby was due, and not too far from her parents who had moved from Muswell Hill to a house in Golders Green, not far from the Great North Road. They wanted to be nearer Derek who had been excused military service on account of a heart murmur which, in the absence of so many men overseas, had gained him rapid promotion to manage a small branch of the bank nearby. Derek had also married the month before war broke out. His wife was called Hilda, and she had given birth to a baby girl only two months before Mark was born.

Ted and Jennifer Lester were a nice, ordinary, middle-class couple who had lived in the same part of London all their married lives: Muswell Hill, near the Broadway. It had been quite a large, double-fronted house and when Derek and then Emily got married they decided it was time to break the ties of a lifetime – as people often do in middle life – and move.

They had found a semi-detached house neatly positioned between the homes of their two children, and near enough to Muswell Hill to keep up with the old ties. The house was in one of the warren of streets that led off the Great North Road; far enough from it for the noise of traffic not to be heard, but near enough for convenience.

Ted Lester was a minor civil servant who had spent all his working life in Whitehall. His weekdays had been taken up with commuting between North London and the seat of government, and his weekends mostly in his garden. He was so keen on gardening that he had acquired an additional allotment which ran alongside the Great North Road, one of many lots made available by a government urging the populace of Britain to dig for victory.

He also had a small car which, since the outbreak of war, stayed mainly in the garage and he travelled to work by tube. His wife worried a good deal about his work which, though not officially listed as dangerous, did mean that his department was in line for a direct hit if the enemy got close enough to bomb the Houses of Parliament. Jennifer was a worrier. She worried about her husband, she worried about her daughter Emily and the fact that her scholastic attainments might drive the young men away. Her parents were proud of Emily, the only member of the family ever to have attended a university; but what was scholarship compared to the benefits of married life, children, a home of one's own and all the satisfaction, the promise of domestic bliss that went with it?

If ever Jennifer Lester had been determined about anything it was to see her daughter married to Edward Blair. He was just the sort of man she had envisaged for a daughter with brains rather than looks as her main asset. He was clever himself but he was also a gentleman, a doctor's son and, thus, a person with status.

Jennifer knew that Emily was not in love with Edward but with his younger brother. But she, Jennifer Lester, considered Jeremy unsuitable as a potential mate. He was attractive, his sexual allure was almost overpowering, even for a woman in her mid-forties who might have thought herself past that sort of thing. Even she, Emily's mother, was not immune to Jeremy Blair's charm: but as husband material? Never.

In Jennifer's view the war, though a catastrophe on a worldwide scale, was a good thing as far as her daughter was concerned. It made Emily see sense and, after Dunkirk and the escalation of the war, the road to respectability seemed inevitable. Edward was going, and Edward might not return. The whole family had in mind Aunt Frances Clarke as an awful warning of what happened to women who missed their chances, who left it too late.

So it was with no small amount of satisfaction that, after an hour's visit, Jennifer Lester kissed her new-born grandson on the top of his little bald head, kissed her daughter on the cheek and said they'd be back to see her the following day.

Then she tucked her arm through her husband's and they walked through the ward, smiling benignly at other new mothers in the self-congratulatory way that proud grandparents have, with an air of relief, of satisfaction at a job well done.

Ted had brought his car to the hospital and, as he edged it carefully out of the car park towards Edgware Road, the sirens sounded. Night was just falling. It was eight o'clock in the evening, about the time the German bombers chose for their raids.

'Hell,' Ted said, looking anxiously up at the darkening sky. 'Perhaps we'd better go back inside the hospital?'

'Really, Ted,' his wife gazed at him with contempt, 'this isn't *Whitehall*. We'll be home in ten minutes.'

Ted Lester was a man rather timid by nature. The war

had frightened him: the thought of the disintegration of civilization, the destruction of his conformist, cosy world. His relief at being too old for call-up was tempered by his position in the heart of the war machine that ran the country: the corridors of power in Whitehall. Ted had absolutely nothing to do with running the war. He was but a tiny cog in this vast machine. In fact, his brief was the protection of the public highways in the event of widescale devastation or occupation. He spent hours in a small room, fortunately a basement, which was situated in a vast modern building at the back of Westminster Abbey, making plans of all the public highways in the south of England, the main arterial roads, and the smaller ones leading off them. He would gaze at his work with pride before locking it safely in the drawer at five o'clock sharp when the time came to catch the tube to go home.

But this was a Saturday and he'd spent most of it in his allotment which was full of fine sprouting cabbages, new potatoes, lettuces, radishes and green peas, with a precious crop of tomatoes in a tiny utility greenhouse: his pride and joy. He'd gone home, washed, had tea, got out the car and, for the second time, taken his wife to visit their newborn grandson.

Ted decided to avoid the Great North Road, because of its proximity to the main railway, and went instead through a maze of roads with which, because of his calling, he was familiar. Finally he crossed the Great North Road and made a dash up the avenue that led into Uphill Crescent where he and his wife now lived.

The drone of aeroplanes overhead was intense and frightening. The sky by this time was quite dark yet lit up by the beams of the search lights operated by the various ack-ack stations that surrounded the capital trying to identify the bombers as they crossed the sky.

Even Jennifer was unusually silent and tense as Ted negotiated, with some skill, his way home.

With a great sigh of relief Ted let Jennifer out, put the car in the garage, locked it and then ran into the house, calling to his wife to get down to the shelter in the back garden.

'Oh, *Ted*,' Jennifer said scornfully. 'The raid is nearly over by now. It's the *City* they're after . . .'

These were the last words that Jennifer Lester ever uttered. The following morning her body, with that of her husband and the family pet dog, was dug out of the rubble of their home and laid reverently in the makeshift morgue at the bottom of the road.

Catherine linked her arm through that of Geoffrey's daughter-in-law, as much for support as comfort. The poor girl literally seemed to need holding up physically as she watched the coffins of her parents gently slide into the ground in the Jewish cemetery at Golders Green.

There were few mourners besides Derek and his wife. Maybe the news had not got around or, maybe, people felt they had other duties, other things on their minds in those dark days of the war. Maybe the Lesters, after all, had not had as many friends as they thought.

Catherine rather awkwardly carried a bunch of flowers, and it was only when she saw that hers were the only ones on the coffins that she realized that flowers were not usual at a Jewish funeral.

Hilda Lester had a simple reception at her home after the brief ceremony. There were just tea and cakes and no alcohol. Derek seemed not to have absorbed the shock of the death of his parents, but Emily, who was the last to see them so happy about Mark, was shaken by grief and remorse. She seemed to think that it had been in her power to stop them when, in fact, they had already left the ward when the siren sounded. She locked terrible, and Catherine feared for her health and that of her baby.

Catherine, always there when needed, had hurried down as soon as she heard of the tragedy, a rare and quite useless attack on a closely-packed housing estate in North London. Of course the Germans had been trying to bomb the railway, the main route for supplies to and from the north of England. It was only a couple of miles from the mainline stations of Euston, St Pancras and King's Cross, all of which served the north. The Great North Road itself – that main artery with all its capillaries stretching east and west, radiating like tiny veins from the massive jugular – might have stood out on the fine summer evening, attracting a shoal of bombs from a keen-eyed bomb aimer a mile up in the sky, anxious to get home.

No one would ever know. Certainly it was a night on which much of London was bombed and the stories of the homeless, the dead and wounded so legion that the deaths of a Mr and Mrs Lester were mere statistics.

Catherine had never met Derek and his wife before. She felt curiously uncomfortable in the company of people she didn't know. In Netherwick she was accustomed to being known, and to knowing everyone. However, she thought that Emily, too, seemed uncomfortable and whispered to her: 'Don't you think we had better get back and see to the baby?'

'Oh yes,' Emily replied, hand to mouth as though she had forgotten the existence of Mark, left in the care of a neighbour.

Hurried farewells were made and then they left to return to the house not far from the hospital where Mark had been born.

Once they were there Emily seemed to relax. She had

started to breast feed Mark but all her milk had stopped as if turned off by a tap with the shock of her parents' deaths, and he was now fed with a bottle.

Mark was a healthy, full-term baby and he rested contentedly in the arms of his mother. In a strange way he seemed to know about the tragedy, to be pleased to see her again and to be trying to comfort her. Holding him tight Emily realized he was doubly precious now because, with her parents dead and Edward away, not yet aware of the birth of his son, he was all that she had.

Catherine, happy to be away from the small crowd of mourners, bustled about in the practical, capable way that she had. She liked to be needed and she was good at managing. She was only shy in the company of strangers; she was after all a provincial woman who had rarely visited London.

'Trust me to visit here in wartime,' she said with a smile, handing Emily a cup of freshly brewed tea. As a northerner, tea was an indispensable adjunct to civilization as Catherine knew it, and vast quantities were consumed by her in the course of every day.

'We drink an awful lot of this at the WVS,' she said, sitting down in front of the unlit fire in the grate.

'It's *very* good of you to come,' Emily said shyly. 'I don't really know what I'd have done without you.'

'Of course I had to come!' Catherine said, leaning forwards. 'Geoffrey would have come too; but he had his patients.'

'I suppose, also, someone had to stay behind with the children,' Emily said sympathetically. 'They're still quite small aren't they?'

'Well, we do have a woman who looks after them and, besides, in Netherwick we're a very close-knit community,' Catherine murmured, leaning back in her chair, feeling relaxed for the first time for forty-eight hours. 'In your situation, now, you would never be alone. People would be knocking on your door with offers of help at every minute of the day and night, whereas here,' she scratched her arms and looked around, 'it's like being on an island, isn't it? An island surrounded by millions of people, all of whom are isolated from the rest?'

Emily carefully removed Mark from one arm to the other as she altered the position of the feeding bottle.

'I never thought of it like that,' she said, raising her eyes. 'I thought it was because we were only in furnished accommodation and hadn't been here very long. We don't know any of our neighbours. But in Muswell Hill . . .' She paused and her eyes immediately filled with tears. 'Well, we'd lived there all our lives. My parents should *never* have moved. If they hadn't . . .' her voice faltered and she lowered the bottle, 'they wouldn't be dead.'

'Now, now,' Catherine said, springing up and taking the feeding bottle from her hand. 'You can't think like that, love. There's no earthly point in it. Here, let me take him,' and, skilfully, Catherine eased the baby into her own arms and tilted the bottle to his mouth, smiling down at him as his little hands enthusiastically grabbed the sides. 'He's a *love*,' Catherine crooned. 'He's a little, little love.'

Mark seemed to smile back at her and kicked his feet with joy. 'I could eat him,' Catherine went on. 'I love babies. Of course, as you know, I'm much younger than Geoffrey, only a few years older than you.'

'Would you have liked more children?' Emily was glad to change the subject from herself.

'Other things being equal, yes. But the twins were a handful, even though I had help, and Geoffrey, well,' she paused for a few seconds to smile at Mark again, tipping the bottle ever higher as he drank, 'well, Geoffrey was too old to have young children. I realize that now. He loved them, but they were too much for him. Young children need young parents and Geoffrey . . .' she looked thoughtfully across at Emily, 'of course you met him just that once.'

'I liked him,' Emily said firmly. 'I know about the difficulties with Edward and Jeremy; but I liked him.'

'He liked you too.' Catherine shifted the weight of Mark more evenly in her arms. 'My, he weighs a ton this baby. No, Geoffrey liked you and he said, well,' swiftly she glanced at Emily, 'he said why don't you come and live with us, for a while, you know, to get over the shock of your parents' deaths and until you decide what you want to do?'

'Doctor Blair said that?' Emily said with amazement. 'Well, you do surprise me.'

'Geoffrey is a *very* good man,' Catherine said defensively.

'Oh I don't mean that.' Emily felt the blood rush to her face. 'Don't think I doubt his goodness, but Edward said he always had an uneasy relationship with his father. I think it's very *generous* of the doctor to want his son's wife and baby to stay, I mean live.'

'Yes, live,' Catherine said, 'for as long as you like.'

Emily decided very quickly to go and stay, for a time at least, with her father-in-law and his wife in the Dales town of Netherwick. Perhaps she was afraid that the incident which had resulted in the death of her parents could occur again – Edgware and Golders Green were very close and the bombs often fell indiscriminately as if to terrify the population. What had happened once could happen twice. Maybe she feared for the safety of herself and her newborn son or, maybe, she disliked the furnished digs which she shared with a much older couple who, although kind, were quite unable to cope with small babies.

Whatever the reason, it didn't take her very long to accept the invitation, and, as soon as the arrangements could be made, she boarded the train at King's Cross with Mark clasped tightly in her arms. Hundreds of soldiers, who were travelling home on leave, accompanied them north.

It was a wartime journey undertaken mostly in the dark and it seemed to last a long time. Emily, Catherine and the baby were given seats, largely through the courtesy of two soldiers who surrendered theirs in order to stand in the corridor.

'Very kind . . .'

'No trouble at all, love . . .'

'Aren't people *kind*?' Emily whispered to Catherine as the train journeyed through the night, creeping along the main railway line as though trying to escape unnoticed in the dark, halting at junctions, at darkened railway stations, sometimes for inexplicable lengths of time that seemed like eternity.

'People *are* very kind,' Catherine whispered back, glancing at the soldiers swaying in the corridor outside their compartment. God knew they probably needed rest as much as anyone.

'They say war unites people, brings them together. But in Netherwick you'll find people are always like this. They'll do anything for strangers; well, almost anything,' she added.

'I'd never been to a Jewish funeral,' Catherine said conversationally as the train stopped in yet another junction. Somewhere along the corridor a group of soldiers were singing softly.

Emily looked at her sharply. 'Surely Edward told you I was Jewish?'

'He didn't, but his brother did.'

'Did it matter to Edward's father?' Emily looked at her dispassionately, her smooth, white brow unfurrowed by apprehension or alarm.

'Not at all! No dear, of course it didn't. We have no prejudice against Jews. I do want you to believe that. It was just at the ceremony,' she shrugged, 'I felt so foolish being the only one with flowers.'

'It was a nice gesture,' Emily said. 'You couldn't be expected to know.'

'Also there's the problem of the food,' Catherine said hesitatingly.

'Oh, we're not kosher!' Emily laughed and leaned back against the seat which was old, much used and smelt of must and sweat. But what did that matter in wartime? At least it was a seat. Across Europe, it had been rumoured in the community, Jews were being herded in cattle trains and sent to concentration camps. 'You don't need to worry at all about that, Catherine,' she murmured. 'We are not orthodox. I was married in a register office. It's not that I'm ashamed of my Jewishness. I just don't think about it. It's never been very important to me. Maybe I'll become more conscious of it if Hitler does invade . . .'

'Oh, for heaven's sake don't say that!' Catherine cried. 'Don't even *think* of it.' Then she leaned towards the tired woman clutching the sleeping baby and whispered. 'At any rate if he did you'd be quite safe in Netherwick. You'd come to no harm at all there.'

Emily let her head lie back against the old worn seat of the coach, and allowed the gentle roll of the train to lull her to sleep while, next to her, Catherine kept an anxious watch on the baby to be sure he didn't fall.

Netherwick was reached in the middle of the following morning after a change and another lengthy wait at

Leeds. Passenger trains in wartime were frequently shunted into sidings for hours on end to allow trains carrying troops and vital equipment to pass. Emily leaned forwards as the little train puffed importantly across the terrain which already showed the undulating hills of the Yorkshire Dales, an area she had never visited. Despite the fact of it being their home town, neither Jeremy nor Edward seemed particularly attached to it. Or, rather, they disliked the town, but approved of the beautiful countryside surrounding it.

As the train came into Netherwick station Emily rose and drew down the window. She could see that it was a small town, its roofs mainly tiled with grey slate, wispy smoke trailing from the many uniform chimney stacks. Netherwick was completely surrounded by hills interspersed by valleys with narrow winding roads. On one side of the town these led towards Lancashire and the Lake District. On another across the moors into Ilkley and neighbouring Skipton. On yet another Harrogate and, finally, into Warfedale and the heartland of the Dales.

It was a grey day, unseasonally cold; the dark clouds seemed to scud ominously across the sky. Emily felt herself in the grip of a sudden fear, of foreboding, and she thought this dour town cut off from the outside world was no place for her and her baby. What would Edward say if he knew? Would he wish her to live in a place where he'd been unhappy? Yet, surely, he would be happy to know she and Mark were being looked after?

Catherine, however, was obviously delighted to be home. As the train slowly approached the place where she had been born, she jumped up, sticking her head through the window and started frantically to wave. '*Geoffrey*'s here, Emily!' she said, almost bursting with excitement as she turned back towards her. 'Geoffrey *himself* has come to welcome us!' This was, undoubtedly, an honour.

'Oh.' Nervously Emily looked furtively into the carriage mirror, carefully clasping Mark but anxious, nevertheless, to make herself look presentable for that strange, awesome creature who was Mark's grandfather. She had only once before met Doctor Blair when Jeremy had received his DFC, and what a stiff, brooding figure she had thought him to be, exuding little joy even over the honour bestowed on his son.

She tugged this way and that at her hat, tucking away a stray wisp of hair beneath it. She looked pale, but it had been a long journey and now she also felt slightly sick.

As the train drew to a halt a porter ran alongside their door, obviously on the instructions of Doctor Blair who followed slowly behind him. He wore a grey lightweight summer overcoat and a grey homburg squarely on his head. He was so like Edward to look at that, involuntarily, Emily swallowed; they were the same height, had the same complexion, the same heavy moustache obscuring the upper lip, and the same cold, unfriendly blue eyes. Though, in the father's case, they were partly obscured by his spectacles, which glistened in the light.

Geoffrey raised an arm stiffly in greeting, pipe clenched firmly between his teeth. Catherine excitedly unfastened the catch on the door and as she stepped down from the train she looked back to be sure that Emily and the baby were all right. She reached up to take Mark from Emily's arms and, as she did, Geoffrey looked curiously at the little face, almost hidden in his shawl, and then, gently, he drew it back so that he could see the baby more clearly.

But Mark Blair, oblivious of the fact that this was his

first meeting with his grandfather slept on regardless, a faint smile playing round his lips, little hands clenched tightly, confidently to his chest.

Geoffrey gave a smile of satisfaction, kissed Catherine punctiliously on each cheek and then turned to Emily, one arm extended.

'Welcome to Netherwick, Emily,' he said bending to kiss her, also on the cheek, his hat in one hand, pipe in the other. 'I hope you'll be very, very happy here.'

'Oh, thank you, Doctor Blair,' Emily said, feeling bewilderment and yet, at the same time, gratitude as she returned his bleak kiss. 'I'm *sure* I shall.'

And at first, she was. Emily was gratified by the unexpected warmth she received from her in-laws, especially Catherine. Geoffrey, she could see, was a taciturn man, very much as Edward had described him, obviously nervous and hypochondriacal, wary of chills, over-protective of himself and his health.

But Catherine was delightful; charming, warm and, despite her own youth, determined to replace, in her heart and affections, the mother Emily had lost. She knew all about babies and she loved them. Mark was a particularly winsome, good baby who fitted in not only with his new family but with the twins who, although his uncle and aunt, were still children themselves.

Tansy, who was impulsive about everything, decided from the moment she saw her that she would adore Emily. Gilbert was polite, but more reserved. He was not interested in small babies and he also resented the intrusion of another adult, and having to make way for two more members of the household. There was plenty of room, but Gilbert enjoyed his space, his creature comforts and, above all, routine.

* * *

And so the war years passed, too slowly for those whose loved ones were far away, many unheard of for years; too quickly for those who were bereaved, who knew that a son, husband, even a close friend or member of the family had been killed and would never be seen again.

Edward managed to write regularly to his wife and his letters were delivered in batches, as were hers to him. But after the fall of Singapore in February 1942 all contact with Jeremy ceased abruptly and his fate remained unknown, his name absent from the lists that were sent regularly from one combatant to another through the Red Cross.

Geoffrey worried incessantly about the fate of his middle son. Because of his nature he feared the worst. He had lapses of memory and black depressions, times when he was unable to work. Gradually his colleagues shouldered more of the burdens of the practice though there were long periods when Geoffrey was completely normal, sanguine, even philosophical. At these times, no news, in his opinion, was good news. While the name of Squadron Leader Jeremy Blair remained off the lists of the dead or wounded which emanated regularly from the Far East, there was hope.

For Catherine, on the other hand, not to know was worse than knowing the truth, however bad, and she fretted and worried about Jeremy and Edward in equal measure. But the one who remained calmest of all was Emily, sustained, surprisingly, by something as unexpected as it was precious: the slow revelation of love, a process which began almost at the time of Edward's first letter home from overseas.

She had never known of course before they were married what kind of a letter writer Edward was. There was never any need for them to correspond. She received her first letter from him about a month after their wedding when already she had begun to suspect she was pregnant with Mark. His letters were tender, even passionate. She had not realized he had such literary flair. He was able to express in writing, with great lyricism and beauty, an emotion that he had only awkwardly and with a great deal of clumsiness been able to put into practice. Soon the memory of the wedding night – their only physical encounter – was obliterated by the emotions conjured up by his words, and gradually, imperceptibly she fell in love with her husband until, eventually, she longed to see him again.

One never knew where the letters were from in those early days of the war but after the years of set-backs – the fall of Singapore, the losses in Russia, north Africa and the Middle East – a feeling of defeat gradually turned into one of hope. After Singapore there was El Alamein, and then the tide of the war began to turn. This continued throughout 1943 and now, in the summer of 1944, Emily knew that Edward was in Italy, taking part in the allied march on Rome, crawling along the peninsula with his regiment of tanks, still safe, still unscathed.

Soon, soon, perhaps, he might be home.

Tansy knocked timidly on the door of Emily's room, then, hearing a cheerful 'come in', she gently turned the handle and put her head round.

Tansy had been brought up to respect people's privacy so, even though she was on the best of terms with Emily, she always did as she had been taught and knocked first before entering.

Tansy loved Emily. She had just had her tenth birthday and she could hardly remember the time when Emily had not been with them or Mark, now almost three and rushing about on his sturdy little legs bumping into everything, everyone he came in contact with. Mark was clumsy but cheerful and he brought cheer. He was appealing, beguiling, into everything, always causing trouble and everyone loved him.

Emily's room was the large room at the back of the house which had been Edward's as a boy. It had been his den whenever he was home. It was in that room that Emily had grown to love Edward as she perused his neatly written letters, page after page, pouring out his passion, his yearning for her and Mark, and above all his love.

As Emily opened the door Tansy stood there with her arms behind her back. Her little pink tongue swept along her lower lip and her expression was artful.

'You've got another letter!' Emily said, thrusting out her hand. '*Give* it to me!'

Tansy squealed with laughter and ran into the room, dodging past Emily and pretending to hide behind the bed.

'Give it to me, *please*, Tansy,' Emily said, her pleasure turning swiftly to frustration. 'I haven't heard from him for *six weeks*!'

'All right, then,' Tansy said, reluctantly releasing the letter in its buff envelope. Then, as Emily tore open the flap, Tansy lay on Emily's bed and looked at the ceiling listening to Emily turning the pages, sensing her concentration, envying her.

Tansy was a little jealous of Edward, the brother she could hardly remember. She had been five when Edward joined up. Vaguely she could remember him with his moustache, but she knew that she confused him in her mind with her father. Everyone said that her father and Edward were so alike.

She still had, however, a very strong recollection of

Jeremy. Her memory of him was acute: that of a tall good-looking man who was fun for a child to be with.

But Jeremy had been missing for a long time and even Tansy knew that now it was doubtful he would ever return.

Emily finished turning the pages of the letter, sitting in her chair by the window, oblivious to the presence of Tansy on her bed, one leg crossed over the other, revealing her bottom and her frilly pink knickers made by Catherine who was a deft and clever needlewoman and made nearly all her daughter's and some of her son's, clothes.

'And so, my darling,' Edward concluded his letter, 'I feel it won't be very long now until we are reunited. I think the years we have been apart will make that reunion all the more worthwhile because, through the power of the written word, our exchange of letters, I think we know, understand and, certainly, love each other more than we ever did before.'

Much much more, Emily thought, letting the pages drop into her lap. She knew that people sometimes fell in love with people they had never met, strangers with whom they corresponded by post. One of her friends in Netherwick had written to a prisoner of war she had never met through the Red Cross and they had even become engaged by post, without ever having set eyes on each other.

Emily had more than two hundred letters from Edward carefully numbered in their envelopes and arranged in boxes in one of her cupboards. Two hundred. She never knew when he got the time, or opportunity, to write them; but, to her, they were an essential symbol of their love. And she had written as many back, maybe more. Sometimes she wrote one a day because to her it was like a dialogue that kept her close to Edward and made the war years at least tolerable for her.

'Is it a nice letter?' Tansy turned her head sideways, eyes scarcely concealing her jealousy.

'Yes,' Emily smiled. 'They're always nice because Edward writes beautiful letters. If only I'd known . . .'

'Known what?' Tansy eager for her attention, jumped off the bed as Emily's voice trailed away.

'Known that before we married.'

'What difference would that have made?' Tansy curled up on a pouffe at Emily's feet. Emily put out her hand and fondled the mop of tightly curled hair on Tansy's head. 'You wouldn't understand, darling. Not just yet.'

She leaned forwards and kissed her, and Tansy warmly responded, leaning her cheek against Emily's.

'I do *love* you,' Tansy burst out suddenly. 'You won't go, will you, when Edward comes back?'

'Of course I shan't.' Emily clung to her young body as though, through it, she could feel Edward's. 'We shall probably stay in Netherwick.'

'Oh really?' Tansy jumped up and began to swing on the end of the bed post.

'Edward talks about getting a schoolmaster's job here, or near here. He says the war has made him value his roots.' She stopped and looked fondly at the restless, mobile young girl. 'It's difficult to explain.'

'I can understand,' Tansy said crossly. 'After all I *am* ten years old.' She drew herself up as if to disclose her full maturity. 'Of course I can understand.'

'Well.' Emily got up and carefully tucked the pages of the letter back into its envelope. In time, after she had read it through two or three more times, she would answer it, and then she would number it and put it by the side of its predecessor. 'Well,' she looked at Tansy again, 'there *is* the possibility that Jeremy will not return. We don't know, do we, if he's alive or dead? There's been nothing for years. If he is dead . . . if he doesn't come back Edward feels that his father will need all the support he can get. He has taken Jeremy's loss so badly. Edward would like to help make up for that. To find a home with me and Mark, somewhere near here.'

'Oh, I'd *like* that too,' Tansy said fervently, then, tentatively after a pause, she asked shyly, 'Would you have other babies when Edward comes back?'

'Well,' Emily said, also feeling shy, 'that would depend.'

'On what?' Tansy asked curiously.

'On a lot of things.' Emily turned away, but in her heart she knew the answer. The drama of the wedding night could never be repeated. Now that they knew each other so much better it would be impossible for him to hurt her so much again.

'The answer is "yes, I hope so".' Emily turned to her with a smile that made her face radiant, as though the sun had suddenly shone on it. 'Now you go and get on with whatever it is you have to do, because I must write to Edward.' And as if she had already forgotten Tansy, she drew his letter out to read it to herself again.

After the destruction of the ancient and venerable monastery of Monte Cassino, bombed by the allied troops to rubble and provoking a storm of hostile criticism round the world, the British Army had pressed on towards Rome. Already they had encircled the Eternal City set on its seven hills which they could see from the plain.

Although every step of the way was hard fought for, there was already a feeling of victory among the troops. Victory after long, bitter years of war, much of it in the desert and all of it over hostile terrain, which had to be taken inch by inch. The collapse of Rome would surely be followed swiftly by the fall of Berlin and then the whole of the Axis side would disintegrate – if not this year, then the next.

Edward had fought a long, hard and gruelling war as a tank commander. He had seen men die and he had seen them terribly wounded and mutilated. He had lost close comrades, many of them friends, but he himself had sustained only a small cut when he had scrambled over the beach at Salerno after his tank got caught in a sandbank. That was the nearest he had come to being killed, because the allied advance was greeted by relentless enemy opposition.

Now, at last, Rome was in sight and, on that halcyon day in June 1944, Edward sat with his back to his tank reading the latest batch of letters from Emily, this time accompanied by some recent snaps of Mark as well as of Emily and his family.

As he drew out her picture he kissed it and put it in his shirt pocket, then he inspected the other photographs before reading her letter.

Mark. It was incredible to think that he had never seen his son. It was nearly his birthday and he would be three. When he got home Mark might be four or five. Edward kissed the picture of his cheerful little son and put it in his pocket next to Emily and then he gazed at the recent photo of his father and Catherine sitting on the garden bench with Tansy and Gilbert sitting cross-legged in front of them, hands clasped over their knees.

It was rather a stilted photo, a trifle blurred in the way that such photos sometimes are. They all appeared to be trying hard to look happy. They all had fixed smiles except his father who hadn't made the effort to try and smile at all. Maybe that was a day on which he felt depressed.

Yes, his father's melancholy showed through in the photograph, Edward thought, scrutinizing it closely. He had been deeply affected by Jeremy's fate. There was not even an attempt to smile as the others watched 'the birdie'. Catherine had her hand in his and Tansy leaned forwards while Gilbert looked away from the camera as though something had caught his eye. They were handsome children, both of them. They looked to him nearly grown up. Maybe it was the war that had made them mature so quickly.

Edward put that picture with the others in his breast pocket and then he took out a cigarette, lit it and expelled smoke into the cerulean Italian sky. He had a deep feeling of contentment in his heart. The sky was blue, the war was well on the way to being won on all of its fronts and he knew that his wife, who had not loved him when they married, was in love with him now. Through the strength of their letters a deep, unbreakable bond had been created. He knew that for certain, and what had sustained him through months of fighting and danger was the knowledge that, when he got back, Emily would be there waiting for him.

'Darling Edward,' (she began, her first letter dated sometime in April) 'As usual I got yours this morning and immediately started to answer it. When I hear from you, darling, I feel that I must instantly communicate with you as though we were together and having a normal conversation. The war news is good, darling, and everyone in Netherwick feels more cheerful. Some people, of course, have had bad news and know for certain that their loved ones are dead. There is still no news of our beloved Jeremy. One or two other people in the town are still missing too, and some are dead. But your father never ceases to believe that Jeremy is alive. He says he believes, but he does not look as though he does. Sometimes I pity poor Catherine because he can be very hard to live with.

Tom Thackery says your father is filled with guilt for the past and has tried to get him to see a psychiatrist! But your father, typically, says he doesn't believe in such nonsense. It doesn't affect his work as much as it did and he sees more patients, though I suspect Tom takes on more than we know. Your father takes a sleeping pill at night, so Tom makes all the night calls.

The main thing, my darling, is that we are all alive and well, except poor Jeremy, and how can we know the truth? Little Mark is a bundle of joy and trouble and the twins are like his elder brother and sister. Gilbert is especially good with him, caring, and likes to help him to make things and to try and read. Gilbert is such a *serious* boy – a bit like you. Geoffrey is determined he will go on to medical school and I think Gilbert wants to himself – *not* like you! Tansy is more mischievous and sometimes she teases Mark until he cries out of rage and frustration. Tansy is a tomboy. Gilbert is rather more thoughtful and, sometimes, I think he's missing out on his childhood. He is so studious, so anxious to please his father!

I love it here in Netherwick, darling Edward. Sometimes I can't believe I've been here nearly three years. It will soon be the anniversary of the deaths of Mum and Dad. The only thing I miss about being away from London is that I can't visit their grave; Derek and Hilda go regularly however. Hilda is having another baby. That will make three.

I sometimes think, darling Edward . . .'

Edward looked up, aware of a buzzing around him. A large bee hovered over a yellow flower which clung, despite all odds, to a craggy escarpment beside which the tank was parked. Around him the men lay in the sunshine. It was early morning and not yet hot enough to take cover from the heat which was already beginning to shimmer above the ground. He watched a lizard slither across the tank, disappearing in one of the many crevices, maybe in search of shade.

Suddenly one of the men in front of him cried out and, jumping up, pointed towards the sky to where a low-flying plane was coming at them only a few hundred feet, or so it seemed, above the ground. Edward started to get up but, all at once, there was a strange whirring in his ears, the ground tilted beneath him and a huge orange ball began to revolve in the sky. At its centre he saw quite clearly the picture of his son: the infant Mark whom he had never seen and now knew he never would.

Afterwards, when the dust and debris cleared, his body was found close to his companions; but it was only identified by the pictures of his family, miraculously safe and intact in his breast pocket, close to his heart.

PART TWO

The Mills of God

1945–1953

Chapter 7

Netherwick, as a town, had been relatively unaffected by the war and, in many ways, had never lost its normality, its momentum. It had experienced the same shortages as other parts of Britain – but even this was relative. There was always plenty of good farm produce – eggs, butter and milk, even beef, pork and chickens – to be had by those in the know. Yet, like any other city or town, Netherwick had shared in the national trauma and, like any other, it took its time to recover as new industries opened or old ones closed, and men came back from the services to resume their pre-war occupations. Yet some citizens of Netherwick would never see the place of their birth again, and some returned maimed in body and soul; sometimes both. It was the lot of Doctor Blair and other medical men in the town to look after these just as it had been after 1918. The year the First World War ended Geoffrey Blair had been thirty, a young father, a proud and happy husband who seemed to stand at the threshold of a life of opportunity and plenty.

In 1945 he was fifty-seven, a grandfather and a man weighed down not only by personal cares and grief but by the melancholic nature of his own temperament that had been with him since childhood.

Geoffrey Blair was not singular in having moments of black despair when, for no reason at all, the world seemed a dull, hopeless place. When he was young it was thought that his intelligence was to blame; he was a myopic, introspective young boy who did not seem to enjoy the games and pastimes of his peers. He blamed his poor eyesight for lack of skill with a ball, and he despised those of his contemporaries who could not delight as he did in the classics, great works of literature or scientific subjects. Geoffrey Blair had lost both his parents before he was eighteen. When he was fifteen his father, also a doctor, had died in an epidemic of scarlet fever. All his life, however, he had suffered from moods of such blackness and despair that he had shut himself up in his room, sometimes for days on end. The year Geoffrey went up to medical school his mother died of pneumonia which she had neglected, maybe out of a desire to join the husband she had adored. Geoffrey was left at eighteen on his own, comparatively wealthy but prey to the critical heritage, the same depressive malady which had afflicted his father.

Prior to the 1914–18 war little was known about depression or the way to treat it. Some people thought it was a form of insanity and that such afflicted persons should be put away. But the work of Sigmund Freud and his colleagues was helped into prominence by the experience of doctors and surgeons in the First World War in treating victims of shock, gas or those whose brains had been damaged in battle.

Geoffrey Blair had little time for, or interest in, the work of psychiatrists whose methods he tended to denigrate, in common with a lot of his medical colleagues. He linked his own particular moods with some malaise of the soul; to him they were spiritual, not physical or mental, and the cure for him was to remain as quiet as he could and not be irritated or worried by trouble of any kind.

When he was on his own he used to be able to cope with his moods much better. He would lock his surgery door at night and remain in his warm study, sometimes not even going to bed but sitting in a chair staring at the wall in front of him.

The excitement of his new young wife, the rediscovery of physical love and the birth of his twins allowed him a respite from depression, a remission which lasted approximately two years. But since the holiday with his sons in 1935, his moods had been more severe than ever and he knew that his irritation with his family, his choleric temperament, had worsened.

Geoffrey Blair had a profound sense of guilt about his sons, both of whom now appeared to be dead. Edward had been killed outside Rome and his son Jeremy had not been heard of since the fall of Singapore. He was not officially reported dead, just missing, presumed dead. Not knowing the whereabouts of his body was even worse than knowing that the bones of Edward at least rested in a well-kept grave on the hills outside the Eternal City.

After the death of Edward, Geoffrey withdrew into himself for so many weeks that Tom Thackery was consulted about having him committed to a home. He was not violent, but silent. He walked like a man in a trance, acknowledging no one and slept sitting up in his chair. Tom, who shouldered most of the work of the practice, had not wanted to commit his friend and senior partner. He told Catherine that, as long as she and the family could cope, Geoffrey should remain at home where his chances of complete recovery were much better.

In time Geoffrey did improve and this improvement came largely with the help of Edward's widow, Emily, who found caring for her father-in-law a way of sublimating her own grief.

Emily was a treasure whom the beleaguered Blair

family much appreciated. Her own grief at the death of a husband she had learned to love too late can only be imagined. But, in fact, tending to her young son and helping his grandfather comforted her. Through the care of others she learned not how to forget the memory of Edward or her love for him, but how to put that grief in perspective as part of the process of life.

By the end of the war Catherine Blair, who was herself only a young woman of thirty-four, had streaks of white in her hair and a lined, prematurely aged face. She too felt guilty that at one time she had not done more to bring father and his elder sons together. She saw herself now as having been too selfish, too concentrated on herself and her own children, too possessive of Geoffrey who, after all, had other responsibilities.

The common-sense, practical approach of Emily was of profound help and significance to Catherine, as well as to all the people in the Blair household in the years after Edward's death in 1944 and beyond.

By Christmas 1945 Emily felt that she was as much part of the family as anyone else; that she at last had found her roots and that she, too, belonged.

Geoffrey Blair gradually emerged from the acute stage of his depression and began to see patients again; just his private patients by appointment. Another doctor had been taken on, a refugee from the bombing, like Emily, who had lost his wife through tuberculosis and whose children were grown up. His name was Terence Fulbright and he was a pleasant, gentle practitioner of the old school who believed in plenty of fresh air and castor oil as the main adjuncts to healthy living. Doctor Fulbright had originally come from the north of England and he was quickly accepted by the people of Netherwick and liked by them.

There were those, however, who swore by Doctor Blair. He had delivered their children and looked after their ills and as soon as he was fit, they were glad to see him again. They found in him the virtues of medical practice they had liked and needed. He was a good listener, a good diagnostician and he cared. Also, since he had lost his two sons, he seemed to have acquired a dimension that he hadn't had before: a depth of understanding and sympathy that was of help to those who were themselves bereaved.

Thus he knew that Mrs Lulworth's back pains were a symptom of her grief over the death of her husband on the very day the war ended, not in battle but of cancer in the local hospital, although he was not a young man and had lived a full life. Doctor Blair listened to Mrs Lulworth's heart and chest through his stethoscope, percussed her back and then told her to put her clothes on behind the screen while he went back to his desk to make notes.

'Well, Mary,' he said to her, looking up as she emerged from behind the screen. 'Your chest is perfectly sound; heart and lungs: nothing wrong with them. Just because George died of cancer there's no need to think *you've* got it too.' He looked at her over his writing spectacles with a kindly smile and handed her a prescription. 'These will help to soothe your nerves while you get over the period of bereavement for George, which is perfectly natural. Come and see me again in six weeks' time, Mary.'

'Thank you, Doctor Blair,' Mary Lulworth said in the grateful, obsequious tone of voice that patients seem to reserve for doctors, fastening her coat, and taking the piece of paper from his hand. 'I'm so glad you're back again. Nothing really wrong, I hope?' She looked at him anxiously.

'Just a touch of indigestion, Mary,' he said smiling blandly at her and patting his chest. 'A touch of wind *and* advancing old age.'

'You're not an *old* man, Doctor Blair!' Mary Lulworth protested. 'I shouldn't think you were much older than me.'

In fact Geoffrey Blair was considerably younger, but he made no comment. He knew he looked old and he felt old. Sometimes he felt very old indeed.

'No word I suppose . . .' Mrs Lulworth left a finger at her lips, name unspoken.

Doctor Blair shook his head, experiencing the familiar lump in his throat, the slight pain in the chest every time Jeremy's fate was even referred to.

'We don't despair,' he said, with a shrug of the shoulders.

'You hear of people who seem to come back from the dead,' Mrs Lulworth said, with an encouraging smile. 'You know what they say: "no news is good news".'

'I shan't give up hope until I have proof that Jeremy is dead,' the doctor said. 'Illogical as it is I feel, in my bones, that somewhere – I don't know where – my son is alive and that one day he will be returned to us.'

He then sharply and uncharacteristically turned his back on his patient, leaving her to show herself out.

Mary Lulworth was the first of the patients Geoffrey Blair saw that afternoon, on a cold raw day in January 1946.

His private patients were mainly the older, wealthier segment of the population and no doubt these would continue even after the introduction of a National Health Service, which was being bitterly resisted by the medical fraternity which had a habit of resisting reforms that threatened to deprive them of the fat of the land.

Geoffrey Blair would never resist the introduction of a

National Health Service nor welcome it. He would remain outside it and concentrate exclusively on those patients who wished to retain his services on a private basis. Tom Thackery and Terry Fulbright could see to the rest.

When he had seen his last patient for the day Doctor Blair leaned back in his chair and closed his eyes, running a hand over his brow as he did. He was very tired. He was tired and Mary Lulworth had thought he was older than she was; and she was sixty-six! He thus looked ten years older than he was; but what did it matter? He got so little joy out of life that sometimes he hoped he had not long to live. But then he thought of the twins, his hopes for the future and he felt better. Tansy was a charming, attractive girl who would marry well and Gilbert already wanted to be a doctor.

One should count one's blessings, Geoffrey thought, heaving himself out of his chair and gathering up the medical records of the people he had seen that afternoon to give to his receptionist. He was about to open the door when she opened it for him and popped her head round the door.

'There's a gentleman to see you, Doctor Blair,' she said, giving him a peculiar look.

'My surgery is finished for the day, Anita,' he replied firmly. 'Ask him to make another appointment would you? Or, if it's an emergency . . .'

'It's someone from the *Ministry*, Doctor Blair.' Anita continued to look very mysterious. 'He said it was very important.'

Geoffrey Blair felt a spasm of horror, dread of the unknown, as he threw open the door and looked at the white-faced official in regulation raincoat and trilby, clutching a briefcase with some old, indecipherable initials on it.

He rose to his feet and took off his hat as the doctor entered the waiting room.

'Doctor Blair, sir?'

'I am Doctor Blair.' Geoffrey put a hand on the desk for support.

'Then I would like to tell you immediately I have some very good news for you, sir.'

'Have ...' the doctor began, as if he did not understand.

'Your son, Squadron Leader Jeremy Blair, is alive and on his way home to England by a military transport plane at this very moment, Doctor Blair.'

'Please come this way, sir, madam,' the white-coated orderly said, leading the way into the ward. Ahead of them, in rows of identical hospital beds, covered with white counterpanes, lay the still figures of the seriously ill or wounded who had been returned from hitherto undiscovered theatres of war. Pockets of lost or abandoned troops had been found, particularly in the Far East, many months after the war had ended with the surrender of Japan after the second atom bomb fell in August 1945 on Nagasaki.

It was yet unclear to Doctor Blair and his family how Jeremy had escaped from the jaws of death; but what, now, did it matter? He at least was alive.

'The Squadron Leader has been *very* ill,' the orderly said in a whisper as they started to walk past the still figures in the beds. Some had their arms suspended by pulleys from the ceiling, some their legs. Some had cages over what were, too obviously, stumps and some had bandages round their eyes and heads. But the figure before which the orderly finally stopped lay quite still in his bed with no obvious sign of injury.

Yet he was so emaciated that he looked like a skeleton

whose place should really have been in the morgue. His eyes were closed and deep sunken cheeks accentuated the prominent bones, his nose and his mouth which hung slightly open. His head was almost completely bald but what stubble was left seemed to be grey.

The ward orderly stopped by the side of the bed and looked at Jeremy Blair's father and sister-in-law with pity.

'This is not my son,' Geoffrey said, after he had spent some minutes staring at the recumbent figure. 'My son would only be twenty-nine years of age. This is the body of an old man.'

'I'm afraid it *is* Squadron Leader Blair,' the ward orderly said, yet the expression on his face seemed to reflect the father's doubts. He looked carefully at the charts which hung on the end of the bed and then nodded. 'Identity verified by documents. He was found in delirium on the Island of Takatu which is off the coast of Java in November of last year. He has spent some time in hospital in India before he was brought over here.'

'It can't be my son,' Geoffrey said, continuing to gaze owlishly at the patient through his thick-lensed spectacles. 'It can't possibly. I'm a doctor, you know,' he added severely.

'I do, but he *is* getting better, Doctor Blair,' the ward orderly said in a tone of respect. 'He was to all intents and purposes, dead when they found him. He has suffered from frequent bouts of malaria and consequent dehydration. Some of the men who were with him were dead. They had been cut off from supplies for many weeks. I believe the Squadron Leader was one of the few to survive . . . on account of his youth,' the ward orderly added lamely, looking with a similar air of incomprehension as the father at the skeletal figure in the bed in front of them.

'Will he *live*?' Geoffrey enquired slowly.

'The prognosis is good.' The orderly passed him the notes. 'He has survived so far and this includes a long journey by plane. But he will need a lot of care. He hasn't spoken to us yet. He can't remember anything. But maybe, if he sees you . . .'

Geoffrey Blair in his life as a medical man had seen many unpleasant and, indeed, shocking sights. He had seen death in all its forms, its grotesqueness and, by now, he would have thought he was, if not impervious, at least accustomed to illness in its many manifestations. But he felt he could not advance an inch nearer the bed and finally the orderly, observing his obvious distress, brought him a chair.

'If you would rather have a word with Doctor Lightfoot, Doctor Blair? And, maybe, see the Squadron Leader again when you feel more reassured.'

Geoffrey took the seat but continued to shake his head. 'It is not my son,' he said. 'It was too cruel to give me hope. There has been a mistake.'

By this time Emily, almost as fearful and just as distressed as Geoffrey, had crept nearer the bed and had stood for some time looking down at the face which was the nearest thing to a cadaver she had ever seen. The skin was the texture of parchment and of the same yellowish hue and, as yet, it was impossible to see the eyes which remained closed. And yet . . .

She leaned closer and, suddenly, the eyes opened and they were of a deep cerulean blue; the eyes of a young man. They appeared to have difficulty at first in focusing on her and then, for a long, long time they gazed at her before closing again.

But in them, in that instance, she had seen recognition; she had seen a spark which seemed briefly to flicker and then die.

'It *is* Jeremy,' she said slowly, as if to herself, reaching out to take his hand. 'Jeremy, this is Emily, Edward's wife.'

But the eyes remained shut and, as she held his thin emaciated hand the tears began to trickle slowly from her eyes as if she were weeping not only for him but for those millions who had perished or been mutilated by war.

Tansy slowly turned the handle of the door and popped her head round it. Jeremy was asleep, but he had been reading and the open book lay on his lap. He was propped high against the pillows and there was a half-smile on his face which was now far more recognizable than it had been three months before when his father and Emily had visited him at the military hospital near Southampton.

Jeremy's memory about events in the recent past was negligible, but the remote past he could recall quite clearly and he had known his father and Emily almost at once. From that moment he began to get better. It was as though the recognition and love of his family had given him the will to live.

They still did not know precisely what had happened to Jeremy during the war, how he had managed to escape from Singapore and remain free. All they knew was that he had formed part of a fighting group which had harassed the Japanese on the occupied islands around Java and the Philippines. At first they had been supplied by other pockets of indigenous resistance, but then these had stopped. One day Jeremy's memory would return in full, but it would take time. Time and patience, the medical officer had told them. In six months' time, maybe a year, he would be the man he had been before the war.

But would he?

Tansy stood shyly at the bottom of the bed with a posy of flowers which she had picked herself clasped behind her back. She gazed intently at the man who lay in the bed and then, timidly, she crept up to the table by the bedside and put her posy on it, preparing to tip-toe out again.

But when she turned she saw that the eyes, the deep clear blue eyes were gazing at her, the rest of his face dimly lit by a half-smile.

It had taken a long time for Jeremy Blair to smile. Even now no one had heard him laugh. Before the war he had always been full of laughter and jokes; but no more. He never laughed and he never joked. All that was behind him.

Yet Jeremy was now recognizable, no longer the skeleton he had once been; a man so near death that his blood pressure reading was the lowest the hospital had ever recorded in someone who was still alive.

Jeremy was brought back to Netherwick, a place he had never liked and where he had never felt at home, by military ambulance in February of 1946, four months after his discovery in Java and a month after his reunion with his father. He was taken immediately to his old room high up in the house which, in the much more distant past had belonged to the live-in maid. It was not the most convenient room for an invalid as it involved going up and down three flights of stairs a dozen times a day or more; but everyone felt that Jeremy would be happy there. That he would like his old room best.

But everyone was wrong. Jeremy did not like his old room; it had, it seemed, too many bad memories for him of holidays that he had not enjoyed when he was a boy. It was then that his father realized the extent of Jeremy's unhappy childhood; so unhappy, it seemed, that he didn't even want to sleep in his old room. And such knowledge his father had not even been aware of.

After a week, and with her consent, Jeremy was moved down to Emily's room on the first floor which was light and airy and had views over the town. Emily moved into the smaller room next door which had been Mark's, as she shared with the nurse the duties of looking after Jeremy. Mark moved upstairs to Jeremy's old room which made him feel very grown up indeed, as it was a large, long room under the eaves where all sorts of exciting games could be hatched and enacted. For a boy of not quite five, it was a paradise.

For a long time both brother and sister continued to gaze silently at each other and then Jeremy said: 'What mischief are you up to now, young Tansy?' He struggled to raise himself onto one arm.

'No mischief,' Tansy said virtuously, taking up the flowers and presenting them to him. 'I picked these for you.'

She gazed at him with the eyes of love, but Jeremy had eyes only for the flowers – daffodils, tulips, irises and cornflowers whose blue matched his eyes – gathered by her fresh from the garden and tied with blue ribbon.

'How kind you are, Tansy,' Jeremy said, reaching out for her hand. 'You bring me a little gift each day.'

'To make you better,' Tansy said leaning against his bed, staring at him with that air of fascination that Jeremy always induced in her, as if he were a visitor from an alien planet.

She remembered him being brought back to the house, the ambulance going slowly up the drive and, it seemed, many people helping to take out his stretcher and carry him indoors. She had watched, rather awestruck, from her window which overlooked the front of the house, and she remembered thinking he had come home to die because of the careful way they carried the stretcher, as though it had been a bier, as she had seen coffins being carried into church.

For a few days everyone had fussed over Jeremy, several specialists came from Manchester and Leeds to examine him. She herself had no chance to see him, even to greet him, as grave-faced people moved quickly but silently in and out of his room.

And then one day she was taken in by her mother to see him and, at that moment, she knew that she was, yet again, violently and irrevocably in love. Once it had been Emily, now, undoubtedly, it was Jeremy.

He had looked so heroic leaning back on his white pillows, his face ashen, eyes hollowed out. That day they had been closed, but as soon as she came into the room he opened them and smiled at her in recognition.

That, *that* was the moment of love.

Despite the fact that he was her half-brother, Tansy knew she would always feel like this about Jeremy and that she would be jealous of any woman who had him for her own. Perhaps, now, no one ever would. He had something wrong with his legs and difficulty in walking. He had bad headaches and easily forgot things. What the doctors were trying to find out now was how much was temporary and how much permanent. Whether, in fact, Jeremy Blair would, as the Southampton surgeons had predicted, ever be a completely well man again.

Tansy and Jeremy never spoke much because Jeremy was supposed to remain quiet. It tired him terribly to talk and that was when he began to forget.

So now he lay and looked at her flowers with an expression of unutterable sweetness, almost of nostalgia, as though he were remembering all the years of the good life before the war when flowers and colours and passions predominated.

That is, if he could remember them. His memory was patchy and no one quite knew. One of the neuro-surgeons had recommended a psychiatrist, but Geoffrey Blair would not allow one to cross his doorstep. Jeremy had to rely on his talking companions instead.

Of them all he preferred Tansy, because she was light and laughter in his life and, next, he liked Emily because she was quiet and grave and sensible and seemed to know what to say and do. The person he least liked was the regular nurse, Sister Fairweather, who had been a ward sister at Geoffrey's old hospital and was now retired. She was the old-school kind of nurse who treated patients like recalcitrant children: to be seen and not heard.

As for his father; what was one to make of that enigmatic man, who would sit and gaze at his son shaking his head as though he saw the earth of the grave opening under him? That was very disquieting indeed. Geoffrey Blair depressed his son and his visits were unwelcome. The two had always had difficulty in communication and they still had. War and injury had done nothing to alter that.

'Tansy,' Jeremy said suddenly, looking up at her from his contemplation of the flowers. 'Where's Edward?'

Tansy's whole face always mirrored her mind. She knew that it immediately registered guilt, confusion, uncertainty. Jeremy did not know that Edward was dead and it was, apparently, vitally important for his welfare, even perhaps his sanity, that he should not be told. That much had been instilled in her by her mother, father and Emily. No mention must be made of Edward's fate until Jeremy was stronger.

Jeremy reached out and gripped her hand so fiercely that, momentarily, she winced. 'Edward's dead, isn't he, Tansy? *Isn't* he? Tell me the truth.'

Tansy didn't reply but tried to wriggle her hand from his grasp. 'Come on, Tansy,' Jeremy said more gently, 'everyone is trying to hide the truth from me, but I want to know.'

'I can't say anything,' Tansy said, 'I don't know anything about it.'

Jeremy flung her hand away from him in anger and she hung her head in fear and remorse. Looking at her Jeremy felt remorse too. She was the one person in the household with whom he felt entirely at ease. Everyone else, even Emily, he thought was pitying him or trying to hide something from him.

'Come here,' Jeremy said, gently reaching out an arm and encircling her shoulders with it as she came, reluctantly, to stand by the side of the bed. 'I'm sorry I asked.' He leaned across to kiss her. 'There, I won't make it difficult for you. You see, I know!'

Impulsively Tansy turned towards him and kissed his cheek. She remembered when Jeremy had first come to the house and how thin and frightening he had been. She had thought then that at any minute he would die, and it was only gradually that she realized her frequent visits were helping to make him well again. The love that she'd felt began to grow; a deep, important, but ultimately helpless love because she knew that it could never be anything else. Now for a while he hugged her and then, releasing her, he sank back on his bed, as if too tired to go on. Thankfully, timidly, she tip-toed out of the room.

Later that same day Emily entered the invalid's room and found him sitting in a chair by the window. She stopped and looked at him in amazement.

'Who helped you out of bed?' she enquired. 'I thought you were not supposed to get up for a few more weeks?'

'I got myself up.' Jeremy, still very pale, looked at her proudly. 'I was determined to do it and I did.'

'Tom will be very cross,' Emily said, trying to make her expression severe, but Jeremy only smiled.

'Tom won't know, I will say *you* helped me.'

'Oh . . . you!' Emily went across as if to give him a playful smack, Jeremy caught her hand and the look in his eyes first surprised, then frightened her.

'Come and sit down beside me,' he said gently, pointing to the chair opposite. He continued to hold her hand so tightly that she had to lean over for the chair and pull it towards her. Then, her hand still in his, she sat down and smoothed her skirt over her knees.

'What is it?' she asked.

'I know about Edward. I'm sorry. I'm very, very sorry. I should have gone, not him.'

'Oh *no*!' Emily said impulsively.

'Edward had a child, he had you. I had no one. Jill got married to someone else almost as soon as I went to Singapore. Why Edward and not me?'

'We all thought you had died in 1941,' Emily said in a low, sad voice. 'We thought Edward would come through the war. It was just before D-Day while he and his platoon were waiting outside Rome to enter it. A stray Stuka dive-bomber saw them and made a run, knocking out almost the entire platoon of tanks and men.'

'I'm dreadfully, dreadfully sorry,' he said still tightly holding her hand.

'Did your father tell you?' she asked softly.

'No, no one told me. I asked Tansy this morning and she got so frightened I knew I was right. I'd already guessed, you know. All the stories you were telling me about Edward being "busy" I sensed were false. I'm an invalid, not a child, and I knew Edward would come and see me if he were alive. Don't blame Tansy. I knew. Did he ever see Mark?' His expression as he looked at her was full of tenderness and compassion.

'I never saw him again after our wedding night,' she said with a sob in her voice. 'He had forty-eight hours embarkation leave and we got married. He went to North Africa and then to Italy. We wrote a lot . . . we, well, I,' Emily lowered her head as if trying to find the right words, 'I learned to love Edward after were were married; I didn't before. I think you knew that. But he wrote so many lovely letters to me and I realized what a good, gentle, plucky man he was; how lucky I was to have him, and how good our time would be after the war. We were all convinced he would survive, but he never came back. He went all through the North African campaign and half-way up Italy without a scratch. But . . . that's the way . . .'

Suddenly she leaned her head against Jeremy's chest weeping uncontrollably as, slowly, his hand closed over her head and started gently stroking her hair.

Chapter 8

The fact that Jeremy Blair knew the truth about the death of his brother seemed to ease the tension in the Blair household that had permeated it since the arrival of the invalid. So precarious had been his state of health, so fragile the balance of his mind, that no word of Edward's death was allowed to reach him. Yet the keeping of the secret had engendered stress among those entrusted with it and so, in a way, had impeded Jeremy's recovery.

Now that everything was out in the open he began to get better much more quickly and it was considered obligatory on the part of the family, and therapeutic to Jeremy, to spend a part of each day talking about Edward. It was cathartic and helpful for the whole of the family. However, as the weeks turned into months and the end of the year drew close it was possible for the doctors now to agree on one thing: despite his youth, his resolution and his strength Jeremy would never make a complete recovery from the prolonged effects of malnutrition, dehydration and trauma experienced overseas.

His entire neurological system had been affected, causing at times a weakness in the limbs that prevented him from walking for days at a time. His frequent headaches, blackouts and periods of depression meant he would never again be able to hold down a job requiring any degree of concentration. Even had he wanted to, he would never be able to return to the bank.

Jeremy received this verdict sitting with his father in his bedroom in December 1946, a year after he had been flown back to England. Together they read the lengthy report of the neurosurgeons and their conclusion: Jeremy would be permanently unfit for normal work and would be recommended for a full disability pension from the government.

'In other words I'm a write-off,' Jeremy said, his voice full of bitterness as his father let the paper fall on the floor and sat gazing at it as if unaware of Jeremy's presence; as if the verdict had been delivered not to his son but to him.

'Dad?' Jeremy prompted, worried about his father's silence.

'It's my fault entirely.' Geoffrey Blair sat back in his chair continuing to gaze in front of him. 'I was not a good father to you boys.'

'Dad, that has nothing to do with it,' Jeremy struck the desk with some violence, 'nothing at all.'

'You would not have volunteered to go to the war.'

'But I would have *had* to go to the war. I would have *had* to have joined up, Dad, Edward too. We were of age.'

'But *you* might not have chosen the air force.'

'But Edward didn't, and look what happened to him.'

'It's all my fault. It's the judgement of God,' his father said, striking his breast in a *mea-culpa*, whereupon Jeremy felt a bleakness, a sense of despair engulf his soul as his eyes met those of his father.

That night Jeremy lay in bed trying to focus his eyes on a book. He had never had much pleasure in reading and he did not now. He found concentration very difficult and if he managed a page a day that was quite good going. But he could not concentrate because his mind was so busy racing at great speed over the events of the past, the years before the war and the war itself. With a small group of men he had escaped from Singapore and they had met with a band of guerrillas and joined them in trying to outwit the Japs.

On one level it had resembled a perpetual game of Boy Scouts and that appealed to Jeremy. He enjoyed the rigours of the jungle and the camaraderie of the life in the open air. But the Japanese were a cunning and relentless foe who had a way of seeking out these brave bands of guerrillas and destroying them with the utmost ruthlessness. After one attack Jeremy, who had barely escaped with his life, watched his former comrades, European and Asian, being summarily beheaded in the pitiless sun without trial.

It was after that that his physical strength began to fail, owing to repeated attacks of malaria, to scarcity of proper food and supplies, little fresh water and a diet of bean-shoots and rice.

All too often he lay in a mountain cave fighting for his life, waging war with illness and death by starvation and fever rather than with a physical, visible enemy.

It was then that he had felt he would never survive the war and, sometimes, he longed for death.

There was a movement by the door and Jeremy, brought back to reality, lowered his book. Emily entered very quietly and crossed the room seeming to think that he was asleep, his book fallen on his bedclothes. She raised the book and was about to put a marker in it and place it on the table beside him when she suddenly looked at him and saw those blue eyes open, the still pallid cheeks creased in a smile.

'I was hoping you would come,' Jeremy whispered as Emily leaned over him to straighten his sheets. She stopped and looked at him, his face a few inches from hers and the expression in his eyes was one she had seen before.

But it was wrong; wrong. Sharply she drew back from him but he caught at her hand and, with the other, touched her breast. She was in her nightclothes, her hair bound into a thick plait and tied by a single ribbon. Jeremy thought she looked so ethereally lovely that even to touch her would almost be like sacrilege; but he had been sorely tempted to do what he just had for a long time. It was no sudden impulse.

He knew that his feelings were reciprocated; that Emily did her best to avoid intimate contact with him, being alone with him for too long in the room. He now got dressed during the day and had started having intensive physiotherapy. He didn't need looking after half as much as he had and Emily was beginning to wonder, now that the war was over, what she would do with her own life; what the future held for herself and Mark. She had a war widow's pension and a child allowance, that that was all.

She thought she would have to return to teaching.

But tonight she did not repulse him and the pressure of his hand on her almost naked breast infused her with a desire that she had thought was dead. She had never been satisfied in love and, after Edward's death, thought she never would. It was too late.

Impulsively Emily leaned forwards and Jeremy drew her breast out of her nightgown altogether, putting the tip of it in his mouth as though he were a child she was succouring.

It was a sensation so exquisite that a tremor passed down her body and she lay on the bed beside him while he still clasped her breast in his hand. He began to bare her other breast, but she drew back and cried: 'We can't do this, Jeremy. It's *wrong*.'

Jeremy left his hand on her breast which was round and full. He thought back to before the war and remembered she had been considered flat-chested. He could recall this fact particularly well.

'When did you grow breasts like this?' Jeremy enquired in a conversational tone. 'I'm sure you didn't have any before the war.'

'Oh, so you noticed?' Emily said attempting, not altogether successfully, a light banter.

'Oh yes, I noticed.'

'And did you notice that I liked you then?'

'Oh yes, I did. I was a bounder in those days. Anyway, I thought you would be good for Edward.'

'Because I wore glasses and was flat-chested?' She smiled and, drawing her dressing gown tightly, almost provocatively across her bosom, slipped off the bed.

She went over to the mirror which stood on the washstand and ran her hands through her hair. Her face was flushed and the breast that he had fondled was red above her nightdress. She plastered her hair back against her head and turned to him, leaning against the mahogany washstand for support.

'Jeremy, we can't do this,' she said in a breathless voice.

'Why not?'

'You know why not. Your father would be *very* angry.'

'Oh that,' Jeremy said casually as if what his father thought were a matter of indifference to him.

'I would hate it too.'

'I don't think you would.'

'No, I . . . know what you mean.' She felt herself blushing. 'But I'm Edward's widow. I'm your sister-in-law. It's not right.'

'It's not against the Bible, if that's what's worrying you.'

'But it doesn't *seem* right.'

'It seems right to me,' Jeremy said, beckoning her to

come over to him. 'I think Edward would have wished it too. He would have wanted me to look after you, and you to look after me.'

'Are you sure?' she said tremulously, walking slowly towards the bed, her eyes full of indecision.

'Sure,' he said. 'Quite sure.'

When she lay in his arms and he rested in hers it seemed that the fusion of their bodies was so good, so natural, that it couldn't be wrong. It was so different from her wedding night that it was difficult to think of it as the same experience. But then she had known that Jeremy would be far more skilled than his brother. He had had a lot of practice. Some men delighted in pleasing women and the thought that perhaps she had never really loved Edward at all, despite the letters, made her feel terribly guilty. She also felt guilty about the fact that, while making love to Jeremy, she had forgotten her husband.

Jeremy, as if sensing her confusion, began to stroke her brow, looking tenderly down at her face.

'You really are very pretty, you know,' he said teasingly. 'I used to think you were a plain little thing.'

'*And* flat-chested.'

'With glasses!'

She tried playfully to slap him but she was pinioned beneath his body. 'We shouldn't joke about it,' she said wriggling a little. 'I feel horribly guilty about Edward.'

At that he drew away from her and lay on his front beside her, one arm still loosely round her waist. The light was still on and their faces were hot and excited, glistening with sweat, although it was cold in the room. He put his chin on the pillow and avoided looking at her.

'There is no need to feel guilty about Edward, Emily,' he murmured. 'I feel he knows and he approves. He wants us to be together.'

'Your father wouldn't think that.'

'Good heavens!' Jeremy cried, thumping the pillow. 'Edward has been dead for two and a half years. You have fully served out the term of your widowhood. Father can't expect more.'

'But what can the future actually hold for us, Jeremy?'

'Who knows?' he murmured, drawing her into his arms again.

Gilbert Blair was a solitary, introspective youth who bore more than a passing resemblance, physically and temperamentally, to his dead half-brother, Edward. He seemed unmoved by the highs or the lows of life which he lived rather like a ship pursuing its course through calm seas on an even keel.

Like his father, Gilbert, too, seemed old for his age and when he was thirteen he looked fifteen. The twins celebrated their thirteenth birthday in January 1947. Catherine always had a party for them and made a fuss and this time it was attended by Jeremy who watched the jollifications, ate the tea and participated in as many of the games as he could from a chair in the corner of the lounge. There Emily hovered solicitously around him, watched rather jealously by Tansy who would have liked to look after Jeremy herself.

Gilbert rarely took part in any games except the clever ones which needed a certain intelligence and, understandably, there were hardly any of these. In fact, Catherine decided, watching the two distinct groups of children – those clustered around Gilbert and those around Tansy, but both looking rather bored – children's parties should be a thing of the past.

'I think this will be the last one,' she said to her mother who always came to help Catherine on such occasions. Her husband had died the year before the war and Jean

Wills, who had given up her work in the factory to look after him in his last illness, took up part-time work instead. She helped out at the Co-op from time to time and she worked behind the bar of The King's Head. All her children were married; her daughters Ethel and Deidre had two children each, and her son Colin was the father of four. Colin still worked at the mill where the Wills family had worked for generations; but the two daughters had moved out of the district with their husbands and families, and were seen about two or three times a year.

Jeans Wills was a gregarious woman who loved family life and now she lived on her own in the small house in Castle Street where she had lived all her married life, where her children had been born and where her husband had died. She saw more of Catherine than of any of her children and she liked to come up to the Blair house and help out. It made her feel useful. She was very much in awe of her son-in-law and still referred to him as 'the doctor'. She would never have dreamt of calling him by his Christian name. 'Doctor Blair' he was to her, and 'Doctor Blair' he would remain. She always referred to him obliquely as 'Doctor Blair' or 'Catherine's husband', or, merely, 'the doctor'.

Catherine and her mother now stood, arms akimbo, at the side of the room watching an attempt on Tansy's part to organize pass the parcel, a game much despised by Gilbert and his crowd of intellectual friends, all scholarship boys at the Grammar School, and destined for better lives than most of their parents enjoyed.

'We can't just have *girls*!' Tansy stamped her foot in a tantrum and Catherine was about to intervene when Jeremy got up and, walking slowly across the room assisted, as always, by a stick, squatted down by himself in the middle.

'I'll play,' he said. 'If you girls, or those who want to play, form a ring, I'll start it off.'

The girls rushed excitedly towards Jeremy, each one jockeying for position to be next to him. Tansy let this unseemly scene pass without comment then, when they were all seated and Jean was about to give the parcel to Jeremy, while Emily took her place at the piano, fingers poised over the keys, Tansy said to the girl sitting on the right of Jeremy: 'Do you mind letting *me* sit there, please?'

The girl pursed her mouth stubbornly and was about to refuse when Jeremy nudged her and said softly in her ear, 'Go on, be a sport. It *is* her birthday.' Grudgingly the girl slithered on her bottom across the carpet and everyone had, in their turn, to shift to make way for Tansy who, face flushed with victory and pleasure, squatted next to Jeremy.

At a signal from Catherine, Emily then struck the keys with her fingers to the rousing tune of 'The British Grenadiers', watched apprehensively by the group on the floor who passed the parcel around as though it had been a hot cake.

Catherine rejoined her mother and the two women sat side by side enjoying the scene. The boys at the far corner of the large lounge stared apathetically, slightly disparagingly, at the excited group on the floor, though one or two of them looked as though they wished they had joined them. Gilbert was chatting to his best friend, Norman Lard, and seemed to be taking no interest in the proceedings at all.

'The doctor' had briefly appeared for tea, and was now in his consulting room taking his evening surgery. Outside it was dark and soon one or two parents from outlying districts would be calling to collect their offspring while the rest of the party, most of whom only lived a short distance away, would walk home in twos and threes as they did after school.

Jeremy, his face expressing his contentment, was happily and with great agility passing the parcel from one to the other.

'He's the life and soul of the party,' her mother remarked to Catherine. 'You'd never think he was permanently disabled.'

'No you wouldn't,' Catherine nodded in agreement, watching Jeremy with her young daughter beside him. 'Tansy adores him. Sometimes I think her interest in him is . . .' she paused and looked at her mother, 'too close.'

'How do you mean, love?' Jean's expression was one of bewilderment.

'Well, she's a little bit in love with him. She doesn't think of him as a brother.'

'Oh dear.' Jean's look of bewilderment turned to shock. 'You can't have *that*!'

'She's very young, of course; but she *is* very possessive about Jeremy. Did you notice the way she sat next to him during tea, and insisted on doing the same just now? She visits his room as soon as she comes home from school and says goodbye to him before she leaves in the morning.'

'Does her *father* say anything about it?'

'Her father doesn't notice,' Catherine said with a grimace. 'You know him. All he notices at the moment is how Gilbert is doing and how many marks he gets in his tests. If he took one tenth of the notice of Tansy that he takes of Gilbert she might not be so fond of Jeremy. She's a girl who loves to be admired. You know that, Mum, don't you?'

'And rightly,' Tansy's grandmother said proudly. 'There's a lot to admire. She's a lovely girl and she knows it. She'll marry when she's young, I'll warrant you, and then you'll have her off your hands!'

Marriage, Catherine thought wryly, her gaze returning to the centre of the lounge. The war was supposed to have revolutionized society, but for a girl, it was still apparently the only thing that mattered. Tansy was not a scholar and no one paid much attention to her education. Providing she could read, write and count it was thought sufficient until she was eventually snapped up in the marriage market. But Gilbert; Gilbert was a different matter. Gilbert was poked, prodded and coached – all quite unnecessarily in his mother's opinion – to encourage his natural ability with one end in view: that Gilbert Blair should follow his father into the medical profession.

The game of pass the parcel was coming to an end and everyone was getting very excited about who would be the winner of the coveted prize at the end. Even the apathetic boys in the far corner had stopped what they were doing or saying to watch the outcome of the game. As tension rose each member in the circle slowly passed the parcel to her neighbour anxious for the music to stop and thus win the prize, while Emily thumped the keys of the old piano, which was badly in need of tuning.

Suddenly she stopped just the split second that Tansy had passed the parcel to Jeremy. At that moment Emily turned round and called out.

'Jeremy's the winner.'

'He is *not*!' Tansy said in fury, attempting to seize the parcel from his lap.

'But you had given it to him, Tansy,' Emily said, rising from her piano stool and coming over to the pair in the centre of the floor.

'I was just *giving* it to him. It was still mine.'

'Yes, but it was in *his* lap.' Emily's smile had turned to a frown.

'You stopped on purpose at that moment,' Tansy cried. 'You did it deliberately because *you* want Jeremy to win. You want him to have everything! Sometimes I really *hate* you and I wish you'd go away!'

Tansy rose swiftly from the floor and flounced out of the room while Jeremy sat, looking rather foolish, staring at the parcel in his lap.

Emily leaned down and, taking it from him, gave him a hand to help him up. 'Take no notice of Tansy,' she murmured. 'She's spoiled.'

'I *beg* your pardon?' Catherine, arms still akimbo, walked towards them. 'My daughter is not spoiled.'

'Well, I think she is,' Emily said. 'She gets her way the whole time and has everything she wants. Look how, today, she elbowed that girl out of the way to sit next to Jeremy. She hogged him too at tea.'

'Oh *please*.' Jeremy hobbled to his feet with Emily's help, brushing the dust off the seat of his pants. 'What *does* it matter? It's her birthday. Let's say she won, and let's give her the prize.'

'No.' Emily pursed her lips firmly while Mark, who was one of those who had taken part in the game, hung on to her hand, a finger in his mouth., 'I don't think she *should* be given the prize. I don't think she should have her own way all the time. I don't care if it's her birthday or not. It's not good for her.'

'Hear, hear,' Gilbert said, strolling towards them. 'Tansy gets her own way in everything; she *is* spoiled. Give Jeremy the prize.'

'You keep out of this please, Gilbert,' his mother said, a note of warning in her voice. 'You had absolutely nothing to do with it at all.'

'Yes, but I see the way Tansy is given in to all the time,' Gilbert replied. 'You'd have to be blind not to.'

'Look,' Jeremy put out his hands and handed the

parcel to the girl on his other side, '*you* take the prize, please. It's yours.' And the astonished girl clutched the box to her bosom and, in the unexpected joy of the moment, burst into tears.

'This party is becoming a riot,' Catherine said crossly, looking at the weeping girl who was being comforted and fussed over by her friends. 'I think we'd better have a quiet sing-song. Emily, would you oblige?'

'It's nearly time for them to go,' Jean said and then smiled with relief as the doorbell sounded. 'That will be one of the parents. Just as well. They're all tired.'

Emily went back to the piano, clearly still annoyed, and began to play a few bars of music; but the party mood was over and some children made for the door, while others wandered restlessly around the floor. The girl who had been given the parcel was breathlessly unwrapping it with the help of her friends. Catherine decided that there would never be another party. Her children were clearly too old now for games.

That night as Tansy lay in bed, her face still stained with tears, despite washing it, her mother crept into her room and up to the side of the bed. Tansy sniffed and Catherine put out a hand to smooth her daughter's brow and untangle the wet, sticky hair on her forehead.

'Are you all right now, duck?' she asked. 'Feeling better?'

'No,' Tansy said tearfully. 'I don't like Emily.'

'But you *love* Emily.' Catherine bent over her and stared into her eyes, so red with weeping.

'I don't love her any more!'

'But why not?'

'I can't tell you,' Tansy said. 'I just don't like her and I wish she'd go away.'

'Is it because of Jeremy?'

'Oh, you know, then?' Tansy said, looking cautiously at her mother.

'Know? Know what?' Catherine felt a sudden spasm of alarm.

'I thought you knew,' Tansy went on slyly.

'Thought I knew *what*, Tansy?' Catherine realized her heart was beginning to beat faster. 'Don't talk in riddles.'

'They go to bed together,' Tansy dropped her voice as though she'd said something shameful, 'I've seen them.'

'Oh, no! You must be mistaken.' Catherine sharply removed her hand from Tansy's head and stood up, straightening the skirt of her dress. 'Emily has looked after Jeremy for a long time. It's not like that.'

'It is,' Tansy insisted. 'She loves him. She get into his bed and they lie together, kissing and cuddling.'

'Do they know *you* know?'

Tansy noticed, with some satisfaction, the apprehension in her mother's eyes. 'No, I don't think so.' She shook her head. 'I went in one day just before Christmas to give Jeremy a mince pie and I tip-toed into the room because sometimes he is asleep. But they were both in bed together. Their arms were round each other. They didn't even see me, so I crept out again.'

'Your father must *never* know this.' Catherine began to walk abstractedly up and down the room, her hand now on her own brow. 'If he did it would kill him. Promise you won't tell your dad?'

'Promise, Mother.' Tansy virtuously nodded her head. 'But why?'

'It would upset him because of Edward.'

'But Edward's dead.'

'Yes, but it would still upset your father. I can't explain why. When you're older you'll know.'

'I think you should get rid of Emily,' Tansy said with a

note of satisfaction in her voice. 'Otherwise I know she's going to bring trouble to this house.'

Jeremy said. 'What's the matter?'

'It's Tansy.' As Emily turned her eyes towards him he could see how troubled they were.

'She *is* spoiled. You were right to say what you did.'

'I wasn't. It *was* her birthday. Ever since that day she has avoided me, and we used to be such friends.'

'You will again,' Jeremy said running his hand over her flat, taut stomach.

'I think she knows about us.'

'How *could* she?' Jeremy, looking surprised, raised himself on one elbow.

'She's been odd towards me since before Christmas. It's as though she is jealous of me. You know how much she loves you.'

'Yes, but,' Jeremy started to laugh, 'she's a child. What you're suggesting is quite preposterous.'

'I'm not *suggesting* anything,' Emily said. 'Tansy is only thirteen, but it is a very emotional age. She knows we're close. She guesses it, and, understandably, she's jealous. It's a wonder the rest of the family haven't guessed too.'

'Then what are we to do?' Jeremy tenderly put a finger under her chin. 'There's no need at all for secrecy. We are both adult and free to do as we like.'

'Well, we think that, but will the others?' Emily got out of bed and sat on the edge of it, her back to him, her hair, in its long thick plait, wound over her shoulder. She had grown rather buxom of late and this, in Jeremy's eyes, made her even more desirable. Suddenly he reached out and touched her back.

'You're not *pregnant* by any chance, are you?' he asked.

'I think I am,' Emily said and, as she put her head in

her hands, her voice shook. 'I'm two months late.'

'But, Emily,' excitedly Jeremy turned her towards him, 'that's wonderful. Don't you realize what it means to me, a cripple, an invalid, to father a child?'

'You should have had no doubts on that score,' she said raising her head and giving him a wry smile, 'it's the only part of you that works properly.'

'Well, I'll thank you for that,' Jeremy playfully, glee-fully, tapped her bottom, but he drew her towards him and made her lie beside him again. 'I'm absolutely thrilled. I really am.'

'I don't know for *sure*.'

'It sounds sure to me. I was just thinking how your figure had filled out from the skinny little thing you were before the war. It's the most wonderful thing that has ever happened to me, Emily, apart from loving you. I feel complete as a man.'

'Your father won't like it.'

'I can't think why not.' Jeremy looked at her in surprise. 'He likes you.'

'Yes, but not as your mistress. He thinks I should be loyal to Edward. I know he does.'

'How do you know?'

'Because of the things he says to me when we're alone. He would be horrified if he knew I was sleeping with Edward's brother, having his child. Edward's memory is sacred to him, enshrined. You've no idea quite how.'

'Then what are we to do?' Jeremy scratched his head in perplexity. 'Creep away?'

'We can't do that. They'll have to know, because if I am pregnant the baby will be born in about six months' time. I thought we should try and get somewhere else to live, Jeremy. Move out of here so that if there is a fuss we shan't be too upset.'

'But my darling,' Jeremy lay on his back and reached for a cigarette which he lit with a hand that slightly shook. Any nervous tension made him tremble. He had to live a very quiet life or he shook all over. 'My darling Emily, what will we live on? I have a small disability pension and you have a small widow's one. We're impoverished, darling, whereas here my father has a large house and plenty of money.'

'But your father won't want us. I know. I know how he feels about Edward. He feels guilty about him.'

'And so he wants to punish you and me?'

'I don't know what it is.' Emily shrugged and, taking the cigarette from his lips, inhaled it deeply. 'Your father is a very complex man. I don't understand him and I don't think I ever will. But I do think that, in his eyes, you and I sleeping together will seem to him like incest.'

'That is absolutely absurd.' Jeremy reached for the cigarette again.

'I thought I might start teaching.'

'What, if you're pregnant?'

'Well, by next September the baby will be born. If you are home you can look after it.'

'Home where?' Jeremy's smile was sarcastic.

'I thought we could rent a cottage or, maybe, get a council house. We should probably qualify for one. I could teach and you could housekeep.'

'I'm not going to be the dogsbody at home for anybody,' Jeremy said vehemently. 'For you or anyone else. My physiotherapist said that quite soon I should be able to get a job of some kind.'

'Such as what?' She looked at him curiously.

'Something on the land, maybe. Something not too difficult or taxing. I thought I could be a shepherd.'

'A *shepherd*?'

'Does the idea surprise you?' His voice was now

sarcastic. 'The dashing ex-Squadron Leader looking after the lambs and the sheep?'

'It doesn't surprise me at all. I simply never thought of it. Would you like it?'

'I think I might. Up there alone on the moors. After all, it is not very demanding work.'

'Could you stand the solitude?'

'If I had you to come home to at night I shouldn't mind.'

He put his arm round her and, as she closed her eyes, she could feel his breath on her cheek and his hand slipped between her thighs.

'Let's make love,' he whispered, 'it's the best way to forget.'

Emily sighed but she nodded her head and smiled compliantly without opening her eyes.

If only life could always be that simple.

Chapter 9

It was true that Doctor Blair was inordinately proud of his son Gilbert. He supervised his homework every night and examined him on subjects studied at school that day. His joy in Gilbert and the promise he showed helped to keep those black moods at bay. The end of the war, the gradual slackening of controls, the continued recovery of Jeremy, Gilbert's development as a scholar and Tansy's as a pretty girl with a strong personality, gave Geoffrey Blair a new dimension to his life. It was too much introspection that made him gloomy and life was too promising for that.

Tansy loved her father. She loved her brother too, but she resented the way her father and Gilbert were always closeted together and she sought out her father more and more, anxious for a greater share of his attention. Tansy often envied those of her friends who were only children and wished she were one of them. That way she would have the exclusive love of her parents without having to share.

The best time to see her father was before evening surgery. She had stopped going into Jeremy's room when she came home from school and now she went to see her father instead. They became accustomed to taking tea together and she would toast bread and crumpets in front of the fire, spreading them thickly with butter from one of the outlying farms. The doctor was accustomed to receiving presents from grateful patients and had done without very little during the war: sides of ham, joints of pork or beef, pounds of butter, bread freshly baked with white flour – all these were the luxuries which those who had some power over the community, on whom the community depended for its welfare, could enjoy.

Tansy would tell her father about her day; little things, not tasks of scholarship or achievement which Gilbert used to talk to him about much later. These more solemn encounters took place after evening surgery and family dinner, when Gilbert had done his prep and he and his father went into his father's study together and closed the door.

For his part Geoffrey enjoyed these moments of precious communication with both his children and looked forward to Tansy's knock on the door, every afternoon at about the same time.

Now, about a month after the thirteenth birthday party, in the course of Tansy's customary call Geoffrey sat back in his chair watching her, the firelight reflected in her eyes, her face alive and vital, the blonde halo formed by her hair. She would be married when she was eighteen, his little darling. Some young man would want her. For a moment Geoffrey's eyes clouded with jealousy; but then he reflected that it was unreasonable to expect to cling on to her all her life. For her spinsterhood would be no fun. It was a taint, a blot on any family to have an unmarried daughter living at home. Marriage was socially significant, a prerequisite if any woman wished to have standing in society and be taken seriously.

Tansy jumped up and came over to her father carrying the luscious, dripping crumpets on a plate. She handed him the plate and then she went over to the table on which the maid had placed the tea things: tea in a large pewter pot, two porcelain cups, a bowl of sugar and a porcelain milk jug.

'Two lumps, Daddy,' she enquired, 'as usual?' and

popped them into the cup without waiting for a reply.

'Thank you, darling,' Geoffrey said, putting down the paper which he usually read at the same hour each day, even though he had spent much of the last few minutes surreptitiously watching his daughter, whose movements seemed to fascinate him.

As far as his duties permitted he was a man who liked routine; he found that it suited his moods and his temperament better. Three-thirty to five was a very nice time of the day when he read the paper, attended to any items of personal correspondence, the paying of domestic bills and so forth, and had tea with his daughter who, in his eyes, grew more and more delightful every day, continuously revealing new and unexpected aspects of her character.

Gilbert was his pride but Tansy was his pet; his hobby; his indulgence. Catherine was his prop and he leaned on her, no longer seeing in her that vivacious, young, nubile woman whom he had lusted after sufficiently to disturb his life of seclusion. He no longer lusted after her or, indeed, thought of her in that way; she had ceased to be a mistress and had become an anchor. Her youthful age, compared to his, was immaterial. She could have been any age; the future, and his happiness, lay not in her but in his younger children: Gilbert and Tansy.

For a while father and daughter sat in companionable silence eating crumpets and drinking tea. The glow from the fire illuminated their faces and outside the night was falling softly, as it did in the country, with lights appearing in the windows of houses, and the mists of evening merging with the smoke of freshly lit fires.

'What did you do today, my darling?' Geoffrey enquired, dabbing at the butter on his chin with a napkin.

'Usual thing,' Tansy said off-handedly. 'Boring school.

We had an art lesson, though. I like art.'

'I would like you to pass your exams, Tansy,' her father said with a look of disapproval on his face. 'You may never need to use your School Certificate, and I hope you won't need to, but the world is not what it was and a woman with no qualifications may find difficulties in life.'

'I don't know what you mean, Daddy,' Tansy said looking puzzled. 'You mean we may not have enough money?'

'Of course we've plenty of money!' Geoffrey exclaimed rather testily. 'But I don't want you to remain a spinster at home all your life. You're a pretty girl and you'll marry. On the other hand one can't just presume you're going to get married and have a family as soon as you leave school. You wouldn't particularly want that, would you?'

'I never thought about it, to be truthful,' Tansy said, springing to her feet to pour more tea.

'You'd like some sort of job, maybe. A secretarial one would be interesting and pay quite well. But, if you want to do that, you have to have a School Certificate.'

'I don't see why.' Tansy set her jaw in a stubborn line that was familiar to her father. 'Why should I want to be a secretary?'

'For the reasons I said, Tansy.' Geoffrey began to feel a trifle exasperated, even with his darling, his pet. He found ambition in a woman incongruous and displeasing, unless it was a strict financial necessity, but to have *no* ideas at all . . . 'Do you expect me just to keep you until you get married?'

'I can be helpful in the house,' Tansy said with a beguiling smile. 'Mummy is sure to need me.'

'Oh you're a witch,' her father said fondly, reaching over and drawing her to him while, willingly, she put her head on his knee. 'What would I do without you, Tansy mine? My joy.' He tilted her head so that it was at an angle and gazed at her face.

'I thought *Gilbert* was your joy, Daddy,' Tansy said playfully. 'You are far more ambitious for him than you are for me.'

'Of course I am, that is perfectly natural. Gilbert is a boy. He will have a living to earn, and career satisfaction is important in that regard. With your open contempt for scholarship I don't expect you to want to be a doctor or to go to university; but I would like you to be a woman of accomplishment, an adornment to your husband.'

'You sound terribly old fashioned, Daddy,' Tansy said raising her head from her father's lap and studying his face. 'Don't you realize the war has changed attitudes to women in many ways? Miss Cartwright said it has. She wants all her girls to go into the sixth form.' Miss Cartwright was Tansy's greatly respected form teacher.

'Whatever Miss Cartwright says, I *still* believe a woman's place is in the home,' Geoffrey said firmly, 'and she likes it that way. It is the natural order, where she belongs; where your mother and Emily – well, to a certain extent Emily – belong.'

Tansy abruptly sat upright, moving away from her father. 'What do you mean "to a certain extent Emily"?'

'Well, Emily's situation is different,' her father's tone was cautious. 'She *is* a widow and I don't quite know what we are going to do with her.'

Tansy leaned forwards hugging her knees. '*Do* with her?'

'Well, she came to us when Mark was very small.' Geoffrey removed his glasses, and began to polish them, blinking myopically as he did. 'Her parents had been tragically killed in an air raid and she needed a home. I'm awfully fond of Emily, don't misunderstand me, please. She's my daughter-in-law, Edward's widow, my grandson's mother. Naturally she occupies a firm position in my heart and that of my family. But she is still young. She trained as a teacher and with so many other responsibilities – Jeremy being one – I can't guarantee to keep Emily for the rest of my life.'

Tansy rose and walked over to the window in order to draw the curtains now that night was encroaching. 'You can't just *throw* her out, Daddy,' she murmured, standing by the window and looking into the garden, neatly dug over in preparation for the spring. Below her the streetlights of Netherwick were beginning to twinkle one by one as the lamplighter rode round on his bicycle, touching each with his magic wand. It was a sight which, ever since she had been a little girl, sent a surge of emotion through her breast. She loved Netherwick, her native town, fiercely and passionately and for her this was one of the sights – the lights coming on on a winter's evening – that she loved best.

'I would never *throw* Emily out,' Geoffrey said, resuming his spectacles, now gleaming to his satisfaction. 'I'm not talking of that at all. But I shall undoubtedly have to provide a home for Jeremy for the rest of my life and that must be my primary consideration.'

Tansy scarcely heard what her father was saying for, as he was speaking, Emily appeared from the surgery entrance and slowly crossed the tarmac drive towards the house. Her arms were folded and she appeared deep in thought.

'Is Doctor Thackery taking surgery, Daddy?'

'Not that I know of, why?' her father asked, reaching for his tobacco and beginning the time-honoured formula of pressing it tightly into the bowl of his pipe.

'I just wondered,' Tansy said casually. 'I've just seen Emily come out and go over to the house.'

'Why should she do that?' Geoffrey said without taking his eyes off his pipe which he put to his mouth and began to light. 'Why should she want to see Tom? Is she ill?' he enquired between puffs.

'I don't know, Daddy.' Tansy carefully drew the curtains across, her heart thumping with excitement. There was something in her voice that caught the attention of her father. He gave his pipe a final puff to make sure the tobacco would draw well then he took it in his hand and pointed to a chair.

'What's the matter, Tansy?' he asked in the kind, encouraging tone he used when he knew patients were reluctant to tell him their symptoms. 'Have you something on your mind?'

Tansy hung her head, an uncharacteristic gesture that in itself was enough to alarm her father. A blush stole up her cheeks, and that too was unlike her. 'Tansy,' Geoffrey said anxiously. 'I feel you're hiding something. Is it to do with Emily?'

Tansy, mindful of her mother's words, put her hands to her face in an effort to cool her cheeks. 'It will kill your father,' her mother had said. 'It will kill your father if he knows.'

'It's nothing to do with me, Daddy.' Tansy gazed boldly at him with bright eyes and flaming cheeks.

'What hasn't? Come on, Tansy,' her father banged the arm of his leather chair, 'I must know what you're driving at. Is Emily ill? Is there something the matter? Something I don't know, but should?'

Tansy turned her eyes to the floor counting the contours of the pattern in the carpet as she so often had before when confronted by awkward questions from her awesome father. The little whirls and balls seemed to move about in frenzied confusion before her eyes. 'It's nothing I'm exactly *sure* about,' she said at last.

'*What* isn't? Stop talking in riddles.' Geoffrey's tone was testier than ever.

'Haven't you noticed that Emily is getting rather fat, Daddy?' she said at last. 'I thought you, of all people . . .'

Geoffrey Blair didn't know how he got through the rest of the day, except that his habits as a creature of routine helped him. He had his surgery at five, supper at seven, a visit to make in the town and then an hour with Gilbert, going over his prep. All this he did carefully and as conscientiously as always, but his mind was in a turmoil.

Catherine knew that Geoffrey had something on his mind, but not what it was. She thought he and Tansy had had a row during the afternoon tea time together, but Tansy took care never to be alone with her mother, hastening out to choir practice at the church as soon as supper was over.

Gilbert thought his father was edgy too, and that there was something wrong with his prep. He had got his usual excellent results in his tests that week in maths, physics and biology, so he couldn't think what was the matter. Maybe his father had one of his moods coming on and, if so, this was an occasion for caution, not to be too demanding or ask too many questions.

However, Geoffrey inspected Gilbert's results with his usual thoroughness, went over his prep, smiled at him across his desk and then when everything was complete said in a voice empty of emotion, 'Would you go upstairs and see if you can find Emily? Ask her to come and see me, Gilbert. Oh, and if your mother's about I would be grateful if she could step in and see me too.'

All very formal, rather strange, decidedly ominous. Gilbert gathered up his books and said, 'Is anything the matter, Father?'

'Not that I know of,' his father said reaching for his pipe. 'We shall see.'

Emily felt no alarm as Gilbert knocked at her door and gave her his father's message. She was darning some socks of Mark's and mending a shirt of Jeremy's, listening to a play on the wireless.

'My dad wants to see you,' Gilbert said standing on the threshold of the door, his school books clasped under his arm. 'He's in his study.'

'Oh?' Emily looked up and turned down the volume. 'Did he say why?'

'I have no idea.' Gilbert backed out of her room to continue on his way to his, his mind preoccupied with thoughts of his own.

Emily pondered for a moment and passed a hand across her stomach which she held well in with a corset. She knew it was beginning to show and she should have said something before. She'd been tempted to confide in Catherine of whom she was very fond; but twice she had tried and twice she had failed. The words just wouldn't come. The trouble was that she and Jeremy had no plans, no money and, despite his bluff, she knew he was also afraid of his father; afraid that he'd think he'd defiled Edward's widow, however old-fashioned the notion may have sounded to others.

Yet, in a strange way, unknown to Emily, Jeremy knew how his father would react, and why. He felt as though he had committed an act of incest, as though he had slept with his sister and not his sister-in-law. That was really why Jeremy Blair was afraid of his father's wrath because he would consider it justified. Emily wished Jeremy were with her now, but he was asleep. It had been one of his bad days with nausea and a headache and he'd gone to bed early. Sighing she rose, combed her hair, looked at her pale face in the mirror and went reluctantly to the door.

When she got to Geoffrey's study she found that Catherine had been called too and they arrived on the threshold together.

Catherine caught her arm in a friendly way and said, 'What's up?'

Emily shook her head; but she knew. Her fear was confirmed as soon as she saw Geoffrey's face and the way he looked her up and down when she came through the door, his eyes pointedly resting on her stomach. In them she saw an expression she had never seen before, but which she'd heard about from both his sons. She knew now why, all their lives, they had feared him.

'Sit down, Emily,' he said politely enough, pointing to a chair. Then he looked at his wife in the same detached, though more friendly, manner and put out a hand to indicate a chair for her. 'I'd like you to hear what I've got to say to Emily, my dear. Perhaps you'd tell me if you had any suspicion of it yourself.'

'Suspicion? Of what? What on earth is going on, Geoffrey?' Catherine said nervously and patted both sides of her head as though searching for stray wisps. She was a neat, tidy woman but she'd been in the kitchen baking and her hands were red; traces of flour still adhered to her nails.

'Tell me, Emily,' Geoffrey leaned forwards, ignoring his wife, 'are you expecting a child?'

Emily looked from Catherine to Geoffrey and then back to Catherine again, her eyes now seeking hers for support.

'Good Lord!' Catherine said aghast. 'Are you?' She too studied Emily's figure as though she had never properly looked at it before.

'I am,' Emily said, also nervously patting her hair. 'I should have told you before.'

'Indeed you should,' Geoffrey said angrily, his calm deserting him. He left his chair in his agitation and walked over to the fireplace where he tapped out his cold pipe against the hearthstone. 'It would at *least* have been a civil thing to do, polite as well, seeing that you are a guest in my house.'

'It was difficult to know how to tell you.' Emily felt a lump rise involuntarily in her throat.

'I imagine it was, carrying on a clandestine affair behind the backs of this family.' Geoffrey slowly straightened up and gazed at her coldly. 'I think it is disgraceful, Emily, an abuse of our hospitality, to say nothing of an affront to the memory of Edward. To think of his widow, a woman I have always respected and admired, conducting herself in this way leaves me almost bereft of words. How long has this been going on? For all *I* know, before the death of Edward whom, you led me to suppose, you loved. Do you intend to *marry* the father?' His imperious gaze, his eyes levelled at Emily made him miss the expression on his wife's face.

'I . . . I don't know,' Emily said at last.

'What do you mean, you don't know? I suppose he's a married man. Good God.' Geoffrey paused as if struck by an awful thought. 'I do hope it isn't poor Tom Thackery who has got you in this mess. Tom has always been known as a man for the ladies.'

'*Tom Thackery*?' Emily gasped almost laughing, despite herself.

'Tansy said she saw you coming from the surgery . . .'

'Ah it was *Tansy* . . .' Emily sat back in her chair. 'Now I know.'

'Tansy drew my attention to something I had never noticed,' her father acknowledged after a few seconds' pause. 'That you were putting on weight, that's all. She said nothing about a baby. I do assure you that she is probably too young to realize the significance of what she said.'

'Which I doubt,' Emily said with a bitter note in her voice. 'Your daughter is very jealous of me, Geoffrey. I'm afraid she has been for some time.'

'And why should she be jealous?' Geoffrey stuck his thumbs in the pocket of his waistcoat as if he imagined himself fully in control of the situation.

'Because . . . Tansy loves Jeremy, and so do I. Jeremy is the father of my baby. Jeremy, your son.'

Geoffrey, who had been standing as straight as a ramrod, suddenly crumbled and Catherine who, gnawing the side of her fingernails, had been anxiously watching him, expecting some reaction, but powerless to prevent it, ran and caught him just as he was about to hit his head against the fender.

Tom Thackery, head bent in concentration, listened to the sound of his patient's heartbeat through his stethoscope and then gave Catherine, who was standing anxiously next to him, a reassuring smile.

'I don't think it's a heart attack, Catherine, or if it is it's a very minor one. I can't detect an irregular heart rhythm. I think he fainted; maybe a reaction connected with his neurological condition.'

'What neurological condition?' Catherine had a look of bewilderment on her face as though there were something else Tom hadn't told her.

'His depression. I've always been convinced in my own mind they are due to a chemical imbalance in the brain or the body. So little is known about it. Maybe the shock of what he heard . . .'

'I knew it would harm him if he was told the truth,' Catherine said, turning away from the bed where

Geoffrey lay, peacefully asleep now after a sedative from Tom.

'Then why didn't you *prepare* him?' Tom asked gently.

'*I'd* no idea she was having a baby.' Catherine turned to face him. 'No idea at all. That came from Tansy. I think she just let the remark slip out.'

'But sooner or later Geoffrey would have to have known.' Tom tried to sound reasonable. 'You can't keep a relationship like that secret for ever, especially within the walls of the same house. Anyway there's no point going into the whys and wherefors. However,' Tom got out his notepad. 'I do want Geoffrey to go to hospital for a check-up. Would you like to ring for an ambulance?'

'I'd like to stay with Geoffrey,' Catherine replied. 'I'll get Emily to do that.'

Alone in her room Emily found it hard to keep still. She half thought she should be packing. But where could she go? Mark was asleep and so was Jeremy. She sat on the side of her bed, head in her hands, recalling that awful moment when Geoffrey had slumped to the floor, caught just in time by Catherine who had cradled his head in her arms thinking him dead.

'Just *look* what you've done to my husband!' she'd cried with an expression in her eyes that Emily would never forget. Looking dumbstruck there was little she could do until Catherine had told her to run immediately and telephone Tom Thackery who lived in the next road.

There was no doubt it was one of the worst days in her life: the knowledge that the security and love which she'd found in the Blair household was at an end. Had she been wrong to do what she'd done?

At the sound of Catherine calling her name, she raised her head. She ran quickly to her door and opened it. 'Yes?' she cried out, fearing the worst.

'Tom doesn't think it's a heart attack,' Catherine called

from the other end of the corridor, 'but he would like him to go to hospital for a check. Would you phone for an ambulance, dear?'

Catherine turned on her heels and hurried back to the room that she shared with Geoffrey while Emily ran down the stairs feeling suddenly light-hearted, her spirits raised by the use of the term 'dear'. Surely 'dear' meant Catherine didn't blame her entirely for what had happened? Surely she wouldn't have used an endearment if she meant to eject her from the house?

But maybe it had been a slip of the tongue, a familiar habit because Catherine always called her 'dear'? They had become very close, almost like sisters, in the years she had lived at Glenhadden. They were close to each other in age and, although Emily was more intellectual than Catherine, they shared a lot of the same interests. They were both domesticated women – Emily had had to become that after Edward left for the Continent – and paid the same attention to detail, to the minutiae of daily household tasks and the meticulous care of their children.

Once the ambulance was called for, Emily remained in the hall so that she could admit the ambulance men. It was the maid's night off and the rest of the household was asleep. As soon as the ambulance appeared and the men hurried in with a stretcher Emily led them upstairs and waited while they gently placed their patient on the stretcher and hurried downstairs with him again, followed by Tom and Catherine who was hastily getting into her coat.

'I'll go to the hospital with Tom,' she said, the look of hostility having returned. 'Why don't you go to bed?'

And with that they were gone.

* * *

Sometime in the small hours of the morning Catherine returned, driven back by Tom, but the household was in darkness, even Emily asleep. Catherine thanked Tom, told him she would be all right and went into the house alone, climbing slowly up the stairs to bed.

The hospital would run tests. They were not sure Geoffrey had not suffered a heart attack and they were keeping him in for a few days. Catherine went past Emily's room to her own where, desperately weary, she threw herself on the bed, still with her coat on.

She remained there until Emily crept in in the morning, bringing a hot cup of tea. For a moment she thought that Catherine was dead, stretched out across the bed with her coat on and she almost dropped the tea with shock. But Catherine suddenly moved and, opening her eyes, stared at Emily as if she didn't quite know where she was.

'Why don't you get into bed?' Emily said gently putting the cup and saucer on the table beside the bed. 'You'll be frozen to death.'

'I'm not cold,' Catherine said sitting up and still looking round with bewilderment. 'I didn't know where I was for a moment.'

'I would have stayed up,' Emily said. 'But I thought you might spend the night at the hospital. How's Geoffrey?'

'They seem to think he might have had a very slight heart attack. They call it a spasm or something.' Catherine reached for the cup and put it to her lips, grateful for the comforting warmth of the drink. 'I've never thought his heart was right, you know. For years he's complained of pains in his chest but always when I asked him to do something about it he'd say he had indigestion. I've always had this fear and now it's realized.' Catherine shook her head and, finishing her tea, got off the bed. 'I shan't go to bed now, Emily. I have the children to see to. There is too much to do.' She turned and gave her a rather distant, appraising look as, slowly, she removed her coat. 'We also have to decide what to do about you.'

'Yes, I realize that,' Emily immediately sensed the change in Catherine's attitude, 'I can't tell you how sorry I am.'

'It's a bit late for sorrow now, isn't it?' Emily could never recall having heard her voice so angry and bitter. The 'dear', after all, had been a mistake. Catherine was not going to try and understand her predicament. 'You should have thought of that before. How long did you think you could get away with concealing your pregnancy?'

'I never really thought about it,' Emily said in a low voice. 'I suppose that was irresponsible of me.'

'It was. Very.'

'But before you judge me too harshly, Catherine,' Emily raised her head and looked into those accusing eyes, 'please believe that I love Jeremy. I think I have always loved him, even before I met Edward.'

'You mean that you're now saying you married the wrong man?'

'No, I'm not saying that at all.' Emily made an effort to keep her tone pleasant. 'But I did not love Edward when I married him. The wedding night was dreadful . . . I think I was the first and only woman Edward ever slept with. However, I grew to love Edward and appreciate his qualities through our correspondence which, as you know, was and is very precious to me.'

'Oh well *that's* a relief at least,' Catherine said in a scathing tone which Emily considered untypical. Somehow she had thought Catherine would be more generous and understanding.

'I see I can't really talk to you, Catherine.' Emily reached for the empty cup by the side of the bed. 'Would you like me to go?'

'I should have thought that was obvious.' Catherine went and sat in front of her dressing-table mirror, staring at the reflection of her haggard features, thinking how old she looked, how drab.

'Jeremy, you know, wants the baby,' Emily said. 'He is thrilled about it.'

'Oh I see. It's blackmail, is it?' Catherine's tone was hard.

'Not at all. I am quite prepared to go, and leave Jeremy here.'

'You don't have much option,' Catherine replied, 'as he hasn't a penny, beside his pension. I don't suppose you have much either.' She looked at Emily. 'Perhaps you could go into a home for people in your condition?'

Emily suddenly had a feeling that she would choke, or collapse on the floor as Geoffrey had. In a way she wished she could. Instead she turned her back on Catherine and hurried out of the door, but it was not until she reached the safety of her own room that the tears came and continued, unabated, for some time, with no one to comfort her.

Jean Wills was a kind, gentle woman who had had her fair share of grief and misfortune in life. She had not had the tragedies that seem to strike some people – accidents, premature deaths of loved ones – but her husband had been a difficult, unloving man and, at the end of his life, a very sick one.

Her younger daughter had had a baby out of wedlock which was a disgrace in Netherwick in the thirties, and her elder daughter had married a man who turned into a wife-beater. Her son, Colin, was a sort of middle-of-the-road, complacent kind of man and he married a girl like him and they had settled quite happily in Netherwick not far from the family home in Castle Street. Colin continued to work at the mill and he would probably stay there until he retired, if circumstances and the economy permitted.

It was her middle daughter, Catherine, who had given Jean some of her bitterest as well as her proudest moments. Catherine was not like the others. No one quite knew which member of the family she did resemble, unless it was Grandpa Wills who was considered very bookish, a leading light of the Netherwick Working Men's Institute in the eighties and nineties of the last century.

Catherine was prettier and cleverer than the others. There had always been something distinctive about her which made her stand apart. No one for a moment had thought she would ever go and work in the mill. She seemed destined, in a way hard to explain, for something better.

However, neither did anyone imagine she would marry one of the most prominent doctors in the town and raise herself both socially and financially. To be Mrs Geoffrey Blair was to be quite someone. Not that Jean had, at the time, been particularly pleased about the marriage. In a society that was class-ridden she was obsessed by the nuances of social position less than most. But she was in awe of the doctor; the magic man, the possessor, it seemed, of powers over life and death. Doctor Blair was especially awesome; much older, a widower, a father. The two, accordingly, found communication difficult, but Geoffrey respected his mother-in-law. He always called her Mrs Wills or referred to her as Catherine's mother.

Despite everything, over the years Jean had maintained

a fond and steady relationship with her daughter. She doted on her grandchildren and was loved in return. They thought her house by the side of the canal was particularly delightful and it was a treat for them to go there. They were happy and at ease with their grandmother and they enjoyed visiting her and liked her to come up and see them.

It was on the morning after Geoffrey Blair was taken to hospital that Jean Wills hurried up the hill to see her daughter who telephoned her about the mishap as soon as she came downstairs in the morning. Catherine seemed under even more stress than one would have thought normal on such an occasion. Not only was she worried about Geoffrey, she was bitterly angry about what had happened to him and why. The name Emily was mentioned in this connection and it wasn't until Jean Wills was sitting at the kitchen table with her daughter that she found out what had happened.

'Baby,' she echoed her daughter's words. 'Like our Ethel.' Ethel was the younger daughter who had had a baby when she was sixteen which everyone had thought it best should be adopted.

'Not like our Ethel, Mother,' Catherine said sipping the coffee she had brewed for her mother. 'Our Ethel was sixteen. Emily is over thirty. She should have known *much* better.'

'Poor lass,' Jean Wills said with a sigh.

'How can you *say* that, Mother?' Catherine stood up to wash out her cup, feeling annoyed. 'Don't you think we've been good to her? Geoffrey has kept her for five years and helped to bring up her child. Do you think that is a nice reward for his goodness?'

'She probably couldn't help it,' Jean said, because she always liked to see the best side of people.

'Mother, of course she could *help* it.' Catherine leaned over and banged the table. 'There was no need to take advantage of Jeremy.'

'Perhaps *he* took advantage of her,' her mother said with a wise smile. 'It takes two to make a baby, dear.'

'Well, personally, *I* think Emily is in the wrong.' Catherine got out a pad and pencil from a drawer and went and sat at the kitchen table again. 'Jeremy is supposed to be an invalid.'

She studied her pad and then began swiftly to make a list of the things she had to do that day in her neat handwriting, one after the other. Tasks to do, people to see, shopping, which the maid who was doing the upstairs bedrooms could do while she went to the hospital. Her mother watched her and thought how careworn she looked, how old. After all, she was still under forty herself yet she looked much older. Some people often seemed to grow like their spouses, and it occurred to Jean that her daughter had grown increasingly like her husband, not so much in looks as in behaviour and attitudes. As Geoffrey had always looked at least ten years older than he was so Catherine looked well over forty, with her greying hair and wrinkled skin.

'How do you mean *supposed* to be an invalid?' her mother asked when her daughter paused in her writing. 'He *is* an invalid, isn't he? He has a war pension.'

'Well, he's quite able to make love,' Catherine said sharply. There's nothing wrong with him *there*.'

'Oh.' Her mother's expression became confidential. 'Well *I* remember Mr Fortescue, who came back after the last war with no *legs*, he became a father *twice*. It just shows.'

'Anyway I don't think Jeremy is as ill as he's supposed to be.' Catherine finished her list with a flourish and took off her glasses. 'In my young days we used to call it malingering. I think he should be out getting a job and I'm going to tell him so. This very day.'

'Oh Catherine, love, do be careful.' Her mother put a hand on her arm. 'You've got to be awfully careful. Why don't you leave it until Geoffrey gets back?'

'That's just what I don't want to do, Mother, don't you see?' Catherine glanced at the clock on the kitchen wall. 'I don't want him upset any more. I want it all settled and done with before he gets back.'

As she got up the handle of the door turned and Emily put her head round. 'Is there anything you'd like me to do, Catherine? I'm going into town.'

'Oh, *are* you?' Catherine said spinning round. 'If I were you I'd look for a room. You're not welcome here any more, Emily. I thought I made that plain.'

'Really, Catherine,' Jean said sharply, 'how *can* you say a thing like that?'

'Please keep out of this, Mother,' Catherine replied and seemed about to continue when the kitchen door which had remained partly open, was opened wide.

'I think *I've* got something to say about this,' Jeremy said, using his stick not only to fling open the door, but to point against Catherine. He put one arm around Emily and ushered her protectively to a seat opposite Jean who gave her a good-natured reassuring smile.

'Well, Jeremy,' Catherine said, 'I don't want a confrontation with you here this morning. I've got a very busy day and I have to see your father.'

'But *I've* got a very busy day too,' Jeremy replied, 'and so has Emily if we are to find accommodation in the town.'

'*We*,' Catherine said, then paused abruptly.

'If she goes I go,' Jeremy said. 'I thought you would understand that.'

'Well, I don't know what your father will say.'

Catherine looked doubtfully at her mother who was gazing at the floor.

'My father would probably think I should be with my wife.'

'Your *wife*?' Catherine stared at Emily. 'Are you married?'

'Not yet,' Jeremy answered for her. 'We wanted to announce the whole thing to the family, tell my father, you . . . but I'm afraid Tansy got there before us.'

'You can't blame Tansy,' Catherine said defensively. 'She was only saying what she'd seen, that Emily was putting on weight. If we hadn't all been so busy thinking of other things we'd have noticed it as well. Anyway,' Catherine concluded, taking a seat at the table, 'I don't think your father will be pleased even if you *do* get married.'

'I'm sure he won't.'

'Why did you do it then?'

'Do *what*?' Jeremy looked at her aggressively raising his voice. He was a big man and, leaning on his stick, still standing by Emily's side, he looked menacing.

'Well.' For once words seemed to fail Catherine. Instead she looked pointedly at Emily's stomach. 'You didn't have to go *that* far, did you?'

'It wasn't planned, if that's what you're suggesting.' Emily felt stronger now that Jeremy was with her.

'Well,' Catherine rose and looked at the clock on the wall, 'I must get ready to go to the hospital. I can't discuss this.'

'How *is* Dad?' Jeremy asked.

'As well as can be expected.'

'I suppose you're going to tell me that we brought this on,' Jeremy said.

'Brought what on?' Catherine's tone was sharp.

'Dad's illness.'

'Of course you brought it on.' Catherine leaned over, shaking her finger at him. 'Your father has *never* been a well man. Too much has been asked of him. Too much taken for granted. As for you . . .' she threw Jeremy a withering glance, 'I often wonder how much of that stick business is genuine.'

'Just what do you mean?' Jeremy's voice was vibrant with anger.

'I've noticed you can get on well enough without it – poke it at people, open doors and the like.'

'Do you mean to say you think Jeremy is malingering?' Emily slowly rose from her seat.

'I didn't say it,' Catherine's tone faltered a little. 'But I have wondered, and still do, just how ill he really is.'

'But my father, I suppose, *is* really ill?' Jeremy's tone was derisive.

'Of course he's ill. He's had a heart attack.'

'My father has always used illness when something happens he didn't like.' Jeremy gently pushed Emily on to her chair again. 'Ever since I was small we have had to cope with his black moods, his attacks of indigestion, his need to "lie down". Anything unpleasant comes up and Dad goes down. You know that as well as I do, Catherine. God knows how he ever stood all these years in such high esteem as one of the town's doctors.'

'Emily announced she was pregnant . . . It was a terrible shock.'

'Well,' Jeremy said roughly, 'what business is it of his? It's because I am the father. It horrifies him. He faints.'

'He had a *heart attack*!'

'Well, whatever, he brought it on himself.'

'Like father like son, then,' Catherine shouted at him and, for a moment, Jean thought he was going to strike her with his half-raised stick.

Jean, who had silently witnessed the whole scene rose slowly to her feet. 'I think this conversation has gone quite far enough,' she said in a steady voice. 'If you're not careful you'll start hitting each other. I think you have to take the heat out of this situation; try and see it more clearly.' She looked first at Emily then at Jeremy and gave them an encouraging smile. 'It so happens I live in my house all by myself. You'll want to get away, to have a roof over your heads while this business gets sorted out. You'd both be very welcome in my home indeed.'

Chapter 10

In her fourteenth year Tansy Blair became aware for the first time that one was responsible for the consequences of one's actions; that blame could not be laid at the door of mother, father, brother, even grandmother or nurse, but oneself. In a sense, what happened on that fateful day when her father collapsed turned her from a young girl into a much older and wiser one. It helped her grow up.

Her mother had told her that if her father knew about the relationship between Jeremy and Emily it would kill him, and it very nearly had. He was in hospital for three weeks, not three days as was originally thought, and when he came home he was ordered to bed at once. It would be six months before he could work normally again.

There were three people in the world whom Tansy truly loved: her father, Jeremy and Emily and she had, by her mischief, alienated all three.

It was useless to say she had not meant it because she had. From the day she saw them together in Jeremy's bed and realized their intimacy she wanted her father to know. She wanted Jeremy to be punished for loving someone else even though that someone was Emily. She felt she had been doubly betrayed. She wanted them to be punished, but not to be banished. After they left the Blair house, Tansy knew it would be a long time before she saw them again.

The results of the rift were even more widespread than anyone could have anticipated. Catherine was not really a hard woman and in time she, too, would repent the consequences of her action, her behaviour, the harsh words she had addressed to both Jeremy and Emily. She had been over-protective towards Geoffrey, and it had made her say things she would never normally have said. But she could not forgive her mother for giving the wrongdoers a home, for making it so easy. Because of what they'd done, the way they'd disrupted the house she would have liked them to suffer a little more.

Geoffrey Blair was a puzzle to his doctors. He was ill but he was not desperately ill; not so ill that his recovery should be so slow. Once he was in his private room in the General Hospital, looked after by devoted nurses and competent medical staff, he began to see what it was that some of his patients enjoyed about going to hospital. He was looked after very well indeed. There were no worries, no morning surgeries, no late night visits, no family aggravations. Everything was taken care of, looked after. He was cosseted, pampered and spoilt even more than he was at home and that was saying something as Catherine, always anxious for his health, always solicitous for his welfare, looked after him very well indeed.

Geoffrey Blair was fifty-nine. He had always felt older than his years and now he felt very old indeed. But it helped to know that officially he was ill; he had a heart complaint. For years he suspected he had, but he liked to pass it off as indigestion; he hadn't really wanted to know the truth. Now he had every excuse for taking as much care of himself as he could. He would never return to full-time work but would be semi-retired. He wasn't up to it; he wasn't strong.

A few days after his return Tansy crept into his room and up to his bed. It was the usual time they used to have tea together, just when she returned home from school. She felt so isolated and afraid by the anger of her family, by her loss, that she hoped, at least, that her father would forgive: forgive and understand.

She stood for a long time by the side of his bed watching his chest rise and fall, imagining the damaged heart lying in the protection of his rib-cage. Whatever it looked like, whatever had happened, she was responsible for it; she, Tansy Blair, had nearly killed her father.

Tansy gave a sob and reached impulsively for her father's hand. He snorted, shook his head, rapidly blinked his eyes appearing, momentarily, not to know where he was. Feeling her hand in his he gripped it hard as he saw the large tears rolling down her beautiful, forlorn little face,

'Tansy darling, Tansy, what is it?' Geoffrey struggled to sit up in bed. 'What's the matter?'

'Da . . . Da,' she began like a baby and then she threw herself on the bed across his chest and he took her in his arms and stroked her back tenderly, murmuring: 'There, there, darling. There, there. What *is* it, Tansy?' he asked again when the tears had begun to abate and she pressed her fists in both eyes making the mess look worse than ever. 'What *is* it, my little pet?'

For a moment Tansy stared at her father and then, as she was about to burst into tears again, he shook her fiercely by the arm.

'Tansy, stop it! What is the matter, darling? Remember, I'm not well.'

Tansy opened her eyes wide and extended her arms in a gesture of helplessness. 'All this,' she said at last. 'You, Jeremy, Emily . . . all the people I love. They're gone and I made you ill, Daddy. I nearly killed you.'

'Oh, darling, that is a silly thing to say.' Geoffrey hugged her even closer, his chest heaving with emotion. 'You *didn't* nearly kill me. I was deeply upset by *Emily* . . .'

'But I was the one who told you, Daddy.' She looked at him again, wide-eyed. 'Mummy told me not to tell you.'

'Oh did she?' her father said, still hugging her. 'Then Mummy knew?'

'I told Mummy that they cuddled in Jeremy's bed.' Tansy looked at him helplessly again. 'It was all my fault.'

'Now Tansy Blair,' her father said, pushing her gently away from him, 'I want no more of this. What happened was not your fault. It had nothing to do with you. I have had a weak heart for years, and I knew about it. But the shock that triggered off my heart attack was *not* your fault. It was the fault, I'm sorry to say, of Emily and your brother Jeremy. Sooner or later we were going to know that Emily was going to have a baby. It was only a matter of time. As a doctor I should, perhaps, have noticed it before. I had absolutely no idea, none at all, that she was that kind of woman. Then the shock might have been worse and really might have killed me. Now do you see?' He looked at her and his grey eyes, those dear, tired-looking eyes she loved so much, smiled at her from behind his spectacles, giving him the look of a wise old owl.

'Then it's not *really* my fault?' Tansy asked in a small voice.

'Not at *all* your fault, my darling little girl. It is *their* fault, their sin, their crime . . .'

'Crime,' Tansy cried, clinging to her father.

'Yes, it's a crime. I want you to remember that, Tansy. It is a crime for a man and a woman to sleep together until they are married. It is against the law of God and, in fact, it leads to all kinds of things such as what has happened. In this case it was much worse because Emily was also Jeremy's sister-in-law. Jeremy and Emily have no money and nowhere to live. But for the kindness of your grandmother they would be out on the streets.' Geoffrey seemed to experience a certain amount of self-righteous indignation as he spoke.

Tansy said nothing but remained where she was, pressed against her father's breast, imagining the damaged heart inside it clacketing away like a rusty old pump. But her heart was deeply troubled too at her father's words. Was God so cruel, then, that he put people on the streets when they did things they should not have done? She thought of Jeremy limping along with his stick, of his headaches so bad that sometimes he could not stand the light. Of Emily with her swollen tummy, her hands pressed against her aching back.

'Was it a *kind* thing to do, Daddy,' she murmured, 'to make them leave?' She gazed earnestly into his eyes seeing in them an expression of doubt.

'It was their decision, my darling,' Geoffrey said after a while, after a moment, perhaps, of introspection and self-examination.

'But Mummy *asked* Emily to go, Daddy.'

'Jeremy didn't have to go!' her father said gruffly. 'He was my son. I would never have thrown him out. It was his own wish to leave.'

'But if he loved Emily . . .'

'Love!' her father burst out derisively. 'Love, you say! *That's* not love, my darling. It has another name. Your brother had no right to desire Edward's wife. It's that I can't forgive. That's the real sin, the real crime.'

'Perhaps they couldn't help themselves?' Tansy suggested, sitting beside him on the bed. She was a tall girl, already taller than her mother and she could easily put her arms around her father as she sat close to him.

'You mustn't think like that, Tansy,' her father replied. 'Not now or ever. People *can* help themselves; they *can* do right instead of wrong. This is a lesson I hope that you will learn now so that you will benefit from it in the future. Always do what is right, my darling, never what is underhand or base.

'It is a lesson you must never, never forget.'

Tansy had many occasions to recall her father's words in the months and years that followed the departure of Emily and Jeremy from the Blair household.

'Always do what is right' may have been her father's dictum, but it didn't seem seem to her to tally with the idea of Christian charity, the command to do good to one another, to love those who hate you and pray for those who calumniate you. It didn't seem to square with what she heard in church at Sunday School. It seemed too like the story of the pregnant mother, the Virgin Mary, being turned away from the inn because there was no room.

What seemed cruel to Tansy then, and continued to as she asked her own questions about the morality of what had happened, was that she was forbidden to see not only Emily and Jeremy again, but also her grandmother as long as they lived with her.

Jean Wills no longer came to the house and they no longer went to see her. It was as though a part of the family had been cut off and forgotten; a branch of the tree had been severed and thrown in the stream. Unless something happened they would never see Mark grow up – Mark too was Geoffrey's flesh and blood, but in his biblical anger he appeared to have forgotten this.

Tansy was always to remember that year, 1947, as the year she grew up, that the knowledge of good and evil became reality. She was not convinced that the action of her father and mother was entirely good or that the behaviour of Jeremy and Emily, who were married soon afterwards and well before the birth of their baby daughter, was entirely evil. Many puzzling questions arose for which she failed to find a suitable answer.

If anything, her private judgement was that her parents had behaved badly and her grandmother had behaved well. She was a romantic and, as she had loved both Emily and Jeremy, she came to regret bitterly what had happened and longed to see them again.

Emily had been like a beloved sister, and Mark a much younger brother whom they had watched grow from babyhood. Emily had not only been a companion to her mother, a support to her father and a nurse to Jeremy; she had been more than that: a caring, necessary family friend.

After she left life was not as good as it had been before.

For Tansy it was the beginning of wisdom: the knowledge that sorrow and misfortune formed part of life as much as joy.

Tansy was nearly eighteen before she saw Jeremy and Emily again. After their daughter, whom they named Fern, was born they had gone to live in a village ten miles away, in a tiny hamlet where Emily was fortunate enough to find a job as the one teacher in the village school.

Cragbeck was far enough from Netherwick for no one to have heard of Emily and her sin; her pregnancy outside wedlock, her marriage to a man who was her brother-in-law.

In all the Christian churches marriage of a man's brother to his widow is within the permitted decrees of kinship. But to Geoffrey Blair it was unlawful; maybe some of his fellow citizens instinctively shared this view.

One day in the year 1951, when she was seventeen, Tansy was shopping in the High Street, doing some errands for her mother and idling past the stalls that lined the market place when she saw a familiar figure on the other side of the road, a basket in her hand. It was a cold December day and the rain which had lashed the streets all morning had stopped and, although the pale wintry sun had come out, a bitter wind still blew.

At the moment that Tansy espied Emily from across the cheese stall, Emily looked up from inspecting some cups and saucers on a stall on the other side and stared straight into her eyes. At first she didn't know whether to smile or acknowledge Tansy, and Tansy seemed not to know how to respond either.

They might have passed on their respective ways and lost contact for ever had not Tansy, acting on impulse, flown across the street, causing an oncoming car to brake violently. Emily's face broke into a smile of pleasure when she saw her reaction. Tansy halted just a few feet away from Emily, as if uncertain, now that she had done the deed, how to greet her. At thirteen, when Emily had last seen her, she had been tall for her age but now she towered over her and Emily was the first one to break the ice by exclaiming: 'My, *how* you've grown!'

Shyly Tansy offered her hand remembering, too late, why it was that Emily had left the Blair house. It was because of her. How would she feel about her now?

'How do you do, Emily?' she said rather formally. 'How's Mark?'

'Mark is very well.' Emily looked vaguely around. 'He's about somewhere. We came in to do a little Christmas shopping.'

'And the baby?' Tansy said, feeling shy and awkward and rather wishing she had not acted so impulsively; that she had, perhaps, gone on her way, for what could one say after all this time?

'Well, the baby is no longer a baby,' Emily said shifting

her basket from one arm to another. 'She is four years old. She is at home with Jeremy. Look,' she glanced at her watch and then up at the sky, 'why don't we have a cup of tea? Your father wouldn't mind would he? After all this time? How *is* your father?'

'Father keeps very well,' Tansy said falling into step beside her, realizing how petite Emily was: small, neat and very capable, yet, despite her size, she was a strong woman used to shouldering all kinds of burdens. 'And Mother. She's well too.'

'Are you still at school?'

'Oh no,' Tansy said beginning to relax. 'I managed to get my School Certificate and I had a year in the sixth form. But I left last summer.'

'And Gilbert?'

'Gilbert is going to Leeds University.'

'To study medicine of course?'

'Of course.' Tansy laughed shyly, realizing how good it was to see Emily again.

They went into a nearby tea-shop and Tansy took off her woollen gloves and put her cold hands to her face.

'They have done this place up,' she said, looking around at the gleaming glass and new brass fittings.

'I know,' Emily looked round too. 'Don't forget I've lived in Netherwick ten years.'

'Of *course* you have. I remember you coming with the baby, with Mark.'

'Do you?' Emily said looking up to order tea from the smiling waitress. 'Will you have scones and jam, Tansy?'

'Yes please,' Tansy said. Suddenly it was *very* good to be in the company of Emily. Nothing had changed; she was just the same Emily, always smiling and pleasant. A woman who carefully controlled her emotions. She could see that Emily, too, had found their encounter awkward, but she seemed more relaxed as she took off her gloves and unwound her scarf.

'How is Jeremy?' That was what she really wanted to know and Tansy leaned anxiously across the table so that their heads nearly touched. She felt her heart lurch as Emily gave a little grimace.

'Jeremy hasn't changed all that much since you last saw him. His movements are badly coordinated; he still has headaches that nearly blind him. A couple of years ago I was afraid that he had deteriorated; that he was more seriously ill than we'd all thought. The specialist thought that maybe he had an undiagnosed tumour on the brain.'

'Oh *dear*,' Tansy said clasping her cheeks tightly between her hands and staring at Emily.

'But if it is a tumour,' Emily said with an air of remarkable calm, 'it may well be benign. He doesn't seem to get any worse. They don't know whether to operate or not. An investigation of the brain is a very serious business.'

'I wish Daddy knew all about this,' Tansy said. 'He'd be upset. I can't tell you now, Emily, how bad I feel.'

'Oh *please*.' Emily briefly touched her hand. 'Don't feel guilty about what happened four years ago. I think, in many ways, it happened for the best. Jeremy had become too childlike, too dependent on his father. It was bad for him, and it was a test of his maturity to move out into the unknown with me; and he passed it. He has been working as a labourer at the farm up the road from our cottage and also watching the sheep, and it has done him good. The farmer is a very kind man who realizes that he is not completely well; but there are lots of things he can do. He's particularly good with the milking and with the sheep because he can sit, and he likes it because he can think. He likes ordinary, mundane tasks. But he misses you, Tansy. He often talks about you and Gilbert, wondering how you are.'

'And I miss Jeremy,' Tansy said, adding, 'and you.'

'Then you must come out and see us, that is if you want to.'

'Oh I *want* to,' Tansy said impulsively. 'I've always wanted to.'

'I know, it was your parents.' Emily's smile was one of resignation. 'I understood that quite well, though not exactly why.' She shrugged her neat shoulders. 'It is perfectly legal for a man to marry his brother's widow. In some cultures it is compulsory. It doesn't mean I love Edward any the less. But Edward is dead. Jeremy, who needs me, is alive.'

'I think Father regrets it at times,' Tansy said. 'I'm sure he'd love to see Jeremy again.'

'I don't think Jeremy would see him without me,' Emily said firmly, pursing her lips. 'If he accepts Jeremy he has to accept me *and* our family. We have to make a fresh start.'

When Tansy got home she was full of what had happened in the High Street that afternoon and, on bursting into the kitchen, she called out to her mother; 'Guess who I saw today?'

Her mother studied her daughter's excited face for a few moments and then murmured: 'Jeremy.'

'Not quite.'

'Emily then,' Catherine said with an audible sigh.

'In the High Street! She was out shopping for Christmas.'

'Did you talk to her?' her mother looked up at her from some mince pies she was making.

'We had tea together.'

'You'd better not tell your father, then. Keep it to yourself.'

'Why should I *not* tell my father?' Tansy said boldly, sitting on the kitchen table and swinging her legs. At the same time she reached for one of the crisp mince pies her mother had just baked.

Catherine didn't reply immediately but, sprinkling caster sugar over the newly made mince pies, began to pack them in a tin lined with greaseproof paper. Then she got on with rolling out the next batch and filling them with mince. It was a task she liked; she enjoyed domesticity and housework and particularly that part of it that centred on the kitchen.

Catherine had always found rearing and caring for her family a deeply satisfying task. She knew that, but for her, Geoffrey's illness would have been much worse. He might have died; but because of the way she had cared for him over the years, easing the burdens and worries that with him assumed such gigantic proportions – out of all reason at times – he had survived. Now it was still her task to keep him well and ensure that he didn't take on more than he could cope with. That he had moderate exercise and kept to his diet; not too much tobacco, not too much alcohol. Everything in proportion. Indeed it was a regime that suited Geoffrey very well. He thrived on it.

The maternal, protective role was one that suited Catherine and she loved it. Geoffrey was safe; but the children . . . they were poised to fly the nest. She felt in her mother's heart that Gilbert would never want to be very far away from it; but Tansy . . . Tansy, bold and rather wilful, difficult at times to control, sitting on the table swinging her legs, taking a mince pie without saying 'May I?' Tansy was something else altogether.

Tansy had sat watching her silent mother, similar

thoughts going through her mind. Her mother was a warm, dependable creature, a woman of fierce loyalties, chief of which was to her husband. She knew that her mother cared very much for herself and Gilbert; but, in her scale of priorities, they would always be secondary to her husband.

The life of the house pivoted round its head and Tansy, growing into womanhood, was rather tired of it.

She jumped off the table, dusted her hands and then threw her arms round her mother.

'Why *shouldn't* I tell father?' she asked again, this time as a whisper in her mother's ear. 'Haven't Emily and Jeremy been punished enough? Does it mean that Father will *never* see his own son again? Never want to have anything to do with his own grandson and granddaughter? Fern is four years old now, Mother. Don't *you* think it's unnatural for Father not to want to see her? Why does this vendetta have to last for ever? Is it for life, Mother? If so, I don't see why.'

Slowly Catherine completed her task of folding the tops over the mince pies before putting them carefully in the oven. Tansy thought that her mother, despite the bustle and energy of her life, had begun to move like a much older woman as though she were trying to catch up in years with her father.

Tansy was an impulsive, emotional girl and it was not unusual for her to demonstrate her affection visibly. She was someone who liked to touch, to feel, unlike Gilbert who was as reserved and unemotional as his father. That had never changed.

Catherine gently unfastened Tansy's fingers and slowly turned towards her, part of her face smudged with flour.

'What happened four years ago, Tansy, affected your father very much. He felt that Emily had abused the hospitality he had shown her in this house. He had been

very good to her. She had stayed for four years as a
guest, never had to pay a penny, everything found. Even
the nursery school Mark went to was paid for out of
your father's pocket, and willingly. He didn't begrudge
it for a moment because Emily was his daughter-in-
law and we fully expected to see Edward back again.'
Catherine sighed. 'He seemed to lead a charmed life in
the war. He went right through the campaigns without a
scratch serving in all the major battles in North Africa
and Italy. And then, suddenly, just before D-Day he was
killed. Imagine how that affected your father, a man
whose nerves were never very strong . . . and then
imagine how he felt when Jeremy, who had been
missing for so many years, returned home alive, but sick
in body and mind?

'And what did Emily do? Why,' Catherine's lip curled
in a faint sneer, 'she began to look after Jeremy, to do
what I should have been doing because she did it very
well and she had the time. You can imagine how grateful
we were to her; to have such a noble woman, forgetful
to self and her own grief, repaying Geoffrey's years of
hospitality on such a task. We never dreamed what kind
of person she really was or what she had in mind.'

Catherine paused to turn to the oven again, stooping
low to inspect the progress of the pies whose tempting
aroma filled the large kitchen, reminding Tansy of Santa
Claus and those nostalgic days of childhood Christmases;
stockings on the ends of the beds and an all-pervasive air
of magic about the house. What happy, happy years they
seemed in retrospect now. Just she and Gilbert, Mum
and Dad before the war came with all its horror, its
eventual effect on the life of the family.

'I don't think you can blame people for falling in love.'
Tansy helped her mother to carry the tray to the table

then bent and inhaled the aroma of bubbling hot mince and pastry.

'Oh yes you can, Tansy,' her mother said firmly. 'You *can* avoid the temptation. We all have free will. Jeremy was a sick man and your father thought Emily abused his trust.'

'Oh, abuse. I'm always hearing about abuse!' Tansy cried, shaking her head. 'Do you believe that she didn't really love Jeremy?' She joined her arms and leaned towards her mother as though their roles were reversed, that she was the mother and Catherine the child. How often in the old days had her mother, always the disciplinarian, stooped, seemingly from a great height, to lecture her, berate her or administer a scolding?

'I'm not suggesting she didn't *love* him,' Catherine replied, choosing her words carefully. 'I am saying she should not have put herself in the position where they allowed themselves to *fall* in love; she should not have gone as far as she did. You,' her mother pulled herself up to try, unsuccessfully, to reach Tansy's height, 'you are old enough now, Tansy – you are nearly eighteen after all – to know what I'm talking about. The fact that Emily was actually expecting Jeremy's child is what inflamed your father. And you can't blame him. Edward not long dead and, in that time, his widow had allowed herself to fall in love and become pregnant by another man. Not just any man, but her husband's brother. I think, if you reflect on it, on the enormity of it, you will see why your father was so upset and why he could never bring himself to see Jeremy again, or meet his granddaughter, as long as he remains married to Emily.'

Tansy continued to stare stubbornly at her mother, and Catherine sighed. She knew that expression and that, once again, she had failed to convince her. 'I can see that you don't understand me. All I can say, Tansy, is that if you don't curb your own impulsive and sentimental nature you will bring a lot of trouble on yourself; a very great deal of trouble.'

'If you mean by "impulsive nature", Mother, seeing who I like and going out with my own friends I shall continue to do it. I am nearly eighteen and far too old to be treated like a child. The time Father insists on me coming home is ridiculous! He doesn't set a time limit for Gilbert.'

'Because Gilbert doesn't need a time limit, that's why,' her mother snapped. 'He is always at home working for his scholarship. It must be a great distraction for Gilbert to have you banging round the place at night, out of sorts and with not enough to do.'

'What *can* I do?' Tansy said. 'Do you realize how boring it is for me to be at home every evening? Do you realize all my friends are out having a good time?'

'As far as I know a lot of them spend too much time in the pub, and you're too young. Besides, I never think it's a very seemly thing for a woman to want to do. It's how people get themselves bad reputations. Your father knows what he's doing, believe me.'

'My father does *not* know what he's doing, Mother.' Tansy, working herself up to a real temper, started to thump the table. 'He has no idea at all. He is *totally* out of touch with young people in the same way that he is totally out of touch with Emily and Jeremy. If you ask me if I think he's right, I must tell you, Mother, that I don't. He's a fuddy-duddy and I'm tired of him always looking at the clock to see what time it is, or asking me who I'm with and how long I'll be.'

'I warn you,' her mother said shaking a finger at her, 'I warn you, that's all.' However, her expression showed that, clearly, she was troubled by what her daughter had said and the way she said it.

Tansy flounced out of the room and ran upstairs to her own room, pausing at Gilbert's door as she did. It was already dusk and there was a light under his door, showing that he was at home and, doubtless, bent over his desk studying.

Tansy hovered outside his door and then knocked softly on it. 'Gilbert,' she called, 'can I come in?'

She could hear the sound of his chair being scraped back and then the door being unlocked, which surprised her.

'Gilbert,' Tansy said advancing slowly into the room, her eyes darting mischievously this way and that. 'Have you got a *girl*friend in here?'

'Of course I haven't,' Gilbert said irritatedly, running his hands through his hair. 'It's to keep Father out.'

'Oh, you too,' Tansy whispered conspiratorially, sinking onto his bed and stretching herself out until she lay full length, head propped upon her hands.

'Me too? How do you mean?' Gilbert removed his spectacles and began briskly polishing them.

'I've just had a row with Mother about Father.'

'Surely there was no need for that,' Gilbert was a mild youth untroubled, like his sister, by extremes of emotion.

'I saw Emily today.' The words rushed from Tansy's mouth. 'I saw her in the High Street. She was ever so friendly.'

'Did you speak to her?' Gilbert's air was clearly one of disapproval.

'Yes I did. Of course I did. I had no quarrel with Emily.'

'I wonder she spoke to you.' Gilbert sat down again and, picking up his pen, began to doodle on his pad.

'Why shouldn't she speak to me?' Tansy demanded.

'Because of what you brought about, or have you forgotten?'

A hot blush stung Tansy's face at the memory of what had happened all those years ago, even though then she was a child and now she was grown up. 'The baby was starting to show. It was just a matter of time,' she said.

'All the same . . .'

'Oh, *Gilbert*.' Tansy angrily jumped up and pulled down her jumper over her skirt. 'You are always such a goody-goody. Never do anything wrong. Never *say* anything wrong. Always Father's pet. Mother's good little boy. What would Father say if he knew his precious boy locked the door to keep him out?'

'I simply lock the door to get on with my work,' Gilbert said sulkily. 'Father still feels that I'm a small child who needs to have his homework repeated parrot fashion every day. He takes up so much of my time that I have to shut him out or I'd never do anything. He still expects me to ask him questions and to show him everything I do. That's what I'm sick of.'

'And *I'm* sick of Father's restrictions on my freedom,' Tansy said petulantly. 'He keeps me in like a little girl.'

'Seriously, Tansy.' Gilbert removed his glasses and twirled them about in his hand. 'You must be more serious. You can't just go on like this for ever.'

'Like what?' Tansy demanded.

'Enjoying yourself, doing nothing. Besides,' Gilbert frowned, as if confronted with an impenetrable problem, 'I wonder you don't find it terribly boring. I'd hate to have nothing to do.'

'I have *plenty* to do, thank you,' Tansy retorted. 'Plenty of people to see and talk to. It *may* not compare with a vocation to be a doctor such as *you* have, Gilbert; but I like it. It's my way of life and I find it pleasant. I don't have any great ambition like you.'

'Just to find the right man?' Gilbert suggested.

'Why not?' Tansy looked at him defensively. 'What's wrong with that?'

'Isn't it a bit soon to settle down and marry?'

'Who said anything about *marrying* and settling down?' Tansy replied softly. 'I just want to have a good time. It's true,' she acknowledged, 'I'll probably marry quite early. But that will be just to get away from here; to be independent and my own woman. To get away from Father's perpetually vigilant eye.'

'I wonder what your husband will say to that?' Gilbert was already weary of the conversation and anxious to get back to his studies. He kept glancing at the books on his desk.

'Husband? My husband will be someone like me. Someone who likes what I like and does what I want to do. I'm not going to exchange one gaoler for another.'

'You should get a job.' Gilbert meaningfully flicked through the pages of his biology textbook. 'A job gives you financial independence. It is no bad basis for marriage.'

'Oh, you old man,' Tansy said rushing over to the door. 'You're just as bad as Father.'

After Tansy left the room Gilbert sat thoughtfully staring at the print in his book but not seeing it. Gilbert and his father had many things in common: they were both cautious, frugal, lacking the temperament or impetuosity of Tansy and her mother. Above all they liked a steady life of routine with no ups and downs, highs or lows.

But ever since she'd left school Tansy had been restless. She was only seventeen but she wanted to lead her own life; to see her own friends and do what she liked. Frequently at night the house resounded with the raised, angry voices of Tansy and her father who had stayed up waiting for her to come home.

'But I'm old enough to *know* what I'm doing, Father.'

'No you are *not*!' her father would say. 'And if I had a stick I'd horsewhip you.'

'Don't you *dare* speak to me like that, Father.'

'And don't you *dare* come in after midnight, my girl, ever again.'

And so on and so forth. One evening Gilbert had had to assist his father upstairs and put him to bed after his bad temper had brought on a cardiac spasm.

Gilbert expected that marriage would be the best solution for Tansy. She showed no disposition for further study, even for the shorthand and typing course both her father and mother wanted her to take. She was idle, she was argumentative and she was a nuisance.

Even though he loved her dearly, her brother thought how much quieter, more restful, the house would be without her.

The following day Tansy had tea with her father in the way she used to after coming home from school. Her father had asked her for this meeting and Tansy, fully expecting a reprimand for some misdeed or the other, gazed defensively at him as she came into the room carrying the tray with the tea things as she used to do. Her father sat in his chair in front of the fire puffing away at his pipe, paper on his lap. For a moment Tansy gazed at him wishing, oh how she wished, that the old times could return: the state of innocence and trust between father and daughter.

'I've brought some Christmas cake,' she said, putting the tray down on the table under the window. 'Mum made it in September. She said we'll be tipsy after eating it.'

'Capital,' her father said, chuckling, and his tone of

voice, the slight smile on his face told her that this was going to be a time of healing rather than confrontation. His voice was conciliatory and welcoming and, after she had poured his tea, she put a piece of the rich fruit cake on a plate and, taking it over to him, threw herself on the rug in front of the fire.

'Aren't you going to have any tea or cake, my love?'

'In a minute, Daddy.' She drew her knees up under her chin and gazed into the fire. 'I just wanted to savour this moment alone with you, remembering how it used to be when I came home from school. Those days will never come back again.'

'Little Tansy,' her father said, his voice strong with emotion, 'don't think I don't remember those days too; but they were based on your being a little girl and now you are growing up . . . as you're always telling me.'

'I *know*, Daddy,' Tansy looked wistfully up at him. 'I'm sorry I upset you. I know you only mean it for my own good; but somehow I do feel . . .'

'I know, my darling, I know.' Geoffrey put out a hand to stroke her thick blonde hair combed back from her brow without a parting and secured by a velvet band. Her strong, classical profile was outlined by the fire and suddenly his heart filled with tenderness, and also a love that had in it an element of sorrow because, one day, he would lose her to a man who would love her in a very different way from him.

Tansy got up as if to banish her mournful thoughts and skipped over to the table to help herself to tea. Her very vitality meant that she was always on the move; she had so much energy that she seemed to charge through life never able to sit still for very long.

'Tansy,' her father said as she sat opposite him, hungrily biting into the brandy-soaked Christmas cake, 'I hear that you saw Emily the other day.'

'Ah,' Tansy put down the cake just as she was about to take another large bite, 'so this *is* an interview, a reprimand, after all, Daddy?'

'No it is not, my dear,' her father said rapidly, noting her expression. 'Your mother told me you bumped into her in the street.'

'We had tea together,' Tansy said. 'I felt it would have been rude not to acknowledge her.'

'Maybe you were right.' Her father's tone was off-hand. 'But it is not Emily I am concerned about. It's Jeremy.' He put down his cup and looked into the fire, the expression in his eyes bleak. 'I would so like to see my son again, Tansy. You have no idea how I miss him, how much I want to see him.'

'But, Father,' Tansy cried out in amazement, putting her plate on the floor and dusting the crumbs from her fingers into the fire. 'You have only to ask . . .'

'No, you don't understand.' Geoffrey sadly shook his head from side to side. 'I feel that Jeremy did wrong and he knew how I felt. It is very hard to unscramble something that is so complex, so irrational, maybe, but which affects members of the same family. We each have our fixed positions and now it is necessary for a go-between to act for us. Someone acceptable to both parties.'

Her father stopped and the smile he gave her was so bleak that it tugged at her heart.

'That person is you, Tansy. I would like you to bring us together again, to arrange a meeting . . .'

'Oh, but I'm sure Emily would be delighted.' Tansy jumped up and began to skip about the room like a child. 'The other day she was so sweet, so understanding. Oh I'm so happy.' She bent to kiss her father, encircling his neck with her arms. But, with a force that surprised her, he prised them apart, each hand grasping her wrists.

'Tansy,' he said in a harsh, strong voice. 'You don't understand. This has nothing to do with Emily. What *she* did was quite unpardonable and unforgivable. It is my son I want to see again, my son Jeremy, not the woman he calls his wife.'

Chapter 11

Tansy sat in the middle of the bus that bumped its way through the Dales along the road that wound from Netherwick, Skipton and then on to Rylstone, Linton, Burnsall, Appletreewick, across the ridge to Barden Tower then back over the moors to Netherwick again.

Tansy got off the bus in Grassington and had a cup of coffee at the tea shop in the cobbled square while she waited for another bus to take her to Cragbeck. The little shops were all brightly lit up for Christmas and from the electrical shop came the sound of Christmas carols recorded by a famous Cathedral choir. The huge tree in the centre of the square was hung with coloured lights, and the breaths of the shoppers vaporized in the air as they hurried about their tasks in the chilly morning.

Tansy loved the Dales bus, and the many journeys she had made in it over the years to visit friends who lived in outlying places had made her familiar with every inch of the way, in every season from the lush greenery and meadow land of summer – fields of tall grass flecked with buttercups – to the bare leafless trees and the hard frozen fields of winter.

During the war the Dales bus had been the only means of transport because of petrol rationing and then it only ran two or three times a week. But, because of her father's position as a doctor, Tansy used to accompany him on many of his visits to the distant villages like Starbottom, Hubberholme, and Kilnsey beyond which lay Cragbeck off the Kettlewell road.

The bus that went to Kettlewell left the bus station just

about eleven and Tansy mounted it as the driver was climbing into his seat and wishing her 'good morning' because he was one of her father's patients.

'How's the doctor, Tansy?' he enquired, smiling down at her as she paused by his cab.

'He's very well, thank you.' Tansy knew the man but not his name. Anyway, she had been brought up to be polite to people who might address her because they knew who she was even if she didn't know them.

Tansy took her seat and, within a minute, the bus had turned out of the station and went down the steep road over the bridge, across the Wharf, up past Threshfield to the Kettlewell road.

The road ran through Bluebell Wood, which was full of primroses and bluebells in the spring. Below it ran the River Wharfe which had its source in the hills high above Hubberholme many miles distant yet. Here it was a broad, shallow river, a haunt for anglers who would stride out into mid-stream in their high waders, expertly casting their flies for the elusive trout.

The bus stopped in Kilnsey where some people got off and others got on, including a couple of hikers with packs on their backs. Then it went past the huge over-hanging crag that looked so deceptively near the road, past the road to Arncliffe where it began to climb until it reached the spot where Tansy was to alight. From here to the village of Cragbeck it was only a mile but, as she expected, there, sitting on a wall waiting for her, was Jeremy, his hands resting on his stick, a young collie dog sitting obediently at his feet.

Jeremy rose as the bus stopped, hailed the driver, whom he also seemed to know, and then put out his arms as Tansy ran into them and, for an emotional moment, brother and sister hugged each other.

'My, you've grown,' Jeremy said at last holding her at

a distance to admire her. 'How long is it since I saw you?'

'Four years,' Tansy said feeling rather shy, surprised by the warmth of the hug, his obvious pleasure in seeing her.

'You're a woman now, Tansy,' Jeremy said, waving at the driver with his stick as the bus drove off. 'Four years is a long time.'

Tansy watched the bus disappear over the brow of the hill with some misgiving. It would be four hours before it was back again and she suddenly regretted her father's request and the impulse that had made her come.

Jeremy seemed to notice her expression, so he tucked his arm through hers and pointed to a horse and brightly painted cart which stood by the roadside, the horse contentedly feeding from a bag round its neck.

'Isn't she beautiful?' he said, pointing to the colourful ensemble.

'She's yours?' Tansy enquired, laughing.

'Better than a motorcar, more reliable, cheaper.'

'She's lovely.' Tansy went up to the mare and stroked her sleek chestnut coat. The little trap was painted black and red with shiny brass fittings and someone had obviously taken a lot of time and care doing it up.

'Emily breaks up today for Christmas,' Jeremy said, helping her up the steps into the cart. 'She'll be home when we get there.'

'That's good.' Tansy felt awkward and tongue-tied, and she brushed her hair away from her eyes as Jeremy gently flicked his whip over the mare's flank and, perfectly familiar with the route, she set off up the narrow lane that led to Cragbeck.

It was a beautiful sunny day, the air crisp, the sky azure blue and the skeletal trees standing like rows of sentinels – although of assorted sizes – along the crest of the hills through which they drove. The mare trotted at a brisk pace and, over the high stone walls, Tansy could see sheep, protected from the cold by their heavy coats, grazing contentedly on the thick green pasture.

'Are these your sheep?' Tansy said conversationally and, after a quick glance in her direction, Jeremy tossed his head towards the hills.

'Mine are higher up.'

'Do you take the horse and trap to get there?'

Jeremy looked at her and laughed.

'You *are* a townee,' he said. 'There are no roads to where my sheep graze. I walk or take the horse if I'm too tired or my leg hurts.'

'You do look awfully well,' Tansy said still feeling shy. Her half-brother had filled out from the emaciated, angular figure she remembered from years back, and his hair, always sparse since his illness, was practically white, a fact which surprised her. She knew Jeremy was only in his mid-thirties. But the white hair made him look even more handsome although a lot older, like their father. It seemed to be a family characteristic that the Blair men should look much older than their years. Yet Jeremy had put on about a couple of stones so it was obvious that country life and plenty of fresh air suited him.

Almost as soon as the horse started they could see the roofs of the village of Cragbeck in the distance as it nestled in the shadow of Cragbeck Fell that dominated the valley. The fell was part of the Pennine range that ran from the Midlands to the Scottish border. Cragbeck Fell was famed for its potholes, the long subterranean caverns that ran through the chalky limestone deep underground. Sometimes in the winter it was covered with snow and was a popular haunt for skiers and tobogganers who raced down its icy slopes.

But now the hillside was green and flocks of sheep

grazed upon its slopes while, from the village itself, spirals of smoke twisted into the air which was pungent with the smell of burning wood.

Cragbeck had one small school that served the village and a number of neighbouring hamlets, and it was of the fifty or so pupils of varying ages that Emily was in sole charge.

As they trotted into the village one or two people stopped and hailed Jeremy who returned their greetings before turning up a narrow street, which had room only for the horse and cart, and stopping at the end cottage which backed onto the fell.

It was a double-fronted dwelling with a tiny garden and by the side was a track that led into a field which was where Jeremy kept the horse. As he stopped at the entrance to the track, the front door of the cottage opened and a small girl ran out, straight past Tansy, and flung herself into Jeremy's arms. He threw down his stick, nuzzling her hair with his face, picked her up and hugged her. Then, still with his daughter in his arms, he turned to Tansy who was stroking the head of the horse, to give herself something to do.

'This is Fern, Tansy.' Fern immediately buried her head shyly in her father's shoulder. 'Fern, look up, this is your Auntie Tansy.'

Fern kept her head buried in Jeremy's thick coat and Tansy, feeling shy herself, said:

'Hello, Fern,' in a formal way which she knew sounded silly. Fern, however, decided to overcome her shyness and, turning round, gazed with interest at the stranger, finger in her mouth. She was a delicate-looking child of astonishing physical beauty with pale translucent skin, high cheekbones and thick curly hair that lay matted on her forehead as if it hadn't been combed for days.

She looked, in fact, very much a country child, with a blue jersey over warm woolly trousers and heavy carpet slippers which revealed a pair of bright red socks. ''Lo,' Fern said at last.

'I never think of myself as an auntie,' Tansy said, giving her a friendly smile. 'You must call me Tansy.'

'Tansy,' Fern said, then again. 'Tansy. It's a funny name, Daddy.' She spoke with a Yorkshire accent and, as she gazed at her father, he smiled and hugged her again before putting her down.

'You run back in. You've only got your slippers on. Is Mummy home?'

Fern nodded and, at that moment, Emily appeared at the doorway wearing an apron, her face flushed as though she'd just been at the stove.

She too exclaimed when she saw Fern standing on the muddy road in her slippers and, with a finger pointing sharply towards the ground in a gesture of authority, said: 'Come here this moment, Fern! If those slippers get wet they'll take days to dry.'

'I think it's too late.' Jeremy shook his head with a rueful smile. He then started to undo the horse's halter from the cart, calling over his shoulder, 'I'll just put Polly in the field and I'll be back in a moment, love.'

'Now you leave that cart until someone comes to help you lift it,' Emily said again in a stern, schoolmarmish tone, which was new to Tansy, to whom she now turned: 'He always tries to do too much. Welcome to our little home, Tansy dear.'

Emily spontaneously stretched out her arms and Tansy, coming forwards, kissed her awkwardly on the cheeks, embarrassed by this display of affection because of the message she brought from her father. Strange though it might seem, it had never occurred to her that the presence of Emily would prove a difficulty simply because she was so overjoyed by the invitation she had to extend to Jeremy.

Now that she was here, miles away from Netherwick with four hours to go until she caught the bus back to Grassington, she realized just how difficult her visit might prove to be. Emily was not included in the invitation.

Emily, however, seemed to attribute Tansy's attitude to shyness and, putting an encouraging arm round her shoulder, drew her into the cottage while Fern, finger still firmly in her mouth, followed from behind with fascination at this new relation she had never seen, never been aware of. Fern with an elder brother and lots of playmates of her own age in the village was scarcely a lonely child yet, in the isolation of Cragbeck, she lived a life comparatively sheltered from the world.

The front door led directly into the main room of the cottage which was large and pleasantly furnished with old but not antique pieces: a large sideboard, a chintz-covered sofa with matching armchairs and, under the window, a round polished table on which stood an urn filled with winter berries and twigs, pieces of holly and fir cones.

The blackened grate, in which a large cheerful fire burned, had an oven to one side and the mantelpiece was full of photographs – of Edward, Jeremy, Fern as a baby, Fern and Mark together with Emily, Jeremy and Fern, obviously when she was newly born. There were none of Geoffrey and Catherine Blair, Tansy or Gilbert.

The floor was covered with a worn-looking carpet on which there were bright rag rugs which looked as though they had been recently made.

The cottage was shabby, yet homely; it exuded warmth and friendliness and Tansy felt herself begin to relax.

'It *is* lovely,' she said looking round. 'What a homely place.'

'We think so,' Emily said, looking pleased, 'though of course we don't own it. It is a tied cottage. None of this furniture is ours although I made the rugs and re-covered the chairs.'

'Emily is a wizard,' Jeremy said, stamping his boots on the mat by the door as he came in, 'she has put in so much work in this cottage she has transformed it.'

'It seems a pity not to own it,' Tansy said. 'Who does it belong to?'

'It belongs to my boss,' Jeremy said with a shrug of resignation. 'It goes with the job. If I leave we have to give up the cottage.'

'Unfortunately, if Jeremy goes for treatment to London as planned,' Emily said, 'he will have to give up the job. But there is a possibility that the school will find me a house, or a cottage. There is one that goes with the job but the last headmistress, who was there for thirty years, is still alive and the school authorities haven't the heart to ask her to leave; a decision I respect,' Emily finished, looking at Jeremy who was busy taking his boots off sitting on a chair just inside the door. 'You must be famished, Tansy.' Emily returned her gaze to Tansy. 'It's been a long journey.'

There was an appetizing aroma coming from the kitchen and Tansy decided that indeed she was very hungry.

'We eat in the kitchen,' Emily explained, leading her through another door. 'Usually Jeremy uses the back door when he goes out and comes in, that way he keeps his muddy feet off my new rugs.'

The kitchen was almost as large as the main room. It seemed to have been added on to the cottage – which would explain the oven in the main room – and had an

Aga stove in the corner and a solid deal table in the
centre of the floor which was covered with a tablecloth
laid for four people.

'Where's Mark?' Tansy asked.

'He's on the hills with the sheep,' Jeremy grinned. 'He
offered to keep an eye on them while I went and met
you. I'm a shepherd practically full-time, now. I prefer
it. We have to be careful of snow this winter. At the first
sign of it we get huge drifts on the Fell and sheep can get
lost. My job is to stop this happening so that the sheep
should all be safely in shelter before the snow falls.'

'I can't imagine you as a shepherd,' Tansy said in a
conversational tone, sitting in the chair indicated for her
by Emily. 'I imagine you as a sort of very active man, not
sitting looking at sheep all day long.'

'I *am* a very active man.' Jeremy disappeared inside
the larder by the side of the kitchen, emerging with a
bottle of beer which he proceeded to open and pour into
a pint glass. 'As active as I can be. But I like the life of
contemplation on the hills. You find out things about
yourself and others that you never knew about before.'

'Jeremy's started to write,' Emily said with a note of
pride. 'He gets the ideas during the day and then puts
them down at night.'

'*Write*?' Tansy said with interest. 'Write what?'

'It's a book about my life.' Jeremy sat down next to
her, still in his socks. 'It's a book for reflections, rather
difficult to describe, really. I don't suppose anyone will
ever want to publish it.'

'I think it's very good.' Emily carefully drew a large
pot from the oven with a cloth and carried it to the table.
As she lifted the lid Tansy's taste buds involuntarily
watered in anticipation.

'Hot pot,' Emily said, noticing her expression. 'I pride
myself that I make the best in the village.'

'England,' Jeremy said with relish, raising his glass to his lips. 'Cheers. Nice to have you with us, Tansy.'

'I like being here,' Tansy said. 'I wish I'd come before.'

'Why didn't you?' Emily enquired, holding the ladle in the air before dipping it into the large earthenware pot whose surface was encrusted with slices of golden potato.

'You shouldn't ask her that,' Jeremy chided. 'I know why she didn't come. So do you.'

Emily said nothing but labled the stew onto the plate. 'Help yourself to cabbage,' she said to Tansy, pointing to a dish in the centre of the table.

'It's all going to change now anyway,' Tansy felt herself almost choking with excitement, 'I'm here because Daddy asked me to come.'

'*Father* asked you to come?' Jeremy slowly replaced his glass on the table, an expression of amazement on his face.

'Daddy says he wants everything to be forgiven and forgotten. He misses you very much.'

'He actually said that? Well, well,' Jeremy said, the look of amazement turning to pleasure.

'I hope you won't go running off to see him,' Emily said sharply to her husband. 'Just because he beckons.'

'Oh, Emily,' Jeremy looked at her with surprise, 'that is *not* a very nice or conciliatory thing to say.'

'Nevertheless it's true.' Emily finished serving the food and then, replacing the lid on the pot, lifted it with the help of the oven cloth and put it back on top of the Aga. 'I hope *you're* not going to forgive your father so lightly after what he did to us.'

'What is there to forgive?' he said eventually, his voice vibrating with anger. 'Father did absolutely nothing. It was Catherine who was responsible for what happened,' he glanced apologetically at Tansy. 'I'm sorry to speak about your mother like this, Tansy, and you certainly were too young to remember what happened. But it was she who asked Emily to leave the house, and it was my decision to go with her. *My* quarrel is with Catherine, not with Dad.'

'Well, I don't know.' Emily, who had been listening to him with signs of heightened tension, put her knife and fork on her plate and sat back in her chair, arms folded. 'You mean you don't think your *father* was behind it?'

'I'm certain he wasn't. He may have agreed with Catherine, but he didn't expect me to go away, or you,' Jeremy added as an afterthought.

'He never asked you to come back, did he?'

'It was very difficult for him. He was ill. He depended so much on Catherine. I can see just what sort of dilemma Dad was in.'

'Well, I've never heard *anything* like it.'

Tansy could never have imagined the normally placid Emily being so angry. The hot pot lay untouched on her plate in front of her and then she pushed it away as if she would eat no more.

'I don't know what it is you don't understand.' Jeremy also appeared angry and Tansy saw little Fern look with apprehension from one parent to the other. Perhaps these differences of opinion were a common occurrence. 'I would have thought it *perfectly* clear.'

'You mean *you* think we've been here all these years living in poverty in a furnished cottage because of the whim of your *stepmother*? Shame on you, Jeremy!'

'I think that had a lot to do with it.' Jeremy looked her straight in the eyes. 'I'm not saying it was the *only* reason. Anyway, I don't think we have been living in poverty. We both earn and we only pay tiny rent.'

'Life hasn't been easy.'

'But it hasn't been *hard*.' Jeremy's expression seemed

to be asking her to see reason. 'Come on, Emily, you have often said how lucky we were.'

'Relatively lucky,' Emily acknowledged in a chilly voice, 'in that we had each other. We each supported the other.'

'And we don't want to fall out now.' Jeremy got up and went over to her, leaning beside her as a child takes a lesson to a teacher to have it explained. 'All *I* am saying, darling, is that I am glad there is the chance of a reunion with my father. It's going to be a difficult time for us both and you will have some support while I'm in London.'

'Oh,' Tansy said, and then put her hand to her lips, as if to seal them.

'Oh what?' Emily looked at her with interest. 'Were you going to say something?'

'Oh, that's all.'

'You can't just say "oh".'

'Oh, I didn't know Jeremy was going to London,' Tansy improvised hurriedly.

'But I told you he was the day we met in Netherwick. They are hoping to try a new treatment on him.'

'Yes, I'd forgotten.' Tansy avoided Emily's clear, knowing eyes.

'But that's not all is it, Tansy?' Emily prompted, giving her an encouraging smile. 'There's something else, isn't there?'

'What do you mean?' Tansy tried to look away again.

'You said "oh" when Jeremy talked about me having some support from the family. I think you meant to suggest that I will not have that support.'

'I didn't *say* that,' Tansy said quickly. 'It was only that the message from Daddy came for Jeremy and I think he does want to see him first.'

'It's understandable,' Jeremy said, sitting back, having

cleaned his plate. 'After all, he *is* my father.'

'So you're going to see him without me?' As Emily stood up Tansy saw her hands were trembling.

'Yes, why not?'

'Because I think it's contemptible, that's why. You are trying to placate your father and leave me out.'

'I am trying to do nothing of the sort.'

'If you like . . .'

'I think for Jeremy to come by himself *is* the best thing first.' Tansy felt increasingly uncomfortable as well as nervous as the atmosphere deteriorated. 'Daddy did say he wanted to see *you*, Jeremy. He said nothing about Emily.' Furtively Tansy glanced across the kitchen to where Emily was stooping by the oven in the act of bringing out a large pie. Tansy felt guilty because Emily had obviously spent a lot of time preparing for an event that was turning into a disaster. Instead of being the bringer of good news she felt she was sowing the seeds of discord between husband and wife. Taking advantage of the diversion she leaned across to Jeremy and whispered, 'He did mean *you*, just you. He didn't want to see Emily . . . not just yet.' Studiously Tansy gazed at her lap, avoiding Emily's eyes as she carried the dessert to the table.

For the rest of the meal, Emily didn't refer to the matter again and nor did Jeremy. Emily, who had left her main course unfinished, ate some bilberry pie with thick cream that came from the cows of a neighbouring herd.

Tansy was aware that Emily was keeping herself tightly under control, turning the conversation to trivialities so that the matter of Jeremy and his father should not be brought up again.

After lunch, while Emily washed up, Jeremy took Tansy up the Fell to where Mark, huddled against the wall and well wrapped up in a thick anorak, was watching the sheep. Mark remembered Tansy quite well and he and she greeted each other very cordially, though without kissing. He explained to her how he kept count of the sheep and what he did if a sudden snowstorm happened.

Tansy could see that he and Jeremy got on well and that Mark seemed to like and understand his stepfather. She thought that for a boy of twelve he was already remarkably mature.

Mark walked down the Fell with them to the lower meadows, and then he stood – a solemn, sturdy figure, somehow the epitome of the country boy – waving until they were out of sight.

By the time they got back it was three o'clock. Emily was at the ironing board listening to a programme on the wireless. The table was cleared, the dishes from the unsuccessful lunch party all washed up and put away.

There was something in Emily's demeanour now that hadn't been there when Tansy had arrived – a defensiveness, a wariness when she looked either at Tansy or Jeremy – and Tansy wished dearly that her father hadn't made her his emissary.

Emily was restrained in her farewell and shut the door before Jeremy had fastened the horse to the trap and they set off for the main road. As she turned to wave Tansy could see Fern, who had remained all the time with her mother, as though distrusting the visitor. She stood at the window, finger in her mouth, hand raised in farewell; but of Emily there was no sign.

'I think we upset Emily terribly,' Tansy said, when they had left the village. The wind bit into her face and she sensed there would soon be snow. Maybe the village would be cut off as it was most winters, and she thought how snug and cosy it would be inside the cottage.

'Emily can't expect to stand in the way of me and my father,' Jeremy said grimly. 'We made our point and now I think it is time to be friends – all of us, me, Emily, Catherine and Dad. You can't nurse a grudge for ever. It is time for us to be one big happy family, and let bygones be bygones. That's the way it should be.'

Should be or would be? Tansy decided it was best to say nothing further on the subject, but her heart was full of apprehension at the unforeseen consequences of her visit, and the possible trouble it would cause.

Jeremy sat, feet stretched out before the fire roaring in the grate, a tumbler of whisky in his hand. Opposite him sat the man he had not seen for four years. At first, the encounter had been a strange one. Both father and son had greeted each other with an air of mutual embarrassment, of awkwardness, of obvious regret for the past.

The day for the reunion had been chosen shortly before Christmas when Catherine had gone with her mother and Tansy to shop in Leeds. Jeremy had caught the bus to Grassington where Geoffrey had picked him up and, largely in silence, they had driven through the Dales to Netherwick.

'Catherine has left us a spot of lunch,' Geoffrey said, breaking the long silence that had ensued after they had sat down for a pre-lunch drink, facing each other across the fire. Words seemed hard to find.

'That's very good of her,' Jeremy said.

'Something cold. Quite simple. Maybe hot soup to start.'

'When will Catherine be back?' Jeremy, feeling nervous, looked at the clock on the mantelpiece of his father's study.

'They're catching quite a late afternoon train. They'll take a taxi from the station. They'll have plenty of time.

All the same . . .' Geoffrey sucked at his pipe and puffed a thick stream of smoke into the air. 'I wish you'd stay a few days or, at least, the night.'

'I couldn't stay a few days, Father,' Jeremy said. 'There are the sheep and there's Christmas. Fern is just beginning to be the age when she appreciates it.'

'Of course, of course,' Geoffrey said gruffly, as if to disguise the fact that he had never seen his grand-daughter. 'How quickly one forgets that age.'

'I hope you'll see her quite soon, Father.'

'I'd like that,' Geoffrey said, but Jeremy detected a lack of enthusiasm in his voice.

Once more a long pause ensued as if each were thinking of the past.

'Well . . .' Geoffrey said and then paused, pushing his tobacco firmly in the bowl of his pipe.

'Well . . .' Jeremy put his glass to his lips. 'It's been a long time, Father.'

'Too long,' Geoffrey said with unexpected emotion. 'I blame myself . . .'

'You can't blame yourself, Father. You weren't even there. Catherine had the row with Emily. In a sense it was nothing to do with either of us.'

'Quite,' Geoffrey said as though unexpectedly granted a reprieve. 'Women . . .'

'Catherine literally pushed Emily out of the house. She left me with no alternative but to go too.'

'Naturally.' Geoffrey studied the ceiling. 'Though you can't blame Catherine entirely. Emily's news was a very great shock. I thought, we *both* thought, she so revered Edward.'

'She did and still does.' Jeremy gazed at his father. 'But Edward had been dead for a long time. Over two years. *I'm* as much to blame as Emily.'

'You were very vulnerable,' his father said, as if anxious

to make excuses for him. 'You were a very ill man.'

'Do you still think Emily took advantage of me?'

'Who am I to say? However, it was Eve who seduced Adam . . .'

'Oh, *Father*,' Jeremy shifted uncomfortably in his chair, 'that *is* unfair.'

'Nevertheless,' Geoffrey gave him a meaningful look, 'the Bible isn't so very wrong, you know. Myth it may be but it is also full of old, ancient wisdom. It is the man who is vulnerable, the woman who ensnares. You have only to look at myself and Catherine . . . oh, I admit I was very taken by her; but I was a lonely man with two young sons.'

'And she set her cap at you?' Jeremy thought that he and his father had never been so frank with each other.

'Undoubtedly, not that I regret it. Don't think that for a moment. But for that I would never have had Gilbert and Tansy; but neither would I have lost the love of my two elder sons, and that meant a very great deal to me.'

Jeremy said nothing for a moment or two, unwilling to speak and undecided as to what to say; but it was dawning on him that there was some truth in what his father was suggesting. Both he and his father had been seduced by women who knew what they wanted and intended to get it. And both had gained a lot from their marriages – Catherine social advancement, respectability, money. Emily, security, a man who had willingly married her when she was pregnant. Maybe she had become pregnant deliberately? The idea had never occurred to him before.

'What you did was for the best, but we were too young to know it.' Jeremy was anxious to reassure his father. 'It was natural for you to think it was better for us to be with young relations than alone with you. You were generous, self-sacrificing . . . and how badly we repaid you. We owe *you* an apology. You don't have to apologize to us.'

'How do you mean?' Geoffrey was very alert now to the way the conversation was going. It seemed to be reinterpreting the past in a way that exonerated him. Maybe he wasn't so guilty after all. Why had he spent all those years blaming himself for what had happened to his sons? If it was not *his* fault but Catherine's . . . and how much he had suffered. For what?

'We were both horrible when you remarried, Father; we were not nice to you and beastly to Catherine. She, on the other hand, could, I believe, have behaved better towards us. She could have been more understanding. After the twins were born she seemed to exclude us, to prevent us from seeing you. We were never made to feel very welcome at home.'

'Catherine was not much older than Edward,' Geoffrey nodded his head sagaciously, 'that was the trouble. She was jealous. I know she wanted to exclude you, and I let her. That was very weak of me . . . and weak of me to allow her to let you leave this house with Emily when you were a very sick man. That's why I wanted to see you so much again, Jeremy; to apologize for the past and try and make a better future.'

'Oh, Father,' Jeremy said, his heart full of emotion. 'What is past is past. As for the future . . . it has already been decided that I must go to London for an operation at the Hospital for Nervous Diseases. There is new hope for my condition if I submit to surgery; a very new technique to remove the tumour that's pressing on my brain. The only thing is when; as Emily and I have to give up our home which is tied to my job.'

'Will Emily go with you to London?' his father asked.

'No. Not yet anyway. She likes her job; but there is no vacant house at the moment until the old teacher dies.

Emily is very happy at Cragbeck.'

'But how can you live in London by yourself?'

'I have my pension. I thought I'd get a room near the hospital, because I must continue to have treatment there for about six months after the op.'

'Dear boy,' Geoffrey said reaching out his hand. 'You must let me do all I can to help you. I can ensure that you have no worries about money. That really *is* the least I can do to make up to you for the past.'

In the course of the afternoon father and son became closer than they had ever been before. It was as though an entirely new understanding grew up between them and, although neither was consciously aware of the fact, their enhanced relationship, their bond, was based on an implied criticism of the women whom each of them had married: Catherine and Emily. Each woman was seen as Eve who, tempted by the serpent, had seduced two innocent and well-meaning men. It was the Biblical story all over again.

When Catherine came home she could sense at once what had happened by the way that they looked at her as she entered the room, by Geoffrey's lack of a kiss and Jeremy's frosty politeness as he shook her by the hand.

Still, she didn't care. She had ploughed other fields and it was many years since Geoffrey had desired her as a wife. She had made a place in the home that was essential to the welfare of the others who lived there.

'Jeremy's going to stay the night,' Geoffrey said enthusiastically. 'Is there a bed made up, my dear?'

'No, but there soon will be.' Catherine gave Jeremy a friendly smile while Tansy made much of her brother, remaining for several minutes after greeting him with her arms entwined round his neck.

Catherine felt excluded from the family group, all

related by blood, and she went into the kitchen to prepare the evening roast and instruct the maid to put fresh sheets on the bed in the spare room.

Yes, she knew what had happened; the rapport between the two who had not spoken for four years was too obvious. They had found refuge in each other by blaming the women. Probably most of the censure had been about her because she had told Emily to leave.

It was so simple to say that now.

Yet dinner still managed to be an occasion of celebration. A bottle of wine was opened, a rare occurrence in the Blair household, and Geoffrey, surrounded by his family, forgot how much he had done in the past to blight the lives of those he loved. After all, he was a victim too.

The following morning Geoffrey drove his son to Grassington to catch the Dales bus. He didn't offer to drive him right home and Jeremy knew why. His father didn't want to see Emily and he knew the feeling was mutual: Emily didn't want to see Geoffrey.

It was a subject they had carefully avoided. Emily had hardly been mentioned between them, and Catherine had never so much as asked after her, though she enquired about Mark and wanted to be told all about Fern. If Tansy was embarrassed she didn't show it and, anyway, the main thing was that her father and brother should be reconciled. Maybe a lot that had happened to Emily was her own fault; she was always a very proud, self-contained, solitary kind of woman. It was quite easy to rationalize unpleasant facts when one needed to.

As soon as Jeremy alighted from the bus along the Kettlewell road, Emily, who had brought the horse and trap to meet him, could sense the difference. There was a new dynamism and energy about him but, also, a new wariness as he kissed her. She could feel the lack of response in his lips.

However, Fern was waiting for her father too, so there was no need for words except for Jeremy to say the visit had been a good one and he was glad it had taken place. It was not until Fern and Mark were both in bed and Emily and Jeremy were sitting in front of the fire much later on that Emily said:

'So the visit went well?'

'Very well.' Jeremy leaned forwards to poke the ashes of the fire. Next to him Emily sat with her head resting on her hand, staring at the dying embers in the grate. When the fire went out it became very chilly as there was no other heating in the house. That day Mark had brought the sheep down from the hills, just in case there was snow. 'Dad is going to give us some money.' He turned, poker still in his hand, to gaze at his wife.

'Us?' Emily said in surprise.

'Well, me when I go to London. He said he doesn't want us to worry about money.'

'That's very good of him.'

'I thought so.'

'Did he mention me?'

Jeremy looked at her in surprise. 'Of course he mentioned you.'

'Did he ask when he was going to see me?'

Jeremy turned and started playing with the embers in the grate again. 'Not exactly. I think he wants time . . .'

'I suppose he still regards me as the scarlet woman and you the blameless victim.'

'Oh, don't be silly, Emily,' Jeremy said, shaking his head with irritation. 'What happened happened a long time ago. It is all in the past. You've got a bee in your bonnet about all this.'

'Still, he could have brought you all the way home, if only to say "hello" to me. It would have been polite.'

'Well, he didn't.'

'Because he didn't want to.'

'I tell you, the subject never came up. He met me in Grassington and he took me back to Grassington. Really, dear,' Jeremy reached out to take her hand which was cold, 'you mustn't read too much into this. You're terribly prickly. My reunion with Dad is very important to me. Besides, he's getting old.'

'What *I* read into the situation is that your father has not forgiven *me*.'

Emily got up, hugging herself because she was cold. She went to the mantelpiece to wind the clock and put the guard in front of the fire just in case a stray spark flew out onto the rug.

'Father has very complex feelings about you . . . *and* about Catherine.'

'About *Catherine*?' Emily looked at him in amazement.

'Well Catherine was the one who threw us out.'

'Oh *she's* guilty too, then? Poor Catherine. How I sympathize with her.'

'"Poor Catherine",' Jeremy said derisively, mimicking her voice. He too rose, rubbing his hands together because of the cold. '"Poor Catherine" has quite a lot to answer for.'

'I can just see you two men,' Emily said with a smile. 'Commiserating with each other on what you have suffered at the hands of women.'

Jeremy didn't answer but, as he followed her up the stairs to bed, putting out the lights, he marvelled at her prescience.

Later as they lay in bed they snuggled up together because they always did to keep warm. It was not necessarily a prelude to lovemaking and tonight Emily knew Jeremy would not even try. There was a new vitality about him that had nothing to do with her. It was as though his visit to his father had brought about a radical, possibly unwelcome change. She wanted Jeremy to be more alive, but not without her.

'Did your dad think the operation a good idea?' she enquired, staring at his profile in the moonlight which, after lurking for some time behind the Fell, streamed onto the bed through the windows.

'He felt it was a chance I should take. It is free. I shall be in the hands of the best surgeons and there is a very good chance it will work. Dad provides the financial support we badly need and, do you know, I suddenly decided today to take my book down and work on it there?'

'You mean try and get it published?'

'Why not?'

'No reason why not. I just thought . . .'

'It was unpublishable?'

'I thought you were writing it for yourself.'

'My dear, I'd rather be an author than a shepherd. Look at Richard Hilary. He became famous. My book is very much like his, except that I'm still alive, and intend to remain so.'

'I'm glad for you, Jeremy, really glad,' Emily said after a pause; but she could feel the goose pimples rise on her skin and knew it wasn't just because of the cold.

As Jeremy clasped her even closer the warmth of his body seemed to penetrate hers, infusing it with his energy and fire.

'It was really *nice* to see Father again,' he murmured, his voice already drowsy with sleep. 'In a way I think the break has done us good. We understand each other a lot better and he seems full of optimism about my future.'

'That *is* good news,' Emily replied, feeling his hold on her slacken as he drifted off.

Long after he fell asleep she remained awake wondering what it would be like when he was gone for so long, and whether this future that he planned for himself would include her.

Chapter 12

From across the table Michael Garrett found his gaze returning to the birthday girl, eighteen-year-old Tansy. For one so young she seemed to him to have a particular sophistication and allure, a wordly, almost knowing air that surprised him because of what he knew about her. She was the kind of girl he was used to meeting at parties around the world, and yet she was a local girl who had scarcely ever been out of Netherwick. Not that Tansy was a stranger to Major Garrett who had made the army his career. The Garrett and the Blair families had known one another for years, along with the Todds, the Wentworths, the Hamleys and other prosperous families who also sat round the table at the dinner party in honour of the Blair twins' eighteenth birthday.

About half a dozen names had formed, as it were, the *crème de la crème* of Netherwick society, establishing themselves in positions of prominence and respectability since the fortunes of the town had taken an upward turn in the latter years of the nineteenth century. The development of more advanced methods of weaving and spinning and, more importantly, the advent of the internal combustion engine to aid mechanization, had led to a burst of prosperity as new mills and factories opened up, as well as businesses to service them.

The Mayor of Netherwick sat on Catherine's right and his wife sat between Doctor Blair and Peter Wentworth, who ran the biggest mill in town where the Wills family had worked for so many years. If Catherine felt any embarrassment about this, and there was no reason why she should in a town of shifting degrees of social stratification, she certainly did not show it.

Michael's father, George Garrett, had inherited the Garrett Great Engineering Company from his father who had started it almost at the same time as the Hon Charles Stewart Rolls and Henry Royce were developing their 10-hp two-cylinder motor car in Manchester. The Garretts had gone into manufacturing small parts for motor cars and had extended this to a point when, during the Second World War, they were one of the largest producers of engineering parts for troop carriers, tanks and other military vehicles in the country.

The main plant of the growing business was outside Leeds and it was known that George would have liked Michael to join him and his eldest son, Robert, in the business; but Michael had enjoyed the war, enjoyed soldiering and stayed on in the regular army.

Michael Garrett had seen Tansy only infrequently in the last ten years, much of which he had spent abroad; and he had only reluctantly come to the dinner party in place of his brother who was skiing with his family in Switzerland. Now he was glad he'd come and, although he made little contribution to the discussion at table, he was aware of Tansy and knew that she was aware of him.

Michael was a stocky, tough-looking man of about five foot ten. He was dark-jowled, had brown eyes peering from under a low brow and crinkling black hair cut close to his scalp in military style. He was not, strictly speaking, handsome. Indeed, he looked rather fierce; but he had a strong masculine appeal that attracted women and had broken quite a few hearts.

As he glowered over the table, impervious to the need to charm, it was not only Tansy among the women present who felt the force of his personality; even the older ones seemed flustered by his glances too.

But on the whole, the younger people at the table – Tansy, Gilbert, Michael and Rosalind Wentworth, who was a school friend of Tansy – contributed little to the conversation which was dominated mostly by the grown-ups, all of whom had views on a number of subjects which were forcefully expressed.

The White Swan was a country house hotel on the edge of Ilkley Moor from where it commanded an imposing position looking away from the town upwards towards Wharfedale. Far below ran the River Wharfe, leaving its quiet sanctuary of moor and dale in the course of its slow, relentless journey to the sea. The White Swan had been virtually taken over by the Blairs for the twins' dinner party and the dance that was to follow, and many of the guests had booked themselves in there for the night.

Just before ten the head waiter arrived in the dining room to inform Doctor and Mrs Blair that guests were already beginning to arrive for the dance which was mainly for younger people. With a startled exclamation Catherine stood up, beckoned to her husband and the twins and, excusing herself to the rest of the guests, made her way quickly out of the room followed by her family.

'Attractive girl,' Michael remarked to Helen Thackery who was there with her husband, Geoffrey's partner.

'Tansy you mean?' Helen said, following his gaze. 'Surely you've known her for years and years?'

'Yes, but I haven't seen her for years and years,' Michael said, producing his cigarette case and offering it to her. 'In fact I don't think I've seen her since the end of the war.'

'Oh, there will be a difference, then.' Helen, who was

an attractive woman herself in her mid-forties, smiled at him. 'She's very popular.'

'Is she still at school?'

'Oh no. No ambitions there, to her father's regret, although it has always seemed to us that his hopes have obviously been centred on Gilbert. He is just content for Tansy to marry well and settle down.'

Michael smiled at her through the smoke of his cigarette and Helen looked at him closely before turning her head away, intent on something her neighbour was saying. But her thoughts remained on Michael. She decided that, despite his strong sexual attraction, his mouth looked cruel and his eyes were cold. He was the kind of man capable of causing chaos in the hearts of women susceptible to a certain kind of charm that was inherently sadistic: the type of person who delighted in conquest and then cared little for what he had caught.

Michael rather worried Helen because she had seen the way he looked at Tansy, a much younger, more vulnerable woman. Michael would be very attractive to someone like Tansy who resented the influence of her father yet, at the same time, needed a father-figure. She knew he was a bachelor, a soldier and, instinctively, she knew he was dangerous. For her Tansy and Gilbert were like family, and she didn't want anyone or anything to hurt them.

When she looked up she saw Michael studying her carefully.

'Penny for your thoughts,' he said. 'Anything wrong?'

'Oh nothing,' she replied, laughing a little falsely. 'It's just that sometimes we worry about Tansy, you see, we all love her but one would have thought that she might have done something else before she married – you know, nursing, secretarial, something like that. I imagine

Tansy to be the sort of girl who would like to see the world.'

'Then she should marry the right sort of man,' Michael said with a chuckle, finishing his coffee. 'Someone who likes to see the world too.'

Helen knew then that Michael Garrett was interested in Tansy Blair.

But he was not alone, nor without competition. Young men in business, of about twenty-three or twenty-five, wanted to take her out, and boys of her own age or a little older tried too; but very few of them got past her father. Only those whose credentials were absolutely impeccable had a hope of getting Doctor Blair's blessing and, maybe, Michael Garrett would be one of them? As a soldier he would be used to making strategic moves in order to get his own way. She decided that she didn't like him; she was a little afraid of him and his power.

Just then the company broke up and, in twos and threes, the dinner guests began to stroll towards the door, in the direction of the ballroom from which music could already be heard.

Downstairs there was a cacophony of sound and movement as young people either arrived, or were delivered by parents to the door and, watching them from the top of the stairs, Catherine was reminded of those children's parties she used to give so religiously year after year and how glad she was when, after their thirteenth birthday, they came to an end. After that it was a visit to the cinema in Leeds and tea at the Grand.

The next big event would be their twenty-first. She knew some people had said too much of a fuss was being made of the eighteenth, and yet it was a milestone. Gilbert had been awarded a scholarship and would go to Leeds University in the autumn and Tansy ... well,

Tansy was a woman now and sometimes her mother felt
not only proud of her but anxious and worried too.

Greeting the guests, she was flanked on one side by
Geoffrey and on the other by Gilbert, bespectacled and
studious-looking like his father, obviously ill-at-ease in
his first evening suit. Tansy, however, looked as though
she was quite used to grown-up dances. She wore a long
green taffeta dress with a simple V neckline to show off
the even row of pearls her parents had given her for her
birthday. A striking sash of electrifying colours – black,
red and purple – bound her slim waist and then cascaded
behind her in ribbons, not unlike the plumage of a
peacock. And, like a peacock too, she attracted more
attention than lesser birds, however bright and gay;
every eye in the room seemed riveted on her.

There was no formal reception of the guests, as this
was intended to be a party for young people. For a while
the older dinner guests circulated, danced a few numbers
rather staidly with one another and then either went up
to the bar or left.

Tansy had her first dance with her father, her second
with her brother and her third with Matthew Todd, the
son of the Mayor. She was just finishing the number
with Matthew when Michael Garrett, who had been
hovering on the edge of the circle of dancers constantly
eyeing her, strode across the floor and held out his hand.

'May I, before anyone else claims you?'

He was only just in time because a number of other
young men had bounded towards her with the same
intention and fell back forlornly as Tansy, thanking
Matthew Todd, turned to Michael. Deftly his arms
encircled her waist and he led her back onto the floor so
that they were one of the first couples to begin the
quickstep.

They danced very well together, immediately in tune. Her father had little dancing skill and her brother none at all. Matthew was much taller than she was and had appeared ill-at-ease, and clumsy. But Michael was only a little taller than she and, from the moment the music started, their movements synchronized perfectly.

They didn't exchange a word during the dance and when it finished a number of young men began to hover round Tansy but Michael said at once, without letting go her hand: 'Again?'

Tansy looked uncertain; after all she was the hostess but, without waiting for an answer, Michael pulled her onto the floor and, almost as if it were obeying a signal from him, the band started a slow foxtrot. His arms once more encircled her, though this time more tightly, and he laid his cheek against hers.

Tansy felt nervous and her eyes darted around to see if her father were watching. Michael seemed aware of her tension and murmured in her ear, 'Relax. I told my father to take yours to the bar. There is no one looking.'

'How do you know?' Tansy murmured, acutely sensitive to the touch of his skin against hers.

'I know that your father watches you like a hawk. I saw him at dinner and then my mother told me he seldom lets you out of his sight.'

'He only does it for the best,' Tansy said, feeling suddenly rather silly.

'I can see why he thinks someone is going to snatch you from him,' Michael raised his head and smiled into her eyes, 'but he has to let you go sometime.'

'Sometime,' Tansy murmured, still uncomfortable.

When the dance finished Michael seemed disinclined to let her go; but Jonathan Leggatt claimed her, a rather determined boy who was going to study medicine with Gilbert. He had made several attempts to dance with her already. He too was a hopeless dancer and kept apologizing all through the waltz until he stood heavily on Tansy's foot, which was encased only in a toeless sandal and, involuntarily, she cried out in pain. They stopped dancing at once and she hobbled to the edge of the dance floor while Jonathan hurried by her side apologizing profusely.

'It's quite all right,' Tansy smiled reassuringly at him as she sat down, rubbing her damaged foot. 'Please *don't* worry about it, Jonathan.'

But Jonathan was worried. Tall and gangly, his face was very red and she contrasted him suddenly in her mind with Michael, ten years his senior, it was true; but how differently Michael would have coped with the situation. However, with Michael, an accomplished dancer, it would never have happened.

As she looked up there he was standing just behind Jonathan, one hand in the pocket of his well-cut evening jacket, the other held a cigarette which, with a sardonic smile, he put to his lips as though to say: 'What *can* you expect?'

'Perhaps I could get you something to drink?' Jonathan suggested anxiously.

'Lemonade would be *lovely*,' Tansy said, just to get rid of him and, as he hurried away to the bar, Michael sauntered over to her, casually edging his way past the group of young men who hung about hoping for the next dance.

'Shall I get you a doctor?' he enquired.

'I don't think that's really necessary.' Tansy realized he was joking and, finishing massaging her foot, put on her sandal.

'That's what comes of choosing younger men.' Michael took the chair next to her which had become unexpectedly vacant.

'I didn't choose him, he chose me – besides, he's a friend of my brother's. I could hardly say no.'

'For the rest of the evening I insist that, for safety's sake, you dance only with me. That is, if your foot's all right.'

'Oh I couldn't possibly do that.' Tansy tested her foot by standing upright.

'Why not?'

'It's my party. It would look very rude.'

'You mean someone might tell your father?'

'No I don't,' Tansy snapped at him, feeling annoyed. 'I don't think that at all. But how can I spend the whole evening dancing with one man whom I hardly know?'

'That's not true. I have known you since you were a little girl.'

'Yes, but that's not "knowing". You must be at least ten years older than me. I know that you have always seemed much older, even when I was small.'

'Ah, then you *do* remember me?'

'Of course I remember you, Michael.'

He was looking at her strangely and she suddenly felt rather confused, and a little alarmed by his earnest, steady gaze. He had been looking at her a lot during dinner too, but one thing she knew about Michael Garrett was that he liked women: he was a flirt. She hadn't taken much notice of him and decided it would be prudent not to do so now. As if reading her thoughts Michael said with studied casualness: 'I think a glass of champagne is called for to heal the sore foot. Let's go to the lounge.'

'Jonathan's gone for some lemonade.' Tansy looked around in the direction of the bar for a sight of her former partner.

'You don't want to have anything more to do with that clod-hopping fool, surely?' Michael said acidly. 'He'll probably spill it down your dress,' and, delicately, he took her by the hand and led her away from the crowd, out of the ballroom and into one of the lounges which was half empty. She had actually found walking quite painful and was relieved not to be dancing.

'It's exquisite, by the way,' he said as he helped her into a seat. 'The dress. Surely it's not from Netherwick?'

'It isn't as a matter of fact,' Tansy arranged the skirt carefully over her knees, 'but I don't see why it couldn't be.'

'It couldn't possibly be from Netherwick.' Michael beckoned to a waiter who was on his way to the door and held up a hand.

'Sir?'

'A bottle of your best champagne please, waiter.'

'A whole bottle, sir?' the waiter asked, as if he hadn't heard correctly.

'That's what I said. I assume you have champagne?'

'Of course, sir.'

'Then a bottle of Krug, or Bollinger. Make sure it's a good vintage.'

The waiter hurried off and Tansy lay back thankfully in her chair and studied Michael's face. 'You embarrassed that poor man.'

'My dear, you don't understand; *that's* what waiters are there for. He should know whether he's got champagne and interpret my wishes without question. A bottle indeed! You'd think there was something extraordinary about asking for one: "a *whole* bottle, sir?"'

'This isn't London.'

'I'll say it isn't.' Michael drew a flat silver cigarette-case from his breast pocket and offered it to Tansy who shook her head.

'You don't? Of course you wouldn't.'

Tansy didn't answer but showed by her expression

that she took exception to his remark.

'I'm sorry,' he said, leaning forwards and putting a hand over hers. 'That was *very* rude of me. Uncalled for. You know, Tansy,' he moved nearer to her, his hand still on hers. It seemed rather a natural, brotherly gesture. 'I do like you and we *are* old family friends.'

'There's still no need to be rude,' Tansy said. 'You can say some quite rude things.'

'I know,' he looked contrite. 'I don't mean to, honestly.'

'You also try to belittle me by remarks about my father. Do you think I don't mind the fact that he watches me all the time? I hate it and I have done all I can to rebel against it. Now that I am eighteen it will be much more difficult for him to control me as he used to. I know he only does it out of the best of motives and for my own good, because he loves me. I know he does, but he makes a fool of me.'

'I don't think *anyone* could make a fool of you, Tansy,' Michael said with real warmth and friendliness in his voice. 'You have no idea how attractive you have become, or, rather, perhaps you do if the number of men waiting to dance with you was anything to go by. However, you have a special sort of attraction for me. Your maturity quite amazed me. I would *never* belittle you. Never.'

'That's good to know,' Tansy said briskly, but suddenly a curious kind of happiness swept over her that was like nothing she had ever felt before.

At that moment the champagne arrived in a bucket with two glasses. It was brought by a different waiter who had obviously been called upon to take over because of his expertise in dealing with champagne and awkward customers. With a practised smile at Michael he first presented it to him for his approval and, at a nod from Michael, he deftly eased the cork from the bottle. Without spilling a drop he expertly filled first one glass and then the other. The first one he handed to Tansy, the second to Michael.

'Thank you,' Michael said, taking the bill from the tray and handing the man a note. 'Please keep the change.'

'Thank you, sir,' the waiter said bowing and then, putting the white napkin professionally over the neck of the bottle in the bucket, moved across the room.

'A war veteran if you ask me.' Michael held up the glass towards Tansy.

'How do you mean?'

'He is older, he knows what he is doing. You only get that through experience, Tansy. Happy birthday.'

As he drank from his glass he looked at her over the rim, and she knew that, from now on, her life would be different.

The whirlwind romance between Tansy Blair and Michael Garrett soon became the talk of Netherwick. From the night of her eighteenth birthday, life consisted of being taken to dinners, lunches and parties of all kinds in Michael's snappy red MG in which he'd driven up from his barracks near London.

The day after the party, from which he had taken her home, Michael had called her and suggested a date for that night. From then on they saw each other every day until one afternoon as she was waiting to go out her father appeared in the hall.

'Will you come into my study for a moment, Tansy?'

'I'm just waiting for Michael, Daddy.'

'I know that, but I'd like a word with you first, dear.'

She had no option but to follow him into his study and when he asked her to sit she said she would prefer to stand.

Absent-mindedly, it seemed, her father began to fill his pipe and, as she would not sit, he remained standing in front of the fire which roared up the chimney. How well Tansy knew this slow, thoughtful procedure, refined by her father over the years when he was playing for time. It could precede pleasant or unpleasant news, a statement or merely an item of information, important or unimportant. It could be a gentle reprimand, or praise for something she had done at school when she was smaller but, whatever the occasion, ever since she was little she could recall her father slowly, carefully, filling the bowl of his pipe with tobacco, pressing it down with his short stubby forefinger and then lighting it, waiting for it to draw and expelling the first mouthful of smoke in the air before starting to speak.

So she knew now that, Michael or no Michael, she had to wait. 'Now, Tansy,' her father said at last, the ritual complete, the first puff spiralling upwards. 'What is this I hear about Michael Garrett?'

'What about Michael, Daddy?' She shifted from one foot to the other on her booted feet because it was cold even in his warm study. But she was also nervous, a little apprehensive.

'I hear you are seeing him every day. That's a *lot*, Tansy.'

'It's only for a short time, Daddy. His leave finishes next week.'

'Nevertheless, my dear, have you asked yourself whether or not it's a good thing to do?'

'I don't see why not.'

'Michael is *much* older than you are.'

'I know. We're not going to get *married*, Daddy.'

'Oh I'm glad to hear that,' her father said with a note of irony in his voice. 'Just friends?'

'What else?' Tansy glanced anxiously at the clock on

the mantelpiece, her ears attuned for the sound of the front door bell. 'We have known Michael and his family all our lives.'

'I know that, Tansy.' Her father kept his tone quiet and agreeable. 'But every day, for nearly a week, is quite often, is it not?'

'Michael hardly knows anyone here. He has been away for such a long time.'

'But what do you do when you go out, Tansy?'

For the first time a blush flared on her cheeks and she resented her father's implied suggestion.

'We eat at restaurants, we go to the cinema. Last night we went to a dance. Today we're going for a drive.'

'I would be very glad if you told Michael, Tansy, that after today you can't go on seeing him every day.'

'Why not, Daddy?'

'Because it is not seemly. Your mother tells me that people are already talking about it. Michael has a very distinctive car which is seen, with you in it, all over the place. I can't have it, Tansy. I can't have you losing your reputation.'

'That's a *ridiculous* thing to say, Daddy!' Tansy said angrily, stamping her feet, aware of how long ago it was since she had dared to argue with her father. 'Michael behaves perfectly correctly towards me. I am just a friend. Someone he likes to go out with. I don't know what you're thinking, but he is very bored in Netherwick.'

'Oh, is he?'

'Yes,' she thrust her chin defiantly in the air, 'like Jeremy and Edward. He has never liked the place. He finds it insular. He served in the war and he travelled all over the world.'

'I know that, my dear, and I *like* Michael and his family. Please, please, don't misunderstand me. However, I think you are too young to be seen constantly in the company of a much older man. It is quite natural if people talk and assume what they do.'

'What do they assume, Daddy?' Tansy's eyes narrowed.

'They *assume* that you must feel something for each other or else you wouldn't spend so much time together. Even your mother is worried by the implication and I, for one, think you are too young and Michael too old to be alone together all the time. If he wants to see you again before he goes ask him here for dinner. Tomorrow if you please. I'd like a talk with that young man.'

'Oh please, Daddy, *no*!' Tansy suddenly lost control of herself and rushed over to her father clawing at his arm. 'You make such a fool of me. The first time he talked to me at my party Michael knew about you.'

'What about me?' her father said, his pipe, again by time-honoured procedure, now quite cold again.

'That you kept your eye on me. That you watched me constantly. He said everyone knew about it.'

'I am not ashamed of it,' Doctor Blair said loftily, 'and I wonder that a man from a family like his is not aware of how we feel. I'm sure *his* father would protect a daughter if he had one; especially if she were a girl of your age. There was a daughter, but she died very young. No, Tansy, I want this to be quite clear, to you and to Michael, and I want him *here* to dinner tomorrow night and let him know exactly what I think.'

'Of course I shan't go,' Michael said, sitting in the front seat of his car, his arm casually around her. As she didn't reply he looked at her. 'Do you mind?'

'I just think it will cause a row if you don't, but I do know how you feel. *I* feel awful.' Tansy had a rug on her knee, but her cheeks were blue with cold. They had gone up through the woods to Storiths and had parked in a clearing from where they could look directly onto Bolton Abbey, and the gentle curve round that ancient building made by the River Wharfe below them.

'If you father starts dictating to us now, Tansy, our relationship will never recover. I'm *not* going to be dressed down like a schoolboy merely because I want to see his daughter every day.'

'It's because you're *not* a schoolboy that he wants to see you.' Tansy rubbed her hands together and blew into them to try and keep out the cold. Beyond the woods, on either side of the river the blue sky tinged with pink and white seemed to rise above them like a canopy, while birds swooped gracefully in and out of the trees, down to the ground and up again, in search of food left by walkers on the river bank.

Tansy felt Michael's mouth upon her cheek as his arm tightened around her shoulder. She turned her face towards him and he kissed her lips gently at first and then more passionately with the expertise of a practised lover. She knew that he wanted her but that he would not force her; not only through fear of her father, but also because he had already told her that his feeling for her was special.

'I love you,' Michael said as their lips parted, and he held her face tightly between his hands, bringing it close to his and looking into her eyes. 'I have never loved a woman as I love you.'

'Michael,' Tansy said, feeling both exultation and despair because of what he had said. 'Michael, what shall we do?'

'I'm going to go back to London,' Michael said firmly after a moment or two, still gazing at her. 'I don't want your father to threaten us. I'm not going to risk a dressing down by him. Besides, my love . . .' he gripped her hand, almost crushing it as if to convey the power and strength of his emotions, 'I don't think I can last out much longer like this. You know how I feel about you, and I think I should go away for a while and reflect about what has happened between us in such a short time. And maybe you should reflect too, and decide how you feel about me and what you want to do.'

Tansy nodded. She felt confidence in him. He was, after all, so wise, so mature, such a match for her father.

The following day Michael Garrett left Netherwick to spend the rest of his leave in London. But if Tansy's mind was in a turmoil, his was too. He saw himself as a sophisticated man of the world who liked living dangerously; he liked fast women and fast cars. He never in his life had dreamt that he would fall in love with a teenager, a virgin with no experience who had scarcely ever left her little home town in the Yorkshire Dales, except for trips to the sea. He was at home in Mayfair, Soho and knew all the drinking clubs and low dives in the West End. Tansy had never even been to London, or further south than Sheffield where her Aunt Deidre lived, her mother's elder sister.

Yet it was not the innocence or inexperience of Tansy that Michael fell in love with; they were disadvantages to a man who had had mistresses in Cairo, Alexandria and Athens as well as London. He had fallen in love with Tansy on the night of her eighteenth birthday party when she came into the room with her parents and her brother wearing her bright green taffeta dress with its swirling sash. She'd paused and looked about her, poised and at ease, like a queen, yet brimming with life and vitality, her brown yellow-flecked eyes alight with expectation, her fair curls tossing about on her head. This was Tansy Blair who was eighteen yet who could pass for twenty-three or -four. She was tall and slim and, although she was just out of school, she had the air of a woman of the world.

Geoffrey Blair received the news that Michael had gone with apparent equanimity. Yet, in his heart he rejoiced that what had seemed a dangerous affair had been snuffed out, possibly by his action in inviting Michael to dinner. He liked the Garretts but he didn't want his daughter to marry a soldier, to wander around the world leaving him, possibly, for years at a time. If she married young he would rather it were to someone who had a good job or a career, who lived in Netherwick and who wanted to stay there.

With that he put the whole business out of his mind, little realizing how much he was deceiving himself or how far the affair between his daughter and his friend's son had progressed in a very short time.

'Darling Tansy,' (Michael wrote a few weeks later) 'I have decided to leave the army. It is nothing to do with you, although knowing you has influenced it indirectly. I have been thinking along these lines for some time. Some people like the life of an army wife but I do not think you would be one. I feel I shall be sent abroad again, possibly to the Far East, and that will take me too far away from you. Having just got to know you I can't bear the thought of being so far away from you. Tell me, if I get forty-eight hours' leave and come up to Leeds, can you meet me there without telling your father?'

Tansy put down the letter and gazed out of the window of her bedroom which looked over the town of Netherwick and the surrounding hills. It was a view familiar to her from her earliest memories when she had shared this room with her twin. They were separated when they were about five and Gilbert went to the room along the hall, which had been Edward's, and which was still his.

Gilbert's room had a view over the garden and the gardens of the other houses in the road; it was the kind of quiet scholarly ambience that suited Gilbert.

But Tansy loved the grey slate roofs and the smoke that curled up from the chimneys, the haze in summertime and the mist in winter. All this was timeless, familiar. All this was a reminder of a safe and secure childhood; a happy one basking in the love of her mother and father, her grandmother and numerous friends.

Tansy knew that ever since she met Michael there was a threat that all this would change. Michael represented excitement, even danger; it was like catapulting one's life into a void with a person one scarcely knew, to experiences and sensations that one could only guess at.

Yet ever since she'd met Michael he had obsessed her; his image seemed constantly in front of her mind dominating her thoughts and, sometimes, seeming to control her actions. Even before he had told her he loved her she knew that, whatever happened, her girlhood was over.

After Michael had gone, no one mentioned his name again. It was as though there was a conspiracy between her parents, an almost child-like form of delusion that would banish him from Tansy's mind if no one spoke of him.

But his letters had begun to arrive almost at once and, aware of her parents' true feelings, Tansy asked Doreen the maid who was her friend to slip away letters for her in her pocket and give them to her when the family were not around. She didn't want to break the spell Michael had cast over her.

Tansy leaned on the window sill, head in her hands. It was mid-morning and the citizens of Netherwick were going about their business: in the shops, factories, mills, offices, in the hospital, in her father's surgery. Yet here she was with time on her hands. All her friends had got jobs and she knew that people wondered why she hadn't. But she was in love. All she had was time on her hands; time spent waiting for Michael.

But to go to *Leeds* for a secret assignation. That was something else. What did he meant, forty-eight hours? Did he mean . . . She took a deep breath, raised her arms and stretched. Had the time come already for that great, that momentous decision?

Tansy's mother said to her later that day, 'I don't know what's the matter with you lately. You're getting terribly absent-minded.'

'Sorry, Mother,' Tansy said. 'What did I do now, or not do?'

'You forgot your grandmother's birthday.'

'I didn't,' Tansy said indignantly, sitting on the kitchen table, a mug of coffee in her hands. 'It's tomorrow.'

'Oh, I thought you'd forgotten. You usually mention it and you hadn't.'

'I've a card and a present for Gran upstairs. I bought her a pair of gloves in the market. Is she coming here or are we going to her?'

'She's coming for tea. But, seriously, Tansy you *are* very absent-minded lately. You're always mooning about the place. I can't understand a young girl with nothing to do. I do think it's time you looked for a job, anything, just to keep you occupied.'

'I thought I would try and get a job in Leeds, Mother.' Tansy looked out of the window so as to avoid her mother seeing the expression in her eyes.

'*Leeds*?' her mother said with a gasp. 'Why Leeds?'

'I've hardly ever been there. I've hardly ever been away from Netherwick, Mother. I've been too protected. I thought I could get a better job in Leeds with better money. As a matter of fact I'm going to go up next week and see one or two of the employment agencies. I want to know what there is on offer for a girl without any qualifications.'

'Nowt I should think,' her mother said, not attempting to hide her displeasure. 'Leeds . . . your father won't be pleased at all.'

She had imagined he would be in uniform. She thought his stocky, powerful figure would look very good in khaki. But he was wearing cavalry twill trousers and a blazer, crisp white shirt and a crested tie. He sat on one of the benches in an alcove, his knees crossed, cigarette in one hand, flicking through the pages of a magazine. He looked very worldly, sophisticated, dangerous . . . Tansy stood for a while in the doorway looking at him and, then, as she began to walk towards him he saw her and, throwing down the magazine, sprang to his feet tossing his half-smoked cigarette into an ash tray.

'Tansy,' he cried, coming to her, arms outstretched and, as she felt his cheek against hers, she remembered their first dance together, their first intimate contact. In many ways it had been like the loss of innocence.

He held her away from him and then drew her face towards his as if to kiss her mouth, but she looked around and shook her head.

'Of course,' Michael nodded, smiling. 'Your father.'

'Oh, Michael, don't be wicked,' she said playfully, tapping his wrist. 'You take the micky the whole time.'

'It's true though, isn't it? I bet you didn't tell him you were coming here?'

'I said I was going into Leeds, but not to meet you. I'm *supposed* to be looking for a job.'

'A job?' Michael looked puzzled.

'My mother says I must get a job. She says I haven't enough to do. She's never stopped working in her life and she doesn't like idle hands.'

'I see.' Michael seemed preoccupied and looked at his watch. 'Let's have lunch then we can decide how to spend the rest of our time. I've an awful lot to tell you.'

Over lunch in a corner of the dining room at the Grand, Tansy felt as if they had never been apart. She had rather been dreading their first meeting after their separation, but then there had been the letters. It was true that letters did bring people together, and she remembered how Emily had told her about the long correspondence with Edward. She felt she knew Michael better now than she had a few weeks ago and that their intimacy had increased. She knew now, without any doubt, that she was in love.

'Why didn't you want to come to Netherwick?' Tansy asked as he returned the menu to the waiter after ordering their meal.

'I thought it would be more fun like this,' he said, eyes shining. 'Don't you?'

'Yes.' She gazed at him and her expression told him everything.

She wore a blue cotton dress under a lightweight spring coat of white lambswool and to him she looked the very epitome of innocence and desirability. It was that fascinating combination of naiveté and self-assurance that had first captivated him. He knew that other people in the dining room were looking at them and he was proud of the impression he knew they made: two young people in love, with the whole world before them.

'What was it you've got to tell me?' Tansy asked, as the wine waiter presented a bottle to Michael for his inspection. He nodded and, as the waiter poured a small amount into his glass, he sipped it and pronounced it first class. The waiter filled Tansy's glass before moving back to Michael.

'This is very grand,' Tansy said, leaning excitedly towards him. 'I've only ever had tea in the Grand. Never lunch.'

'How about dinner?' he said, smiling at her.

'No, I have to go home.'

'You *what*?' Michael had been in the act of lighting a fresh cigarette and he looked at her with an expression of such dismay that it seemed to freeze her heart.

'Michael,' Tansy said resting her hand in his, 'of *course* I have to go back. I can't stay *here*.'

Michael, looking angry, said nothing and impulsively drained all the wine in his glass at a gulp.

'I don't know what you thought, Michael,' Tansy continued in a low voice. 'But meeting you here doesn't mean . . . I'm not *that* sort of girl,' she said and, releasing his hand, stared at him.

'I didn't suggest for a moment that you were,' Michael's expression softened. 'You completely mis-understood me. I love you, Tansy. I told you I loved you at the time of your birthday. I am in love with you. Love at first sight. I haven't been able to get you out of my mind.'

'Nor me you,' Tansy said ungrammatically, staring at him with frank adoration.

'I wanted to meet you here and not at Netherwick because I can't bear the stifling attitude of both our families – mine as well as yours. I can't bear to think of going out with you with the whole town knowing and talking about it.'

'I know what you mean.' Tansy stuck her spoon into the grapefruit they had ordered as first course. 'Your little MG . . .'

'Exactly, Tansy.' Michael put down his spoon and joined his hands on the table. 'I am twenty-nine. I have been in the army for eleven years. This year I am not going to renew my commission. I want to leave the army and travel. How . . . how does that strike you, Tansy?'

'Travel?' she looked up at him. 'Travel where?'

'I went to Australia just after the war. I liked it a lot. There is a lot of opportunity there for business.'

'What sort of business?'

'Any business. But I want to get into business before I'm too old to learn the ropes. I'm used to giving orders, taking command.'

'Maybe your father . . .'

'I want to have *nothing* to do with my father's business. I am not interested in the products they make. Besides, Bob is well in control there. I want to start afresh, Tansy . . . a new life, and I want to start it with you. I'm asking you to marry me and come with me because I know that you are the woman I want in my life. I have no doubt of that at all.'

Tansy had known he would propose; but had not thought it would happen yet, not in a crowded dining room at lunch-time in Leeds. In her fantasies she had imagined they might be walking on the moors or sitting in the front seat of his MG, the wind blowing in their faces. She had a very girlish romantic idea of what proposals and marriage were about because she had spent much of the last few weeks dreaming about it.

'I know it's very sudden,' Michael said, misinterpreting her silence, the expression on her face. 'But I'm that sort of person. I'm very impulsive; however, about you I have not been impulsive. I know.'

'You haven't known me long,' Tansy said.

'I have. I've known you all my life. When I saw you I knew that I'd been waiting for you to grow up . . . really,

Tansy, don't look at me like that.'

She had a smile on her lips as though she couldn't take him seriously. 'I don't know what to say,' she said at last.

'But you do *love* me, don't you?'

He said the word so loudly that heads were turned and Tansy, blushing, lowered her head and hissed across the table: 'Everyone's listening.'

'Tansy, you're making it very hard for me,' Michael hissed back.

'Then let's wait until after we've had our lunch,' Tansy said, prosaically and resumed the dissection of her half grapefruit. 'Tell me about the army.'

There was not much Michael could think of to tell her about the army. His mouth felt dry, the lunch unappetizing. He had chosen the moment badly. He felt wounded, put in his place by a slip of a girl who seemed to find his emotions amusing. Yet he had never proposed marriage to anyone in his life. He, a man of the world, of experience, of knowing the ways of women, had bungled.

After a while, as if thinking a change of subject might help, Tansy said: 'Jeremy is going to have an operation, in London.'

'Oh, really?' Michael mopped his lips and took a fresh sip of wine. 'You like him, don't you?'

'Of course I like him! He's my brother. But he's been ill ever since he came back from the Far East. There's a benign tumour sitting on his brain and they are going to remove it.'

'How ghastly,' Michael said, grimacing.

'It *sounds* ghastly, but if the operation is successful Jeremy will be able to lead a normal life. Part of his brain is not functioning properly because of the tumour. He can't walk properly, has bad headaches and periods of forgetfulness.'

'Isn't it a risky thing?'

'He wants to take the risk. He feels it is worth taking.'

'Does Emily?'

'She seems to. We don't see Emily much. Dad won't have her in the house. I see her when I can because I like her.'

'And does Jeremy accept that?' Michael nearly whistled with incredulity. 'His father's attitude?'

'He seems to.' Tansy too looked puzzled. 'I didn't expect he would; but he seems awfully pleased to see Dad again. Dad hasn't actually *said* he won't have Emily, but he never invites her and Jeremy never asks if he can bring her. I don't think they ever talk about her. It's a strange situation; but they seem to understand each other.'

The change of subject did break the ice and, by the time lunch was finished and they were settled in a corner of the lounge, away from prying eyes and listening ears, with a tray of coffee in front of them, Michael felt at ease again with Tansy and put his hand over hers. 'I was asking you to marry me.'

'I know.'

'You were making it very dificult for me.'

'I wasn't.' Impulsively she bent to kiss the back of his hand. 'I thought you would ask me, but not just yet. I don't think I'm really ready, Michael.'

'Then when will you be?'

'I don't know. I don't feel I want to leave Netherwick or my family. I don't know if I'd really like Australia. I've been thinking about what you said. I think if you were coming home to work in your family business it would make all the difference to how I felt.'

'Oh, you just want me to be like everyone else?' Michael's voice was scornful. 'Nine to five, golf at weekends, drinks with the boys afterwards?'

'Yes,' Tansy said, staring at him. 'That's exactly what I do want. It's the kind of life I like. And I know it's what my parents want. We want the same thing. It may be boring to you; but I could never leave Netherwick. I don't think you understand, Michael, just how much it means to me.'

Chapter 13

Jeremy sat rather nervously in the foyer of the publishing house feeling both out of place and slightly uncomfortable in the good suit that his father had insisted on buying him for this important interview. It was difficult to remember now that, before the war, Jeremy Blair was considered a bit of a dandy, a snappy dresser who worked in a bank, played cricket for his club, drove a fast car and had a lot of friends of both sexes.

Yes, a great deal had happened since then. For so long he had been used to casual trousers and a jacket or sweater that his new suit seemed strange, and he fiddled uncomfortably with the knot of his tie as if it might choke him.

The exterior of the publishing house was very smart, the interior even smarter; glass, chrome, copies of books by successful authors and a very superior receptionist, who had taken his name, sitting at a desk. She was so superior that he had to repeat it twice before she remembered it, thus seeking to emphasize his insignificance in the grand world of the bestseller, of which this particular company had quite a few.

'Mrs Hornsby will not keep you waiting long Mr, er,' the receptionist looked at her notepad to check the name, 'Norton.'

'That's all right,' Jeremy said, hands straying to the knot of his tie again. 'I know I'm early.'

'Are you new to London, Mr Norton?' the receptionist said with a patronizing smile.

'No I'm not,' Jeremy replied. 'I lived here before the war and I've recently taken up residence again.'

'How interesting,' the receptionist said, but her tone of voice sounded insincere. Jeremy felt he disliked her very much and turned his mind, instead, to Mrs Hornsby, wondering what she would be like.

It had been a very exciting moment when he received her letter:

Dear Mr Norton,

A Shepherd in the Hills

I have now had a chance to look at this manuscript which you kindly submitted to us and I am very pleased to tell you that I agree with our outside readers who have praised it highly. Naturally it reminded us of Richard Hilary's *The Last Enemy* although, thankfully, you have been spared the fate that eventually befell him.

I don't want to raise your hopes too highly, as I am not yet in a position to make an offer of publication, but if you could spare the time I wonder if you would like to discuss the manuscript with me over lunch on 14 March? I look forward to hearing from you.

(signed) J. R. Hornsby (Mrs)

That, at the time, was one of the great days of Jeremy's life. Coming after months of uncertainty and pain following his operation, it had been just the tonic, not only that he needed, but that the doctors had promised him.

Suddenly he looked up as an attractive young woman appeared in the reception and smiled at him.

'Mr Norton?'

'Mrs Hornsby?' He stood up, not yet able to move without the aid of his stick which he saw the young woman glance at instinctively, the familiar expression of pity in her eyes he so hated.

'No, I'm Jill Hornsby's secretary. She wondered if you'd like to have a chat in her office before going out to lunch? There *is* a lift,' she said looking again at his stick.

Jeremy followed her out of the reception into the hall where people were just emerging from the lift on their way to lunch.

The got into the lift and stood smiling awkwardly at each other as it took them to the top floor of the building in Mayfair which had once been someone's substantial town house.

'Smart offices you've got,' Jeremy said as they walked along the corridor before stopping at a door with a nameplate on it.

'This house used to belong to Lord Hargreaves,' the girl said. 'The family emigrated to Canada just before the war.'

'How wise,' Jeremy replied acidly as the secretary opened a door and stood back to admit him into a room with a pretty view of Berkeley Square, glimpsed at the end of the street.

'Mr Norton, Jill,' the girl said, and closed the door behind her. Jeremy held out his hand as a woman of about his age looked up, then, removing her glasses, rose from her chair.

'How do you do Mr . . .' the woman stopped and Jeremy clapsed her hand and held it.

'Jill,' he said. 'Jill Dashwood.'

'*Jeremy*,' Jill gasped. 'I simply *don't* believe it.'

'We've both aged a bit,' Jeremy said with a chuckle that broke the tension between them. 'If my arithmetic is right it's about twelve years since we became engaged . . . an engagement, incidentally, which has never been officially broken off.'

'Oh, *Jeremy*,' Jill said, smiling with relief and pulling

him down on to a sofa by the side of her desk. 'You, the author of *A Shepherd in the Hills*! The very *last* person I expected.'

'Didn't my war experience give you a clue?' he said wryly, reaching in his pocket for a cigarette.

'Buy why did you use a pseudonym?' Jill realized that they were still tightly holding hands.

'Everyone said it was the best thing. I don't know why.' Jeremy shrugged. 'Maybe a bit too personal, because of Dad. There was quite a lot of trouble when I married Emily. She was Edward's wife.'

'Oh dear, you must tell me *all* about it over lunch.' Jill glanced at her watch.

'And you must tell me all about *you*!' Jeremy rose slowly and for a long time he stood gazing down at her, as if recalling the past.

The restaurant was a small, fashionable place not far from Berkeley Square, the sort of place where publishers, literary agents and other luminaries of the arts world like to congregate. Jill obviously ate there a lot and was recognized by the manager who personally conducted her to a table in the corner.

Jill was not very tall but, as she had been when he first knew her, she was still a smart, well-groomed woman, attractive rather than beautiful. She had been Jill Dashwood and her father had been killed in Spain where he had been a war correspondent. The family seemed to have had an unusual background and Jeremy thought she was different when he first met her. She was a pilot officer in the WAAF and they had a very passionate love affair during their brief engagement. After he went to Singapore he never heard from her again. Eventually he learned that she'd married another flier and, during lunch, he asked what had become of him.

'Divorce, I'm afraid,' Jill said off-handedly, tossing back her thick, well-cut auburn hair which she'd worn in a wartime roll when he first met her. Otherwise he couldn't remember very much about her because his memory of her became confused with other women and, of course, since then there had been his illness and Emily. 'It was a wartime marriage; but it survived to the peace. We only got divorced in 1950.'

'Do you have any children?'

'Two, two girls, both at boarding school. Tim, my ex-husband, and I had a very civilized divorce and he left me the house we'd lived in in St John's Wood. You must come and visit it, Jeremy.'

'I'd like that,' Jeremy said sincerely.

'With Emily of course,' Jill added. 'Is she with you in London? I gather you are living in London from your address?'

'I had a brain operation nearly a year ago,' Jeremy said. 'I came to London for the op and stayed for treatment.'

'I gather it was a success?' Jill was very matter-of-fact about the whole thing, which Jeremy liked.

'Almost totally, except for my legs. It was a benign tumour pressing on my brain. They felt they had progressed enough in brain surgery to do something about it. It had an immediate effect on my memory, awful headaches and periods of depression and so on; but I still don't walk too well and may have to keep the old stick for the rest of my life.'

'It looks rather attractive, actually,' Jill said with an admiring smile. 'Distinctly Byronic. I noticed it almost before I noticed who you were.'

She looked at him in a strange kind of way and he realized that they still liked each other.

He was very glad indeed that he'd met her again.

They enjoyed lunch, a mutual exchange of reminiscences and the fact that they would be working together.

'Of course we'll take the book,' she told him.

'But you said in your letter . . .'

'The power is mine.' She gave him a curt, professional smile. 'It's our way of hedging our bets. We like to meet prospective authors before we take them on. If you had been unpromotable I might have decided not to. You know, someone who only had one book in him and could be a bit of a pest. There are some people like that. But you're going to make it.

'Won't Emily be pleased?' she added, looking at him.

Emily read the letter from Jeremy telling her not only that his book was to be published, but that the publisher was his old friend and former fiancée Jill Dashwood, whom Emily had met the time Jeremy got his medal.

Of course she remembered Jill Dashwood: cool, composed, elegant and very sexy in her WAAF uniform. Emily was then married to Edward; but it was not Edward she had loved, but Jeremy. She, however, was not Jeremy's type and he had never pretended she was. She was the one who had pretended; but then when she saw Jill, she knew immediately that she was Jeremy's type; that they went together as she, Emily, and Jeremy never had.

Emily studied the letter for a long time before she put it on the table and then she got up and glanced at the clock. Time for tea.

Fern had been sent to school in Netherwick because she was a bright child and needed proper schooling. She stayed with her grandparents because she was, after all, Geoffrey's granddaughter and all was forgiven. But Emily, personally, had not been forgiven or her deed forgotten. She agreed to the arrangement because it would have been unfair to Fern not to; but it had all been arranged by Jeremy and she had not yet been asked to the house. It was as though she didn't exist and one day, she knew, she would lose her daughter.

Somehow, now, everyone seemed to accept it, even she. It was the price she had to pay for doing something Geoffrey Blair didn't think she should have done. It was the woman who took the blame, who suffered.

Geoffrey had also agreed to pay for Mark to be sent to boarding school, much against his own wish. He was a country boy who loved the outdoors, and when Jeremy gave up shepherding Mark would have liked to take over his stepfather's job. It was then that Geoffrey had stepped in with his offer and, at the same time, Emily's school, rather than lose its excellent headteacher who was so much better qualified than they had a right to expect, offered her a house without waiting for the former headteacher to die and vacate hers.

Getting her solitary tea and eating it, Emily knew that she had cause for gratitude rather than complaint. Jeremy's operation had been seventy per cent successful. Another, in a year or two's time, might cure him completely, so advanced were the techniques of the brain surgeons, largely thanks to the lessons learned from the war. Fern and Mark had both been able to go to good schools because of Jeremy's reconciliation with his father, who had also given him an allowance which had enabled him to find a flat in Bloomsbury not far from the hospital where he attended daily physiotherapy sessions. His progress had been swift due to his renewed appetite for life, his unexpected happiness at being back in the big city.

Jeremy had wanted Emily to join him; but Cragbeck had become a way of life to her and she enjoyed being its schoolmistress. She felt she had to think of her own life as well as Jeremy's because she was convinced that, one day, he would want to return to Cragbeck and write. If Jeremy was the man she thought he was he needed to return here, and she needed to stay so that she could support him when he did.

Yet, somehow, the news about Jill Dashwood, now divorced and the mother of two children, caused her disquiet. She vividly remembered Jill and wondered if she'd changed. Jill was a factor that she could not possibly have known about or considerd when she decided to stay in Cragbeck rather than be with Jeremy in London.

Over her tea Emily re-read the letter and then, glancing again at the clock which governed her day, she got out a pile of exercise books and began to correct the prep of her charges, some of whom might, thanks to her, well be good enough to qualify one day for grammar school. She decided to put Jill Dashwood firmly out of her mind.

The following day was a Saturday and Emily had an appointment in Netherwick with the dentist. One of the pleasures in visiting the dentist, in fact her only one, was the knowledge that she would see Tansy with whom she kept in touch.

Reacting to the promptings of her family Tansy now worked as a receptionist for Robert Smiles who had a substantial dental practice in Netherwick. In a way it was a very good job for Tansy who had no qualifications other than a rather mediocre School Certificate. Yet she had charm and a pleasant, smiling manner which particularly endeared her to Mr Smiles' patients, most of whom were used to the rather bad-tempered manner of the woman who had been Tansy's predecessor.

Having decided to work, Tansy had taken to her job with zest. She was also learning to type so that she could help out with the paperwork engendered by the requirements of the National Health Service. She introduced a personal touch to the waiting room, decorating it with flowers and pictures and ensuring that the chairs were comfortable and the magazines not too out of date. Everyone liked her. People actually looked forward to going to the dentist to see Tansy, but some thought that she was capable of better things. She was too much under the thumb of her father who prevented her from expressing herself fully.

Tansy and Emily had become close in the past year because Jeremy's departure for London and his operation coincided with the rupture of Tansy's romance with Michael Garrett. The abruptness of its termination had amazed Emily merely, it seemed, because Tansy had preferred life in Netherwick as a married woman rather than somewhere far from home, like Australia.

Emily, twice married, experienced, warm-hearted and sympathetic was a far better confidant than any of Tansy's girlfriends, certainly than her own mother. Emily would listen to Tansy, help to try and console her; but the gist of her opinion was simple: Michael was too old for her, too peripatetic, too set in his ways and demanding. Michael Garrett would never have done as a husband for her. She was well rid of him.

Emily's appointment with Mr Smiles was at twelve, and afterwards she and Tansy went to a local café to lunch together as they usually did after Emily's treatment.

'How was it today?' Tansy enquired, looking hungrily at the menu.

'He's nearly finished,' Emily said, tenderly feeling her mouth. 'I think I'll just have soup.'

'I'm *starving*.' Tansy leaned enthusiastically across the table. 'Any news?'

'News? What news?' Emily asked, smiling.

'There's always *news*,' Tansy replied.

'There's good news from Jeremy,' Emily, a note of caution in her voice, drew the much-read letter from her handbag. 'He's going to have his book published.'

'Oh, I can't *believe* it,' Tansy cried, brushing her hair back from her head and reaching for the letter. 'May I see?'

'Of course.' Emily handed her the letter. 'A lot of it's personal, but I don't mind you reading it.'

'Oh,' Tansy said, abashed, handing back the letter, 'I thought it was from the publisher.'

'No, read it,' Emily insisted. 'It's quite a remarkable coincidence really. You won't remember, you were too small but, before he went to Singapore, Jeremy was engaged to a girl called Jill Dashwood. She was very pretty, naturally, and also in the WAAF. However, after Jeremy went missing she met someone else and eventually married him.'

'Oh,' Tansy said trying to take the news in. 'What is the connection with his book?'

'The coincidence is,' Emily replied, 'that Jill, now divorced, happens to be an editor at the publishing house where Jeremy sent his manuscript. He knew absolutely nothing about that, beforehand, of course.

'Jill didn't know it was Jeremy because he submitted the manuscript under a pseudonym, but she had good reports from her readers and decided to read it herself. *Then* she wanted to meet this unknown author . . .'

'Well . . .' Tansy rapidly scanned the letter. 'How exciting.' She handed the letter back to Emily, much of it unread. 'Do you think she would have taken it if she hadn't known him?'

'She told him she would; but she wanted to meet him before making up her mind. She was amazed when she knew it was Jeremy. She'd changed her name too, through marriage. Jeremy talks in his letter about settling permanently in London. I don't know if you read that bit.' Emily started on her soup while Tansy tackled a huge plate of sausages and chips. 'I don't think I'd like that.'

'Really, you like Cragbeck as much as that?'

'I love it,' Emily said. 'And I love my school.'

'I would have thought with Daddy and Mummy being so horrible you would be glad to get away.'

'Oh they're not *horrible*,' Emily said. 'They completely ignore me, and that's not "horrible". They have done a lot for Jeremy and my children. I can't complain; but I don't want to leave Cragbeck and go to live in London again. That I know for sure. Besides I'm also sure that one day Jeremy will want to come back. He loves the place, but is temporarily dazzled by the bright lights.'

'Maybe Jeremy *will* be a famous author?' Tansy wondered.

'Maybe he will,' Emily's tone was laconic. 'Jill apparently is keen to tutor him. She regards him as a find, a feather in her cap.'

Emily's voice suddenly faltered and Tansy put down her knife and fork on her now empty plate, joined her hands on the table and looked at her steadily. 'You don't actually *like* Jill, do you?'

'It would be very unfair to say I positively disliked her.' Emily blushed faintly. 'I am very grateful to her for what she is doing, and can do, for Jeremy. It is just the lift he needs; but she is or was, exceptionally pretty and she is divorced. I would not be human if I didn't feel a little apprehensive, a little jealous. I'm sure her looks haven't deteriorated in the last ten years or so and she *was* very attractive. Jeremy's kind of woman.'

'You're attractive too,' Tansy said stubbornly.

'In a different way, perhaps.' Emily immediately felt self-conscious. 'But I let myself go, and I know that I could never touch Jill. If it's the kind of life that Jeremy wants . . . well, I'm not sure what I should do, or what I can do. I'm a fatalist, I expect.'

'But Jeremy loves *you*. He quarrelled with Daddy for you. He left home for you . . .'

'Yes, but that was some time ago. He has since resumed his relationship with his father which, of course, I'm very pleased about for him; but the last year has put a strain on our marriage. I also think Jeremy resents me not going to London to look after him.'

'Oh, I'm sure he doesn't,' Tansy protested.

'He says as much in the letter. I think you skimmed over that bit. He feels I could have tried to get a job in London. I could have easily, of course, and better paid, more responsibility.'

'*Go* then,' Tansy urged, 'and don't let him fall into the clutches of the dreaded Jill.'

'I can't, and I don't want to,' Emily said firmly. 'I am nearly forty and I know what I want to do with my life. I want to make Cragbeck village school my life. If I can I would like to buy my own house or cottage and spend the rest of my life there. I love it and my children love it. My husband loves it too and, once he has got over the glamour and excitement of London, I feel he will come back to Cragbeck and realize where his real roots are.'

Tansy had her doubts about the wisdom of what Emily had said. She felt rather sad as she wandered slowly back to the surgery where Mr Smiles' partner saw patients in the afternoon. Tansy worked alternate Saturdays, but she didn't mind. If she worked a Saturday she had Monday off and then she went into Leeds or Bradford, shopping with her mother or grandmother. Sometimes they stayed until evening and took Gilbert out to dinner as he was now in his first year of studies as a medical student and lived in hall. Usually he came home for the weekends so that he could report to his father, who took his usual keen interest in everything his son did.

These had been happy years for Geoffrey Blair, years that had seen the fulfilment of two of his ambitions, and his state of mind was reflected in his health. He had been reconciled with his elder son and seen his younger go to medical school and, although he still had days when melancholy confined him to his study, on the whole there were fewer of them, and his family were grateful for this.

But Emily was a problem, at least to Tansy who was very fond of her sister-in-law. She had never got over the feeling that she was, at least partly, responsible for what had happened to her. One could never really rid oneself of guilt, Tansy thought, opening the surgery door and then she stopped, her heart literally missing a beat, for sitting in one of the chairs reading a magazine was Michael Garrett. She hadn't seen him since they had parted on rather bad terms after lunch at the Grand over a year before. Michael looked up as the door opened and, perfectly at ease – he had the advantage of her there – rose from his seat and came over to her.

'Hello, Tansy. I heard you were here.'

'Hello,' Tansy said, smiling awkwardly. 'Have you come to make an appointment with Mr Smiles?'

After taking off her coat and hanging it on a peg behind the door, she went to her desk and thumbed through the appointment book with an air of studied casualness before looking up and saying: 'He could see you on Tuesday afternoon at three, or is it more urgent?'

'Tuesday's fine,' Michael said with aplomb, getting out his diary. 'I thought I should have a check-up.' He made a note in pencil in his diary before shutting it and slipping it into his breast-pocket. He watched Tansy carefully as she wrote his name in the ledger and then the door opened and the first patient for the afternoon came in.

'Please go straight in,' Tansy said, after ticking the patient's name in the book. 'Mr Crowther will see you now.'

The patient smiled and slipped past Michael through the door into the surgery. Michael, however, showed no signs of leaving and produced his cigarette case.

'Not in here, if you don't mind,' Tansy said with a polite smile, as though she were addressing a stranger. 'Neither Mr Smiles or Mr Crowther like patients to smoke.'

'But I'm not a patient, yet.'

'They don't like smoking in the reception. I'm sorry.' Tansy sat down and drew the appointments book towards her so that she could get out the records of the patients whom Mr Crowther was due to see that afternoon.

Yet she was aware of Michael, of his presence and the memories of the time she imagined herself in love with him. Or had she imagined it? She'd hoped he would write but he never did and, gradually, she learned that he had left the army and gone abroad.

'I've been in Australia,' Michael said, coming over to her desk. 'Did you miss me?'

'No.' Tansy looked at him coldly. 'Not at all.'

'I missed you.'

'I find that hard to believe.' She rose and went to the drawer where the records were kept neatly filed and then she turned and said, 'I can't really talk here personally, Michael, I'm afraid. I have a job to do.'

'Still Daddy's girl?' Michael taunted, standing just behind her.

'Oh do shut up,' she cried, looking over her shoulder, 'and please leave.'

The next thing she heard was the door closing and she leaned her head against the cool steel of the filing cabinet trying to recover her composure.

The rest of the afternoon passed too slowly for Tansy who realized she was much more upset than she ever thought she would be by Michael Garrett's reappearance. She was sure that she had got him completely out of her mind. She had learned only gradually that Michael had a reputation and that there were a few bruised hearts in Netherwick besides hers and heaven knew how many others round the world.

And now he was back. Well, she for one was not interested.

At five o'clock Mr Crowther put his head round the door and asked if there were any more patients.

'That's all, Mr Crowther,' Tansy said, putting the cover back on the typewriter on which she'd been practising for the past hour.

'We'll wrap it up for the day then, Tansy.'

'Yes, Mr Crowther. Shall I lock up?'

'If you would.' Mr Crowther looked at his watch. 'My wife is waiting for me. I'll slip out the back way.'

'Very good, Mr Crowther. Have a nice weekend.'

'You too, Tansy,' Mr Crowther said with a smile and a wave and returned to the surgery.

Tansy had already got out the records for the patients expected on Monday, ready for the part-time receptionist who helped out on her days off, or when she was on holiday. She looked round to ensure that everything was neat and tidy, the magazines in a pile and then she popped her head through the surgery door, looked round to see that everything there was all right, shut the door and locked it. Then she went through the reception and put the lights out before opening the street door, going out into the street and locking that.

She popped the keys into her bag and started towards the town when she saw a familiar car parked by the edge of the kerb and behind the wheel sat the person she had thought about so much, dreamed about so often and tried unsuccessfully to put out of her heart.

'You don't know how often I've thought about you,' Michael said, in the corner of the bar of the King's Head where they'd eventually gone. She'd refused an invitation to dinner, saying she already had a date. It wasn't true, but she didn't want to make herself too available to someone who had already hurt her once.

'Is that so, Michael,' Tansy said in a quiet, sceptical voice, not wishing to draw attention to herself in a place where it was possible she would know many people, or they would know her, particularly on a Saturday night.

'But it's true, Tansy,' Michael said, equally quietly but sounding indignant. 'Don't forget you walked out on me. You started the row that day in the Grand.'

It was true they had had heated words over lunch; but he had upset her by his mocking words which had begun again as soon as he saw her in the surgery. He couldn't resist jibes about her father, and she couldn't stand them.

'I think we agreed mutually that we couldn't get on,' Tansy said. 'Anyway, I've discovered since then you have a bit of a reputation in Netherwick.'

'Oh have I?' Michael said contemptuously. 'That doesn't take much doing. I suppose you've been told I seduced every woman in town.'

'Not *quite* every woman,' Tansy said cautiously. 'But you did seem to know a few.'

'It's not unnatural is it, Tansy?' Michael's face looked earnest, thoughtful. 'I'm a normal man. I like women. They like me. I have it's true taken out quite a few girls in Netherwick and elsewhere; but I have never asked any of them to marry me.'

'You didn't ask me properly,' Tansy said, even more quietly.

'I did,' he insisted, 'I told you I loved you. I don't say that to many women, I assure you. I was sure we would marry; I *did* ask you that day at the Grand. I felt very excited. I thought you felt the same. I came up especially to see you and then all you could tell me was that you could never live anywhere but Netherwick. It was a bit of a turn-off, Tansy.'

'I can't stand the way you're always knocking my father,' Tansy said heatedly shaking her head to emphasize her point. 'He has nothing to do with me.'

'But he *has*, Tansy.' Michael leaned towards her. 'Your father has blighted your girlhood and youth, and will continue to do so unless you resist him.'

'How *can* you say that?'

'I can because I know him and my parents know him. Everyone knows him. He is a tyrant who makes his entire family do his bidding, but you won't admit it.'

Tansy made as if to get up, but Michael took her by her arm and pulled her down beside him again. I shan't even say "hello" in the street if you don't hear me out this time.'

There was something so compelling in his tone that Tansy was forced, despite herself, to sit down. She was breathing heavily and she grasped the glass of sherry that he had bought her and tossed the contents down her throat. Michael, who was drinking draught beer, grimaced with quiet satisfaction and called out to the barmaid. 'Another Amontillado, please, dear.'

'Coming up,' she replied cheerfully.

'I can see you're angry, Tansy, but listen to me,' Michael went on. 'I have come back just to see *you*. I have left the army and I've spent the last six months in Australia. My father, as you may have heard, is unwell and I felt I had to come home and see him; but I'm going back and . . . if you like, I want you to come with me.'

'To Australia?' Tansy exclaimed in a voice so loud that interested faces were turned towards them.

'As my wife, Tansy,' Michael whispered. 'I'm sure we'll get on. I have never stopped thinking about you and I know you feel the same about me. I can tell it by the way you react to me. You ran away from me that day in Leeds because you thought I wanted to take you to bed; well I did and I do, but not unless you want it too and, if you like, I'm prepared to wait until we're married if it's what you want, just to reassure you. Just to let you know that, to me, you are very special and I'm thinking along permanent lines.'

It was a funny sort of proposal delivered in such a quiet tone that Tansy sat staring at him in amazement, feeling as if she had been lifted about fifteen feet in the air. She had felt like this before when he first kissed her in the red MG, made her open her mouth and feel his hot, wet tongue, so unlike the chaste, boyish kisses she had been used to before. She had known even then that there was something serious about his feeling for her, that he wanted to go to bed with her. Then, perhaps, she would have become pregnant and what would her father have said?

It was this fear, this holding back from Michael because of what her father might have thought, that had been the cause of all the trouble and misunderstanding the year before. Tentatively she put out her hand and touched Michael's. 'Thank you,' she said in a low voice. 'I know what that cost you.'

He gripped her hand, swallowed hard and smiled. '*Where* did you say you were having dinner tonight?'

Michael Garrett stood in front of Doctor Blair and watched him with the pipe – the unrolling of the pouch, the slow flaking of the tobacco, the pressing of it into the bowl, the lighting, the expulsion of smoke – he had heard all about the routine from Tansy and she had warned him not to be intimidated by it.

Finally Doctor Blair looked up from his chair by the fireside, although it was summer and, instead of a fire in the grate there was a large bowl of flowers: marigolds, hollyhocks, sweet williams, lupins and scabeous. Catherine had an instinctive flair when it came to arranging flowers.

'Now, Michael,' Doctor Blair sat comfortably back in his chair puffing away. 'What can I do for you?'

'I would like to marry your daughter, sir.'

The doctor said nothing but went on puffing steadily, his eyes not on his putative son-in-law but on some bird on the lawn, or object in the garden that appeared to have taken his fancy. The light shining on his spectacles made it difficult for Michael exactly to determine his expression, but when Geoffrey Blair removed his pipe from his mouth and looked at him it was enigmatic.

'So I heard.'

'I suppose you think I should have asked your permission first, Doctor Blair; but I had to be sure Tansy wanted to marry me.'

'Naturally,' Geoffrey said, but his expression remained frozen.

'Tansy does want to marry me, Doctor Blair, and she,

I, we . . .' for the first time Michael faltered, 'would like your blessing, and your permission, of course, sir.'

'Which you have to have as she is under age.' There was a cutting edge in Geoffrey's voice.

'She felt sure you would wish her happiness and, as you have known my father . . .'

'But it is not your father who wishes to marry my daughter, young man,' Doctor Blair continued in the same unfriendly tone, 'and I must tell you that I consider you too old.'

'Too *old*, sir?' Michael spluttered.

'Yes. Tansy is nineteen and you are thirty. That is a very big difference. You will soon tire of a woman who is undeveloped when you marry her, and she will grow bored with you.'

'I assure you, sir, that Tansy and I have given a lot of thought to this.'

'You surprise me.' Doctor Blair rose, his chin defiantly in the air. 'I understood you had only recently returned from Australia. How much, in your case is, "a lot"?'

'It was love at first sight, Doctor Blair.' Michael, beginning to get angry, raised his voice. 'At her eighteenth birthday party. We had a misunderstanding last year, but that has all now been put right. I may not know Tansy very well, but I have known her since she was a little girl, and you have known my father . . .'

'There you go again. I like your father very much, Michael,' Doctor Blair said in a kinder tone '*and* your mother; but I still don't consider you suitable as a husband for Tansy, and I shall try and get her to change her opinion about you.'

'But what have I *done*?' Michael implored.

'Naturally nothing that I know of, except that I understand you have acquired a reputation here as a ladies' man; but it is primarily your age. Your age and the fact you intend to take Tansy back to Australia with you. That I simply can't allow.'

'But you can't stop it.'

'I can stop it for two years,' Doctor Blair said, and Michael could see those short-sighted eyes glinting dangerously. 'By that time she may have forgotten you, or met someone else because I don't think you would be the kind of person to wish to hang about. At nearly thirty-two you must think it high time you were married. I do too; but not to my daughter.'

'And if we elope . . .' Michael found that in his anger he had begun to splutter, and he had promised himself that if the interview proved difficult he would keep control of himself.

'*If* you elope,' the doctor said evenly, 'the consequences will be very serious. I would never have anything to do with my daughter again, ever. Besides,' he looked at Michael with a slight smile on his lips, 'I don't think she would agree.'

Catherine Blair sat by the window with her needlework on her lap, her nimble fingers darting in and out with the various coloured threads used in the tapestry she was embroidering from a pattern designed by herself. She was a clever needlewoman and, in recent years, since she had stopped having to make her children's clothes, she had become even more devoted to this particular craft.

In the far corner of the sitting room Geoffrey sat turning over the pages of the evening paper; but she knew that, after the row with Tansy, his mind was not on his task.

Catherine could never recall hearing Tansy actually *scream* at her father and, for a while, her mother even thought she might strike him. Frequently Geoffrey had clutched at his heart but even this threat had not been enough to stop Tansy, who accused him of ruining her life.

She had then told him that, whatever he said, she was determined to marry Michael Garrett. She had made up her mind and so had he. She told her father that if he refused permission she would go to London until she was twenty-one and would not care if she never saw him again. She had then flounced out of the house to Michael, who had been waiting outside for her in his car, which had driven off at speed.

The evening meal had been a quiet, dismal affair with Tansy's place left empty and Geoffrey glancing frequently at the door. Now, Catherine knew, it was her task to undo the harm Geoffrey had done and try and save her daughter's happiness, and his.

'Anything in the papers?' Catherine asked, looking at her husband over the spectacles she used for close work.

'Nothing,' Geoffrey said, not raising his head to look at her. His demeanour worried her. She knew that what was happening to Tansy would, inevitably, have an effect on his health; but she had spent her life trying to protect her husband from the consequences of normal events that happened around him and she knew she couldn't go on doing it for ever. One day he would either have to adapt . . . or take the consequences.

'Geoffrey,' Catherine removed her spectacles and carefully smoothed her tapestry over her knees, 'we must have a talk about Tansy.'

'There's nothing to discuss,' Geoffrey said.

'I think there *is*, Geoffrey . . .' Catherine stared at him. 'Please look at me when I'm talking.'

'Oh, Catherine.' Geoffrey threw down the paper and turned an angry face to her. 'What *is* it you want to discuss?'

'You know perfectly well, Geoffrey, only you want to avoid it, as you always do.'

'My dear, I haven't gone through life avoiding things.' Geoffrey reached instinctively for his tobacco pouch and Catherine, her nerves already on edge, burst out: 'Geoffrey, for *God's* sake put that damn pouch down and concentrate on me, for a change.'

'Catherine,' Geoffrey said reproachfully, his hand still on his pouch but going no further.

'You know quite well you only start fiddling with your pipe to play for time. I am sick and tired of seeing that pouch brought out every time anyone in this house has something important to say.'

She watched as Geoffrey's other hand strayed towards his heart, but she knew that that gesture too was instinctive. 'And don't clutch your heart either, please, Geoffrey. Tom Thackery says you are a very strong man. You just use illness as an excuse and for putting off things you don't like.'

'Tom Thackery says that?' Geoffrey looked at her indignantly.

'Well, not in so many words; but I know it. Now today you had a very stormy interview with Tansy and you survived *that*.'

'Just,' Geoffrey muttered peevishly.

'She is nearly twenty. Geoffrey. She will do what she wants to do and you know it.'

'Michael Garrett is too old for her; besides, I don't like him.'

'*Why* don't you like him? You have always got on very well with George and Felicity.'

'Michael is too mature for Tansy, too old. He will make her grow up too fast. Also he has had too many women, if stories I've heard are anything to go by. I don't like that sort of thing for my daughter.'

'But Michael is nearly thirty-one, Geoffrey. It would be rather odd if he had had *no* girlfriends.'

'I don't mean *that*.' Geoffrey vigorously rubbed his eyes under his spectacles with annoyance. 'You know quite well what I mean. He's also not at all settled. He wants to go to Australia. Why does he want to go to *Australia*?' He looked owlishly at his wife, his face by now quite animated.

'How should I know? He likes the climate, I expect. They say it is the land of opportunity.'

'Opportunity my foot! He has plenty of opportunity here in Netherwick.'

'Really, Geoffrey!' Catherine started to laugh.

'Really *what*, Catherine? Plenty is going on in Netherwick, in Yorkshire generally and in Leeds. George Garrett actually wants Michael to work for the family firm. He has offered him a job, but Michael doesn't want it.'

'I understand he doesn't get on very well with his brother. Bob is managing director. He wants to start up on his own.'

'Oh you know everything, don't you?'

'Well I do know quite a lot because Tansy's happiness is at stake. I would like you to think about this, Geoffrey, and to realize how unreasonable to our daughter your attitude is. You will alienate her and she will not love you. If she does marry Michael, and she seems determined to, and goes to Australia, we may never see her again.'

Catherine rose and, coming over to her husband, put her hand on his shoulder. 'And I tell you this, dear, that, if that is the case, you will have only yourself to blame.'

Tansy and Michael came out of a long kiss in the front seat of the MG. They were bucket seats and not very comfortable and, as they rearranged themselves, Michael sighed, 'Can't keep this up for long.'

'It won't be long,' Tansy said, her eyes alight with love. 'Mummy is working on him.'

'Well, she'd better work fast.'

'She says Dad will agree if you stay here.'

'Then I say "no"! I shan't be blackmailed by your father. You know me, Tansy.'

There was a prolonged silence between them.

Three weeks had elapsed since the row with her father during which time he told everyone he thought he had had a mild heart attack. For once no one actually believed him and Tom Thackery reported a negative ECG.

But George Garrett had been to see him, and spent a long time with him, and Catherine and her mother had reported to Tansy a positive response from her father *if* Michael agreed to give up the idea, for the time being, of going abroad.

'Just England,' Tansy said winsomely. 'Not even Netherwick.'

'That *is* decent of your father.' Michael managed, however, to smile. 'You know I don't get on with Bob. There's no point staying in England if I don't work for Garretts. If I went south I'd get some grotty job as a rep. Anyway, Tansy, I don't see why your father should dictate to me what I do or where I go. I'm too old to be told what to do.'

'I agree with you, darling,' Tansy said, reaching for his hand. 'But I *would* like a proper wedding in a white veil with Daddy giving me away and everyone being happy. I would like that, and so, I think, would you and your parents. If we start wrong, Michael, everything will *be* wrong . . .'

'You really want it?' Michael folded her hand tightly in his.

'Yes I do. If it doesn't work out then, after we're married, we can go to Australia, or anywhere you like. No one can stop us then.'

'So this is just for now?'

'Just for now,' Tansy promised.

'Yippee!' Michael cried, throwing his hands first in the air and then enfolding her in his arms.

PART THREE

Critical Heritage

1953–1955

Chapter 14

The wedding of Tansy Blair and Michael Garrett was the social event of the Netherwick season. But it had an interest that went far outside, and not only the town and local papers, but the *Yorkshire Post* and one or two county magazines sent reporters and photographers.

It was the kind of wedding that every conventional bride dreams about: a beautiful dress, a church full of relations and family friends, her father to give her away, a full peal of bells, a church choir which sang beautifully and, above all, a happy, handsome, smiling groom, clearly as in love as his bride.

It was said that half the women who came to watch the bride and groom leave the church envied Tansy; but, as a statistic, it was impossible to check. It was not a day for statistics, anyway, but a happy, hauntingly beautiful day that promised happiness for those involved; happiness ever after.

It was a late summer wedding arranged very soon after Geoffrey Blair had finally, if grudgingly, given his consent. It had made George Garrett decide to retire from the business and leave everything in the hands of his two sons. What was doubtful was that the brothers would live happily ever after. Gilbert acted as best man to his brother-in-law, whose own brother, Bob, was on holiday, a fact which some considered not only a significant snub, but a bad omen too.

And so, at the age of nineteen and a half, Tansy Blair became Mrs Michael Garrett and moved into a house a block away from her father's that the families had bought for her and Michael. Michael had demurred at first. He would have preferred to be nearer Leeds, further away from the in-laws; but once he had submitted to his father-in-law's blackmail he seemed to accept everything else with amazingly good grace: a junior position to his brother in the business and a house in Netherwick five minutes away from the Blairs. Everyone decided that Michael must be very much in love indeed.

For Tansy it was a dream come true, one that would have seemed unbelievable a few months before. She and Michael flew to the Caribbean for their honeymoon and had the stylish, much photographed sort of honeymoon that rich young couples had who could afford the fare, the luxurious hotel and all the little extras of a fairy-tale.

While they were away a team of workmen, supervised by the two excited mothers, moved into the detached house on Sycamore Drive and turned it into a home to fit in with the dream honeymoon when the couple returned. There was central heating, fitted carpets, a kitchen with all modern gadgets, draped curtains at the windows and a huge double bed in the main bedroom; one room along the corridor had no bed at all, but was clearly intended for a cot.

The house was painted inside and out, the garden newly planted and every room was full of fresh flowers when Tansy and Michael returned to Netherwick at the beginning of October to begin their married life together in earnest.

And for a time all went well. Tansy gave coffee mornings and tea parties for her girlfriends, some of them newly-weds like herself. Michael went to the office every day in the new Aston Martin his father had bought him to replace the red MG which was now considered unsuitable for a married man.

Even Michael decided he liked his new status. He had

his own office, his own secretary and even his own workload which was separate from his brother's. He had to consult him in all financial matters but was given an amount of freedom in making decisions that was unusual for a new recruit to a business, even a family one.

George became president of the Group and went into the office once or twice a week, mainly to enjoy a hearty lunch at the Grand with his sons. He was then chauffeured back to Netherwick and a game of golf, or a round of bridge in the clubhouse with his cronies.

The things that Michael, a long time bachelor, had thought he wouldn't like about marriage in fact he liked. He liked going out in the morning and coming home at night which he did regularly, every day at six o'clock. He liked the glass or two of sherry with Tansy while they exchanged news about their day, and then he liked the intimate little dinner she had prepared just for the two of them, consumed before the early retirement to bed.

He liked the fact that he had been the first to instruct Tansy in the art of lovemaking and she was a good pupil. She was a girl with no inhibitions, no false prudery. She was even more sensual than he expected and he felt he was more in love with her than at the time of their marriage. By the following spring she told him she was pregnant and that made everything seem just about perfect; as perfect as it could be. They were pleased, the parents were overjoyed, a beautiful draped cot was ordered for the vacant spot along the corridor just down from the master bedroom. Everything was going as planned – but could it last?

Even Geoffrey Blair was happy, although he worried about his daughter and fussed over her ante-natal care, insisting on a gynaecologist from Leeds to look after her, and annoying the local doctors in the process.

It was about the time that Tansy announced her

pregnancy that Jeremy's book was published to a chorus of press attention carefully prepared by the publisher well in advance. There was an American sale, a serialization and a possible film deal in the offing. There was a new two-book contract, interviews in the press and one on TV.

It looked as though Jeremy Blair was set on a path as happy as the one his sister was making two hundred miles away in Netherwick, and most of the family descended on London for the party given in his honour at his publisher's Mayfair headquarters.

There were blown-up pictures of Jeremy looking extraordinarily handsome with his striking white hair, the firm square jaw, the eyes staring serenely into some far distant spot: possibly sheep on another hill?

For this was the story of the worldly man whose experiences had made him a contemplative. He had searched into his soul on those lonely hills; he had drunk bitterly from the dregs of life.

It was difficult to reconcile this image with the current pictures of Jeremy in his smart grey Daks trousers, the expensive tweed jacket that came from an exclusive store in Piccadilly. He wore a check shirt and a woollen tie and looked like a man who, having indeed drained the dregs, had now thrown them away and drank more frequently from a glass with bubbles at the top.

As Jeremy limped about with the aid of his stick, the image was right, and the prospect of great fame did not seem too remote on that spring day when family, friends and admirers gathered round him as he signed copies of his book and directed interested foreign publishers to the foreign rights department.

As Tansy had entered the room she stood for a moment, her arm through Michael's, trying to take it all in. In Berkeley Square the trees were just coming into leaf, their little tendrils glinting in the late afternoon sun which shone through the windows onto the soft pile carpet, onto the highly polished furniture, the tall champagne glasses, the *objets d'art* and ornaments resplendent in the boardroom. The sophisticated, glittering crowd of people, mainly young or very old and distinguished-looking who gathered round Jeremy, seemed to pay homage to his celebrity.

It was all a very long way away from Netherwick.

They had last seen Jeremy at their wedding and, as they entered, he spotted them immediately and, hailing them, came over to greet them, kissing Tansy on the cheek.

'It's marvellous news about the baby,' he said. 'When is the date?'

'In about seven months' time.'

'You look extremely well.'

'I feel fine.' Tansy smiled at Jeremy and then at a woman who stood just behind him, whom she knew at once was Jill.

'This is Jill,' Jeremy said bringing her forward.

'I thought it must be.' Tansy shook her head. 'How do you do? May I introduce my husband, Michael.'

'I'm delighted to meet you both,' Jill said with a quiet, insidious kind of charm. 'I've heard so much about you, especially Tansy. You have a very special place in Jeremy's heart.'

'And he in mine,' Tansy said, looking around. 'Have you met our father?'

Geoffrey was never very far away from Tansy. If ever there was a party or a gathering attended by them both one could expect that Geoffrey would be shadowing his daughter, never far from call, especially now that she was going to have a baby. As he'd always been over-concerned about his own health, he now worried incessantly about hers. It irritated Michael but he put up with it. He tolerated it as he tolerated so much else that annoyed him about the Blairs, from Geoffrey's over-possessiveness to Catherine's over-bearing solicitousness.

Some days Michael couldn't help but wonder if the good days were over and the troublesome ones were about to start.

Jill shook hands warmly with Catherine and Geoffrey, congratulating them on their son's talent, and saying how good it was to see them again. Geoffrey modestly disclaimed any connection with Jeremy's writing. In fact, he said, there was no literary talent that he knew of at all in the family.

'Jeremy is going to be a great writer,' Jill affirmed, putting a beautiful hand with long manicured nails on his arm. 'Everyone is crazy about his book. We have even sold it to the French, and they scarcely ever buy anything.'

'The French,' Geoffrey said, with the wonder on his face of the traditional country bumpkin. 'Did you hear that, Catherine? Jeremy's book is to be *translated* into Fench!'

'French,' Catherine repeated, again admiringly, but her eyes were busily scanning the crowd. 'Have you seen Emily anywhere?' she asked Jill. 'Jeremy's wife.'

'Oh, I think she went off with her daughter,' Jill said, also looking round. 'Not really the place for a little girl.'

'You mean they've *gone*?' Tansy's face was perplexed. 'But we were supposed to meet her here.'

'I think she's coming back,' Jill said rather off-handedly. 'I really wouldn't know.' Looking over Tansy's shoulder she appeared to see someone she recognized because suddenly her face lit up and, standing on tiptoe, she waved and grabbing Jeremy she said in an urgent voice: 'Jeremy, do come and meet Paul Eizberger. He is one of the most influential editors in . . .'

The town or country was lost in the noise of voices made by too many people in too small a space. But with the already practised smile of one touched by fame Jeremy disappeared into the crowd with Jill.

'Are you all right?' Michael asked Tansy anxiously. 'It's terribly *hot* in here.'

'I feel absolutely fine,' Tansy replied, 'but let's go and stand by the window. Where do you think Emily could have gone to?'

'I don't know anyone here at all,' Geoffrey Blair grumbled, leaning on Catherine's supportive arm as they followed Tansy and Michael. 'And it's awfully hot.'

'You wanted to come, dear,' Catherine said, with a glance at Michael. 'I *did* say I thought you shouldn't.'

'Of course I had to come to Jeremy's party. My son, a famous author! Never did I think I'd live to see the day. Where did you say Emily was?' he looked around. 'I suppose I'd better at least say hello.'

Tansy thought that Emily had probably gone in order to avoid meeting her father. Their brief encounters were never pleasant. 'She's probably taken Fern to bed,' she said.

Emily avoided these family gatherings. She felt patronized by them and she clearly hated Geoffrey. She had attended Tansy's wedding with Jeremy because Fern was one of the bridesmaids, but she never spoke to Geoffrey. They nodded from a distance and that was all.

Geoffrey told everyone he was quite willing to make it up with Emily and, in a sense, this was true now that Jeremy was firmly back in the fold. It was Emily who did not want to make it up with her father-in-law, a fact that Jeremy reproached her for. He said she was stubborn. But Emily was prickly. She had been offended and now she felt cast out by Jeremy who had another life. It was not surprising that she left the party as soon as she decently could.

After a while, as the crowd in the room seemed to get even bigger, Geoffrey said he had had enough and he and Tansy decided to walk back to the hotel. They all went in search of Jeremy and found him sitting in a corner smoking and chatting with authorly animation to three people who were lapping up his words. Jill sat on the arm of his chair, a hand resting casually on his shoulder.

'We're off now.' Tansy tried raising her voice above the hubub. Jeremy lifted his head and waved.

'Any chance . . .' Michael began, but the noise was too much even for him. 'We're eating at the Connaught,' he bellowed through cupped hands. Jeremy nodded as if he understood, and Jill smiled too. As she did her hand tightened on his shoulder and Tansy thought of Emily who had left early with Fern. Emily who, clearly, had learned a lot that day merely by watching Jeremy's behaviour with Jill.

'There's nothing you can do about it,' Michael said as they prepared for sleep. 'If they're having an affair, they're having an affair.'

'I don't know how you can *say* such a thing!' Tansy said, looking at him indignantly.

'Besides, Emily's so dowdy compared to Jill.'

'But you can't just toss someone aside when you're tired of them.'

'Some people do,' Michael said nonchalantly, taking off his shirt.

'You don't *approve* of it, Michael, do you?' Tansy sat on the bed and began to roll down her stockings. 'You don't actually *approve* of adultery and people having affairs?'

'My darling, you have to be realistic.' Michael scratched his bare chest, looking thoughtfully at himself in the mirror. 'You told me ages ago that Emily and Jeremy had not been getting on.'

'It's all because of Daddy,' Tansy said, stepping out of her suspender belt. 'He caused this rift between Jeremy and Emily. I could see it coming. In fact I was part of it.'

'How?' Michael let his gaze linger on his wife's nearly naked body. He came and sat beside her putting a hand on her thigh.

'Well,' Tansy looked at him ruefully, 'Daddy asked me to take a message to Jeremy that he wanted to see him. It was years ago. I was so excited because there'd been a rift for so many years . . . I never thought that he would exclude Emily whom he never forgave, as Edward's widow, for looking at another man.'

Michael put his tongue on her shoulder and gently let it run round the back of her neck. 'You're enticing me,' he murmured. 'You don't want to talk about your family at all.'

Jeremy said: 'I really will have to go. She'll wonder where I am.'

Jill sighed and put on the light, glancing at the clock and rubbing her eyes, because they'd fallen asleep. 'She'll *know.*'

'She doesn't have to know.' Jeremy got out of bed and sat on the side. 'Not yet. I'll tell her the party went on very late.'

'I tell you she knows. I saw it in her eyes when she looked at me.'

'I think you're imagining things, Jill.'

Jeremy felt tired and he had a headache; too much to drink, too much adulation. Both went to the head. He groped round for the glasses that he now had to wear;

like father, like son, but whereas they made Geoffrey look like an old owl, they made Jeremy look interesting.

'Anyway you've got to tell her sometime,' Jill said, as she held up the clock and began to wind the alarm. Party or no party, she had a heavy day to come at the office.

'Tell her what?' Jeremy looked up at her sharply, straightening his spectacles.

'That you're staying in London, silly. What did you think I meant?' Jill began to unfasten her hair which she'd worn in a smart chignon for the party.

'Nothing,' Jeremy reached for his trousers and dragged them on.

'You are, aren't you?' Jill demanded.

'Yes I am. You know I am.'

'Did you talk to your father about it?'

'Not yet; but I should think I'll be in a position to keep myself quite soon.'

Jill frowned. 'Money takes ages to get through. That's why authors are always complaining about it. Now I could keep you *here*, very comfortably indeed. You wouldn't need to pay any rent.'

'Jill,' Jeremy said, with a note of irritation in his voice. 'You promised you wouldn't bring that up again.'

'I said I wouldn't bring it up again *yet*, but when I see your wife, Jeremy, I honestly think you've nothing in common.' Jill looked thoughtfully up at the ceiling. 'She was never a beauty but she has changed for the worse since you got your medal, hasn't she? You remember the party we had in London? Your parents came.'

'I remember. I also remember you and I were engaged,' Jeremy had an edge to his voice.

'So?' Jill looked at him sharply.

'Well, you didn't wait for me very long, did you? Shortly after that I went abroad.'

'Darling, I waited at least two years, for Christ's sake!'

Jill said bitterly. 'I wasn't made of stone, you know.'

'You said you married Jim in 1943.'

'I did.'

'Well that's not two years.'

'It's long enough,' Jill said, flinging herself full length on the bed, 'and why on earth rake up the past *now*?'

'Because of Emily,' Jeremy sat down suddenly on the bed. 'You've no idea how much I feel I owe her.'

Emily went back alone to the Dales. She travelled with Fern in a third-class compartment, changing at Crewe. She'd hated every minute of her visit to London and knew she should never have gone. Every instinct had told her to stay at home and not subject herself to such punishment.

But Fern was excited at the idea of her father being a celebrity and Emily, always scrupulous, had thought she owed it to her.

It had been worse than expected. She scarcely ever thought of clothes or fashion these days and realized only the day before they were due to go that she had nothing to wear. So she wore a pre-war suit with a white blouse, but the skirt no longer fastened at the waist and she knew she looked a frump.

She never thought about appearance much in Cragbeck as long as she looked neat enough for school and her clothes were clean. Too much reading had made her eyes worse and the frames she had got for her glasses were issued on the National Health.

The point was that she didn't actually care or, rather, she hadn't cared until she saw Jill and all those elegant fashion-conscious women in their beautiful clothes; all those *young* women fawning over Jeremy. Then she cared.

He'd only come back at four in the morning, saying

the party had gone on for hours. But she could smell Jill and her perfume and knew that he was lying. She'd said: 'Why don't you tell me you're having an affair with Jill?' And he'd replied, 'Oh for God's sake shut up and let me get some sleep.' He'd had much too much to drink. He was still not a completely well man and he couldn't take it.

So Emily left before he woke up, telling Fern to dress quietly and not wake her father. They were going home.

It was a long journey back. The train from Crewe to Leeds was a stopping train and the one from Leeds to Netherwick seemed to crawl — a journey that she normally loved took an eternity.

It was nightfull when they reached Netherwick and they were both exhausted. She toyed with the idea of taking a taxi to Cragbeck but it would cost pounds. So she rang Jean Wills who said that, of course, she and Fern must come to her for the night, and then trudged up the cobblestones to her house.

'You look absolutely dreadful,' Jean said as she admitted them.

'It was a *very* long journey.' Emily thankfully took off the unbecoming hat she had bought in Netherwick at the last minute from a second-hand shop. She hadn't realized that no one at that smart London party would wear a hat because, at Tansy's fashionable wedding, everyone had worn a hat and she hadn't one to wear. She always seemed to get things wrong.

'I thought you weren't coming back for days.' Jean bustled around. It was seven o'clock and she had just been about to start her evening meal. 'I thought you were having a holiday.'

'Jeremy's too busy,' Emily said, running her hands over her face and gazing at Jean. 'He lives in a different world from me now, Jean. You've no idea how much he's changed.'

Jean said nothing, conscious of Fern's pale, tired little face staring at them.

They had soup, and bacon and eggs. It was a good north country meal and Emily and Fern enjoyed it. Afterwards Fern went straight to bed and Emily stayed to help with the washing-up though Jean told her she should go to bed too. 'What's Fern doing tomorrow?' she asked.

'She'll come home with me as it's still school holidays,' Emily said. 'The Blairs aren't home yet. They're living it up in a very expensive London hotel.'

'Oh.' Jean looked thoughtful as she bustled about by the draining board.

'I don't like my daughter staying with the Blairs anyway,' Emily had a note of grim determination in her voice, 'and I'm going to put a stop to it.'

'What will she do?'

'I don't know yet; but if her father is earning all the money he's supposed to be making from his book he can pay to send her to boarding school. There's a very good school at Harrogate, in fact there are two or three. But I want my daughter out of the Blairs' influence. I don't like it and I don't like *them*.'

'Don't forget Catherine is my daughter, and Tansy is my granddaughter,' Jean said defensively.

'I don't regard Tansy as a Blair,' Emily replied, 'though she has done me a bad turn or two in my time. But she hasn't meant it. Tansy is a good girl, and I only hope she's happy with that man.'

'That man?' Jean looked at her, eyebrows raised. 'Do you mean Michael?'

'I do mean Michael,' Emily said. 'Michael Garrett. He's

not a good man. Anyone can see it. I don't like Geoffrey Blair, but he was right to oppose the marriage. I should have advised her more strongly against it myself because Tansy confided in me; but I didn't know Michael. I had never met him until just before the wedding and I didn't see what I see now.'

Jean sat down on one of the chairs in the kitchen with her tea cloth in her hand. 'Goodness me, Emily,' she said. 'I think your visit to London has turned you. You seem against everyone.'

'It's not that,' Emily said, taking a seat next to her. 'It's just that, suddenly, I see things in a new way, Jean. You know, the one good thing about Jeremy's book is its honesty. There on the hills he really did look into himself and try and discover what kind of person he was. He made an honest effort and it is a good book.

'But I think it will be the only good book he writes. He has been corrupted by London and by his father. In order to get to London he had to play up to his father. He needed the money. He wanted to get away, and his father was the only one who could help him.'

'But he had to have that operation.' Jean looked at her doubtfully. 'And maybe you *should* have gone with him.'

'Maybe I should, but maybe what has happened would have happened anyway.' Emily stopped for a minute, aware of the birdsong in the small yard behind the house. She loved the sound of the evening blackbird and if it was good here it would be a thousand times better and stronger in Cragbeck where the air was cleaner. She smiled suddenly, released from her terrible burden.

'Jeremy is having an affair with a woman he used to be engaged to.'

'Get away,' Jean said, looking scandalized.

'She's the editor at his publishers. She's the one who

helped him get the book published. They were engaged during the war. I met her when I was still married to Edward and she was an officer in the WAAF. I remember the patronizing look she gave me at a party Geoffrey Blair gave for Jeremy at Lyons Corner House in Piccadilly after the ceremony. She gave me almost exactly the same look last night at her office party in Berkeley Square. She hasn't changed at all; but I have. I may not have been beautiful or smart. I was never that; but people told me I was pleasing. After all, two men loved me and married me.

'But Jill's eyes seemed to tell me that I'd let myself go. I was shabby and dowdy and had no place by the side of a successful author like Jeremy. I'm also a little older than Jeremy and, by worldly standards, the standards of a woman like her, that's old. She seemed to tell me: "You're old and shabby, Emily, go back to the Yorkshire Dales". And that's exactly where I'm going.'

Timidly Jean reached out and put her hand over Emily's. 'Oh dear, oh dear, you *do* sound sad,' she said. 'I just don't know what to say, I really don't.'

Bob Garrett was three years older than his brother Michael and the two had never got on. Even as boys they fought and quarrelled constantly and, in despair at their mother's failure to cope with two warring youngsters, George sent them to different boarding schools. There had been a sister in the middle, Joyce, but she had died young from tuberculosis.

Bob and Michael were, however, both tough stocky boys who grew into tough stocky men and neither of them had shown the least sign of the illness that killed their only sister, which came from their mother's side of the family.

Felicity Garrett was a frail, rather beautiful woman

who suffered from 'nerves'. She had found her nerves an extremely good weapon, indeed the only weapon, with which to fight the menfolk in her family who were all forceful personalities driven, in various degrees, by ambition.

The father of the family, George, was what might be termed a benevolent tyrant. That is he terrorized his family and his workforce but, in his eyes, for good reasons. He felt that they would feel better, do better and work better if they obeyed his instructions. He was genuinely a family man who loved his family, and his sorrow when his only daughter died was pitiful to see and remembered by many, especially Geoffrey Blair who had treated both daughter and subsequently father and mother. If was for this reason that George remained in Geoffrey's debt. He could never forget how good and compassionate Geoffrey had been when Joyce died.

In the year that his son married and joined the family firm, George Garrett was only fifty-seven. But due, perhaps, to his choleric temperament he had acquired a heart condition and Geoffrey had told him many years ago to take it easy.

George had spent most of his life building up the business which he inherited from an equally tyrannical and choleric father who had, indeed, succumbed to a coronary thrombosis at a comparatively early age. George liked life and wanted to live as long as he could. He liked playing golf, bridge and enjoying the fruits of his years of hard labour with his wife, and it was their habit to take an annual cruise to healthier climes which were, incidentally, also of great benefit to Felicity's fragile nerves.

George Garrett intended that both his sons should join the family business after their war service, but only Bob wanted to. He had served in the navy, and had no wish to prolong his career after years spent on the North Atlantic convoys. He had been torpedoed twice and mentioned in dispatches, so that there was no doubt about his bravery. In 1945 he joined the Garrett Great Engineering Co and, in the year of his brother's marriage, he became its managing director.

The Garretts had a number of senior employees, some of whom had been with the company all their lives and could be relied upon to steer the young Garrett along the right lines, with tact and a sure knowledge of the market.

Bob, however, had discovered in himself, or thought he had, an unusual gift for business, and took little notice of anything that was said to him or any advice he was given. Two years after the end of the war he had married a pretty Irish girl called Claire and they had two young children. They lived in a large house on the edge of a golf course outside Leeds, and had a wide circle of friends and acquaintances.

Bob had done everything he could to stop his father encouraging Michael to come into the firm and he thought he had succeeded. He was thus less than pleased when Doctor Blair made it one of the conditions of allowing his under-age daughter to marry that Michael should stay in England, and even more astonished that Michael had agreed. It had been unlike Michael to knuckle under to that sort of pressure because he was a very independent, stubborn man, like his father and brother, and it was known that he liked neither England nor Netherwick.

When he heard the news Bob could foresee nothing but trouble.

The day that Michael arrived back from the party in London for Jeremy he found Bob in a particularly black mood. Michael was in charge of new product development, a position created by Bob to shunt his brother into a position of minor importance, as Garrett Engineering was well set along the path it had taken for years, and appeared to have no intention of diversion. It made parts for lorries, trucks and cars and would continue to do so. Michael, however, had spent the first six months of his career in the business taking his position very seriously indeed, and he had employed a small team of men to work constructively on new ways for Garrett Engineering to branch out; new products they could make and new avenues which they could explore.

Before Michael went to London he left a folder on his brother's desk containing the summation of his team's hard, continuous work and thought. The plans were all there: costed and explained to the tiniest detail. And it had all been done in six months. Michael had sent a copy to his father as president of the company and, independently of Bob, George had told him by telephone how pleased he was; how overjoyed to have his sons at last united in the business.

Michael had only been in his office for a few minutes sorting through his mail, reading messages left for him by his secretary, when the intercom buzzed and Bob's voice came on the other end asking him briskly if he would come to his office at once.

'Could I just have five minutes to look through the post, Bob?' Michael enquired amiably. After all he had been away for nearly a week, staying in one of London's best hotels, enjoying himself, and he felt relaxed and at ease.

'I said *at once*,' Bob barked into the phone, 'the mail can wait.'

Michael's instinct was to ignore his brother. He felt his hackles rising at the very sound of his voice, but part of the reason he had been in London was also to do business, and he had had one or two very satisfactory meetings while Tansy saw London and the shops in the company of her father and mother. Even though it was the Easter vacation Gilbert had not gone to the party. He had taken up mountaineering as a sport and had gone climbing in the Lake District.

Michael sorted through a few more letters and was about to leave the office when the intercom buzzed again. Rather than provoke a fresh row with Bob he left it buzzing and sauntered along the corridor to the office of the managing director, not bothering to knock as he went into his room.

Bob still had his finger pressed angrily on the intercom button as Michael walked in and, when he saw who it was, he flicked off the switch and rose to his feet.

'So it's you. At last.'

'What's got into you?' Michael said, going to the window and staring out onto the industrial scene before him with its mixture of new and old buildings, bombed or derelict sites and the canal winding sluggishly past, its muddy waters carrying the flotsam and jetsam of a busy, industrial city.

'God, how I *hate* Leeds,' Michael said, turning to face Bob. 'The very sight of the place depresses me.'

'It's a pity you didn't stay in Australia as you said you would.' Bob slammed Michael's report, obviously well-thumbed, down in front of him. 'If *that's* all you can produce in six months you're wasting your time here.'

'Oh?' Michael lifted his eyebrows and, ignoring the report, went over and slumped in one of his brother's comfortable new chairs. The offices of the Garrett Great Engineering Company, built on the site of the old building, was practically brand new. A tall tower of chrome and plate glass had risen like a phoenix from the ashes of nineteenth-century Leeds.

'*And* employing people to work on it! What a waste of the firm's money.'

'What exactly are you getting at, Bob?' Michael crossed one leg over the other. 'Or are you just intent on needling me?'

'I simply don't like your ideas, Michael,' Bob said, continuing to sit at his desk, clasping his hands in front of him. In appearance the brothers were alike to look at except that Bob had the colouring of his mother, and his straight hair was combed into neat but sparse strands on top of his head. The men were about the same height and the same build; they both had brown eyes but Michael's hair was brown. Nevertheless it was easy to tell they were brothers.

'Your ideas,' Bob went on, 'are way, way out. It would mean a completely new product line; retooling, reassembling. Television!' He thumped the report with his fist. 'Leave that to others.'

'Well I don't want to leave it to others,' Michael said in an equable tone of voice. 'I don't agree with you and nor does Dad. He phoned me in London to tell me he was very excited about my ideas.'

'He *what*?' Bob, clearly furious at being kept in the dark, rose to his feet.

'He didn't think you'd share his opinion, and he told me so. He knows how you feel, but he thinks you're wrong, and so do I, Bob.'

Michael got up from his chair and once again sauntered over to the window. 'You want to continue as we've been going all these years. The job you created for me was a red herring, meant to deceive Dad and deceive me. Dad is all for innovation, and so am I. You're not.

Well Dad thinks, and I think, that we should have a new company specially to deal with communications and that the head office should be moved to London.'

'Where of course, *you'll* go,' Bob sneered.

'Eventually, if Tansy wants to.'

'If she gets her father's permission, you mean,' Bob said.

'Tansy is now my wife,' Michael refused to let himself be rattled, 'and I hope she will be guided by me and do what I want to do, because she will see it's for the best. I don't think there'd be any problem there after the baby is born.'

'Have you been studying our cash flow by any chance?' Bob flung another document over to Michael. 'Cash flow is the flow of money in and out of a business.' His tone was heavy with sarcasm. 'Well *I* have news for you, Michael. Ours is none too good. Too much is flowing out and not enough in and to pay three men, besides yourself, to think up ideas that have nothing to do with anything we have experience of is, I think, a complete waste of money.'

Michael ignored the report, leaving it lying on the table by the side of his chair, an expensive glass table that had been crafted especially for the new building.

'The cash flow is one of the reasons I want to expand into other fields,' Michael said. 'You don't seem to realize, Bob, that the motor industry is changing. You're simply not keeping abreast with developments. The whole new mechanization and concept of the combustion engine will undergo a radical revolution in the next ten years and we won't be ready for it. You'll go on making the same old things in the same old way and one day our business will go under. You mark my words.'

He got up and, turning his back on his brother, walked over to the door.

'To think that this time last year you were in Australia,' Bob shouted after him. 'For God's sake why didn't you *stay* there?'

Michael spent most of the rest of the day on the telephone. He then had a meeting with his ideas team and told them to press ahead with the plans they had been working on. He put through several calls to London and made appointments for the following week.

When he got home he was dead tired and Tansy could see that the first day back at work had been a hard one.

'Bad day?' she said sympathetically, bringing him his sherry as he lay slumped in the chair. 'Well, you expected it.'

She knew Bob was a problem. From the day that Michael had started working for Garretts, Bob had made difficulties that Tansy was sure would, eventually, erupt into a major disagreement. In fact if Michael hadn't had the firm support of his father she thought it would have happened already. But what would happen if George died? The business might go down altogether. According to Michael, Bob had no proven business ability, couldn't think on a large scale, had no real idea of forward planning.

Tansy didn't much like Bob, or his wife Claire. They were the kind of socially aspiring, ambitious young marrieds that she so hoped she and Michael would not become. Both Claire and Bob hunted and Tansy hated blood sports, but generally they were both so keen on sport of every kind that they talked of little else. It was typical that they should have arranged a holiday to coincide with Tansy and Michael's wedding.

It was like a deliberate snub.

Michael sipped his sherry while he watched the television news. His chin was slumped on his chest and Tansy thought at one time that he was asleep.

'Are you all right?' she asked anxiously, sitting next to him.

'Television!' Michael said almost to himself. 'Bob can't see that that is the obvious development, the way forward. Making parts for television. Why can't he understand?'

'I don't know,' Tansy shook her head.

'Television is going to be *the* great big leisure industry of the years to come. It will eclipse the cinema and forms of entertainment as we know them today. One day it will be in colour; they're already experimenting. Why doesn't Bob want to get into TV or, at least, let me get into TV?' He shook his head. 'It beats me.' Michael suddenly looked at her and held out his hand. 'How are you today darling? Did you have a good day?'

'Fine.' Tansy leaned over to kiss him. 'Only I don't want you worried. I also don't want you to spend the rest of our married life fighting with Bob.' She looked at him intently. 'Maybe we should have gone to Australia?'

'Are you serious?'

'No, just kidding.' The look on his face worried her – she hadn't expected to be taken so seriously – and she got up and crossed the room towards the kitchen.

'Dinner in about a quarter of an hour,' she said, glancing at him over her shoulder. 'I'll bring you another drink.'

Tansy had been joking about Australia, and she wished she had never mentioned it because, over the next few months, Michael's relations with his brother deteriorated even further. Bob, with the help of the old senior executives who had been with the firm for years, managed to convince even George Garrett that Michael was on the trail of a gigantic red herring and vetoed all the plans he had set his heart on.

George, who was nervous about upsetting his older son, said they were all for diversification, but communications was another field altogether. They should stick to what they knew and develop along those lines: they should keep abreast with the motor industry, which was what they knew best.

By the summer the half year-results for the Garrett Great Engineering Company were very bad and, for the first time in its history, the company was in the red. The product development department was closed down and Michael's colleagues were sacked at a board meeting without reference to him. It had been agreed at the start that he should serve with the firm for two years before being given a seat on the board.

After the meeting Michael resigned from the family firm, having been with it just over a year. He arrived home early one afternoon when Tansy was resting and she immediately knew something was wrong.

'What is it?' she enquired anxiously, sitting upright in bed as the door opened and Michael, whom she had heard running up the stairs, burst in. He stood by the door gazing at her for a minute and then he walked over to her and sat on the bed beside her.

'Are you all right, darling?'

'Of course.'

'Then why are you lying down?'

'I usually do at this time of day, Michael. The doctor said I should put my feet up.'

'Nothing wrong?'

'Nothing at all.' She took his hand and smiled at him reassuringly. 'But there *is* something wrong with you.'

'I've resigned,' he said keeping tight hold of her hand. 'It's all over, finished. I can't take it any more.'

Tansy clasped his hand in hers and, for several seconds, said nothing.

Well, marriage had its ups and downs and this was the first real down.

'It's never been right, has it?' she said at last. 'You should never have worked with your brother.'

'I said at the time,' Michael began, but Tansy went on as though she were talking to herself:

'You did it for me. Your instinct was to get away, but you stayed here for me. You hated the family firm and Netherwick stifles you. Oh I know it does, Michael.' She put a finger firmly on his mouth to stop him from speaking. 'You needn't tell me. I *know* it does.'

'It's just that there's nothing to *do* here, darling,' Michael said gently. 'After that week in London . . .'

'I know – theatres, cinemas, restuarants. I could see how much you enjoyed it. Oh, Michael, I thought we might have to move to London, one day in the future . . . but now.'

Michael reached into his pocket and carefully drew a letter from it. 'By extraordinary coincidence I heard only yesterday from Banks Bros in Australia,' he said handing her the letter. 'They were the people I worked for when I was there. Read it.'

Slowly, feeling her heart beating fast, Tansy unfolded the letter and slowly read the contents.

Chapter 15

Gilbert Blair bent over his father and peered carefully at his face. Sometimes it was hard to know whether his father was genuinely asleep or bluffing. He was certainly ill but, undoubtedly, he liked people to think he was worse than he was.

Tansy and Michael had put their house up for sale and intended to move to Australia, lock, stock and barrel. The day following the announcement Geoffrey was taken to hospital. Coincidence? One could never be sure.

'Father,' Gilbert said in a whisper. He could see his father's eyes moving beneath his lids and knew he was awake. 'Father, Tansy's had a little boy.'

The eyes then moved very rapidly and his father opened his eyes. 'Boy?' he said, his eyelashes fluttering. 'Is she all right?'

'She's fine.'

'That's good.'

'She's in the same hospital as you, Dad; only in the maternity wing,' Gilbert said with a heavy attempt at humour. 'I don't think they'll admit you there just yet.'

Geoffrey didn't find his son's remark funny and the flicker of his eyes beneath the lids stopped as though he had, indeed, suddenly fallen asleep. Gilbert knew he was under heavy sedation.

His father was a strange man and, although he loved him, he couldn't understand him. As far as Gilbert was concerned, what Tansy did with her life was her own affair. They had had a very long talk about it after Gilbert was summoned home following his father's heart attack. Gilbert realized then what he hadn't before: that Tansy and Michael had deliberately stayed in Netherwick to please their father; that, in a way, the old man had blackmailed them into doing what he wanted before he would let them marry.

Why hadn't Tansy run away? Gilbert didn't know. He realized then that, in his single-minded pursuit of his own career, he had cut himself off from the life of his family. He had been so bound up in his studies, in his books, that they had become the reality, and people unreal to him.

Gilbert Blair, at twenty, thought he had a lot to learn; the sort of information that could not be found solely in books.

Tansy was a young strong woman who, after an excellent, trouble-free pregnancy, had an easy, trouble-free birth. Baby Roger Garrett came into the world at a little over eight pounds and was an immediate joy to his father and mother because the rest of their life was in turmoil.

Geoffrey Blair's heart attack had been a shock. Michael had already accepted the job and they had put the house on the market before announcing their intentions. They thought that way it would be easier for him to take the news; but it was not.

Curiously enough this crisis in their lives at first brought Tansy and Michael very much together. Tansy knew that she couldn't spend the rest of her life being blackmailed by the weakness of her father's heart and the use he made of it. Michael was now her first priority. Michael, and Roger.

But still Tansy felt guilty. She loved her father and she didn't want him to die, or to feel in any way responsible for his death. One day he would die naturally anyway, after all he was sixty-six and had been in poor health for years, and then she would feel free to do as she liked.

Besides, bringing Roger back to a house that had a FOR SALE notice on the outside seemed all wrong. Was it fair to take a small baby half-way round the world away from his grandparents on both sides, all his relations and family friends, away from his roots?

Tansy first put her misgivings to Michael when he was about to book the air-tickets for their flight to Sydney.

'What do you mean, you can come along later?' Michael demanded, already in his shirt sleeves studying the brief for his new job.

'Roger is awfully young, darling, to fly half-way round the world.'

'Babies do it all the time, Tansy.'

'Yes, but it *is* a very long journey. Supposing something happened? I'd like him to be a little older.'

'But, Tansy, I start this job next month. It's all arranged.'

'We haven't even *sold* the house, Michael.'

'But Dad is going to look after that. Everything is arranged, Tansy.'

'I might never see my father again,' Tansy said, with a stricken expression on her face. 'Can't you see how I feel?'

'Ah *that's* it.' Michael sat back and rolled up his sleeves. 'Daddy's little girl.'

'That is a very unfair thing to say, Michael,' Tansy felt close to tears. It was probably an old wives' tale but she had heard that if you upset yourself it soured the milk, and she loved feeding her baby. It seemed to her the epitome of motherhood; that bond made between parent and child which was supposed to endure for life. She knew she must not get upset for Roger's sake; but it was very hard not to. It was also very hard to feel that, by going to Australia, she might kill her father.

Michael left the following month for Australia and Tansy stayed behind. It had not been an easy month and the joy they had had in their child and each other seemed to have evaporated. Tansy's milk did dry up and Roger was put on a bottle. She felt she had failed, in a way, both husband and baby; but she had kept the love of her father.

As he sat under the huge elm in the garden in the warm September sunshine, gazing at his grandson lying in his pram, Tansy felt that she had done the right thing. His happiness, which was so transparent, seemed paramount. But it was only for a while. Only until he got stronger and then she would follow Michael.

As if in tune with her thoughts Geoffrey Blair gave a deep sigh and put his hand out, groping for hers. She reached for his hand which was so thin, the skin like old wrinkled parchment. Even his bones seemed to have shrunk and made him seem smaller.

'It is so good to have you here with me, darling Tansy,' her father said. 'I can't tell you what it means to me, or thank you enough for staying with me for a while until I get better.'

'That's all right, Daddy.' Tansy squeezed his hand gently because it was so delicate she felt she might crush it. 'I wanted to.'

'Did you really?' He may have been ill but he missed nothing and his knowing, intelligent eyes blinked at her shrewdly behind his glasses. 'You mean you didn't want to go with Michael?'

'Not particularly Daddy, to be honest.'

'But you will go eventually, of course?' He sounded hopeful that her reply might be in the negative, but she was quick to disappoint him.

'Of course I shall have to. I'm hoping that after a while Michael will find that Australia is not all he thinks it is. That it is too far away, and he will want to come back. However, I don't think he'll ever come back to Netherwick, Daddy. Not after the row with his father.'

There was a silence, a moment during which both father and daughter appeared to be lost in thought. Between them in the pram Roger opened his eyes, stretched out his baby arms with his tight little clenched pink fists and yawned. He looked a thoroughly happy and contented baby and Tansy wondered how, indeed, he would have reacted to the long journey, the strangeness and uncertainty of a new country, however well looked after he might have been. Their first weeks or months would have been spent in a hotel.

Here in Netherwick he had his roots and his mother had hers. She looked guiltily at her father who seemed able to read her mind.

'I suppose you really *are* happy with Michael, Tansy?' he said a little wistfully.

'Of course I am, Daddy!' If anyone had said this other than her father she would have resented it deeply. 'The last month wasn't easy because, of course, he wanted me to go with him. He couldn't understand my attitude. But once we're together again everything will be fine.'

'You don't sound too sure, darling,' Geoffrey insisted.

'I am *very* sure, Daddy. I love Michael and he loves me.'

'Well I'm glad to hear it,' her father said not very convincingly and settled back in his chair. 'George was extremely upset with Michael. He has a weak heart, as I have. He said Michael used language a man should never use to anyone, never mind his father! It showed him a violent side of Michael he didn't like, and I hope he never shows this side to you, darling.'

'Michael thought *he* was very badly treated by his father, who changed sides. First he supported Michael then he went over to Bob. Michael wants to save the company. He thinks that what will happen soon is that Garretts will have to be sold in order to pay its debts and the family, instead of being wealthy, will be paupers.'

'Oh, I don't think it will come to that.'

'You don't know anything about it, Daddy, if you don't mind me saying so. Michael has a very good head for business, and I don't say that just because I love him. I know.'

'Well,' Geoffrey, in a placatory gesture, reached for her hand again, 'the main thing is that I have you and my dear little grandson for a few more weeks. Longer I hope. That's a bonus that I didn't expect.'

The feel of her hand in his was comforting to Geoffrey who had a foreboding that he had not much longer to live. How nice it would be if he could persuade her to stay here with him. One big happy family, living in the same house; the way he wanted it to be.

From the house Catherine watched father, daughter and grandson together on the lawn. The news that Tansy was not to go with Michael but would stay behind for a while had had an astonishing effect on Geoffrey whose ECG became almost normal, and he was discharged from hospital within a few days. Yet the whole affair had upset Catherine and made her feel her age. She knew how much Geoffrey depended on Tansy and it worried her that he could so easily get his own way.

It had been put about that the baby was not ready to travel. He was too small, too young; but there were those in the town who thought differently, and the rumour quickly spread that the marriage of Tansy and Michael Garrett was not going well. Such a pity they said. She was not yet twenty-one. Tongues wagged.

Catherine knew all about the rumours. It was also true that Michael and Tansy *had* seriously disagreed because Michael expected his wife to go with him. On the other hand, perhaps Tansy was right. Roger would have been flying at only six weeks old, and it was an awfully long way for a tiny baby to go. Supposing he was taken ill? Supposing Tansy was? No, better by far to stay until Roger was a little older, a little stronger and Geoffrey was better too. All in all, Catherine tried to comfort herself, it made good sense.

She turned at a noise from inside and saw Gilbert opening the fridge. 'Do you want a drink, Gilbert?' she asked.

'Have you any lemonade, Mother?'

'No, dear. We don't keep lemonade but, if you like, I can get some.'

'It's all right, I'll have milk.' Gilbert poured the bottle into a glass and put it to his lips.

'Hot,' he said.

'Very hot for climbing, dear.' His mother's expression was worried. She hated this hobby of Gilbert's and wished he had taken up any other sport but that; even caving, which she hated too, and which was very popular in the Dales. He was to leave in a few days for Switzerland on his first climbing holiday in the Alps with a group of friends from the university.

'It's *ideal* for climbing, Mother,' Gilbert drained the last drop of milk. 'Now don't worry.' He went across to her and put his arms around her. 'We have had a lot of training in the Lake District and Snowdonia. We are only going on easy slopes. I shan't do anything the least bit dangerous, I promise you.'

'I couldn't *bear* to lose you, Gilbert.' Impulsively his mother clasped him to her. 'Suddenly the world seems so insecure – your father ill, Tansy about to go half-way round the world. You, choosing a dangerous sport like mountain climbing.' She gazed anxiously up at his care-free, smiling face. 'I can't understand it. You were always such a *careful* boy. Never even liked sport because of your sight. Don't your glasses get in the way?'

'Climbing is an ideal sport for people who wear glasses, Mother,' Gilbert said, pushing them firmly up his nose. 'It is far better than football or hockey or rugger.'

'Well I don't like it and I wish you'd stop it,' his mother said with a sigh. 'Now I suppose I'd better get tea and take it out to Tansy and your father.'

'As for Tansy going half-way round the world,' Gilbert said quietly, 'I don't for a moment think she will.'

'But of course she will.' Catherine looked at him in surprise. 'Michael has a job there. It's where his work is. She loves him.'

'Yes I know all that; but I don't think she'll go. I'm sure she doesn't want to go.'

'But how can she not go?' Now Catherine looked perplexed.

'I think she'll find an excuse, maybe Father's health, and then Michael will have to come back again, won't he?'

'I think you're being a bit naughty. I can see you smiling,' Catherine said reprovingly; but as she got the cake out of the tin and brewed the tea in the pot she couldn't help wondering if Gilbert were right. They were twins and such people often had an intuitive understanding of each other.

'Come here Gilbert, and take this tray out for me,' she said. 'There's a dear.'

As Catherine and Gilbert came over the lawn with

the tea things Tansy got up to help them, setting up the folding table, making sure the legs were straight. Geoffrey, tucked up in his chair with a rug around him, despite the heat surveyed the scene with pleasure and took his cold pipe out of his mouth.

He had been strictly forbidden to smoke after his last heart attack. No smoking and no drinking, he was warned, if he wanted to live to see his grandson grow up. So he used his pipe as a dummy, keeping it in his mouth most of the day and sucking at it like a baby. He found it most soothing.

'This is delightful,' Geoffrey said, beaming around him, 'to have my whole family here with me. How infrequently it happens.'

'Not your whole family, Daddy,' Tansy corrected him. 'There's Jeremy, Fern, Mark . . .'

'Jeremy,' her father said plaintively, the smile vanishing from his face. 'Why does Jeremy never come and see us? Has he left Emily? He never comes home now. Is it that woman? That Jill? Why doesn't someone explain things to me?'

'Nobody knows the answer, Father.' Gilbert took a huge chunk of cake from the plate. Despite his glasses he was a good-looking boy and, although they were not identical, he and Tansy resembled each other enough for people to see they were twins.

'Nobody,' Catherine echoed, passing Geoffrey his cup of tea.

'Do *you* see Emily?' Geoffrey looked accusingly at his daughter.

'She came to see me in hospital.' Tansy put down her cup and looked searchingly at her father. 'Daddy, why don't *you* invite Emily to the house? Why won't *you* be reconciled with her? She's very unhappy.'

'She deserves to be,' Geoffrey said with satisfaction.

'She is reaping what she sowed.'

'But, Daddy, that is most unfair,' Tansy cried. 'Jeremy is openly living with Jill, yet he is married to Emily. Why don't you disapprove of *that*? Emily didn't do anything wrong. Why blame her?'

'She did wrong.' Geoffrey's hand crept towards his heart. 'Please don't upset me, Tansy. I tell you if Jeremy has left her she deserves it. She is getting her comeuppance.'

Gilbert, sitting in a deck chair, his eyes half closed, took in his father's words but said nothing. He felt a spasm of pity, not only for Emily but also for Tansy and anyone who dared to cross the path of that beloved, but severe and obdurate parent.

Driving along the Dales road in her new car Tansy remembered the day she had gone there by bus and Jeremy had met her with the pony and trap. It seemed such a long time ago because so much had happened. Then she seemed but a child. Now she was married, had a baby and was shortly to leave for Australia. Or was she?

Michael's latest letter had not been quite so enthusiastic. The company had, to his thinking, misrepresented itself. It was not situated in Sydney but in a place which seemed to resemble Netherwick, in being small and out of the way. That in itself was sufficient to detract from its glamour as far as Michael was concerned. Michael said that to have a house worth living in they would have to build it themselves. It was that sort of place. However, there was plenty of scope for improvement, and Australia was still a relatively young and underpopulated country where fortunes could be made.

Tansy hadn't seen Emily since her brief visit to the hospital and she worried increasingly about her. She felt that Emily was isolated from the family, a family that had not, on the whole, been good to her. She hadn't seen her since Roger was born, and he was now four months old.

She turned off the Kettlewell road, vividly recalling the day she and Jeremy had trotted along in the cart, the cold making their faces tingle, the wind blowing in their hair. And then she saw Cragbeck just as she had that day, lying so peacefully in the folds of the hills, a small hamlet which, under another name, had become celebrated in Jeremy's book *A Shepherd in the Hills* describing his life there after the war. There was talk of making a film or documentary about it. There had been an American sale and one or two European publishers had bought translation rights, but *A Shepherd in the Hills* had not made Jeremy famous. It had not been on the bestseller lists, or even sold particularly well. It had received what was called 'critical acclaim', which generally meant books that were written about and talked about rather than read. People liked to have a copy on their bookshelves or lying casually about where others could see it, but they would not have read it.

However, *A Shepherd in the Hills* made Jeremy's a name to look out for. Almost overnight he became a member of the literary establishment and his liaison with Jill did him no harm at all. He was seen with her, looking tweedy and intellectual, at publishing parties and other places where the London literati gathered. It was said he was working on a new book. With Jill's support, both moral and financial, his future seemed bright.

How bright was Emily's, Tansy wondered, stopping the car outside the house the school had bought for her, on her assurance that she intended to make her life in Cragbeck. She would be with the school until she retired. Emily had felt too insecure to take chances. Neither

Jeremy nor she had money. That, as much as anything else, had maybe pushed him into Jill's arms.

That had seemed to set the seal on Emily's break with Jeremy. Tansy wondered if she regretted her attachment to Cragbeck, or ever would?

It was a nice house that had once been the vicarage when the village had its own church. But now that was the village hall, and people worshipped in the village further down the valley which had also amalgamated with the one beyond it. Fewer people worshipped these days and one incumbent had to serve a number of parishes.

The old vicarage was quite a large house, the biggest in the village and, maybe, the authorities had given it to her in the expectation that she would be living there with her husband and two children. Perhaps they would not have given it to her at all if they had sensed a divorce was in the offing. But Jeremy had never mentioned divorce, and Fern had not yet quite developed into the aloof young miss she would become, formed by the expensive private school her grandfather had paid for, and despising country life and country living.

Mark had been sent to public school in the south of England. He, too, seemed to have grown away from his mother. He had lost his love of the Dales, his passion for the countryside and watching sheep. His friends at school were the children of the wealthy, many living in the metropolis or in country houses set in acres of land.

Emily didn't come to the door as Tansy got out of the car and, for a moment, she wondered if she had mistaken the day arranged over the telephone the week before. She stood at the door and knocked for a while, and then she went round to the back where she found Emily hanging washing on the line, pegs in her mouth which fell out with surprise when she saw Tansy.

'So early! she exclaimed then looked at her watch. 'Good heavens I'd no idea of the time. How *rude* you must think me.'

'Not at all,' Tansy said, going up to kiss her. 'I am a bit early. You said twelve and it's a quarter to.'

'I thought it was about ten,' Emily said, impatiently tugging off her apron. 'It just shows what very little idea of time one has here. Did you bring Roger with you?'

'No, he has a snivel so Mummy is looking after him. Anyway I wanted to see you. Maybe we could have a walk after lunch?'

'That would be nice.' Emily stood back, ushering Tansy through the back door into the kitchen where the washing tub stood in the middle of the floor. 'I was praying for a fine day.'

'I was too. Can I help?'

'No, you sit down. I expect you'd like a coffee?'

'I would actually,' Tansy said. 'I didn't have time before I left.'

'Have you still got your house, then?'

'Why, yes.' Tansy paused, staring at Emily. 'Where did you think I was living?'

'I thought you might have sold it and be staying with your parents. When do you hope to fly out?'

'I'm not sure yet.' Tansy pointedly studied the rings on her fingers. 'Nothing's decided.'

The years had taught Emily tact, so she said nothing until they were sitting after lunch in the conservatory at the front of the house which overlooked the pleasant garden that had once belonged to the vicarage. On one side of them was the village hall and on the other open fields.

'It *is* a heavenly spot.' Tansy put up her hand to shade her eyes. The house faced south and the sun shone directly into the conservatory, making it feel quite hot although it was a chilly autumn day.

'It *is* lovely,' Emily agreed. 'It consoles me for a lot.'

Tansy gazed at her, not quite knowing how to reply. 'Has Jeremy seen it?'

'Jeremy hasn't been up here since his publication party; and just after that he moved in with Jill. Sometimes I wonder if he will ever return to Cragbeck.'

'You must feel very sad,' Tansy said in a voice full of sympathy. 'Very bitter.'

'Sad, not bitter,' Emily corrected her and, swallowing her coffee, set the cup down beside her. 'There's no point in bitterness, but one can't help sadness. I feel I've lost not only my husband; but will soon lose my children. Fern was never very happy here, but Mark loved it. Fern always yearned for the big world and loved going away. She particularly likes staying with Jeremy and Jill, because Jill's girls are about her age. That's part of Fern's life that has absolutely nothing to do with me, and I feel completely cut off and excluded from it. But I'm not lonely and I do love this house, although it's far too big for me.' Emily paused, looking at Tansy fondly. 'You know, I shall miss you terribly. What shall I do when you go?'

'I may not go,' Tansy said, without realizing what she was going to say. 'Look, shall we take that walk?'

She stood up abruptly and Emily rose with her. The sun which had appeared briefly during lunch was now obscured behind a bank of cloud and, as they set out on their walk, they shivered. Emily had bought a mongrel pup for company called Spot which ran in front of them smelling the ground, the rabbit droppings and the clumps of cow dung with ecstasy. They kept to the footpath by the side of the fell and the beck that ultimately ran into the Wharfe.

There was a strong hint of autumn in the air and,

already, some of the trees were almost bare. But the beauty of the scene tugged at Tansy's heart and she felt a lump come into a throat.

'I sense you're having some sort of struggle,' Emily said, halting as Spot plunged into the beck, chasing an imaginary rabbit. 'Do you want to talk about it? It's about Australia, I suppose?'

'I don't really want to go.' Tansy struggled hard to control her emotion. 'I know now that I definitely don't. Before I pretended it was because of Roger. I've taken the house off the market.'

'Have you told Michael?' Emily enquired gently.

'No. I had a letter from him last week saying that things were not as rosy as he thought they would be. The factory is not in Sydney but in some remote place in the outback and facilities are very primitive. Even more primitive than Netherwick, Michael said, so you can imagine what he means by that!'

'So isn't he going to stay, or what?'

'Well he's going to stay; there's not much else he can do because he has a contract, but he doesn't sound very happy.'

'He still wants you to go, though?'

'Oh yes. Very much. He says we'll live in Sydney and he'll commute and come home at weekends. Life would be very lonely for me then, you know, not knowing anyone. In Netherwick I know *everyone*.'

'But, Tansy, you'll have a lovely time.' Emily put a hand on her arm and pressed it. 'You'll meet lots of young, attractive people, like yourselves. It will be a whole new life opening up. You can't live in Netherwick if Michael can't find work here. You mustn't hesitate . . . or, is it your father? Is that really what's stopping you?' There was no mistaking her meaning.

'Well,' Tansy hedged, 'Father, of course, isn't *happy*

about me going, never has been; but he doesn't know about Michael's letter. Mum does though.'

'And what does she think?'

'She's unhappy too. She thinks I should stay here and so do I.'

'But, Tansy,' Emily's voice acquired a sudden urgency, 'what about your marriage? What about Michael?'

'Well, I love him of course . . .' Tansy voice trailed off and Emily gently shook her.

'Tansy, what are you doing? What are you saying? Don't you realize that if you don't go to Michael your marriage will founder, as mine did? If I'd gone to London with Jeremy as he wanted me to, there would be no Jill. We'd still be living together instead of being on the brink of divorce.'

'Do you really think so?' Tansy felt the lump in her throat again and tears welled up behind her eyes.

'I *know* so, Tansy. Jeremy and I were very close, very loving. We had a good sexual relationship, a deep bond. I should never, ever, have let him go alone. I relied on the bond but it wasn't enough. He needed me to look after him when he came out of hospital and I wasn't there. You have no idea how much I reproach myself for it. I was selfish and I didn't think of him. No wonder he went straight into the arms of another woman who showed him some sympathy.

'Tansy, you *must* go to Michael. Go *now*! Take the baby and go before it's too late. He's an attractive man and he'll find someone else. Don't risk it. I don't blame Jeremy for what happened to us. Jeremy stuck by me when Catherine asked me to leave and, yet, when he needed me in London I didn't go.'

'I think you're too hard on yourself,' Tansy said at last. 'You needed to work. You had a good job here.'

'I could have got one in London, maybe something

better, teaching my subject, classics. There's a shortage of teachers and they would have taken me; but I loved Cragbeck too much and it made me selfish. What's more, Tansy, I know that *you* are not selfish. You are very loving and giving, but I do know your father and I think he has a hold over you that you must break. Break it please, before it is too late. Go to Michael, Tansy. Michael needs you.'

Bob Garrett and his wife Claire were fanatical about sport. If they were not on the golf course they went hunting or playing squash or badminton at the local sports club. Every night before he came home from the office Bob worked out in a gym, and, as soon as it opened every morning, he was the first through the door at the public swimming pool.

Bob was a thrusting, ambitious man and, to him, personal health, welfare and financial security were synonymous. He made no decisions before he had thoroughly spied out the land or tested the market, and the main difference between him and his brother Michael was that one was instinctive and the other a bit of a plodder.

It had always been like this, the brothers rivalling each other in games, schoolwork, and for their parents' affection and attention all their lives. The consequence was that they hated each other.

Bob was extremely glad when Michael decided to stay on in the army. He had prepared himself carefully for succeeding his father as the head of the Garrett Great Engineering Co and he'd spent the first two years after his demob learning the business from the bottom. His rage may, therefore, be imagined when Michael had suddenly decided to enter the firm as an already established high-flyer, with no experience whatever, given a department all his own, and sent the firm careering in all directions.

Bob knew that Michael was an interloper, a flash-in-the-pan who threatened the security of them all. With his wild ideas the Garrett Great Engineering Co might well go under altogether. In Bob's carefully considered opinion the best thing to do with bad figures was to retrench and keep afloat with the help of heavy borrowings from the bank. It was no time to start spinning the wheel.

After Michael had gone things did slowly start to improve. Many of the new models of cars were flash-in-the-pan too, and soon disappeared from the production lines. The popularity of television was certainly causing a surprise, but the sets were large and cumbersome and colour when it came, *if* it came, would be extremely expensive and the quality not very good. Besides, Bob reasoned, there were so many invested interests working against television: the cinema industry, theatres, clubs and the leisure entertainment in general. They would never allow a machine to take over the whole huge entertainment world merely by pressing a button; to become as widespread and as popular as people said it would be.

Bob and Claire Garrett had bought a nice house that they could afford in a respected suburb of Leeds. They had two children and would not have any more; one of each sex. They had what they wanted and were contented with life. When Michael left the business they were more contented than ever.

In the autumn their great delight was the hunt. There they considered they met the right kind of people, mixed with the county set and made good connections. Many of the landed gentry still had large houses and estates in Yorkshire, and it was good to be associated with people like this and to ensure that one's children went to school with theirs.

One frosty morning in November Bob and Claire were dressed to go hunting. Claire always wore a hard black cap, but Bob wore a top hat. People said it was dangerous to do this and that there should be more protection for the head, but Bob took no notice. He was a good rider, a careful jumper and, above all, a cautious man; he would never take risks or attempt a fence he knew he couldn't jump. Thus his philosophy of life was extended to every aspect of it.

Bob preened himself in the mirror, satisfied with his appearance as a prosperous, successful man of the world. The business was turning the corner; the children were doing well at school and he had his eye on an even larger house that had once belonged to an earl whose family had fallen on hard times. He could imagine the hunt meeting there; enjoying a stirrup-cup before it began its forage into land owned by him and he, perhaps as master, leading the assorted members of the prosperous middle class who largely made up the hunt; people like him.

'Do you think Tansy will ever *go* to Australia?' Claire said, peering over his shoulder as she flicked at a speck of mascara which had lodged itself into the corner of her eye.

'Mother says she's going *after* Christmas,' Bob replied, rearranging his cravat. 'The plane is booked.'

'Is the house up for sale again?'

'I don't know.' Bob turned around with an air of indifference. 'Why, do you want to buy it?'

'No *fear*,' Claire said. '*That* pokey little place? Much too near your mother and father as well. Besides, I thought you'd set your heart on Endells?'

Endells was the mansion, set in fifty acres of woodland, which had once been the home of the earls of that name whose impecunious descendant now lived in a decrepit block of flats in West Kensington.

'I hear Michael is not happy in Australia,' Claire said as an aside.

'Well, he's not coming back *here*,' Bob said firmly, getting his topper out of the hat box and carefully brushing it.

'Could you stop him if he wanted to?'

'I could and I would,' Bob said firmly. 'I will never, ever allow Michael a place in Garrett Engineering, even on the shop floor. That I have made perfectly clear to Father.'

'Well let's hope he settles down then.' Claire was finally satisfied with her own appearance and pulled her well-cut riding jacket down over her slim hips.

It was true she was an Irish beauty, who had been the cloakroom girl in a nightclub in Leeds when Bob met her and, to her credit, she had kept her figure and her looks. Elocution lessons had eliminated most of her Irish vowels, and she studied the art of flower arranging and attended Cordon Bleu cookery classes where she met the kind of women who either hunted or whose husbands did: the sort that she and her husband wanted to be associated with.

When Bob and Claire got to the hunt in their shooting brake, their two large labradors barking loudly and enthusiastically in the back, the hunt was gathering in the yard of the farm where most of the members stabled their horses. Some with very large houses had their own stables and, one day, Bob and Claire would at Endells. It was a prospect which they both looked forward to.

They parked their car with similar cars which also had

large dogs barking, or small ones yapping away. It was a scene of noise and pleasant confusion, colourful and redolent of pictures of old England. No other country seemed to organize the hunt in quite the same way as the English, who had built a veritable aristocracy around it.

Bob went over to the stable where his and Claire's horses were kept and, as he did, one of the grooms greeted him at the stable door of his horse, Porter.

'Porter has gone a bit lame, Mr Garrett,' the man said. 'I don't think he should go out today.'

'When did this happen?' Bob said, striding through the stable door. 'Careless on the morning run, were you?'

'I was not, Mr Garrett,' the lad said, flushing. 'I noticed it last night and I thought today I'd call the vet.'

'And did you?' Bob impatiently hit his thigh with his crop.

'Well . . .' the groom scratched his head. 'Porter does seem a bit better this morning.'

'Well, let's see, then, let's see.' Bob was aware of the sounds in the yard as the hounds arrived and the farmer's family carried round trays with the stirrup-cup.

'You can't actually *see* anything, Mr Garrett,' the groom said. 'And when you start off he's all right. Maybe it's a touch of rheumatism, I rubbed him last night and this morning.'

'Maybe that did the trick, then,' Bob said in a kinder voice, now that he seemed to be getting his way. 'If I find him going lame I'll come straight back. Don't worry.'

'I'd be *very* careful, Mr Garrett.' The groom still looked worried. 'If there were another horse I'd suggest you borrowed that, but everyone has turned up today.'

'I'd rather ride Porter,' Bob replied. 'I'm used to him.'

As the groom led him outside and saddled him Bob

grinned at the horse and rubbed its nose. 'We'll be fine together Porter, won't we old boy?'

The hunt went through some of the finest, but also some of the most difficult country in that part of Yorkshire. There were many copses, hedges and streams in the path of those chasing the helpless fox who, in this particular case, may be said to have had an advantage over his pursuers. In fact the fox usually got away and the North Wolseley Hunt didn't have much of a reputation; but this in no way detracted from the enjoyment of the members who liked nothing better than galloping over the fine countryside on a chilly winter's day, even if it meant chasing after a non-existent prey.

'What's the matter?' Claire enquired testily as Bob eventually rode up on his horse who appeared to be moving quite well.

'The groom said Porter had gone lame; but I think he's all right,' Bob replied.

'He looks all right to me,' Claire said, staring at the horse's legs as if she were an expert. 'People were asking where you were.'

Just then the horn sounded and, without even the chance of a drink, Bob set off in the rear of the hunt and in the wake of his wife who quickly moved up to the front in order to be seen riding alongside the master.

This, however, was one of those days when the master saw, or pretended to see, a real live quarry and, with a shout he encouraged his horse, with a flick of his crop, to gallop faster.

'The fox, the fox,' Claire cried, looking behind her for Bob, who seemed to be finding difficulty in making the pace.

Porter *was* lame. There was no doubt about it. They had scarcely gone a few furlongs when the horse began to limp and Bob, sick with frustration and rage, knew he would have to turn back. He was not a cruel man and to force a lame horse to hunt was not only cruel but senseless. If it had to be put down it would cost him a packet to buy another.

So Bob, with the sounds of the hunt ringing in his ears, disconsolately turned Porter back towards the farm giving him a sympathetic pat on the flank.

Suddenly Bob heard his wife call and, glancing over his shoulder, observed her galloping towards him waving her crop in the air and pointing angrily in the direction of the hunt.

The sight seemed immediately to alarm Porter who whinnied and unexpectedly broke into a canter. The faster Claire came towards him, the faster the lame horse tried to go until its legs buckled under it and it fell heavily on top of its rider, who had no chance at all to get away.

PART FOUR

The Pride of the Family

1958–1961

Chapter 16

'Gilbert Wills Blair,' the voice intoned and Gilbert, wearing his academic gown and hood over a dark suit, stepped onto the rostrum and bowed to the chancellor of the university.

In the auditorium his parents and sister, smiling, clapped loudly. Gilbert Wills Blair, Bachelor of Medicine, Bachelor of Surgery; first-class honours in both. The pride of the family.

Gilbert gave a modest grin in the direction of his family and, later, when the degree ceremony was over, he joined them outside the hall where they stood talking to the Wentworths whose daughter, Rosalind, had graduated in English at the same time as Gilbert.

'Well done, Gilbert, well done, Rosalind,' exclaimed the families in unison as the pair, who had met during the ceremony, came over to them clutching the scrolls of their awards in their hands.

'First-class honours.' Peter Wentworth warmly shook Gilbert by the hand. 'Your parents are very proud of you.'

'*And* a special prize,' Geoffrey said, beaming at his son. 'For the best student of his year.'

'Really Father.' Gilbert looked nervously around in case any of his contemporaries could overhear this paean of parental praise.

'Rosalind did awfully well too,' Catherine intervened quickly. 'I understand you want to teach, Rosalind?'

'I'm not sure,' Rosalind replied. 'I'd quite like to get into publishing.'

'Well, my daughter-in-law is the person to ask about that,' Geoffrey said. 'Why don't you drop her a line?'

To Tansy it still seemed very odd to hear Jill being referred to as 'daughter-in-law'; but in fact she had been for two years. Jeremy and Emily had a quick, clean divorce with Jeremy admitting adultery, naming Jill as the co-respondent. In days gone by it would have been considered shameful to be named as the other woman and people had done their best to conceal it. But that was long ago. In the post-war world morals had changed, as much as attitudes towards divorce and remarriage, and only the churches now seemed to consider dissolution of marriage sinful, or even anything to be ashamed about.

Geoffrey liked Jill. She was the sort of smart, pretty woman he had always admired and she quite unashamedly played up to him, angling for his approval by sending him the latest book published by her firm with a note: 'I thought you would like to see this', or 'Yours was the first name that sprang to my mind.'

She always called him 'Father' and he liked that too. Emily never had – it was always familiarly Geoffrey or, sometimes, Doctor Blair.

But Tansy, alone of all the family, didn't like Jill. She thought her superficial and wondered that no one else seemed to see through her. Nor did she feel that Jeremy was particularly happy with her and, certainly, he hadn't produced much work. He hadn't produced any. He was kept by Jill; but if this irked him he didn't show it.

After the graduation ceremony there was a dinner at the Grand. Michael joined them from the office and as he came, late as usual, into the dining room Tansy remembered when they'd lunched there just before their relationship had broken up.

Now, five years later, they were more married than

ever and, in addition to Roger, had two more children: Julia born in 1955 after Michael came back from Australia following Bob's fall, and Francis, the baby, six months old, always called Frank.

'Sorry,' Michael said, adjusting his tie as he stopped to kiss his wife, his mother-in-law and shake hands with everyone else. 'I nearly didn't make it at all.'

'Things going all right, Michael?' Geoffrey enquired gruffly. He still didn't like his son-in-law but, above all, he hated his habit of being late for everything as though to emphasize his own self-importance.

'Very well, thank you, Doctor Blair,' Michael said politely, stopping the waiter and asking for a whisky and soda. 'At last the London office is all sewn up.'

'But, surely, you're not going to live there?' Catherine looked sharply over her half-moon spectacles through which she was reading the menu.

Michael wriggled in his seat, glancing anxiously at his wife. 'Well, it's a moot point at the moment. However, Tansy and I aren't going to quarrel over it. We shall come to some compromise. Besides, I have Bob to think of.'

'Tansy still doesn't want to leave Netherwick, I expect.' Dorothy Wentworth gave her husband a knowing glance. 'Personally I'd jump at the chance to live in London.'

'That's because you weren't born here, my dear,' Peter Wentworth said. 'People who are born in Netherwick have it in their blood.'

'Well I don't,' Michael said shortly, 'and *I* was born here.'

'Neither had my two elder sons,' Geoffrey added, 'although in my opinion Jeremy would love to come back. He gets no inspiration in the city. No wonder, always going to parties.'

Tansy sat listening, saying little, thinking. She was always thinking these days because so many decisions had to be made. Life with Michael was anything but dull, yet it was peace she craved. Peace to be with her children and live the sort of domestic life her mother lived and which she, lacking any other ambition, had always wanted.

Only, if this had been her goal, she had certainly married the wrong man.

'How *is* Bob?' Peter Wentworth leaned towards Michael. 'I hear he's made some progress?'

'Bob will never walk again,' Michael lowered his voice. 'His spinal cord was completely shattered. However, I have promised him he can come back to the business whenever he wants to. He's paid a full salary and, as a director and major shareholder receiving dividends, he can do what he likes.'

'By any standards Michael has been very good to Bob,' Catherine insisted, looking at him. '*And* after what he did to you.'

'I was never one for revenge, Catherine,' Michael murmured, accepting wine from the waiter as he started his first course although the others were already on their entrée. 'The inconvenience to me was infinitesimal compared to what happened to poor Bob.'

'I understood he was warned not to ride the horse.' Geoffrey looked pointedly at Michael.

'Yes, but he was on his way back, realizing it was lame. Unfortunately it was Claire, who had come to find him, who startled Bob's already nervous mount.'

'Terrible thing,' Dorothy said in a shocked voice. 'It ruined his life.'

Tansy thought that Dorothy didn't realize just how true that was. Bob had not the emotional resources to accept a tragedy like that and he had not yet got over it, perhaps never would. He had become morose and difficult, drank a lot and, two years after the accident, his wife had left him, taking the children with her.

Michael had indeed been very good to Bob and when he had flown home from Australia, on hearing the news of the accident, he had taken control both of the business and the family in an admirable way. In addition, a year after Bob's accident their father died and, the following year, Claire had left Bob. She said she could tolerate anything but a man who drank, as her own father had been an alcoholic and she didn't want a husband who was one too.

Bob had been unable to manage on his own. Michael had arranged for him first to go into a private nursing home and then to live with their mother in the old family home, with a full-time nurse for Bob and plenty of help in the house.

Michael was averse to discussing his family and his personal life, and the conversation soon drifted on to other subjects, the careers of the new graduates being the main topic.

However, after the party broke up and they got back to their own home Tansy said:

'Your mother will miss you terribly if you go back to London, Michael.'

'What do you mean if *I* go, Tansy?' Michael said undoing his tie. 'You mean – *we* go.'

'You know I don't want to go to London, Michael. I hate the city.' Tansy flopped on the bed feeling dejected and morose despite the joy of Gilbert's degree day. Or, in a way, perhaps that had something to do with it; she seemed to have achieved so little compared with Gilbert. Gilbert was poised on the threshold of a brilliant, exciting life whereas she was already settled into a pattern that many would consider humdrum.

Michael didn't answer at once which, in itself, was an ominous sign, but proceeded steadily with his undressing, after which he went into the bathroom, from which she could hear the familiar noises as he vigorously brushed his teeth.

When angry about something, Michael shouted. He liked to get his own way by bawling at people. In a way he lived on his nerves, just as his mother did on hers. If Michael didn't shout it was even worse because he seemed to bottle everything up and when the row began it was twice as bad.

Tansy was in bed by the time Michael came back and climbed in beside her. Then he lay there, his head propped against his pillows, arms crossed.

'It was a very nice day,' Tansy said uneasily, because Michael frightened her a bit at times. 'Dad is awfully proud of Gilbert.'

'I think we're all proud of Gilbert,' Michael replied. 'He's a fine man and he's going to be a fine doctor. I personally am exceedingly proud to have him as a brother-in-law.'

'That's very generous of you, Michael.' Tansy glanced at him in surprise, but he remained with his arms folded and the air of someone who was on the brink of a row; after five years she knew all the signs.

'Tansy,' Michael said after a while. 'I know what you're thinking; but I am not going to have a row with you tonight or any night about this subject. If you want to continue as my wife you must come with me to London. If you don't, well . . .' He gave her a meaningful look and Tansy immediately thought of the children and of little Frank sleeping in his crib in the nursery next door, within earshot of his parents' room.

'You *are* threatening me then, aren't you, Michael?'

'No I am not.' Michael sighed with exaggerated

patience. 'You are my wife and I love you; but I think your place is by my side, and your duty is to do what I want.' Wearily he passed a hand across his brow. 'I have had a hell of a few years, you know, Tansy. I want a bit of peace.'

'I know that, Michael.' Tansy nervously, placatingly, put a hand on his arm. 'I'll see.'

'No "I'll see", Tansy,' Michael said firmly, turning his back on her as he prepared for sleep, drawing up the bedclothes until they covered his shoulders. 'I insist on it and that is all. You simply have no choice . . . that is, if you want things to continue as they are.'

The solicitor said: 'Do I take it that you want to file for divorce, Mrs Garrett?' Yet he looked puzzled. He was a man she'd gone to Leeds to consult, one who knew nothing about her, her husband or her family. He did, however, seem familiar with the name Garrett Engineering and its rapid progress in the last few years.

'No, I just want to know what my rights are.'

The solicitor spread out his fingers in a deprecating manner. 'Well, of course you do not *have* to do what your husband demands if you don't want to. This is not the time of Queen Victoria or even . . .' the solicitor, who was not a young man, cleared his throat, regretfully in Tansy's opinion, 'the years immediately before the last war. Your husband cannot *force* you to do anything.'

'Can he divorce me if I refuse to go?'

'No.' The solicitor looked understandably cautious. 'No; but he might demand a legal separation on the ground of incompatibility. Divorce law, as you know, is exceedingly complex and due for reform. However, you certainly can be sure that he can't divorce you solely on the grounds of your refusal to go to London with him. You might suggest, say, a reasonable compromise.'

'How do you mean "reasonable"?'

'Well, couldn't you go part of the time?'

'My children are very young. I couldn't go backwards and forwards with them.'

The solicitor gave a despairing shrug of his shoulders. 'Well then, Mrs Garrett, I think if you wish to retain the affection of your husband you don't have a great deal of choice.'

'*If* you wish to retain the affection of your husband . . .' The words echoed in Tansy's mind all the way back to Netherwick. She had left her car at the station and gone to Leeds by train. As it chugged back across the valley she realized that every inch of the way was familiar to her: every sight, every hill, valley; every little copse, every mill and factory chimney and then, when the grey slate roofs of Netherwick came in sight, she felt herself suddenly choke and her eyes filled with tears.

Her mother had no doubt about the ethics of the situation.

'But of course, Tansy, you must go with Michael to London. That's where your place is. It's not as though it were Australia, is it, dear? It's not that far. You can come home often.'

'But it won't *be* home, Mother.' She looked at her mother with the pleading eyes of a young girl. 'We won't keep a house in Netherwick. Michael has big ideas for expansion. He might even move the entire operation to the south.'

'Well he *has* saved the company, dear,' Catherine said in a tone of admiration. 'I have to hand it to Michael – one blow after the other and he copes with them all, *and* injects new life into a company that some people say was nearly bankrupt.' Her mother looked at her searchingly over the kitchen table where they were having a cup of tea. 'Do you still love him, Tansy?'

'Of *course* I love Michael.'

'Sometimes I think you have a funny way of showing it.'

'Why do you say that?' Tansy looked sharply at her.

'You never *seem* a very loving couple.'

'We don't have to show affection in public,' Tansy said acidly. 'We do have three children to prove there is another side to our life together, Mother.'

'Oh I know that, dear,' Catherine said hurriedly. 'I can't really explain what I mean. Now then,' she glanced at the clock and got up, smoothing her skirt with her hands, 'Gilbert is coming home tonight.'

'Tonight?' Tansy said with surprise.

'He wants to talk to your father. I think it's something about his work.'

Tansy could see that her mother was worried and, rising, she put an arm anxiously around her shoulder. 'Oh, Mother! I am very selfish aren't I? I thought you seemed preoccupied. Why should I have assumed it was just about me?'

'Well I'm worried about you too, Tansy,' her mother shook her head, 'I don't deny it. I'm sorry about you and Michael, and your father is worried too. I think, and even your father thinks, that you should fit in with Michael's wishes: you should go and live in London and, if that's what he wants, bring up your children there. It's what I would do for a man I loved. It's not just your father, is it, Tansy?'

Tansy folded her arms and leaned against the side of the table. 'How do you mean, Mother?'

'That you don't want to leave him.'

'He *is* nearly seventy, Mother. His health isn't good.'

'Your father will live on his bad health until he's ninety,' her mother replied caustically. 'I have *no* doubt about that.'

On the way home Tansy found herself reflecting on her mother's remark and wondered what she meant.

That evening over dinner Tansy told Michael that if he really wanted to live in London and thought she should of course she would go with him. She only hoped that they might live just a little outside the city; somewhere in the suburbs, like Kent or Sussex, somewhere where they could hear the birds sing and see the trees and flowers grow.

Geoffrey Blair looked up as his son came into the room and immediately his face lit up with pleasure.

'Am I disturbing you, Father?'

'Of course not.' Geoffrey put down the paper and held out a hand. 'I just saw my final patient and was reading the evening paper.'

'How long are you going to go on seeing patients, Father?' Gilbert kissed his father on both cheeks and then sat in the comfortable chair opposite him.

'Until you're ready to join me, my son. I take it that will be sometime next year?'

Gilbert gazed at his father for a moment and then turned his eyes away, clearly the bearer of bad tidings.

'Anyway, I enjoy seeing patients,' Doctor Blair went on. 'It helps to keep me active; in touch with reality. I only see two or three a day. I don't make visits. When you join us I shan't see any at all. You and Tom Thackery will share the load.'

'Father,' Gilbert began and, as his voice faltered, he looked up and his father exclaimed:

'Gilbert! Is anything the matter?'

So much was invested in Gilbert, in his future, that

the slightest thing disturbed his father, the slightest intimation of ill health, of trouble of any kind. He hated him going climbing and intended as soon as he could to put a stop to it. Maybe that would happen when Gilbert got married and, already, Geoffrey Blair was putting out feelers for suitable candidates, like any broker in an eastern marriage market. As far as he could he had mapped out his son's future from the time he was born and, so far, things were going according to plan. So he gazed apprehensively at his normally articulate son who clearly now had difficulty in expressing himself.

'Gilbert?' he asked sharply again.

'Father, I don't want to be a GP.' At last the words tumbled out in a torrent. 'I know it will be a terrible shock, but . . .'

To Geoffrey the words were so redolent of those spoken by Edward so long ago, that he had a feeling of *déjà vu*.

'You don't *want* to be a doctor?' he spluttered.

'Oh no, I *want* to be a doctor, Father; but not a GP. I want to specialize.'

'But you can't,' Geoffrey said in a flat voice. 'All my life I have planned that you would join me in this practice. All my life I have waited to see your name and mine on the brass plaque on the gate. You don't know what it means to me for you to carry on a practice where I have been all my life.'

'But I do, Father, that's why I find it so difficult to express myself. I want to go to London and specialize. I had a long talk with the professor the other day and he is putting me forward for a scholarship to Guy's.'

'Oh, is he?' Geoffrey said bitterly. 'And did *you* tell him what your father expected of you?'

'Yes I did. He said he thought I would be wasted in general practice. I had the highest marks . . .'

'I know your marks were very good, Gilbert, and I was proud of you.' Geoffrey's spectacles had started to mist over with emotion and, as he took them off to clean them, Gilbert saw, to his dismay, tears in his father's eyes. Of course he had known it would not be easy. He had even discussed tactics with the professor, who knew all about Doctor Blair's ambitions for his son. The professor, however, had erred in thinking that the doctor would be even more proud of a son who went on to a career in Harley Street.

'Gastroenterology,' Gilbert said, his voice going hoarse again. 'There is a vacancy for a junior registrar in the department and, after I have finished my houseman's year . . .'

'You know what this will do to me, don't you, Gilbert?' Geoffrey carefully replaced his spectacles on his nose.

'But, Father, Tom Thackery . . .'

'Tom Thackery is *not* Gilbert Blair. My dear boy, I could have sold the practice to Tom Thackery years ago and retired, as my health dictated I should. I have purposely stayed working for you, and now *this* is my reward!'

Geoffrey fell back into his chair and started gasping. Gilbert swallowed but remained where he was. He had already rehearsed this scene and its possible outcome and had vowed not to give in to his father. Never, never, never. His father was sure to use blackmail about his state of health.

Gilbert got up and, instead of going to his father as Geoffrey had anticipated he would, worried about the possible effect of this announcement on his father, he strode towards the door.

'I'll see you at dinner, Father.'

Gilbert crossed the hall to the kitchen where he found

his mother presiding over the preparation of the evening meal. She looked up with pleasure as she saw him and went over to him, putting floury arms round his shoulders and kissing him, eyes smiling fondly up at him.

'Did you see your father?'

'Yes, Mother.' Gilbert kissed her on both cheeks and then went over to the pots on the stove, lifting the lids one by one and inspecting the contents. Gilbert was a 'picker' and when he was a little boy he was always being reprimanded for helping himself to food, prepared and waiting to be served in the kitchen.

'Now now,' his mother said, pretending to be annoyed. Having Gilbert here made up for the disturbing visit Tansy had made in the afternoon. She was sure that one day her daughter's marriage would flounder and the prospect which she had, so far, kept to herself made her very unhappy. She had never really felt Michael and Tansy were suited and that Tansy had been swept off her feet by an older, more sophisticated man, as, in a way, so had she many years before. Now, however, that they were married and the parents of three children, Catherine wanted them to stay together. She dreaded the consequences to Geoffrey's health if they didn't.

'What time is dinner, Mother?' Gilbert put the lid on the last pot. 'I'm starving.'

'When weren't you? I don't think they feed you properly at that hospital.'

'It's the hours,' Gilbert said, perching on a stool by the table. 'Sometimes I'm on duty for twenty-four hours at a stretch. *That's* what makes me hungry.'

'It's all wrong in my opinion,' his mother said, putting the tart she had been making into the oven. 'Anyway, when you join the practice you'll have mother's home cooking again. That will be nice, won't it?' And, smiling,

she raised herself from her knees and went over to was
her hands. As there was no reply from Gilbert she looke
round enquiringly. 'Won't it?' she repeated.

'Mother, I told Father just now I didn't want to joi
the practice. I want to specialize.'

'You want to *what*?' his mother said, turning round a
slowly and carefully, she dried her hands.

'Specialize. There are one or two openings in Londo
for junior registrars. Gastroenterology is one, orthopaedi
another. I'll eventually become a consultant, a surgeon

'Then you won't be coming here at all?' His mother
tone was one of bewilderment. 'How did your fath
take it?'

'Well of course he's upset, but I think he'll get over
After all, to be asked to take higher qualifications is a
honour. Medicine at this level is very competitive. I
have years of study in front of me.'

'By which time your father will be dead,' Catherir
said bluntly. 'He won't ever share your triumph. I thir
it will kill him if you don't come into the practice. I
has talked of nothing but your names together on tl
brass plate at the gate for years.'

'But, Mother,' Gilbert protested angrily, 'this is a for
of blackmail. Don't you see . . .'

'*If* it hadn't been for your father, you would nev
have been a doctor at all.'

'I don't see how you can possibly say that, Mother. I
reasonable. I might have wanted to study medicine ev
if Father had not pushed me into it. Even if I hadr
known how strongly he wished me to succeed whe
Edward had failed. Well he did and I have. What's mo
I got the highest honours.'

'Too good to be a mere GP I suppose,' Catherine sai
echoing some of Geoffrey's bitterness.

'That's not true at all, Mother.' Gilbert, who ha

prepared himself so carefully for this ordeal, who had anticipated every reaction, still felt it unfair that both his parents should oppose him.

'With Tansy going to London and then you . . . I really don't know what it will do to your father.' She began to wring her hands, still a little wet from washing.

'Tansy *is* going to London, then?' Gilbert had not heard this news and, worriedly, ruffled his hair.

'In her case she doesn't have much choice if she wants to stay married. As she has three young children I suppose she does. In your case you *do* have a choice. I was so looking forward to having you home here again, Gilbert. It can be very lonely with your father and his moods. Some days he doesn't speak at all.'

'But, Mother, he is much better.'

'When you're here, or Tansy's here, or people come to call,' his mother said with a catch in her voice, 'he makes an effort; but when he's alone with me he makes no effort at all. Sometimes we don't converse all day long and he sits in front of the fire, not reading, just sunk in gloom. I tell you I don't think I can bear it for much longer.'

'Oh, Mother!' Gilbert got up and put his arms around her. 'I'd no idea things were still so bad.'

'I didn't want to depress you,' Catherine stroked his back while he held her in his arms, 'but I felt that once you had done your houseman's year there would be nothing to stop you coming home, with an established, lucrative practice waiting for you. You have a very comfortable home here, Gilbert. Some doctors have to strive for a long time to get patients. How long will it take you to become a specialist?'

'Years, Mother. You have to climb the ladder.'

'Exactly, living in the hospital, long hours, poor pay for years and years. Is it *worth* it, Gilbert?'

'Well . . . looked at that way . . .' Doubt now showed clearly on his face.

'Besides,' his mother saw the look and hurried on to take advantage of it. '*When* are you going to marry? Tansy already has three children.'

'Mother, I'm only twenty-four. It's not exactly old. Tansy did marry when she was very young.'

'Yes, but it would be nice to settle down. To have your children and Tansy's growing up together. You don't want too much of a gap between cousins.'

'Well, Mother, if she's in London and I'm up here they won't see much of one another.'

'Oh, you'll *stay*, then,' his mother threw her arms more tightly around him. 'I knew you would, Gilbert, I *knew* you would.'

Gilbert gently but firmly prised his mother's fingers from his arms. 'I *can't* promise, Mother. Please don't force me to take a decision I *know* is wrong.'

Crestfallen she removed her hands and for a long time they gazed into each other's eyes. Catherine was the first to break contact. Instinctively she felt she had lost.

Michael pushed open the door of the house and ushered Tansy inside. It was completely empty, but it had been carpeted and was beautifully decorated. Just ready to move into.

'There, darling,' Michael said, closing the door and putting an arm around her waist. 'I know you wanted it to be the home counties, but I fell in love with this house and hoped you would too.'

Leaving Michael standing where he was, Tansy walked through the hall into the front room which ran the whole length of the house, so that there was a view from the front to the small garden at the back. Slowly she walked to the window and looked out. Yes, it was pretty but it was not what she wanted. Across the brick wall, was the garden of the house next door, just like this one.

'It's a very good area,' Michael said, coming up to her. 'Harrods is just round the corner.'

'How convenient.' Tansy didn't try to conceal the sarcasm in her voice.

'Now, Tansy,' Michael said, also in a different, less conciliatory and more peremptory, tone of voice.

'You promised me a large house in Sussex or Kent.'

'In that case we might as well have stayed in Netherwick,' Michael said, his voice continuing to rise. 'Besides, I never "promised" you anything. By the time I get into the City from the country half the day would be gone. Besides, I don't *like* the country, Tansy. I don't want to live there. I like the excitement of towns.'

'Well you should have made it clear, and you didn't!' Tansy snapped back at him. 'You should have been honest and frank, instead of misleading me. Anyway I don't like this house, and I *don't* want to live in the centre of London.'

She turned round and made her way to the middle of the room where she stopped to look back at him. 'If you keep your promise and look for somewhere out of London, I'll consider it; but I don't want to live here. It is not good for the children and it's not good for me.'

'It's very near the park,' Michael said in a voice of growing desperation. 'A stone's throw from . . .'

'I don't care *where* it is, Michael. I'm not living here. I don't like it.'

As Tansy went to the hall Michael shouted after her. 'Well it's too damn bad, Tansy, because I've bought it. It's *our* house and we're living here, whether you like it or not.'

Tansy ran down the hall and out of the front door, down the stone steps that led directly to the pavement. Then she looked round, her heart thumping painfully, not knowing where to go or what direction to take. She felt like a trapped animal who wanted to raise its head and scream for help.

'Tansy,' Michael said, rushing down after her and pulling roughly at her arm. '*Please* don't make an exhibition of yourself.' He looked nervously around at the windows of the houses on either side, at the ones opposite them in the pretty square.

It *was* a pretty square, as London squares went, there was no doubt about that. It was one of the prettiest as well as one of the most fashionable and expensive in the heart of Knightsbridge, with Harrods, indeed, just round the corner.

'This house has cost a lot of money, do you hear?' Michael said in her ear. 'A lot of money and we're going to live here. If you don't like it you can go home without the children. Now come inside and don't make a fool of yourself in the street.'

He propelled her towards the steps which Tansy reluctantly climbed, feeling like a small, rebellious child. As she entered, the walls of the house seemed to close around her, producing in her a feeling of claustrophobia. She was not used to the city and she hated it. Besides, it was *not* what Michael had promised. To get her to London he had set a trap with his lies. She looked defiantly at him as, carefully, he closed the door after them, breathing heavily.

'It's not what you promised,' she insisted.

'Tansy, I haven't had *time*. Don't you realize how busy I've been?'

'You could have left that to me, the house hunting,' she said, leaning against the wall. 'You could have lived in a hotel until we found something I liked. I haven't had much choice in our life together, Michael, but I do think . . .'

'*Not much choice?*' Michael bawled, raising his eyes to the ceiling in mock despair and then he began to laugh. '*You* have dictated our marriage from the day we walked down the aisle. First of all we went on honeymoon to the place you wanted to go to; then we lived where your parents wanted you to live. I didn't want to have children for a while and you started a baby almost immediately. In the end I even went off to Australia by myself and, do you know what Tansy . . .' Michael came over to her until his face, mottled with rage, was only a few inches from hers, '*I* wish to God I'd stayed there. I wish my brother had never fallen and broken his back. God how I wish it! I wish my father hadn't died and left me to cope with all the family problems; my paraplegic brother and my neurotic mother. Sometimes, I confess, I wish I hadn't married you but someone on whom I could lean, who could help *me*, support and understand *me* instead of opposing every bloody move I made, like the spoilt little father's pet she is.'

Tansy reached out and slapped Michael so hard round the face he reeled. Then, like a cornered animal, he leaned forward, stuck out his chin and, assuming the stance of a fighter, bared his knuckles. Tansy thought he would beat her to death, such was the hatred on his face. Suddenly she felt frightened and put her hands on her cheeks.

'I'm sorry,' she said timidly, beginning to tremble. 'I shouldn't have done that.'

Michael remained exactly where he was, quivering, not moving and then as, still frightened, she began to edge away from him along the wall, he lowered his fists and stood upright, passing a hand nervously again and again through his hair. She could see he was trembling.

'My God, I could have killed you then,' he said.

'I know.' Tansy realized she was trembling herself. 'I know and I'm sorry. I provoked you.'

'Never, *never* hit me again, Tansy.'

'No I won't,' she said, still alarmed at what she had done.

'Never, *never*, do you hear?' he repeated.

'Yes, I do!'

'If you ever lay a finger on me again, I'll kill you. I'm sure I will. From now on I want you to do exactly as I tell you because, if you don't . . .'

'I will,' Tansy said, aware of a tremor that ran from her head to her toes.

She realized that Michael had transformed himself into a dangerous stranger; a person with whom she was not in the least familiar and of whom, now, she was very frightened.

Chapter 17

Jeremy lay watching Jill as she walked from the bedroom to the bathroom and back again getting dressed, fixing her hair, making up. This was a very important part of her toilet, and she spent a lot of time on it. She applied moisturiser, cream, make-up base, powder, mascara, eye shadow, rouge and, finally, a deep orange carmine lipstick that seemed to make the mask spring to life like a character from a Venetian carnival.

Jill was not as beautiful now as when she was young, but she was the sort of woman who made the very best of herself so that the contrived effect was still, indeed, one of beauty. Men turned to stare at her and some women envied her. She was most conscious of her appearance and took great care of it.

Whatever time they went to bed — and it was usually quite late due to the nature of Jill's job, entertaining visiting publishers, authors, agents and so on — Jill never had any difficulty rising with the alarm. This went promptly at seven-thirty, and she could be out of the house within the hour. She took a taxi to Berkeley Square and was in her office before nine.

Such was Jill's meticulous, ordered and busy day, as a contrast to Jeremy's which was largely spent sleeping, idling, or drifting around the shops in Knightsbridge and the West End.

What had happened to that much-awaited book? It was still embryonic in Jeremy's mind if, indeed, it existed at all. Jeremy knew that his inactivity irritated Jill and it had been the theme of a heated discussion between them the previous evening. Which was why Jeremy now lay awake watching her. Usually after the alarm he went straight back to sleep.

'Busy, busy,' Jeremy said at last, as Jill looked for the umpteenth time at her watch and put the final touches to her make-up before dabbing perfume behind her ears.

'I wish we could say the same of *everyone*, darling,' Jill replied in a pleasant voice.

'You're referring to me, of course.'

'Jeremy,' Jill put on the coat of her suit, shrugged her shoulders into it, looked at herself again, this time with a smile of approval, and came and stood by the side of the bed. 'I can't really stop to talk about your future again, darling, not just now. After last night . . .'

'I tell you I can't *write* in London,' Jeremy said irritably, shaking a cigarette out of the packet by his bed. 'The words just won't *come*.'

'But the words came *before*, Jeremy.' Jill perched on the side of the bed looking earnestly at him. 'You finished *A Shepherd in the Hills* in London, you told me so yourself.'

'That was different. I was living by myself . . .'

'Ah, well, if you want to live by yourself.' Jill started to get up but Jeremy gripped her by the wrist and she had to stay where she was.

'I don't mean I want to live by myself, you know that. I love you and I need you; but I do think the situation would alter if I had somewhere in the country, some small place where I could go by myself and write, perhaps somewhere like Dorset or Somerset, far enough away from London for me not to be distracted.'

'Ah, at my expense, I suppose.' Jill freed herself and, standing up, once more looked at her watch. 'I can't really talk about this any more, Jeremy. I have an author coming to see me sharp at nine. But, frankly, I feel that as I am out of the house all day and you have the whole place to yourself I can't for the life of me think why you don't take advantage of it.' With that she bent swiftly, kissed him chastely on the lips and was gone.

Jeremy listened to the sound of her steps running downstairs, a pause as she put on her scarf and gloves and, probably, took another look at her immaculate appearance in the mirror to make sure not a hair was out of place. Then the front door closed and he could hear her high heels pattering along the pavement to Avenue Road in search of a taxi. The cup of tea she had on waking was all she allowed herself by way of breakfast.

Jeremy sighed, coughed and put out his cigarette. It was true he had the house to himself all day, and a very nice substantial house it was. A woman came in at nine to clean and see to his needs; he had his own study overlooking a quiet garden and no distractions at all until Jill arrived home, again by taxi, and usually between six and seven o'clock.

But instead of getting up, bathing, shaving, dressing and going to his study, Jeremy usually slept until about eleven, had lunch and breakfast combined in bed brought to him by the daily woman; did his ablutions and loafed about during the afternoon. Sometimes he went to a film in Swiss Cottage, Baker Street or the West End. If the weather was good and there was a match on in the summer he went to Lords.

The only time he even made a pretence of getting on with his novel was when Jill was around at weekends and then he did it so that she would think he was working; but he knew he couldn't bluff her. Jill was one of those extremely well co-ordinated people who knew everything, which was why she had made a success of her job, even her life. Everything had to be co-ordinated and controlled, neat, meticulous and tidy.

Jill was one of those exceptionally lucky people for whom work was not a chore but a pleasure. All documents and correspondence were neatly filed away; her manuscripts were in date order and she couldn't tolerate confusion or irrational behaviour. She regarded most of her authors as wayward children who had, somehow, progressed into adulthood. She nursed the gifted ones, but was quite ruthless with failures and rejected manuscripts unmercifully.

It was really rather extraordinary that she had married Jeremy because, in his lifestyle, he represented everything that she disliked, even pitied. But she had thought he was gifted; he was certainly attractive, and she made him her protégé. It amused her to be seen with this good-looking man, a war hero with, possibly, a brilliant future. Where was that future now?

Jeremy knew he wouldn't sleep that morning after Jill had gone so he got up and was already in his bath when the daily, Jessie, came promptly at nine. She was surprised to see him descend the stairs fully dressed at nine-thirty, and enquired if everything was all right.

'Everything's fine, Jessie,' Jeremy said, smiling at her. 'Just a little breakfast and then I think I'll take a taxi to Harrods.'

'*Harrods*, Mr Blair?' Jessie raised an eyebrow.

'But don't tell Mrs Blair,' he said with a wink. 'If she telephones say I'm in my study working and on no account wish to be disturbed.'

Tansy walked aimlessly round Harrods in the manner of someone who has nothing else to do, with no positive goal or purpose in sight. It was true that Harrods was round the corner from her Knightsbridge home, and she went there frequently for coffee or to lunch with one of the new friends she had acquired through the children's nursery school, or Michael's many business acquaintances.

It was a very different life from Netherwick; it was different in every way. One, for instance, dressed differently. She never wore trousers or sloppy clothes to Harrods, or even in the streets of Knightsbridge because one never knew who one would meet, and, if some of the mothers who had children at the nursery were untidy like her, most of them were not. None of them was ever seen in the street, certainly not in Harrods, looking anything but smart.

Tansy had found it very difficult to accustom herself to London and London ways. To her London had been a place to go for a short holiday; to see Buckingham Palace and the Changing of the Guard, Kew Gardens, the Tower and Trafalgar Square. That had made London an exciting, interesting place to go to, especially in the heady, early days of her marriage when she and Michael were still very much in love, and staying in the best hotels with him was like enjoying a second honeymoon.

By the summer of 1959 Tansy had been married to Michael for six years. Her children Roger, Julia and Frank were five, four and two respectively. Roger and Julia went to nursery school, taken there each morning by the nanny Marge who looked after Frank during the day and took him for walks in Kensington Gardens. Besides Marge, who lived in, there was Clare who came every day to clean and Pru who helped out whenever the Garretts were entertaining, not that Tansy couldn't cook. She had learnt by the side of her mother since she was a small child all the basic rudiments of cookery. But Michael's sophisticated friends liked continental cuisine and Pru was a *cordon bleu* chef.

Once the move had been accomplished, the house

furnished and the staff engaged, there was very little for Tansy to do. Michael, on the other hand, was extraordinarily busy and she knew her inactivity irritated him. When he asked her each evening what she'd done during the day and she replied, 'Oh nothing much,' he lost his temper. So, lately, she had begun to make things up, to tell untruths and say she had done things which she had not done. Michael urged her to go to classes: pottery, cookery, flower arranging, like the other aimless wives of rich, successful men. There were thousands and thousands of things she could do, and no doubt there were, but she didn't want to do them. So she went through her new life like an automaton, obeying Michael, lying to him and always pretending.

One day she knew she would snap, and then she would think of her father and wonder if the depressive streak that ran in his family was beginning to infect her too.

It was the triviality, the meaninglessness of life, that frightened her; why couldn't she be like everyone else? Those busy, busy mothers who flung their children into the nursery school and then went off to their classes, their outings, their coffee mornings, their gossipy lunches. Some of them actually worked.

Tansy liked Harrods because it was possible to fantasize there. She had an account and, as Michael liked her to dress well and expensively, she bought a lot of clothes, and accordingly wasted time trooping in and out of various changing rooms before it was time to lunch.

So this day in the summer she had bought herself a skirt, a cocktail dress, and was just on her way up to the restaurant when she saw someone coming down the opposite escalator and, in a very unladylike way, she yelled:

'*Jeremy!*' Then she waved furiously and Jeremy, who

had been staring at his feet, looked up, saw her and waved joyously back. She then waited on the next landing for him to join her and, at the top of the escalator, they fell into each other's arms so that people who saw them thought it must have been many years since they'd met.

It was, in fact, quite a long time. Jill and Jeremy had had them to dinner soon after they came to London, and Michael and Tansy had them back. But Michael, although he liked Jill, was irritated by Jeremy; and Jill, although she liked Michael, found Tansy rather boring, countryfied and lacking the sort of glitter, the drive and ambition that one expected of one's friends in the city.

Brother and sister embraced and then stared at each other.

'Do you come here often?' Jeremy asked with a smile.

'Very often,' she replied. 'It's just round the corner from our house. Do you?'

'No. I came to get some new shirts and thought I'd stay and have lunch.'

'Have lunch with *me*,' Tansy said linking her arm through his. 'It's lovely to see you.'

'It's lovely to see you too, Tansy,' Jeremy said pressing her close. 'I gather you were on your way to the restuarant?'

'Yes.'

'Then let's both go,' and they got on the escalator again and ascended to the top floor.

There was something very relaxing about Harrods' restaurant. It was spacious and the tables were spread well apart, which was frustrating for eavesdroppers. It was possible to feel at ease and have a quiet meal either on one's own or with friends. Tansy didn't much like eating by herself, but here one could do it without feeling odd or that other people were looking at you all the time. She would often read a paperback or the paper, trying to conceal her loneliness, her lack of attunement with the life of the metropolis.

She had booked a table and she and Jeremy were shown to it immediately and, as they sat down, they looked again at each other and spontaneously burst into laughter.

'What's funny?' Tansy said at last. 'Why are we laughing?'

'I don't know about you, but I feel I'm playing truant,' Jeremy said, ordering a dry Martini while he studied the menu. 'I'm supposed to be in my study working. And you? Why are you laughing?'

'I'm just glad to see you.' Tansy reached out her hand for his. 'Why didn't we think of this before?'

'So you *do* come here often?'

'I practically live here.' Tansy shrugged. 'What else is there to do?'

Jeremy hadn't seen Tansy for several weeks, it might even have been months, and he was rather concerned by her appearance. It was true that she was smartly and fashionably dressed, but she had shed such a lot of weight that her cheeks were almost cavernous and she didn't look well. Her eyes burned brightly, almost as though she had a fever; but it was the loss of weight that worried Jeremy and his face grew suddenly serious.

'Are *you* all right, Tansy?'

'Of course I'm all right,' she said, concerned by the expression on his face. 'Why?'

'You've lost such a lot of weight.'

'I'm not ill. I'm just . . .' she was going to say something and then changed her mind. Jeremy would tell Jill and Jill, who got on very well with their father, would tell him. Jill made a great point of phoning her father- and mother-in-law every week, or popping up to see them and taking them expensive gifts. Tansy never quite knew why Jill did this, unless it was to make up for her own lack of family as she had no brothers and sisters and her own parents were long dead. She thought it was strange for Jill to try so hard to ingratiate herself with her husband's family but, maybe, she too wanted their father's love. He certainly liked and approved of Jill.

'You're unhappy, aren't you, Tans?' Jeremy said leaning towards her. He had called her 'Tans' since she was small, the only member of her family who sometimes used this diminutive.

'Does it show so much?' she asked.

'It does to me because I know you. If you're not ill then you're unhappy. Of course I knew that you didn't want to come to London.'

'It's not my way of life.' Tansy nervously broke her bread roll into tiny crumbs. Jeremy noticed too how white and thin her fingers were, and the large and expensive rings on her wedding finger were loose. 'But then, if you marry someone I suppose you must expect to do what they want to do. I mean a woman must . . . follow her husband and that sort of thing,' she concluded aimlessly.

'Do you *really* think that?' Jeremy got out a cigarette and lit it. 'It doesn't sound like you at all.'

'Well I expect one must,' she replied, 'other people do. Mother said I should do what Michael wanted. If your husband moves, you have to move with him. The wife doesn't have much choice.'

'I suppose you're right,' Jeremy said frowning. He thought that, in his case, he had to do what Jill wanted. 'I think actually you have to follow the one that has the money. In your case,' he pointed at her, 'it's Michael. In mine it's Jill.'

'But you *do* have money of your own,' Tansy said. 'I don't.'

'I only have a small disability pension.'

'I don't have any separate income at all. I think that's what I really resent, this economic dependence on Michael even though he is very generous and I have accounts everywhere and can buy what I like. Michael complains that I don't make enough of my life and the opportunities I have; but what else is there I can do?'

'I would have thought three children was quite a handful,' Jeremy said.

'Yes, but *I* don't look after them. I have a full-time nanny. Roger and Julia are at nursery school and Marge, the nanny, takes Frank in the park twice a day. Sometimes I go with them of course and I pick the children up and so on but . . .' Tansy stopped and her shoulders seemed to slump. 'I don't *have* to. I don't *have* to do anything except be where Michael wants me. Really it's not much of a life. I think,' fearfully she looked up at Jeremy, 'sometimes I think . . .'

'Yes, what do you think Tans?' Jeremy said encouragingly, gently pressing her hand.

'I think of Daddy.' Tansy knew she was near to tears.

'You mean missing Father?' Jeremy said sympathetically.

'No, about Daddy's illness. I'm wondering if I'm suffering from depression too?'

'Oh, darling Tansy,' Jeremy cried. 'You are certainly not suffering from depression.'

'But it can be inherited.'

'Yes; but I'm quite sure that you haven't. I've sometimes thought the same about myself. Maybe that I was depressed, like Dad. But then it blows away like a wind in summer, and you feel OK again. Jill says I'm lazy. I often wondered if I sleep so much because of innate depression, my tumour and so on; but I think that we can, and do, have control over our destiny and if we want to fight this depression we can and, if we don't, we let it win. It suited Dad to let it win. He always got his own way because of it. Did you ever think of that?'

'I know people said it,' Tansy said, staring at the tablecloth. 'But at times I feel so empty, so useless. All dark inside.'

'That's because *Michael* makes you feel empty and useless. Doesn't he? Speak the truth. I'm your brother and you can be frank with me.'

'Michael and I are very different people. I should never have married him. He was older than me, very different from me in every way. It took me a long time to find that out. I think now he despises me.'

'I don't see how he can.'

'Well, he does.'

'What would you *like* to do, Tansy? Go back home?' Jeremy looked earnestly at her across the table.

'Yes.' Tansy's eyes met his. 'I would prefer to live in Netherwick, or somewhere in the Dales. I should have married a farmer, a man who loved the country and small town life like I did.'

'And I should have stayed married to Emily,' Jeremy said in a voice so soft that Tansy could hardly hear him.

'Emily did you say?' she said leaning forwards as if she hadn't heard properly. 'Did you say you should have stayed married to Emily?'

'Jill is like Michael,' Jeremy said in a low, confidential tone. 'I am like you. My illness changed me very much. I thought I yearned for the city and city life but I hate it. I can't write here. I have not written a word since *A Shepherd in the Hills* was published and Jill knows it. She supports me and she is beginning to despise me too. I don't blame her. I'm a parasite. She thought I would turn into a celebrated author, someone she could show off and be proud of.'

'Oh I don't think that at all,' Tansy toyed apathetically with the salad she'd ordered for lunch. 'She always seems very happy with you when we see you.'

'Well we can all act, can't we? Jill would hate to admit she'd made a mistake. Your act with Michael is pretty good too. You look happy enough when you're together.'

'Do you think you'll ever go back to Emily?' Tansy finally abandoned her lunch and sat back in her chair. She noticed that Jeremy smoked and drank all through the meal, and his appetite seemed slender too.

'Do you think Emily would have me?'

'Who am I to say?' Tansy said. 'Although I'm sure she still loves you.'

'*Does* she?'

'I think so. We scarcely ever talk about you; but when we do her expression is soft and her voice kind.'

'Love is as fragile as a butterfly's wings,' Jeremy said sadly. 'One should treasure it. Emily was a good woman, and what I did was very wrong.'

'She understands, though. She saw that for you the temptation was too great but, you know, Jeremy, if you ask me I don't think you'd be happy in Cragbeck.'

'Oh I would,' Jeremy cried. 'That's just it. I long for a place in the country where I can get away and work as I used to work. You've no idea how the words flowed in my head as I sat in the fields with the sheep. I am simply stifled in London. Dried out. I am useless to anyone, including Jill.' He paused while he drew on his cigarette studying the blunt ends of his nails. 'You must come to dinner soon, Tansy, you and Michael. We must see much more of each other and help each other. You and I need each other.'

Before they parted on the ground floor they kissed again and, sadly, Tansy watched Jeremy leave by the exit on the Brompton Road and leap into a taxi. She felt immediately deprived, adrift, and then decided to go and look once more at the blouses and see if she could find one to go with her new skirt.

When she got home the children were there and Tansy sat having tea with them, feeling by now more cheerful than she had for some time. Talking to Jeremy had helped her. She liked Marge, the nanny, who was a woman of her own age brought up with a similar background — her father, too, was a doctor. Yet Marge was a person who, although hailing from the country, liked city life and living in the houses of the well-to-do.

Frank still sat in a high chair and Marge sat next to him feeding him soft boiled egg mixed into a bowl of bread and butter. Frank resembled his mother, even at this young age, whereas Roger and Julia looked more like Michael. Roger also had much of Michael's personality; he was strong and assertive, maybe a bit of a bully at school.

Julia was rather a quiet, ethereal child and her father's favourite. Playing with Julia, having her on his knee and reading her stories brought out the best in Michael. He seemed to have more time for her than the other two; maybe because she was less demanding. Roger would have liked him to go into the park and play football or sail boats on the pond, like the fathers of other boys; but Michael never did. He never had the time. Even at weekends he was working, struggling to compete in a competitive world; preparing to enlarge Garrett Engineering, diversify and, maybe, in a year or two take it to the Unlisted Securities Market. Then, he told Tansy, they would be millionaires.

'I saw my brother in Harrods today,' Tansy said to

Marge as Frank finished his egg, though much of it seemed to have stayed on his face.

'Oh, did you? Good.' Marge carefully wiped Frank's face with a wet cloth. 'I meant to tell you he rang.'

'My brother?' Tansy looked surprised. 'When?'

'About lunch time.'

'But I was eating with him in Harrods at lunch time. You must mean my twin brother, Gilbert.'

'Oh you mean your other brother?' Marge laughed. 'Sorry. Yes, the one who's the doctor. He said he's coming to London for an interview and wondered if he could stay here.'

'Oh that's lovely.' Tansy jumped up feeling suddenly happy, her depression swept away, like the wind in summer by the prospect of good weather. 'When did he say he was coming?'

'He wanted you to telephone,' Marge said. 'I *think* he said next week.'

'That must mean he's persuaded Father.' Tansy rushed over to the telephone. 'I bet *that* wasn't easy.'

Jill Blair liked to do everything well, no matter how mean or trivial the task. If she didn't do a job herself she ensured that nevertheless it was properly done by whoever did it. Naturally she gave extremely good dinner parties without doing anything to prepare them personally – she hadn't the time – but everything else was organized to the minutest detail.

For many years she had employed a woman who ran a small catering service in North London to cook for her and, days in advance, they went over the plans together, which included the menu and the wines. The woman, who was called Pat, did the shopping, the preparations and, on the day itself, the cooking.

Jill never took the credit for the success of her dinner

parties without mentioning Pat. She was very generous in that respect and, on the night of the dinner she gave for Michael and Tansy Blair, Pat was very much in evidence in her white coat serving the simple, beautifully cooked dishes and pouring the wine served at the correct temperatures.

Together with Tansy and Michael was Gilbert Blair, who had, after all, defied his parents and made his own decision to specialize. He had arrived in London a few days before to take up a junior registrar's job at Guy's. The party was completed by a girlfriend of Jill's called Laura Page who was the features editor on a woman's magazine. Jill had started her career in journalism before moving to publishing after the war.

Laura Page was about thirty-five, a tall, elegant woman with blonde hair cropped closely to her head by a fashionable Mayfair hairdresser, a pale face with little make-up and a very light coloured lipstick; an altogether rather bland and pallid exterior which was thrown into sharp relief by a pair of very large spectacles with brilliant orange frames. The effect of this was to shock and electrify the spectator and it never failed to do so. Laura Page was obviously a woman who wanted, and loved, to be noticed. She was witty, amusing and, without being too verbally obtrusive, kept the ball rolling at dinner, diverting Michael when he tried to monopolize the conversation, or encouraging Gilbert who seemed sometimes too reserved to try and say something.

In his years at medical school Gilbert had had little time or inclination for social life. His one passion apart from his work was climbing. It is possible he enjoyed this because it was considered a dangerous sport, far removed from the safety and security of his professional and personal life. After five years as a member of the

university mountaineering club he had climbed some of
the most dangerous and difficult peaks in Europe and
Great Britain and he planned, if he could get leave, to
spend part of the following summer in India.

Laura Page managed to discover, while they were
having their first course, that Gilbert was a keen moun-
taineer and cleverly drew him out about this aspect of
his life. Once he started to talk about something he
knew, Gilbert proved an interesting, even fascinating,
speaker. Tansy, who knew him so well, was amazed at
his volubility and admired Laura's skill in taking him out
of his shell.

Gilbert was a grave but attractive young man, on the
tall side, like his twin, and with horn-rimmed spectacles
which contributed to his earnest and serious demeanour.
The consulting room seemed the ideal ambience for him
but not, perhaps, the slopes of a steep mountain.

Jill's dining room was at the back of the house and
had french doors opening on to the terrace. The night
had been warm and, as they ate, the doors were left
open to allow a pleasant breeze to filter through which
occasionally caused the candles on the table to gutter.

At the conclusion of the meal Pat, as usual, was called
in for praise by Jill – on this occasion for her wonderful
cold consommé, oeufs en gêlée, and roast loin of lamb
served with a variety of vegetables and tiny new
potatoes. Jill kept a small cellar of carefully selected
wines, and with the consommé there had been a dry
Fino sherry, a Montrachet with the eggs and an Aloxe-
Corton with the lamb.

After Pat had retired, glowing with embarrassment,
Jill put her elbows on the table and, her eyes on Tansy,
said:

'It must be *absolutely* heaven just to be a wife and
mother and to have nothing to do. Personally I've never

had the luxury myself. I adore cooking but never have the time.'

Jill's eyes swivelled towards Jeremy, but by now he was used to these snide remarks which his wife never tired of delivering in company, yet always in a pleasant tone of voice and accompanied by a smile to sugar the pill of innuendo.

'Tansy doesn't cook,' Michael said with a smile. 'So there is no point in envying *her*.'

'Tansy doesn't cook? I'm surprised.' Jill's pencil-thin eyebrows shot up. 'I would have thought a country girl . . .'

'I can cook but I don't,' Tansy said, pointedly returning her sister-in-law's stare. 'That is, I don't cook for Michael's elaborate dinner parties when he wants to impress his business colleagues. We have someone like Pat who comes in to do the catering. Of *course* I can cook! My mother was a wonderful cook and taught me a lot.'

'Do *you* cook, Laura dear?' Jill turned enquiringly to her friend, her tone of voice now conciliatory rather than supercilious. 'I remember once the most delicious party . . .'

'I enjoy cooking.' Laura leaned over to allow Jeremy to light the cigarette he had given her. 'But I don't often entertain. No time. Unlike the pair of you I can't call on the services of a marvellous cook.'

'Tell me, do you travel much in your job?' Michael had appeared quite taken by Laura, amused by her many stories of life in the world of journalism. He looked decidedly less bored than he did at most dinner parties.

'I do some travelling,' Laura admitted. 'Why?'

'I wondered if you'd be interested in visiting a new electronics factory we're opening in Birmingham?'

'Electronics.' Laura pulled a face. 'I don't call a visit to Birmingham *travelling* . . .'

'We're working on coloured television. It would be quite a coup for your magazine.'

'Michael has done a complete revamp of the family firm,' Jill said, looking approvingly at him. 'He rescued it when it was practically bankrupt after his brother had had a serious fall. It's a gripping tale.'

'You must tell me about it,' Laura said politely but without obvious interest. 'However, it doesn't *really* seem right for a woman's magazine . . .'

'On the contrary,' Jill said firmly, 'it's very relevant. At least I think so; also the way Tansy made the transition from country girl to sophisticated city woman. You could make it one of those stories.'

Tansy knew that everything Jill said about her would have a double meaning. Jill knew that she remained loyal to Emily and saw a lot of her. Perhaps that made Jill jealous. In fact she and Jill had little in common and seldom met apart from the family. That evening Tansy had worn a striking short dinner dress of midnight blue and, in an effort to hide her pallor, had, unusually for her, spent the afternoon at a beauty parlour having her hair done and her face professionally made up.

'Now I *do* think Gilbert coming to work in London is interesting,' Laura went on. 'Someone at the beginning of his professional life. *That* would interest our readers.'

'I couldn't possibly advertise,' Gilbert quickly interrupted her. 'You'd have to leave me out, I'm afraid. My life, in fact, has been astonishingly dull and boring but Michael *has* done miracles.'

'We didn't ask you here to provide copy for your magazine anyway,' Jeremy said rather angrily, looking towards the open doors. 'Why don't we go outside and sit on the terrace? It's cooler there.'

'Good idea.' Jill rang the bell for the daily woman to come and clear and led the way onto the terrace which was furnished with a wrought-iron table, chairs and a folded umbrella which could be opened out on fine days, but which now flapped in the soft night breeze.

'I think, actually, we should be going soon,' Michael looked at his watch. 'I have an early business meeting. Breakfast at the Savoy.'

'Oh what a pity,' Jill said, but still she looked relieved. 'Won't you have a nightcap?'

'Not tonight,' Michael replied. 'Gilbert, would you like to come with us?'

'Of course,' Gilbert said.

'I didn't want to break up the party.'

'No I must go too.' Laura looked at her watch. 'Goodness it's nearly eleven. A long day for me tomorrow too.'

'Can we give you a lift anywhere?' Michael said casually, 'or have you got your car?'

'Thank you, but I came by taxi. I'll get a taxi back.'

'No, really . . .'

'Laura's on your way,' Jill said with a yawn. 'South Kensington, or just a little out of it.'

'No trouble at all.' Michael impatiently jangled the keys of his car in his pocket. 'We'd gladly give you a lift.'

'That's very kind.'

'*No* trouble . . .'

In the hall there were kisses, handshakes, promises to get in touch again, thanks for the wonderful dinner and so on. Jill and Jeremy stood at the door waving as the Garrett Jaguar drew smoothly away from the kerb and then, when the car had turned the corner, they closed the door and put out the light.

'Well, I think that was very successful.' Jill stood listening for sounds in the kitchen; but all she could hear was the noise of the dishwasher set by Jessie before she left.

'Very.' Jeremy put an arm around her, but Jill

remained stiff and unresponsive. 'You should ask Laura more often.'

'Oh? Do you like her?'

'Very much.' Jeremy lit a cigarette, standing in the hall. 'She's very amusing. Good value.'

'You smoke too much, Jeremy,' Jill said, staring at him. 'Don't you know how bad it is for you?'

'So they say,' Jeremy said. 'Too late I'm afraid. Besides, darling, would you really miss me if I went?'

'What on *earth* is that supposed to mean?' Jill paused at the bottom of the stairs and looked round at him.

'Snuffed it; dead. You know.'

'Of course *I'd* mind if you died. What a silly thing to say.' Jill continued slowly up the stairs as if his statement had made her thoughtful.

Once they were in bed she said: 'Jeremy, I do think you would be a lot happier if you could manage to start working again. I *know* you're not doing any work, and I think you're bored stiff.'

She waited for him to speak but he said nothing. Jeremy lay on his back listening, yet, at the same time, he felt curiously negative and uninvolved about the whole thing as though she were talking to or about someone else.

'Jeremy?' Jill said sharply.

'Yes, I'm listening. What would you like me to do?'

'I'd like you to *write*.' Jill's frustration showed in her high, thin tone of voice. 'I believe in you, Jeremy, and I know you have it in you and can do it. If you like I'm even prepared to *rent* somewhere in the bloody country so that we can see if it *is* writer's block you're suffering from, and if the fresh air would unblock it.'

A place in the country, Jeremy thought, and, immediately, Cragbeck came to his mind nestling at the foot of the fell with smoke spiralling out of the cottage chimneys, the twinkling, clear-watered beck running through the village, and . . . and Emily.

'Are you *listening*?' Jill demanded, even more sharply. 'You never seem to *listen*.'

'I'm listening,' Jeremy said wearily, but by the time she had finished outlining her new plans he was asleep.

Michael drove expertly through Marylebone, crossing the Edgware Road and entering Hyde Park by Marble Arch.

'It's awfully *good* of you to put yourself out,' Laura said. 'Especially as you have an early meeting.'

'No trouble at all,' Michael assured her with a smile, glancing over his shoulder. Then he said to Tansy who was sitting next to him: 'I'll drop you and Gilbert off, darling, and run Laura home. Is that a good idea?'

'That's fine,' Tansy said.

'I hope we haven't kept you out too late, Gilbert?' Michael looked at his brother-in-law in the mirror above the windscreen.

'I'm quite a big boy now, Michael,' Gilbert replied with the merest trace of sarcasm.

'I know tomorrow's an important day.'

'I don't have to be there until nine. I think the first day will just be meeting people, getting to know the ropes.'

'It must be awfully *exciting*,' Laura, sitting next to him, gazed at him admiringly. 'Your first step to being a specialist!'

'It's a long way to go,' Gilbert replied laconically, 'but, yes, it is exciting, I suppose.'

Michael drove round Hyde Park Corner, through Belgravia towards Knightsbridge.

'I suppose your parents are very thrilled?' Laura continued.

There was a pause and Gilbert didn't reply. Michael answered for him: 'Gilbert's father is a general practitioner in Netherwick, their home town, Laura. I think he wanted Gilbert to follow in his footsteps.'

'Dad does understand, though, now,' Tansy intervened. No point in elaborating, to a comparative stranger like Laura, the days of tension and drama that had preceded Gilbert's acceptance of his post as their father had sunk into such a depression that Tom Thackery began to treat him with drugs. But everyone had insisted that Gilbert shouldn't give in. Tansy, seeing the whole thing from a distance, began to realize just how selfish her father was. How difficult it was solely to blame his illness.

'I should hope so,' Laura said. 'It's a great honour to be selected by Guy's.'

'Not if you want your son to follow in your footsteps,' Gilbert added quietly. 'My father placed a high value on his work in our community. He said his life's ambition was to see my name under his on the brass plaque on the gate. I don't think that you, in your situation, can quite understand how my father feels unless you know him. I still can't help feeling that, in a way, I've let him down.'

At that moment Michael stopped the car outside the door of his house and Tansy and Gilbert got out saying good-night to Laura.

'You must come and have dinner with us,' Tansy said, leaning through the car door. 'I'll get your address from Jill.'

'I'll get it when I drop her off,' Michael said without turning his head. Then, to Laura, 'Like to jump in the front with me?'

'Oh I won't bother,' Laura said casually. 'It's only a few minutes.'

'OK.' Michael let out the clutch and drove off.

'That was a nice evening.' Gilbert stood behind Tansy as she opened the front door with the latch key. Inside the house all was still, though she knew that Marge would be awake, perhaps reading in bed until they got in. 'Jill is really much nicer than I thought,' Gilbert added.

'Is she?' Tansy turned on the lights in the lounge and looked to see if there were any messages.

'Don't you like her, Tansy?'

Tansy didn't reply but went into the lounge where a solitary lamp had been left on. There had been a number of telephone messages, inevitably for Michael, and she checked to see there was nothing urgent.

Gilbert threw himself into an armchair and crossed his legs. 'I said "don't you like her?"'

'I was trying not to answer,' Tansy replied, still reading the telephone messages.

'It's because you like Emily. Well you can like Jill too. What happened wasn't your fault.'

'I don't think I could ever be fond of Jill,' Tansy replied at last. 'She was trying very hard to be nice tonight because Michael and you were there; but usually she never misses an opportunity to demean me. Did you hear her remark about wishing she had the leisure to be *just* a wife and mother?'

'I think you read too much into it.'

'You don't know Jill.'

'Jeremy seems happy enough with her.'

Tansy looked at the clock and said wearily: 'It's nearly midnight. I'm awfully tired.'

'You're not answering my questions, Tansy,' Gilbert said insistently. 'It's not like you.'

'Perhaps tomorrow.'

'You worry me, you know.'

'Why?' She sat on the pouffe at his feet and stared up at him, face in her hands.

'I don't think you're happy. You're awfully thin and you have too much make-up on, I guess to try and disguise how pale your face is. I know you and I've never seen you quite like this.'

'It's been a very big change,' Tansy said. Then she got to her feet and wandered to the window, gazing at the square, still lit by gas lamps, and wondering when Michael would be home. 'I'm beginning to think that, perhaps, in many ways it's been good for me. I was too naive, over-protected at Netherwick. I was "Daddy's girl" and Michael was right.'

'Then you don't regret coming to London?'

'I don't *like* London, but I think living here is good for me. One day I hope we'll move to the country when Michael feels more secure. I haven't given Michael much support these last few years. I was too preoccupied with myself.'

'Michael seems to have done all right.'

'But he does need me. I want to give more of myself to Michael and less to thinking about me.'

'That's a very noble objective,' Gilbert replied with a yawn. 'But I don't find it very convincing.' Then he got up and strolled over to his sister. 'Anyway now that I'm here we'll see a lot of each other.'

'And I'm glad to have you,' she said tucking her arm through his.

'You didn't answer my question about Jeremy. *Is* he happy with Jill?'

'Well,' Tansy began then paused. 'Well, if you want to know what I think: I think he'd like to go home to Emily. That's what I really think he'd like to do.'

Gilbert was about to reply when the telephone rang. It

was immediately answered, as Tansy expected, by Marge, who took it off the hook beside her bed and, for a few moments, she and Gilbert waited, listening to the silence. It was very late for a telephone call, even though Michael's business associates rang at all hours of the day and night.

Suddenly they heard Marge come to the top of the stairs and call: 'Doctor Blair, it's for you.'

'For me?' Gilbert said with surprise, turning as Marge, clutching her dressing gown, came running down the stairs and into the lounge. 'Are you *sure* it's for me? I don't know who'd ring at this hour . . .'

'It's your mother, Doctor Blair,' Marge couldn't conceal the expression of distress on her face, 'I'm afraid it's bad news about your father.'

Chapter 18

When Gilbert Blair went back to Netherwick on the
eve of taking up his new job at Guy's, he knew it was
for good. Without even being told, he knew it was
his father's way of making sure his son capitulated;
surrendered to his wishes.

He packed both his suitcases and he and Tansy travelled up on the first train out of King's Cross to Leeds the
following morning. Michael had driven them to the
station, saying he would follow in a few days. Business
always came first with Michael.

Catherine was waiting for them in the car at Leeds
where they learned of the seriousness of Geoffrey's
condition. He was not expected to live.

But Geoffrey, being Geoffrey, did survive. Within a
month he was out of hospital and convalescing, and it
was then that Gilbert told his father the decision he had
come to about his career.

'But, my dear Gilbert,' Geoffrey said when he heard
what his son had to say, 'naturally I am very pleased;
but I don't want you to sacrifice your career for me. I am
much better now.'

'But still, it was a very serious attack, Father; the worst
you've had and, in a way, I feel I'm responsible.'

'But, dear boy,' his father replied in a voice that shook,
as he reached for his hand, 'you are not in the least
responsible. You must feel free to lead your own life,
but,' he added, firmly grasping his son's hand and
tucking it with his under the blanket to warm it against
his frail, emaciated body, 'you've no idea how pleased I

am that, at last, our names will be together on the brass plaque outside the gate. It's what I've always wanted.'

And that, in itself, was sufficient reward for Gilbert and he knew he'd done the right thing.

Not that everyone agreed with him. Michael thought he was succumbing to the same kind of pressure that had practically ruined Tansy's life, and begged him not to turn down the post which was generously being kept open for him for the period of his father's illness. Even a hospital as prestigious as Guy's was anxious not to lose a good candidate. Gilbert's mother also thought her son's sacrifice too great. Tansy loyally supported Gilbert, yet she agreed, in a sense, with Michael. She knew how strong were the strings that joined a child's heart to his or her parents and she also thought that Gilbert, who had been so close to his father, would be happier helping to look after him in his final years.

As for Gilbert, he knew that if his father had died without him doing as he wished, his guilt would have been insupportable. So he wrote formally turning down the offer from Guy's and his name was duly inscribed on the brass plaque, under that of his father's: Dr G. W. Blair, MB, BS.

Tom Thackery was, naturally, glad to have Gilbert in the practice. He thought that it needed a young man with new ideas, yet with the traditional values, the compassion and the time to listen to their ills that the people of Netherwick expected. Despite his ill health, the times when he was unable to take surgery, old Doctor Blair, as he was now referred to, was revered by so many people that neither Tom Thackery nor Terry Fulbright had ever been completely acceptable to them.

The son Gilbert, now, was different, and in the year that Gilbert finally joined his father's practice, 1959, Geoffrey Blair officially retired.

Gilbert quickly put away his dreams of becoming a consultant and settled down to daily life in Netherwick as a GP. He had his first-class medical degrees, his year as a houseman at his old hospital in Leeds; but this was his first real experience of general practice and he leaned very much on the advice of his father and the guidance of Tom Thackery, as Terry Fulbright also retired and moved out of the district.

Gilbert, however, though he resembled his father in so many ways, found that the problems and ailments of much of the population of Netherwick were similar to one another and didn't provide him with that interest, that challenge, that his medical studies had led him to expect.

He knew that many of his patients came to him for reasons other than their symptoms, which would mostly clear up by themselves eventually, anyway. He found he was unable, because he had no time, to get to grips with the few really interesting problems that came along; and that patients who deserved more time didn't get it.

He thus acquired the reputation of being rather an impatient young man who lacked the skills of understanding and communication that his father had, and those who had gladly transferred to him because of who he was were slowly disillusioned.

Gilbert had neither the time, inclination or patience to exchange views about the weather, family history or indulge in the day-to-day gossip of the town. His father had kept patients waiting because they all knew that, when it was their turn, they would get a hearing as long as the one before; but Gilbert was punctual and, as his work load had also increased, was always in a hurry to get on.

Mrs Sharp, for instance, who always had this problem with her back, returned twice in one week to tell Gilbert that the pills he had given her were no good. She even threw them on his desk as she entered his surgery the second time and said: These are *not* what your father gave me, young man, and I tell you they're not doing the job.'

Gilbert, a worried frown on his face, looked at the pills, looked at Mrs Sharp's voluminous set of record cards, and went back to the time that his father had first recommended drugs for her back. He had prescribed pheno-barbitone, which was neither a muscle-relaxant nor anti-inflammatory but a sedative. His father had ascribed her back problem to her nerves and had prescribed a tranquillizer to quieten her down. Yet, obviously, he had been right. The back pains had disappeared. Now, what did he as a young doctor, scientifically trained in the post-war world, as opposed to his father who qualified in 1912, do? Did he go on feeding Mrs Sharp, who was into her fifties, with pills that quietened her mind, or did he try something more radical?

'These are a new kind of drug, Mrs Sharp,' Gilbert said patiently. 'They are for rheumatism and they act directly on the nervous system that transfers pain.'

'Then what did Dr Blair give me?' Mrs Sharp demanded, clearly aggrieved.

'Well,' Gilbert rubbed his head, not wishing to betray his father, 'they were an older kind of drug which had a different approach, and a different effect.'

'I'll have some of *them*, then,' Mrs Sharp said, firmly clutching her handbag on her lap, lips pursed. 'I preferred what your father gave me to what you gave me. I'm sorry, but I know you're still learning.'

And so it went on day after day, week after week, month after month as autumn changed to winter – a winter which was hard, and involved Gilbert in many journeys into the snow-bound Dales – winter eventually gave place to spring, and then it was summer again and Gilbert had been in practice in Netherwick for a year.

His mother knew he was not happy. She knew that he found the daily grind of general practice unfulfilling, and that his nights were spent reading medical books and journals in his room. He seldom went out. He had no girlfriend, or, indeed, many friends at all of either sex. She saw her attractive, clever son, becoming a morose introverted bachelor, of the kind his father had been when she met him. He was loving, dutiful, kind, patient to his parents, especially to his father whose health had improved considerably over the year, but she knew he had the reputation of being rather brusque and off-hand in his medical practice and Catherine deduced that this was because he was frustrated in what he was doing.

Gilbert Blair had been meant for higher things.

'Now that your father's so much better,' Catherine said one morning when Gilbert, having finished surgery, was drinking a cup of coffee with her in the kitchen, 'why don't you consider specializing again, Gilbert? It's not too late, is it?'

Gilbert looked at her over the rim of his cup. 'What made you say that, Mother?'

'I don't think you're very happy, Gilbert. I know you.'

'I'm as happy as I am doing anything, Mother.'

'Yes, but . . .'

'I know.' Gilbert sighed and put down his cup, pushing his spectacles up on his nose. 'I should be married. I should see more people. I should go out more. I . . .'

'Why *don't* you, then, Gilbert? It's not normal in a young man, being as solitary as you are. You could have a wonderful time if you allowed yourself to relax a bit more.' Catherine's expression upset Gilbert and he got up from his chair and went over to his mother, putting his arm around her.

'*You're* not very happy either, are you, Mother? Isn't that what this is all about? Do you know, Mother,' he removed his arm and stood away from her so that he could see her more clearly, 'I never see you anywhere but in the kitchen, or taking something to Father or me. I don't think *you* ever go out and enjoy yourself, now that Tansy doesn't live in Netherwick any more and Gran is dead. You talk about me; what about you? When did you last go into Leeds or Bradford, Harrogate or York to shop?'

'I can't leave your father,' Catherine said, perching on the high stool beside the kitchen table. 'He likes to have me near.'

'But it's *selfish*, Mother.'

'Yes, but your father *is* a bit like that. Besides, I'm used to it.' Catherine swept a stray piece of hair back from her head.

It was true she missed her mother, who had died the year Gilbert had graduated. Catherine's family – her mother, sisters, brothers, her daughter, her husband and her son – were her mainstay. When one died or left home it was as though part of her life went with them. She was a woman without close friends who lived in and for the family.

Looking at his mother Gilbert thought how pale she was. But in fact he never remembered her being any-thing else; pale and hardworking like the wife of some poor man, a mother of a large family with a husband on the dole, as so many of his patients. But in the case of his mother it wasn't necessary. His father had always been careful; he had inherited money and had a success-ful practice. Gilbert knew that money was no problem in the Blair household although they no longer had a live-in maid, because since the war such people hardly existed. But they did have two daily women who came every day apart from Saturday afternoon and Sunday.

There was no need for his mother to look like a working drudge, much paler than she needed to be. The fault was really all his father's, a man who, it was true, had suffered ill health of one sort or another for most of his life; but what sacrifices had he expected of his family in return? In one way or another they'd all paid for it. His mother was a drudge; Tansy was ill-suited in her marriage and he was carrying out the work of a country doctor when he could have been doing the most interesting research into serious medical problems at a famous London hospital.

Gilbert stood in the middle of the floor looking so thoughtful and abstracted that his mother said:

'What's the matter, Gilbert? You look *ever* so strange.'

'I just thought, Mother, maybe we have been too good to Father; we let him get away with too much. He *is* a selfish man.'

His mother looked shocked. 'I don't really think you should talk like that about your father. Besides, he idolizes you; he thinks the world of you.'

'I know, Mother, and I think the world of him.'

'He has given up a lot for you, Gilbert,' his mother continued with a note of reproof. 'Think of all those evenings spent going over your homework with you. Why, his life *was* for you, rather than Tansy or even me. He would be terribly upset if he knew how you spoke about him.'

'But he won't know, Mother,' Gilbert said gently, 'because you and I won't tell him, will we? You and I will say nothing to Father or criticize him in any way and then, when he's dead, we'll realize what empty lives he left us with and, maybe, in our hearts we'll start to reproach him then.'

'Really, Gilbert,' Catherine said, getting up and agitatedly moving things about on the table, as though she had to keep busy. 'I can't listen to any more of this. I have been loyal to your father for over thirty years. I have seldom criticized him or questioned anything he did. I do know that for much of those thirty years he has been a sick man and he has fought very hard against serious illness, both mental and physical. The reason he has endured and survived is because of the care *I* have taken of him and the love he has for his children, particularly *you*, Gilbert, on whom he has set all his hopes for the future. Please don't fail him now.

'I have never seen your father so happy as this past year, having you here, your name under his on the plate as he always wanted.'

'Yes, but now, Mother, you want to change all that?' Gilbert looked even more perplexed. 'You said why didn't I consider specializing again?'

'Because *you're* not happy, dear,' his mother tenderly reached up to pat his cheek. 'That's what I realize now. You did what you did for Dad. Now as he *is* so very much better . . .'

'Mother, he will *never* let me go.' Gilbert found it hard to conceal his bitterness. 'Never, never. If I so much as suggested quiting the practice he would have a relapse. Don't you realize that, Mother?' Gilbert held out his hand and started to enumerate all the incidents in his life, or the life of the family, when some setback had resulted in his father being ill. Finally, ticking off each finger one by one, he got to the end.

'Father made such a fuss when Tansy went to live in London that he has seriously impaired her marriage to Michael and then, just as I was about to start at Guy's, he had his heart attack that brought me back here. I knew that when I came home it was for good.'

'But, Gilbert, your father was *very* happy about Guy's. He was used to the idea. He was proud of you. That had nothing to do with his heart attack.'

'Mother,' Gilbert said, with exaggerated patience, 'this morning I prescribed pheno-barbitone for a lady with a bad back.' As his mother looked at him, puzzled, he went on. 'Pheno-barbitone is a sedative. It had *no* effect at all on the woman's back except that it desensitizes her and makes her feel better.'

'What's wrong with that, then?' his mother asked.

'What is *wrong*, Mother, is that for years and years father has been treating her physical symptoms with a sedative so that now she is so used to it she can't live without it. I tried to put her on another anti-inflammatory drug but it did nothing for her. She wants the old pheno-barbitone back. She's become an addict.'

'I don't know *why* you're telling me this, Gilbert.' His mother looked very unhappy.

'Because it reminded me of Dad. I know he's ill; I know he suffers from depression and also has a bad heart, but the power of his mind is such that he can influence his physical symptoms. I am quite sure he can have a heart attack, now, to order. I only hope that one day it doesn't finally kill him.'

'I think that's a *dreadful* thing to say.' Catherine, by now thoroughly agitated, looked at the clock. 'Goodness, I've forgotten to put his dinner on! He'll be absolutely furious.'

Gilbert gave a deep sigh and was about to begin again, patiently elaborating for his mother the way to a better life when one of the dailies put her head round the door and said: 'Call for you, Dr Blair. It's an emergency.'

*   *   *

Gilbert carefully tied the tourniquet on the farmer's leg and then, when the flow of blood was stemmed, gave him a large shot of morphine.

'You'll have to go to hospital, Mr Monk,' Gilbert said, getting up to survey his handywork. 'I can't stitch this myself.'

'I hope they won't cut it off, Doctor,' the farmer muttered with a grimace.

'No, the saw nearly did that and you were very lucky. I think it will be all right; but you'll probably need a blood transfusion.' Gilbert turned to the farmer's daughter who was hovering anxiously by the side of her father.

'Would you ring for an ambulance, Miss Monk? Tell them it's an emergency.'

'Yes, Doctor,' the young woman said and went quickly out of the kitchen where Farmer Monk's men had carried him after he nearly severed his leg with a circular saw while helping to fell a tree.

The kitchen looked rather as Gilbert imagined a field dressing station must have done in the war. He had never seen quite so much blood, bloodstained cloths and pieces of rag and cotton wool with which Mr Monk's employees and distracted daughter had tried to staunch the wound. He had come just seconds before Monk would have passed out from pain, loss of blood and low blood pressure.

As the morphine began to take effect Monk lay quietly on the floor and Gilbert wandered around the large kitchen looking at the view of the Dales from the windows. Despite the fact that his patient was so badly stricken Gilbert knew he would not die and he experienced a strange feeling that, he recognized, was actually exultation. For the first time for weeks, perhaps months, he was actually happy because he felt he had really done something: he had, literally, saved a man's life. Monk might have slipped into a coma and not recovered. But Gilbert had a great deal of experience in the emergency department of a large hospital, and he had lost no time when he saw Monk's condition. He knew exactly what to do.

And this was really the sort of thing he preferred to do, dealing with real cases, real emergencies; using his skills to save lives and not doling out sedatives to people who had nothing wrong with them.

He knew it was wrong of him to experience such a sense of happiness and fulfilment in these circumstances, and when Eileen Monk came back into the room he readjusted his features to an expression of suitable gravity.

'Your father will be all right, Miss Monk,' he said. 'He's just dozing because I gave him a heavy shot of morphine.'

'Oh thank you, Dr Blair,' the young woman said, and it struck Gilbert, despite her tenseness and understandable anxiety, she was really very pretty. Pretty in a fragile way, very different from his sister and most of the girls he knew. She looked most unlike a farmer's daughter; ethereal and insubstantial.

'We haven't met before, have we?' Gilbert referred to his patient's record card. 'I suppose you know my father?'

'Since I was a small girl,' Eileen Monk said in a low, shy voice. 'He was our family doctor. I hope he's better now?'

'Much better,' Gilbert said, smiling reassuringly at her in an effort to dissipate her unease.

'He looked after Grandad when he was dying. He used to talk sometimes about his children; but mostly he talked about *you*. He was very proud of you, Dr Blair.'

Gilbert turned away, remembering his conversation with his mother. But one accidental near-amputation in a year was not fulfilment. One couldn't go round hoping for this kind of ghastly event just in order to stay emotionally and professionally alive. The place for satisfaction like this was in the casualty section of a large city hospital.

Maybe his vocation was, after all, to be a surgeon.

Just then they heard the sound of the ambulancemen racing up the valley and, in no time, two men bearing a stretcher were rushing into the kitchen and gently lifting Farmer Monk on to it before covering him with a blanket.

'I'll follow in my car,' Gilbert told the men. 'I want to be sure my patient doesn't haemorrhage during the journey.'

'Do you think I could go with the ambulance men?' Eileen looked appealingly at him. 'I'd like to know Dad was all right.'

'Of course, you can come with me!' Gilbert replied cheerily, closing his bag. 'It will be more comfortable for you, and your father will be all right. One of the men will sit with him.'

Within minutes the ambulance had set off, bell ringing, and Gilbert put Eileen Monk into the seat beside him and then followed in the wake of the ambulance.

'Is your mother not in today?'

'Mother's dead,' Eileen said.

'I'm sorry.' Gilbert felt awkward. 'Did she die recently?'

'Just after I was born.'

'Oh dear, I'm sorry. Have you any brothers and sisters?'

'No, there was just me.' She didn't seem sad, just resigned, though he felt she was not someone to whom life had been especially unkind. Yet he felt a sudden urge to help and protect her.

'So you look after the house?'

'I look after Dad and myself.'

'It must be lonely up here.'

'It's what I'm used to,' she said, looking unsmilingly at him.

Gilbert liked her. She was simple and straightforward. What was more he found no difficulty in talking to her, in expressing himself. She was enigmatic but, already, he felt a strange affinity with her. It was also the first time he had been at ease with a mature young woman outside his immediate family.

That night the Wentworths came to dinner and Gilbert compared talking to Rosalind with talking to Eileen, and yet he had known Rosalind all his life, been at university with her. But still he never felt entirely comfortable in her company.

During the meal he found himself thinking constantly of the girl he had met that day and he excused himself to phone the hospital and find out how Anthony Monk was progressing.

'Problems?' Peter Wentworth enquired as Gilbert rejoined them at the table.

'One of the farmers in the Dales nearly cut his leg off today with a circular saw. I was just ringing the hospital to see how he was.'

'Who was that?' Geoffrey looked up with professional interest.

'A fellow called Monk.'

'Oh, Monk,' Geoffrey nodded. 'Anthony Monk. Used to be my patient. Badly hurt?'

'Leg nearly severed just below the knee, Father. Blood pressure low. I did all the usual things and he is recovering.'

'Good boy,' Geoffrey said approvingly but Rosalind shuddered.

'How awful,' she said with a grimace. 'How *do* you cope with that kind of thing?'

'Training,' Gilbert replied. 'Actually I rather enjoyed it; not, of course, the fact that the farmer had cut himself so badly, but that it gave me something I could get my teeth into.'

Peter and Dorothy Wentworth exchanged glances. They both knew, as all Netherwick knew, that Gilbert had given up specializing to please his father and, like many others, they disapproved of it. Gilbert was a young man, one they very much liked and approved of. Nothing would have given them more pleasure than if he were to show an interest in their schoolteacher daughter. They were afraid that, the way she was going on, she would be an old maid.

Rosalind also liked Gilbert. She always had; but to get Gilbert interested in anything besides medicine or mountaineering was very difficult. Everyone had tried to encourage him to mix with the young set in Netherwick, but he always pleaded work as an excuse. He was very hard to get to know. Rosalind knew she was not in love with him because he had never at any time given her any encouragement whatsoever. She was too sensible a girl to lose her heart over someone who had never even asked her out. But, as men in Netherwick went, he was among the most eligible, and if she knew a way to bring him out she would have done so.

It was a good meal cooked by Catherine who, when she put some make-up on and wore a pretty frock, was a handsome woman. Gilbert was glad to see that his talk only that morning seemed to have had an effect on his mother, who discussed going to flower arranging classes with Dorothy Wentworth after the meal.

'Not that you don't arrange flowers beautifully already,' Dorothy said effusively. 'You do everything so well, Catherine.'

'So do *you*, Dorothy.' Catherine looked at her friend of many years with surprise.

'No, not like you. You give your life to it. I have too many other things to do.'

'I think Mother should do more outside the home.' Gilbert stood in front of the fire sipping his coffee. 'I was only telling her so this morning.'

'Outside the home?' His father looked up in alarm. 'What about me?'

'Father, you're fine,' Gilbert said, looking straight at him. 'Everyone agrees that you have never looked better. Or, felt better.'

'That's because I'm retired,' his father said truculently. 'I am able at last to take things easy, to get the rest I need; but I *do* need my wife if I am to be properly looked after.'

'You should get out on the golf course,' Peter Wentworth said jovially. 'I bet you would be good for fifteen holes.'

'Don't be ridiculous,' Geoffrey snapped at him. 'I am in my seventy-third year, Peter, and, never having played golf or attempted to learn, I am not likely to at my time of life. I have plenty to do, thank you. I read a lot. I do *The Times* crossword to keep my mind active, and I take a great interest in my son's career. We shall probably discuss the case of Tony Monk for an hour or so after you've gone.'

It was, in fact, just like the homework sessions, discussing his cases with Father over a nightcap every night. Gilbert had to be very careful to select the ones that would interest his father so as not to give offence. For instance, he wouldn't mention the case of Mrs Sharp because it would seem critical of his father's treatment; but the more he looked into old cases the more he realized that his father had treated many of his patients by sedating them or administering placebos.

Maybe that was the old-fashioned type of medicine that the populace of Netherwick preferred.

On the way out Rosalind said to Gilbert: 'We're having a dance at the tennis club on Saturday week. Maybe you'd like to come?'

'Oh *do* go, Gilbert,' his mother urged him, and, by the expression on her face, Gilbert knew if he did it would give her pleasure.

'May I think about it,' he replied after a pause, 'and let you know?'

Gilbert sat by Tony Monk's bed having examined the wounded leg.

'You're making excellent progress,' he said, tapping it gently. 'You'll be up and about in a week.'

'Rather say a day or two,' Tony Monk said with a grimace. 'I've a lot to do on the farm.'

'Well, you've got to let your leg heal,' Gilbert stood up and reached for his prescription pad, 'or else you'll be back in hospital again. Is Eileen looking after you?'

'She is that,' Tony said fondly. 'She's a champion girl.'

'You're lucky to have a daughter like her,' Gilbert said, and then, after a pause, he asked hesitantly: 'Do you think you could spare her to come to a dance at the tennis club with me next Saturday?'

'Well, if she wants to go of course I can spare her,' Monk said in an equally hesitant, not to say surprised, tone of voice. 'Why don't you ask her yourself on the way out?'

All heads turned as the much sought-after Gilbert Blair walked into the clubhouse for the annual dance with a girl whom few people knew. The Monks lived some ten miles out of Netherwick and Eileen had done very little socializing, certainly not with the tennis club set. But for Gilbert Blair to be seen with *any* girl was an event and Rosalind Wentworth, who knew he had bought two tickets, experienced a pang of jealousy as he came through the door with Eileen, both looking very shy. Rosalind knew her reaction was unreasonable. Gilbert had never in all the years she had known him so much as made a pass at her; but it would have been nice if he had.

At the last moment Rosalind had rung up an old friend from university who came over from Ilkley so that she could pass him off as a boyfriend. But she was very curious to see the girl Gilbert Blair was with and went over to welcome him, first introducing her own partner, Nicholas May.

'Hello,' Gilbert said shaking hands with May, whom he dimly remembered from university. 'This is Eileen Monk.'

'Oh, you're the daughter of the man who cut his leg,' Rosalind said. 'I hope he's better?'

As Eileen looked puzzled Rosalind explained about the dinner party which had taken place the night her father had his accident.

'Did you know Gilbert before that?' she asked while Gilbert was exchanging platitudes with May.

'No.' Eileen was quiet and subdued and, evidently, monosyllabic; but she *was* very pretty. In fact, she was outstandingly pretty and Rosalind knew instinctively that she was the sort of girl Gilbert would be attracted to because, like him, she was withdrawn and had little to say. He would like that kind of girl: serious, pretty, not a talker or a chatterer.

Rosalind turned to throw herself into the arms of Nicholas May, who was waiting to lead her on to the floor for a dance, but inwardly her feeling was one almost of loss, certainly of regret. However, she hid her distress under a carefree smile, and no one would ever have guessed how much she was reproaching herself for not making a determined play for Gilbert Blair much sooner.

Now, she knew, it was too late.

Taking Eileen onto the floor Gilbert tentatively put his arm around her waist.

'I'm a terrible dancer,' he said.

'So am I, Dr Blair.'

'You mustn't call me Dr Blair,' Gilbert said reproachfully. 'Please call me Gilbert.'

'It's very nice of you to ask me out, Gilbert.'

'It's very nice of you to come.'

That was about the end of their conversation, and, as though exhausted by the effort, they danced clumsily together, in total silence; but, for Gilbert, it was bliss. He felt more and more drawn to this pretty, but strange and inarticulate girl. He was aware that she needed him. He couldn't yet say how or why, but no other girl had ever attracted him as Eileen Monk did. He had never been in love and he had never slept with a woman, and, as he had observed the antics of his contemporaries at university, he had often wondered if there were something wrong with him. He knew that women were attracted to him, yet he found it hard to respond. The only one he had ever been able to talk to about this problem had been Tansy, and she had said there was plenty of time; she was sure it would happen to him one day. Love, at some time or other, came to everyone. But Gilbert had known there was a deep void inside himself because he too longed for love; for physical gratification and the joy of children.

Perhaps, then, if he had that he would be reconciled to his lot as a general practitioner in Netherwick and would forget about the glory, the rewards, the satisfaction, of being a consultant in a major London hospital.

After the tennis club dance Gilbert began to date Eileen regularly. First of all he made the excuse that he wanted to see her father, because she was so unforthcoming. He seemed to make little actual impression on her. He wondered, in fact, what she felt about him because she was so uncommunicative. Yet she seemed quietly contented in his company and compliantly fell in with what he wanted to do: go to a film, out for a walk, a drive on the moors. She appeared to have very little will or inclination of her own and yet he didn't feel he dominated her; but that their wishes coincided. He knew, very soon, that he was falling in love with her. With her there was colour in his life; without her there was none.

Gilbert was used to rather strong, forceful women. His mother, his grandmother and Tansy had distinct, powerful personalities. This was undoubtedly why Michael and Tansy clashed because she didn't want to do exactly as she was told and, whereas his mother appeared to be firmly under the thumb of his father, it was in fact her strength that had kept the whole family going for so many years: the house, the practice and their lives ticking over the way they had.

Eileen represented Gilbert's true ideal of woman as soft, feminine, dependent. There would be no clashes with Eileen, but neither did he expect her to be a doormat. He saw men and women as complementary, one incomplete without the other. Having heard the terrible rows that went on between Michael and Tansy as their personalities clashed again and again; having seen the void in Jeremy's life created by his financial dependence on Jill, Gilbert had no wish for that sort of conflict. In his view male and female were counterparts, friends; but it was the man who gently took the lead and gave directions.

He and Eileen agreed on everything and she was always willing to fit in with what he wanted to do; but that, she told him, was because he was busy. It was only fair to let him choose what kind of entertainment he wanted in a life that was dominated by the clock, by routine, by the dependence of his patients on *him*.

All that autumn Gilbert's courtship of the gentle Eileen continued and, as he grew more in love with her, he realized that her own personality was altering, as her own feelings fermented and underwent change.

Eileen was young, she was only nineteen; but she was a farmer's daughter, mature for her age and emotionally strong. Her youth and spiritual strength made for an attractive, yet formidable combination.

One day Gilbert sat in the car outside the farmhouse as dusk was falling and he told her about his life, about his disappointment at not being able to specialize. He spoke more about his past and his dashed hopes than he ever had before. Eileen listened, as she always did, with an air of gravity, tempered with sympathy. In the half light her eyes eagerly watched every movement of his features, often lingering on his lips.

'I'm glad you stayed in Netherwick,' she said when he'd finished. 'Otherwise we'd never have met.'

'I'm glad too, now,' Gilbert admitted. 'It's a very funny thing the part chance plays in our lives. Tell me, Eileen, did you ever have a boyfriend before?'

Boyfriend. The word seemed to make Eileen start.

'Boyfriend,' Gilbert said again, 'someone close to you, like me?'

Then he took her in his arms for the first time and kissed her. He was not very good at it and neither was she. She didn't seem to know what to do and at first kept her lips firmly pressed, closed against his. His hand rested on her breast and he could feel the pounding of her heart. He drew away and said:

'Just try and relax a little, let yourself go; I won't hurt you.' He spoke very gently and quietly, almost in a whisper, as he might encourage a patient fearful of an examination.

'I'd hate my father to come out and find us,' she said, and Gilbert, smiling grimly to himself, let her go.

There was always a father to consider.

The next time he tried, Eileen was more willing. They'd been to the cinema in Netherwick and he parked in the lane leading up to the farm rather than by the farmhouse itself. She nestled quite willingly in his arms, and opened her mouth for his kisses. She was beautiful, so pliable, that Gilbert wanted to crush her and make her his own. He knew that she would probably agree; but that it would never do for one of Netherwick's respected physicians to take advantage of a young woman without any precautions or preparation. It would never do to get her in the family way, and be forced to the altar. Everyone would know about it. He knew that he was ready for marriage, but was she? What would her father say about his daughter leaving him by himself? They were questions to which he did not as yet have the answer.

Gilbert encouraged Eileen to talk about herself, but she had very little to say. She seemed loath to answer questions; but this only inflamed Gilbert's interest in her. A woman who was slow to reveal herself was an exciting challenge. This mysterious, enigmatic quality about Eileen was like the Mona Lisa smile which had baffled countless people over the centuries.

Usually they went out once a week, on a Friday, which was conveniently the night he was not on call. Most nights he volunteered to be on call because Tom Thackery was a family man, and Gilbert, as a bachelor, didn't need so much sleep; but Friday became a regular dating night for him and Eileen. Sometimes on a Saturday or Sunday they went out exploring places which, though familiar to them both, they loved to revisit: the beautiful walk around Malham Tarn, an inland sea; or up through Trollers' Ghyll with its legend of the ghostly 'bargeist' or dog; or a scramble across the moors and past the old lead mines at Hebden Ghyll. Eileen liked walking and she and Gilbert equipped themselves to take the activity seriously with heavy shoes and windproof clothes. They'd take a picnic, thermoses of hot soup and tea, sandwiches and cake, and, gradually, the afternoons became days and they would walk from ten in the morning until the night fell. Eileen liked to listen to Gilbert talk about his work and, because of her absorption in him and concentration on what he was saying, he found he could unburden himself in a way he was unable to with anyone else, either with his mother or Tansy. After Christmas he knew with certainty that he had found his true love. It was now only a matter of time.

Gilbert was to be twenty-seven in the January and he wanted to take Eileen out for a special birthday dinner. His parents, however, expected him to share his birthday with them. They suggested going to London to be with Michael and Tansy; but Gilbert told them that he had other plans, a fact that disappointed them, and mystified his father, who felt that a longstanding family routine — the celebration of the twins' birthday — was being abandoned.

'What does he mean by *other* plans?' Geoffrey demanded of Catherine at breakfast after Gilbert had left for morning surgery.

'Gilbert has a young woman,' Catherine replied.

'A what?' his father said, cupping a hand to his ear.

'A young woman, a girlfriend.'

'Really?' Geoffrey looked surprised, but gratified. 'I'm glad to hear it, but no one ever told me. Why doesn't he introduce us?'

'He's rather shy. So is she.'

'But that's absurd,' Geoffrey said crossly. 'I would like nothing better than for Gilbert to marry. He is nearly twenty-seven. Besides, he will be more settled. This place is big enough for a wife and family.' Geoffrey looked round with a smile of satisfaction. 'It will be nice to have young children about the place again.'

'Geoffrey.' Catherine removed her spectacles and looked guardedly at him. 'You can't assume Gilbert will want to stay on here when he's married.'

'Well it would be ridiculous to waste money on a house!' Geoffrey exclaimed. 'This place is huge. It is right next to the surgery. Couldn't be more convenient. We could have some alterations made so that they can feel independent.'

'Geoffrey, I think you're jumping the gun a bit,' his wife said sharply. 'I said he has a girlfriend. I didn't say they were getting married.'

'Well it must be serious if he doesn't want to spend his birthday with us. This will be one of the few times since he was born that he hasn't.'

In fact there were a good few birthdays when Gilbert had been away at medical school, but Geoffrey had forgotten about them.

For him the past was fused into a nostalgic miasma where everything was pleasant and good and happy; but

Catherine knew that if Tansy had let him down and moved away, he was determined that the same thing would not happen to Gilbert.

'Who *is* this girl, anyway?' Geoffrey looked past the morning paper, which he had resumed reading, to his wife. 'Do I know her?'

'Eileen Monk.'

'Who?' He shook his head. 'No I don't.'

'Of course you do. The daughter of Tony Monk, the farmer.'

'Oh *that* Monk.' Geoffrey slowly put down his paper and stared at his wife. 'The daughter of Barbara Monk?'

'Yes,' Catherine stared fixedly at the table, avoiding her husband's eyes.

'But he can't marry her! Not the daughter of Barbara Monk.'

'Why ever not, Geoffrey?'

'Because she was mad. She killed herself. Insanity like that runs in families.'

'Oh!' Catherine stared at him in shock. 'I think that's *very* unfair to Eileen. There's nothing wrong with her.'

'I don't care; her mother's side was very unstable. I think *her* mother committed suicide as well, that is, the grandmother. Eileen is a very withdrawn, depressed girl, if I recall, I must tell Gilbert to break this relationship off at once.'

'Really, Geoffrey Blair,' Catherine said with an exclamation, getting up from the table and busily beginning to collect the breakfast dishes. 'You'll do no such thing. Is there no end to your meddling? Gilbert is a man of almost twenty-seven years of age, quite able to decide who he will or will not marry.'

'Well he's not marrying the daughter of Barbara Monk. She cut her throat. It was a horrible business, you must remember it. Eileen was a tiny baby. A person must be well and truly mad to do a thing like that. Once I explain what happened in the past to Gilbert he will see sense and drop her.'

'Somehow I don't think he will at all, if I know my son,' Catherine said. 'This is the first serious romance he's ever had that I'm aware of.'

'*How* do you know it's serious?' Geoffrey demanded.

'Because he sees her regularly. They go walking together. They're very close.'

'Has he talked to you about her?'

'Very little. I know who she is – that they go out together but, as you know, there are certain things that Gilbert can be very secretive about. He's shy. He minds his own business. Gilbert will do what he wants to do and let us know in his own time. The Wentworths know because Gilbert takes Eileen to the tennis club. I think they rather hoped he and Rosalind would hit it off.'

'And so he should. Now that *is* a girl he should be keen to marry.' Geoffrey shook a finger at her. 'Perfect. Very nice family, too.'

Catherine sighed and rolled up the napkins putting them in their rings.

'Yes, I think she would be very suitable too. She's a nice girl and I like her. The Wentworths would be more than happy; but what can you do about life, Geoffrey? You can't control it. There is something in Eileen that attracts Gilbert and if he wants to marry her . . .'

'Over my dead body,' Geoffrey said sternly.

'Geoffrey.' Now his wife shook a finger at him. 'I forbid you to try and interfere in Gilbert's romance with Eileen. There is no sense in it. It will only make Gilbert hostile. If he wants to marry her he will, and nothing you can say will stop him.'

Chapter 19

Tansy lay very still, listening to the thump of Michael's heartbeat next to hers. The frantic hammering gradually steadied as his weight increased on her body and then it became quite regular as he fell into a deep sleep, his head lolling across her shoulder onto the pillow.

She never felt tired after making love; in fact, she felt extraordinarily wakeful. Michael had tried to explain this phenomenon early in their marriage by saying that the man had to do all the work to achieve satisfaction. She accepted this then because she had been young and naive, very inexperienced in sexual matters as, indeed, she still was.

But what did satisfaction really mean? Tansy wasn't sure; it was a subject not very much discussed or written about, although there were signs that this attitude was changing. But it was not the sort of thing she'd talk about or, indeed, have anyone with whom to discuss it. She had no really intimate friends and, as a topic of conversation, she knew it would shock both her mother and Emily.

Yet Tansy was grateful to Michael for what he had taught her about physical love. With the freedom, even abandon she'd experienced had come a kind of inner liberation. Maybe before she had been a prude but, after her marriage, she was so no longer. But the main thing to her was that it was a visible expression of her love for Michael and his for her. When they made love she felt much closer, and when they hadn't made love for some time she felt further apart. If he went away for weeks at a time she felt the distance as though it were really an emotional deprivation not just for sex, but for togetherness, for love.

Tansy had realized early on in her married life that men and women had very little in common apart from this one vital act that drew them together. In fact it was what actually kept their marriage alive and, she suspected, many couples like them. Without sex she didn't think she'd even like her husband very much, because, over the years, they had grown further apart in other ways. Even though she grew more accustomed to living in London, and had found more to do with the endless time on her hands, she knew that the home, the children and herself were not the priority with Michael that the business was. She fulfilled her role with him only in one aspect.

But Michael liked to see himself as a family man. He was proud of his children and had a large photograph of them on his desk in the City. He did not have one of her but she had never read any significance into that; that particular group of the three children taken together was a charming one, and the presence near it of either parent would have spoiled it.

Tansy was an understanding, innately submissive wife, who accepted the dictum that the head of the household was Michael. She may, subconsciously, have resented it because in the case of her own home her mother was definitely stronger than her father. Her mother had carried them all for years. But Tansy knew that Michael was the stronger one in every way: he was decisive, dynamic and, over the years, he seemed to have grown more sexually attractive. His centre at the powerhouse of his expanding business suited him; he revelled in it. He was off to work early in the morning and back home late at night.

In between his wife had to live her own life; shop, care for the children and provide the sort of home, the degree of sophisticated entertaining, that Michael expected. She knew that other women also found Michael attractive, especially highly motivated career women, like Jill. Jill liked Michael very much and was always denigrating Jeremy in his presence, in a way that usually embarrassed people, but seemed to amuse Jill. Even Michael was vicariously affronted by it and grumbled about Jill on the way home. Yet Tansy knew he liked her. He liked women and, sometimes, she wondered if he was faithful to her, although she had no reason to think he wasn't.

She grew uncomfortable with Michael's heavy body on top of her and shifted him slightly to one side. He opened his eyes, blinked rapidly a few times, kissed her between the breasts and then, detaching himself from her, turned over and pulled the bedclothes up to his neck.

'Time to get up, Michael,' Tansy said, nudging him.

'What? What time is it?' He opened his eyes and blinked again.

'It's nearly seven. You said you had a breakfast meeting at Claridge's.'

'Hell,' Michael said, 'so I have. What wouldn't I give for a few hours' more sleep?'

'You don't get enough sleep, Michael.' Tansy still lay on her back looking towards the chink in the curtains to see if there was any sign of the dawn; but it was still winter and, suddenly, she felt homesick for Netherwick. Winter made her miss the skeletal trees etched against the skyline, the ploughed fields, the bare hedges and the feel of the keen easterly wind biting in her face.

It was funny the things one did miss; but Yorkshire in the wintertime was one of them.

Michael suddenly threw back the bedclothes and sat on the edge of the bed rubbing his face.

'I thought it was Sunday,' he mumbled. 'You should have stopped me.'

Tansy gave a derisive laugh and put on the light by her side of the bed. 'That wouldn't be easy,' she said. 'You might accuse me of going off sex.'

'I would *never* accuse you of that, Tansy,' Michael said, turning his head and grinning at her. His eyes were bloodshot, his hair stuck straight up on his head and, in the artificial light, his stubble of beard made him look comical; but in a matter of minutes a metamorphosis would occur. Only she knew Michael like this, as he really was.

Michael went into the bathroom and soon she heard the shower, the sound of his electric razor, the noise of the toothbrush. She listened to these sounds every morning except on Sundays when he had a lie in, and she got up first.

The time after Michael went in the morning was one of the best of the day, to be precisely guarded before Frank tried to come into her room or Roger and Julia, neatly dressed for school, popped their heads round the door to say goodbye.

As Michael re-entered the bedroom, vigorously towelling his head, Tansy said: 'Michael, when did you say we could begin to look for a house in the country?'

'I don't believe I gave a date.' Michael began to dress quickly, putting on a shirt, tie and suit she had laid out for him the night before.

'You said "after a year or two". Well it's after that now.'

'Tansy, are you so very unhappy in Knightsbridge?' Michael didn't look at her but started to fasten his tie at the same time, addressing her through the mirror.

'It's very smart. It's fashionable. Some people would give all they owned to live here. Besides,' he turned questioningly to her, 'I thought you'd got more friends?'

'I want animals and chickens.'

'Well you won't have those in the stockbroker belt of Kent or Surrey,' he chuckled.

'No animals?' she said, surprised.

'Maybe a cat.' Michael shrugged on his jacket and hurried over to her, planting a kiss on her forehead.

'Breakfast at Claridge's this morning, darling. Oh, and I'll be late home for dinner tonight.'

Then he was gone, feet hurrying down the staircase, front door banging as he went out into the street.

Tansy sank into a reverie about her life with Michael from their marriage nearly eight years before; about the changes that had occurred and the person she had now become: ostensibly a woman of the world, a mother of three, married to a successful businessman. She knew that some people already called Michael a tycoon and, indeed, his instincts were that of a tycoon, a killer. But to him it was not only money and prestige that mattered: it was being there where the action happened, making it happen and seeing his instincts and judgement, especially about the development of television, vindicated.

Trying to see him objectively and not as her husband, Tansy could not help but admire Michael and his total dedication to his goal. On the way to the top he had not forgotten the curiously named Garrett Great Engineering Company, now a tiny offshoot of the Garrett Corporation with headquarters in the square mile of the City of London where developments on the ruins left by the war were mushrooming. He had not forgotten his elderly mother or his stricken brother, who now lived permanently in a private nursing home where he had every comfort and the best medical care available. Michael dutifully visited his mother and brother nearly every time he went to Leeds and, as long as either lived, they would want for nothing.

As for herself, Tansy knew that inside this stereotype of the successful businessman's wife which she had become, there remained a country girl. She had been a good wife to Michael: she had been obedient and docile; she had smartened herself up for his important friends in the City and their wives and this, in turn, had given her more self-confidence. But she was not happy. She longed to be surrounded by hills and fields, to feel the grass under her feet rather than the hard pavements of the town.

She decided that here and now she would begin a campaign to get Michael to buy her the house outside London he had promised her when they first moved there.

There was a noise at the door like a little mouse scratching and then Frank crawled swiftly across the floor and jumped on his mother's bed. She had had her eyes closed and he thought he would surprise and, perhaps, even frighten her.

'Frank!' she cried clasping him because she had nearly drifted off to sleep again. 'You gave me an awful shock.'

Frank loved his mother dearly. He was, in fact, the most affectionate of her three children. Roger had been rather an aloof, insecure infant who did not seem to want or need the cuddles or caresses that his brother and sister demanded. Frank was Mummy's boy and, as he was not yet four, he had the privilege of staying at home and being with her all day.

He loved to lie in bed with his mother after his father had gone out. His father was a difficult person to talk to: but his mother was easy. She loved to tell him stories about the country and animals, or he would bring her a book and ask her to read to him.

Frank was very like Tansy to look at; he had thick fair curly hair and the brown, luminous eyes of his mother with those little almond flecks which always made people look at her twice as if trying to decide whether it was usual or unusual. Tansy's eyes were very arresting and Frank's were just like them. He had pink skin and freckles, and he was all energy and go from the moment he got up to the time he fell exhausted into bed, except for that precious hour when his father had gone to work, his brother and sister were being taken to school and his adored mother was his alone.

Tansy let her cheek rest against Frank's and then he started to wriggle.

'What is it?' she said.

'Tell me the story of the pony.' Frank stuck his finger in his mouth and pressed closer to her. The pony was a much loved story, which was partly true and partly embellished, about a pony she and Gilbert had shared when they were quite small and had not yet learned to ride. One day the pony disappeared. It had been stolen by some travelling people; but they could make no headway with it because it kept trying to get away and, one day, it did, just as the travelling people were near Settle. It broke out during the night and found its way back to Netherwick just by instinct, where it arrived tired and dishevelled some time later.

The story had been pieced together by the police because Tansy and Gilbert's pony was not the only horse to have been stolen by the gypsies who made their way annually to Appleby for the horse fair, and some of whom were not very scrupulous about how they came by them on the way.

'And did *he* live happily ever after?' Frank enquired

for the umpteenth time, his eyes never leaving his mother's and, no matter how many times Tansy told him this story, Frank always asked the same question.

'He did,' Tansy replied, stroking his hair and kissing his brow. 'Until he was a very old pony and then he just died very quietly in his stall one night and his soul went straight to heaven.'

At this point Frank usually burst into tears; but today he said: '*I* would like a pony, Mummy.'

'Well you'll have one one day,' she promised.

'Why can't I have one now?'

'Because we have nowhere to keep a pony.'

'But people have ponies in the park.'

'Yes, but that means riding them every day. I'm hoping that Daddy will let us live in the country and we can have ponies and dogs and cats . . .'

'Oh, *Mummy*,' Frank cried, sitting upright on the bed. 'Please ask Daddy if we can go soon.'

'I will,' Tansy promised, then, turning to look at the clock, she said: 'I thought I heard Marge come back. Will you go and see?'

That was the start of the ritual of the day. Marge came back from taking Julia and Roger to school. Shortly after that the daily appeared and, while Tansy had her bath, the whole routine of the household began that would only end when she and Michael put out the light some eighteen hours later.

Tansy had a busy day; she met a friend for coffee, a woman whose husband was a successful doctor and who had children at the same school that Roger and Julia went to. Her name was Rachelle and she was half French. In the afternoon Tansy went to look at a couple of London day schools because she preferred to think of keeping Roger and Julia at home rather than letting them board.

One of the boys' schools was in Hampstead and, on the way home, she shopped in Hampstead High Street, buying food for the evening because she wanted to give Michael an especially nice dinner, with all his favourite dishes, to soften him up in order to begin her campaign.

It was Marge's night off and she put the children to bed while the meal was cooking and played with them for a while, waiting for Michael to come home.

Roger felt he should go to bed later than his brother and sister and there was always a fuss about this. Sometimes she gave him an extra half hour or so but, this evening, she wanted there to be quiet in the house when Michael came in. She wanted the dinner to be delicious and seductive to lull him into a pleasurable stupor while she outlined her plans for the move.

By eight-thirty all was quiet in the house; the dinner was prepared, the cold starter in the fridge, the *boeuf bourgignon* simmering in the oven.

Tansy had always been a good cook, taught by her mother how to please men. In London she gradually became quite an accomplished cook, despite what Michael had told Jill, and spent a lot of time over menu preparation with the help of magazines and the plethora of cookery books which were starting to appear. Everyone knew or, if they didn't they were constantly told, that the way to a man's heart was through his stomach.

By nine Michael still was not in and Tansy began to feel annoyed; not worried, because he was not infrequently late, but usually he rang if he was going to be very late.

But by ten she was worried as well, quite off her food, and she began to pace up and down, the palms of her hands damp with apprehension.

At ten-thirty she reckoned she would have heard if there had been an accident. Fear had turned to irritation and, finally, rage and, brusquely, she cleared the table, put off the downstairs lights and went slowly upstairs to bed.

But, of course, she could not sleep or even rest. Anxiety and rage alternated as she turned the pages of her book and tried to read. It was just before one when Tansy heard the key in the latch downstairs and she put down her book wondering whether she should pretend to be asleep and have it out with him in the morning.

But the fury that now gripped her heart made that impossible as she heard him come upstairs and pause before their door until he realized the light was on. Then he opened it normally instead of gently turning the handle as he sometimes did.

'Still awake?' he said with a smile, crossing over and bending to kiss her.

'*Where* have you been?' Tansy put down her book and realized, now that the tension, the worry was over, that she was trembling.

'But, darling, I said . . .'

'You said that you would be late home for dinner but not that you *wouldn't* be home at all.'

'But, Tansy, I'm sure . . .' Michael crossed to the dressing table where, as usual, he inspected his face before beginning to undo his tie.

'Michael, you are a person who always knows what he's doing. I have never ever known you make a mistake or say you would be home for dinner when you knew you wouldn't be. You're not like that.'

Michael undid his tie, threw it over the chair and walked towards her, undoing the cuffs of his shirt. 'Tansy, I am *really* terribly sorry. Let's talk about it tomorrow. It is late and I have had a very busy, tiring day.'

'So have I, Michael.'

'Oh, come on.' Michael took off his shirt and carried it with him to the bathroom where he would put it into the laundry basket. Tansy, half sitting up in bed, listened once again to the familiar routine: the silence that was a prelude to the flush of the lavatory, the brushing of teeth, the gargling, the splash of water on his face. Then he appeared in his pyjamas and, crossing to the dressing table, began methodically to brush his hair.

'I hope we're not having a scene, Tansy. I don't feel like it.'

'Neither do I, Michael.'

'Then don't begin.' She saw him looking at her in the mirror. 'I can see from your face that I've upset you and I'm truly sorry. I didn't realize I said I'd be home. I thought I said I wouldn't. *Please* forgive me. I'll try not to do it again.'

'I had a special meal. I went to a lot of trouble.'

'Truly, darling, I'm sorry.'

Tansy could sense him beginning to grind his teeth with anger. 'But where *were* you, Michael?'

'Oh, Tansy,' he said, wearily getting up from the stool by the dressing table. 'Don't turn into a *nag*. Surely you know that I must have been with some people doing business.'

'You couldn't even *telephone*?'

'I forgot. I'm sorry.'

She saw by the look on his face that he was reaching exasperation point. She knew all about wives who nagged and she had determined she would never be one; but, then, she had never needed to be. Michael, who was so well organized, was still usually very considerate. He had always let her know if something cropped up and he couldn't come home. When she thought of all those wives who, at the coffee mornings and lunches, the tea and drinks parties she attended, did nothing but complain about their husbands, she remembered how superior she always felt. Now at last she began to have some understanding of what made them what they were.

'Never do it again, Michael,' she said, as he climbed into bed.

'Don't worry. I won't.' Michael pecked her carelessly on the cheek, turned his back to her and put off the light.

The following morning Michael banged his fist on the alarm when it rang at seven and murmured: 'I'm not going into the office today, so I'll sleep a bit late.'

'Did something happen last night?' Tansy felt put out at this break in routine.

'Don't be silly, darling,' Michael murmured half asleep. 'I'm going to Zurich this afternoon, and I decided to bring all the stuff I needed home with me.'

'You never *told* me about Zurich.'

Michael didn't reply and she heard the familiar, regular breathing of a person deeply asleep.

Nag, nag, nag, she thought as she went into the bathroom. It would be very easy indeed to become one.

When Michael came down to breakfast Roger and Julia were at school, and Marge had taken Frank to the play group which he attended twice a week. Everything in the dining room was set out as Michael expected it to be; but only one place laid.

'Have you eaten already, darling?' Michael looked at the table with surprise. Then he sat down, briskly unfolding the copy of *The Times* which he had got from the table in the hall.

'Its nearly ten o'clock, Michael.'

'What's the matter, Tansy?' Michael enquired with an abrupt change of tone.

'Nothing. Would you like a cooked breakfast?'

'No, just the usual, thanks.' Michael had already

turned to the business section of *The Times*.

Tansy went into the kitchen and made Michael's toast and coffee herself. From upstairs came the noise of the vacuum. The ritual of the day had started as usual, only in a different way. Michael breakfasting at ten was not normal, and she realized she was becoming routine-minded, like her father. She was getting into a rut.

As she took the tray into the breakfast room Michael looked up and said: 'Won't you have coffee with me, darling, or are you still cross?'

Nag, nag, nag . . . no she mustn't become like them, the people, the dissatisfied women she listened to all day long.

'Why not?' she said with a smile. 'Though I'm having lunch with Jill.'

'How *is* Jill? That brother of yours doing any work yet?' Michael's eyes were once again on the paper.

Tansy ignored his question and poured a cup of coffee for herself as well as him before joining him at the table.

'Michael,' she said hesitantly, 'I thought I'd go up to Netherwick if you're going to be away.'

'Any reason?' He looked up enquiringly from the paper.

'It's our birthday. I haven't been with Gilbert for a long time on our birthday.'

'I hadn't forgotten, Tansy.' There was a gentle reproof in Michael's tone of voice. 'I expect to be back in time for your birthday. I'm only going to Zurich for forty-eight hours.'

'I'd still like to go, Michael, if that's OK with you. I thought I'd take Frank with me. Mother's always complaining she never sees him.'

'Tansy, of course you must go if you want,' Michael said, spreading his toast with butter and marmalade. 'In fact it's a good idea and when you come back we can celebrate then. I may stay on in Switzerland longer, in that case. It will be a break for me too. Now,' Michael threw back his cuff and looked at his watch. 'I had better get my things together or I'll miss the plane.'

Netherwick. It was like breathing clean, pure air again, Tansy thought as the taxi drew away from the station and they began the familiar climb up the hill towards home.

Did she still think of it as home? Yes, she did. It was home and it always would be. Frank leaned forwards with excitement, demanding to be told which was the field the pony had been in, and his mother promised to show it to him as soon as they had said 'hello' to Gran and Grandpa.

Dear Netherwick; dear, familiar place. Even the rain was familiar, welcome. Tansy's eyes filled unexpectedly with tears and she hastily brushed them away in case Frank saw them and wondered what was the matter. He could be frightened by the sight of his mother in tears.

As the taxi drew up at the gate Tansy paid the driver, and Frank, beside himself with excitement, began to clamber out of the car.

'Be careful,' Tansy warned looking anxiously towards the house just as the front door opened, and her mother flew down the drive with the agility of someone her youngest grandson's age. She scooped him up in her arms and gave him two resounding kisses, one to each chubby cheek, before hugging him so hard she left him almost gasping for breath.

Catherine loved children and her main regret was that she had seen so little of her grandchildren since Tansy had moved to London. Visits to Netherwick were infrequent and short. She put Frank down just as his grandfather, too, appeared at the door and Tansy fell into her mother's arms.

'It's a wonderful surprise,' her mother said. 'If you'd have told us the train . . . Is anything *wrong*?'

'Nothing at all, Mum,' Tansy said, kissing her. 'I came on the spur of the moment. Michael's abroad, left early this morning.I wasn't sure myself if I could come today. I had to make arrangements with Marge and then came as soon as I could get away.'

'Are you *sure* there's nothing wrong?' Catherine stood back from her daughter and gazed at her anxiously.

'Of *course* there's nothing wrong! I wanted to be here for my birthday. The first time in about six years.'

'Longer than that,' her mother said and put her arm round Tansy as the daily woman came out to help with the cases. In the doorway Frank had climbed into his grandfather's arms and they had already begun to chat animatedly as Tansy came up with her mother.

Catherine took Frank, and Geoffrey threw his arms around his daughter.

'Darling, what a *wonderful* surprise. You should have told us the train . . .'

'I've been over all this with Mum, Dad!' Tansy disentangled herself from her father's embrace. 'I just didn't know which train we'd be able to catch. I was simply longing to get away.'

'Nothing *wrong*?' her father echoed her mother's words.

'Of *course* there's nothing wrong! How many times must I say it?' She put her arm around his waist as they walked into the house from which came the familiar sounds, the familiar smells: home.

'Oh it's *good* to be back.' Tansy took a deep breath. 'Nothing else smells quite like home.'

Behind her Catherine, one hand holding Frank's, gazed after her daughter, concern still showing on her face. She thought Tansy looked tired and she seemed almost restless with unspent nervous energy.

'Michael sends his love,' Tansy said in an effort to reassure them. She knew they thought her sudden appearance odd. Then, as she walked into the sitting room, she enquired: 'Where's Gilbert?'

'He'll be out on his rounds, dear,' her mother said, glancing at the clock. 'We'll see him after evening surgery.'

'And tomorrow's our birthday!' Tansy turned and again squeezed her mother's waist. '*That's* what I wanted to be home for. Gilbert and I haven't shared a birthday . . .'

'Oh dear,' Catherine said, and stared fixedly at Geoffrey.

'Is there anything the matter, Mother?' Tansy flopped into a chair and kicked off her high heel shoes.

'Well, nothing's the matter *exactly* . . .' her voice trailed off uncertainly.

'Something *is* the matter,' her father said, following them as Frank ran excitedly up and down in front of him.

'Not with Gilbert I hope?' Momentarily Tansy looked anxious.

'There's nothing the matter with Gilbert, dear,' her mother replied, reassuringly, 'or any of us. It's just that he has a girlfriend, and your father is not very happy about it.'

'But that's *wonderful* news,' Tansy cried, clasping her hands. 'Why aren't you happy, Daddy?'

'She's mad,' her father began; but Catherine quickly interrupted him.

'Geoffrey! You promised me you wouldn't use that word again. It's *not* fair, and it's not true.' She turned and looked apologetically at Tansy. 'Good thing you know your father. Gilbert's girlfriend is a very nice, very pretty young lady called Eileen Monk.'

'But I know Eileen Monk,' Tansy exclaimed with surprise. 'She *is* very nice. Don't you *like* her, Daddy?'

'There's insanity in the family,' her father said grimly, putting a finger across his throat. 'Her mother killed herself not long after she was born. Cut her own throat.'

'Well that doesn't mean there's anything wrong with her daughter, Daddy.' Tansy appeared to share her mother's indignation.'Good heavens, I thought that kind of old-fashioned thinking had all gone out with the war.'

'There's a lot in old-fashioned thinking,' her father said, nodding wisely, 'believe you me.'

'And are you having a dinner party tomorrow with Gilbert and Eileen?'

'No we are not,' her mother said, 'that's just the point. Gilbert wants to take Eileen out by himself. Your father is a bit upset about it. Of course, your brother didn't know you were coming home.'

'Oh dear, what a pity!' Tansy looked disappointed for a moment, but it didn't last. 'Well, we'll just have our birthday party another time. How about tonight or the day after?'

'How long can you stay?' Her mother's tone was anxious.

'I'm not sure,' Tansy replied, 'but long enough to have a party.'

Later on, just after tea, Tansy and Gilbert met in the hallway and embraced each other.

'It is absolutely marvellous to see you,' Gilbert said, drawing her into his room. 'But you look pale.'

'It's the journey,' Tansy said wearily. 'Frank needs a terrible lot of entertaining. Wait until you . . .' She stopped and gave him a sly smile.

'Oh they've told you, I suppose.' Gilbert slumped on his bed and lay with his head in his hands.

'Well don't be sad about it, Gilbert.' Tansy sank down on the bed next to him. 'It's nice. She's very pretty, if I remember.'

'She's the most wonderful girl,' Gilbert said in a reverent tone. 'But Dad has this ridiculous bias against the family. Sometimes I think it's Dad who is actually mad, not the Monks. Eileen's mother killed herself . . .'

'I know. They told me.'

'So Dad feels that her daughter must have inherited her suicidal tendency. He wants me not to see her. I tried to tell Dad that a lot more is known now than was known then about post-puerperal depression. Some new mothers really do get suicidal.'

'It's a man's world,' Tansy said grimly. 'That's why no one has ever noticed before.' She took Gilbert's hand and leaned towards him. 'You must resist Dad,' she said urgently. 'Don't let him influence you in this as he has in the past. Don't for a moment let him tell you who you should see or not see, what girlfriends you should have . . .'

Gilbert rose hurriedly from his bed, looking at his watch. 'Time for surgery.' He paused and pushed his glasses up his nose with a forefinger.

'This is really serious, Tansy. This is it. Tomorrow I'm going to ask Eileen to marry me. That's why I wanted her to myself. To make my birthday a really special day.'

Gilbert had arrived back for dinner having had a difficult case up in the Dales, and they had already started the meal without him. Gilbert quickly took his seat after apologizing to his mother.

'That's all right, Gilbert,' Catherine said, ladling the

soup from the tureen in front of her. 'Was it a baby?'

'No it was a little girl who had a bad attack of asthma. Norman Walls' daughter,' he said, glancing at his father who nodded in recognition of the name. 'Luckily we pulled her out of it; but I've sent her to hospital.'

'Never mind, you're here now,' Tansy said, smiling at him. 'And it's lovely to be all together.'

Gilbert began hungrily to spoon his soup. 'What made you come up so unexpectedly? Anything wrong?'

'I wish . . .' Tansy began, looking in exasperation at the ceiling. Then she smiled unexpectedly. 'I *hoped* we'd celebrate our birthday together. Never mind. I do understand.'

'Oh, Tansy, I'm so sorry.' Gilbert put down his spoon and broke into a piece of bread. 'I arranged with Eileen . . .'

'I should think that was something you were *perfectly* able to undo now that your twin has come up especially to celebrate the birthday with you,' Geoffrey said testily. 'Tansy has come *all* this way . . .'

'Really, I don't mind a bit,' Tansy said. 'We can have a nice lunch instead.'

'Why don't you ask Eileen *here*?' Catherine suggested timidly. 'We would love that. She might like it too.'

'No, Mother,' Gilbert replied, an edge to his voice. 'It's all fixed. Table booked.'

'It's a little thoughtless, Gilbert,' his father said.

Finally Gilbert looked angry. 'Dad I *do* have a right to do what I like . . .'

'Of course you do. No one's disputing that, Gilbert; but in this family we have always been accustomed to sharing, you know that. I think it very strange that you so seldom bring Eileen here. It's as though you know there's something wrong but you won't admit it.'

'Dad, I *do* object to that,' Gilbert said, banging down

his spoon. He poured himself a glass of water from the jug in the centre of the table, and as he drank his hand holding the glass shook.

'Nevertheless it's true.' His father finished his soup, dabbed his lips and sat back in his chair, glaring at his son. 'You don't want to admit it.'

'*Please*, Geoffrey, not tonight when Tansy's here.' Catherine looked anxiously at her husband as she got up to clear the plates. Tansy sprang up too and together she and her mother went into the kitchen looking at each other once they were on the other side of the door.

'Your father's really very upset,' Catherine whispered.

'But Gilbert's right, Mum. It's his decision, not *Dad's*,' Tansy whispered back as she allowed her mother to precede her with the roast while she brought in the vegetable dishes on a tray.

Back in the dining room father and son had remained silent, and they both kept their eyes fixedly on Catherine as she carved, and then on Tansy as she served the vegetables.

However, Geoffrey, as he felt was his right as the head of the family, would not let the subject go. He was accustomed to speaking his mind without interference from the family.

'Insanity runs in families,' he said glaring at his son. 'You should know that.'

'Father,' Gilbert, suddenly losing control, banged his fist on the table. 'I have *no* proof, and neither had you, that Eileen's mother was insane. She had puerperal-fever after the birth and that was followed by depression.' He paused and then continued in an even voice punctuated by meaningful pauses. '*You* should know all about depression, Father.'

'I object to that remark, Gilbert,' his father said stiffly. 'No one in my family has ever cut their throat.'

'Oh, *Geoffrey*, Gilbert, please stop this instant,' Catherine pleaded, 'and eat your dinner!'

'But there's a matter of principle, here, Catherine.' Geoffrey looked without appetite at his plate. 'Tansy has come up especially to be with Gilbert on their joint birthday; and Gilbert persists in sharing it with a girl, not his family, and who we scarcely know. Personally I can't understand it.'

'But Gilbert didn't know I was coming up, Daddy. I do think he should be allowed to make his own plans.' Tansy gave Gilbert a conspiratorial smile.

'I think, myself, it's rude,' Geoffrey said.

'I don't,' Tansy replied. 'And I, for one, don't mind a bit.'

'It's just *one* day, Gilbert,' his father pleaded. 'Take her out the following day.'

'No, Father.' Gilbert again banged a fist on the table. 'I have asked Eileen, booked a table, and . . . bought the ring.'

There was a silence that seemed to rebound round the walls of the room as though it were empty.

'You see,' Tansy said, gazing at her parents, her eyes glowing 'it *is* going to be a very special day. Gilbert told me this afternoon and I'm thrilled for him.'

'She hasn't said "yes",' Gilbert said, blushing. 'She may not . . .'

'Oh she'll say "yes" all right,' his father said in a withering tone. 'Quite a step up for the Monk family, marrying a doctor. No doubt but that she'll say "yes".'

'Daddy,' Tansy said sharply. 'You can be *really* horrible when you want to.'

'Tansy!' Catherine cried. 'Mind what you say.'

'Mother, it's *true*.' Tansy leaned earnestly across the table. 'You know it is. This is a great occasion for Gilbert. He has obviously thought long and deeply about what he wants to do, because Gilbert is like that. He is twenty-seven. He wants to be married, to have the happiness that I have, or you and Daddy had. He wants to have children. Why deny those things to Gilbert, why be mean and spiteful about the woman of his choice just because her *mother* committed suicide while the balance of her mind was disturbed after having a baby?'

'It wasn't just her mother,' Geoffrey said stubbornly. 'It was the mother's mother. She killed herself too. Now did you know *that*, Gilbert? Did you know *that*? Insanity runs in the family, through the female line. I haven't seen much of Eileen, you keep her well away from us. But she is an odd girl; unusual, quiet and withdrawn, just like her mother.'

Gilbert quietly drew back his chair from the table, pressed Tansy's arm and left the room, with his mother wailing in the background: 'Oh, *Gilbert*, you haven't finished your dinner . . .'

Gilbert's departure seemed to shake his father, who didn't appear to know whether to continue with his meal or go after his son. In the end he just pushed his plate to one side, and produced his tobacco pouch from his pocket.

'Geoffrey, *please*!' Catherine said sharply. 'Not here! I really can't have you lighting your pipe at table.'

Slowly Tansy rested her arms with deliberation on the table. She gazed first at her mother and then at her father, who was trying to stuff his pouch in his pocket with a rather shamefaced look.

'Daddy,' Tansy said, 'things have really come to a pretty pass when you try and tell Gilbert who he should or should not marry. You did it to me too, Daddy, but I was much younger. However, you did try and stop me and Michael marrying.'

'Tansy!' her mother cried. 'Remember your father's health.'

'I *am* remembering it, Mother,' Tansy replied gently, 'and I *am* trying to be very quiet and reasonable in what I say; but it is true. Michael gave up his chance of a job in Australia because he wanted to marry me, and that changed our lives. I'm not saying it was for the worse, but it did change them.'

'Michael would have come back, anyway, to take over from his brother,' Geoffrey said grumpily. 'Even you can't say *I* was responsible for *that*.'

'No, you weren't responsible, Daddy, certainly not. But you did influence the first years of our lives together, and Michael has never forgotten it. Michael is now quite determined not to give in to me on anything, because he thought he was soft in the beginning. Sometimes it makes things very hard for us.'

'You're not saying you're going to split up, I hope. I *did* ask if there was anything wrong,' Catherine interjected in a tone of horror, jumping to conclusions.

'I'm not saying anything, Mother,' Tansy replied. 'I know marriages change anyway, and Michael has become a very important and powerful businessman; but relationships do deteriorate, especially if you have had a sticky beginning. Ours was hard. I was only nineteen, Michael was over thirty. Whatever Daddy thought was right then, is definitely not right now. Gilbert is a mature man, a doctor, a person in a position of responsibility. He certainly can choose whom he should, or should not, marry.

'Whether there is instability in Eileen's family or not I don't think it's up to you to decide what he does. I remember Eileen quite well and I liked her. But if Gilbert not only likes her but loves her and wants to marry her, that's quite good enough for me. You should be glad on Gilbert's account and I hope that, before the night is out, you will tell him so.'

Tansy got up and swiftly left the room to go in search of her twin while Catherine and Geoffrey sat stiffly in their seats, staring at each other across the table.

As the plane took off from Zurich Airport and, after circling the mountains that surrounded it, began to climb in the sky Michael sat back in his chair and gave a deep sigh. It was a moment he hated no matter how many miles he had flown, and he found the tension remained until the order came to unfasten seat belts. Then he could relax and light a cigarette.

Next to him Laura Page sighed too, and seemed similarly grateful when permission to unfasten seat belts and smoke was announced. She gave Michael a sidelong glance and smiled. 'I can see you're nervous too, Michael.'

'Isn't everyone?' Michael said, groping for her hand. 'Besides, I don't want to lose you.'

As he gripped Laura's hand his head moved as if he wanted to kiss her, but she frowned, shook her head and moved back. 'Not here. Someone might know us. Besides,' she said flirtatiously, 'we've had a lot of kisses these past three days, Michael.'

'Not enough for me,' Michael said, and quickly pecked her cheek, whispering as he did, 'I could never have enough.'

'Oh, *Michael*.' Laura shook her head and released his hand. 'What *are* we going to do?'

Michael didn't reply and, taking out his cigarette case, offered one to Laura, lit hers and then his. The stewardess came round to take orders for drinks and Michael asked for a bottle of champagne.

It had been a wonderful three days, combining business with pleasure; but, thanks to Laura, there was much more pleasure than there was business as it was the first time he and Laura had been away together. Three whole nights on their own, during which they had had very little sleep. In a way it was just as well Tansy wouldn't be home when he arrived or she would notice how tired he was; but he could always lie to Tansy. He had lied and lied to her for years, and she never seemed to notice.

When Michael had married Tansy, with whom he was truly in love, he had vowed to forswear other women; but it was a habit that he had got used to and the vow was soon broken. Michael needed the admiration of many women, the reassurance they gave him and he had had a number of extra-marital affairs before he met Laura.

With Laura he knew at once that it would be serious and, at first, he had tried to avoid involvement. She was a career woman, a successful journalist, and she knew about Tansy and their children.

But it had been hard to keep it on a casual plane with someone like Laura. He slowly realized that her own intentions were very serious indeed but, at the beginning, she had allowed him enough rope not to realize how deeply he was entangling himself.

The rope had gradually shortened and now she was growing impatient.

'I'm not getting any younger, Michael,' was a constant refrain of hers. In vain he tried to explain that children were a tie, a bind, a nuisance. Besides, someone who already had three didn't want any more. But Laura wanted to breed, and that was that. It was a woman's instinct, after all.

'Are you going to tell Tansy when she gets back?' Laura hissed. 'You promised.'

'I'll have to judge the time,' Michael said cautiously, grateful for the noise made by the plane's engine. 'It won't be easy.'

'It's *never* easy, Michael, especially when you've told so many lies, but either . . .'

'I know, I know,' Michael murmured, leaning his head back against the seat, feeling suddenly desperately tired. Laura had said it too often before; 'It's either her or me.'

She no longer wished to be the other woman.

PART FIVE

One for Sorrow,
Two for Joy

1962–1965

Chapter 20

Emily looked at the clock, saw that it was time for supper and put the remainder of the exercise books she was correcting in a neat pile in front of her. Then she removed her reading spectacles, put them on top of the pile and leaned her elbows on her desk gazing, for a moment of utter peacefulness, into the valley that broadened out below her bedroom window.

It was nearly the end of the term. Nearly the summer holidays, and she was going to Switzerland for her first holiday abroad since the war.

Emily was cautious; cautious about money, about her time. The one thing she had not been cautious about was her affair and subsequent marriage to Jeremy. But that was a memory long gone, if not quite forgotten. Everything now was neat, compartmentalized. It was the only way to live when you lived alone; the only way to plan one's life so that, apart from work, it didn't seem empty.

Emily now enjoyed her life; she had grown accustomed to solitude and to spending long spells on her own. Nevertheless she was going to Switzerland with a group from one of the teaching organizations to which she belonged. They were going to do some walking, some sightseeing, and she was looking forward to it very much.

She had tried to persuade her daughter Fern to come with her, but, to a young woman of sixteen, going on holiday with mother was about the most boring thing one could contemplate. Mark was twenty-one and it was many years since they'd spent any holidays together.

Mark was mechanically minded, car mad and, after he had left school, he joined, through the influence of Tansy, Garrett Engineering as an apprentice. Michael Garrett did actually know that his wife's nephew worked for him; but Mark was much too tiny a cog ever to come into direct contact with the Managing Director of the whole group.

So, her children having fled the nest, Emily was now reconciled to spending the rest of her life alone.

She thought she heard a knock on the door which was why she'd glanced at the clock but, as it didn't recur, she decided it was her imagination. Now, however, she was sure; there was a second knock, someone at the door, and she got up and, walking to the window overlooking the garden that was open because of the balmy evening, looked surreptitiously out.

He had the ragged unkempt look of a tramp, someone who had been on the road for weeks; not the urbane man of the world she had last seen at Gilbert's wedding, impeccable in a grey morning suit, acting as best man to his brother.

Just at that moment Jeremy looked up, his eyes catching hers, and she saw that his face was rimmed by a white stubble and that his eyes were red.

'Just a minute,' she called. 'I'll be right down.'

Emily always locked the front door, though many people in the country did not. Some of her pupils had once developed a habit of popping in; or the parents of one of her pupils, wanting to discuss something, would think nothing of going directly to the house instead of hanging about after school, or making an appointment.

She ran down the stairs and turned the key in the lock. Then, without asking him in, she stared very hard at Jeremy for a long while, still finding it hard to take in his appearance.

'You look absolutely *terrible*,' she said at last, standing to one side and motioning him in with a broad sweep of her hand. 'Are you all right?'

Jeremy didn't reply, but came slowly indoors, then he flopped in one of the chairs, both hands hanging down limply on either side.

'Jeremy?' Emily cried sharply. 'What is the matter? Have you been ill? Are you ill *now*?'

Jeremy stared up at her, his red streaked eyes almost sightless. It was an unnerving, even frightening situation for his ex-wife.

'I haven't been well,' he replied at last. 'But that's my fault. I hitch-hiked from London and it wasn't a very good thing to do. I didn't get many lifts and had to do a lot of walking. But I'm entirely to blame. I should have borrowed the money for the fare, or cadged it.'

'Jeremy!' Emily exclaimed, sitting opposite him as she scrutinized him carefully. 'Why should *you* have to hitch-hike from London?'

'Because I've left Jill.' Jeremy shrugged his shoulders in despair. 'I haven't a bean. I left her without a penny to my name, with only the clothes I stood up in. As you see,' he shrugged his shoulders, glancing downwards, 'not much.'

'I don't understand *any* of this,' Emily said, nervously running her hand over her head. 'You're not poverty-stricken are you?'

'I am. Jill accused me of living off her; she said that every penny I had, all the clothes I possessed, every item of value – including my wristwatch – were really hers.' Jeremy held up his arm which was bare. 'So now I have simply the clothes I wear. As you see,' he shrugged helplessly again. 'No luggage.'

Emily felt a terrible rage well up inside her and she kneaded her fist violently into the palm of her hand. 'Then why come to *me*, Jeremy? Why *me*? Why bring this burden to *me*? What have *I* done to merit it? Why didn't you go to your father?'

'I couldn't tell my father I'd left Jill.' Jeremy humbly bowed his head.

'You mean she threw you out,' Emily replied bitterly.

'No, I walked out.' Jeremy lifted his head as though to indicate that some vestiges of his dignity still remained.

'Goaded beyond endurance, by the sound of it.'

'Not for the first time,' Jeremy said in a tone of voice Emily could scarcely hear. 'You don't know what it's been like being Jill's pet dog for all these years.'

'Well, my dear, it's the life you chose,' Emily said, rising and, walking across to the window. 'Don't say it isn't.'

She turned around to face him, acutely aware of him looking at her like a dog begging not to be whipped again by its master. It was pathetic and horrible; but, more to the point, it was not like the Jeremy she'd known at all. However, despite this and remembering the man she had loved, she steeled herself as she answered: 'Jeremy, pray don't think that, just because you have left Jill and we were once married, you can walk in here and resume where you left off, because you can't.'

'I didn't expect it,' he said, humble again. 'Truly. But I had nowhere to go. Could you let me stay here just for a few days, Emily, or I'll become a vagrant? I have absolutely nowhere to go.'

'Tansy?'

'Tansy has her own problems. I couldn't force myself on her.'

'What sort of problems?' Emily asked, sharply again.

'Marital problems.'

'She as well!'

'Yes, she as well. Besides, Michael doesn't like me and I never had much time for him. I have no money, Emily, no clothes and very little pride left now. I have made an absolute mess of my life, and I have no one to blame but myself. I am not begging and I am not apologizing. I am just asking you, as Fern's mother, to give me a bed until I can recover. I really don't feel well, but I promise you that when I'm better I shall be on my way.'

'But what will you *do*, Jeremy? You said you have no money.'

'I have a small pension. I hope to return to the Dales and rent a room. If you ask me what I *really* want to do, I want to go back to what I did best. I have failed as an airman, I have failed as a writer. I want to go back to keeping sheep on the hills. That way I feel I can recover my self-respect.'

'What happened to your career?' Helplessly Emily threw out her arms. 'All those expectations.'

'What happened is that I married Jill,' he replied in a soft, patient tone. 'Jill felt she had made me and could continue to mould me. She pampered me and spoiled me like an overgrown child. I simply dried up. I couldn't work. I followed her around like a puppet on a string. At first she was extremely nice to me, but then she got tired because I didn't produce. *A Shepherd in the Hills* appeared nine years ago; Tansy was pregnant with Roger at the time, because I clearly remember her at my publication party. In those subsequent years she produced two more children; you carved a career for yourself as a teacher. Gilbert qualified as a doctor, married and is, I hear, now expecting a child. I . . .' dramatically Jeremy flung his arms wide again, 'I have done nothing. Nothing, nothing, nothing. I have made no one happy, and contributed to no one's welfare.'

Emily rose and walked briskly into the kitchen where she opened the fridge to see what it contained. She ate frugally and, usually, at this time would have bread and cheese or a slice of ham. She had her main meal at school and that was enough.

'No use feeling sorry for yourself, Jeremy,' she called out. 'I've got a bit of ham here and some cheese. You're welcome to share it.'

As she knelt by the fridge she was aware of Jeremy's shadow darkening the doorway.

'You're *very* good, Emily.'

'No, I'm not,' Emily said, getting to her feet with the plate of ham and a piece of ripe cheddar. 'I'm a practical person and, I hope, a not uncharitable one. It is true we were in love once, married and had a child. It is true you were not a good husband to me, or a good father to Fern. It is true you put yourself before other people; but . . .' she looked at him and smiled for the first time since he'd entered her house, 'you're a human being; you are a man who has known much suffering. You are not a bad man; just a weak man. Fortune has definitely not been kind to you or, maybe, you have not made the best of your advantages.'

She put two knives and two forks on the bare deal table and between them the plate with the ham, a bowl of lettuce and tomatoes and the piece of cheese. Then she went to the tap and drew a jug of water and this she put on the table with two glasses.

'Sit,' she said pointing, 'and eat. Then you must sleep, and when you have slept enough and recovered your health, then we shall talk.'

* * *

Tansy said, in a tone of voice in which there was a new note of determination: '*When* are we going to the country?'

'If I've heard that once . . .' Michael began, and then swore as, trying to swallow his coffee in too much of a hurry, he burnt his mouth.

'But you did promise me, Michael,' Tansy continued in the same flat, strong, demanding monotone. 'You said that, one day, when the business was going really well, we would sell up here and go and live in Sussex or Kent.'

'And you have never stopped talking about it ever since,' Michael snapped back.

'Nevertheless it was a promise,' Tansy insisted. '*I* promised to accept living in Knightsbridge; to be a good wife, mother and housekeeper. To give parties and to entertain. To be a credit to you on public occasions.'

'You make it sound as if we were in church, renewing our vows,' Michael said, but he couldn't help smiling.

'*I* promised all those things, Michael, and I have kept my promises. In return you said we could live in the country and, now that your company is going public, you say you will be a millionaire. I'm very glad, Michael, because success is what you've always wanted, and it's important to you. But I never wanted to be the wife of a millionaire who, in order to get where he has, has had to live and breathe his work. I wanted to live in the country and have chickens. I wanted our children to grow up surrounded by grass, cattle and sheep. I never wanted to spend my days wandering round Harrods, or attending or organizing coffee mornings or lunches for bored, rich women. That's what I've become.' Tansy gazed stonily up at him from the breakfast table. 'A bored, rich woman.'

'Aren't you lucky?' Michael said, rising swiftly from

the table and stooping to peck her on the cheek before retrieving his copy of *The Times*. 'Some people would give their eye teeth just to be you.'

'When will you be home?' Tansy called after him.

'Late,' he shouted back, and he was gone.

Late, as usual, or never. Tansy seldom believed what Michael said now. At one time in their relationship he was a person on whom one could rely absolutely: meticulous, exact, a good time-keeper. But for some while now, as the business had leapfrogged from success to success, he had been the opposite. He had become vague about time, difficult to pin down, unless it was a very important social occasion for business friends and acquaintances. He was never vague about these.

But what a lot of them there were! How *they* had mushroomed, as he became more and more successful, as deal followed deal, acquisition acquisition. And on every occasion there she was: dressed by Hartnell or Amies, Dior or Courrèges as Michael encouraged her to buy couture clothes; her hair styled by Vidal Sassoon or Xavier of Knightsbridge.

Tansy never let Michael down; but he let her down all the time. She had grown to feel it must be part of the act of being a tycoon. The telephone rang but she remained where she was, gazing at the check-patterned tablecloth, at the hard cold piece of toast on her plate.

'Telephone for you, Mrs Garrett,' the daily said. 'It's Mrs Blair.'

Thinking it must be her mother, Tansy got to her feet and hurried into the drawing room so that she could take the call. But it wasn't her mother, it was Jill. Not the calm, competent, cool Jill she was used to, but a woman who sounded very distraught and very frightened.

'Tansy, could you come over immediately?' she said in a breathless voice. 'Something really *awful* has happened.'

Tansy couldn't find out from Jill over the phone what the matter was so she hurried upstairs to dress and, instead of getting her car out of the garage, she took a cab to St John's Wood. As soon as she arrived Jill opened the door and rushed to the gate to greet her, throwing her arms round her neck.

'What on earth . . .' Tansy began, taking her in her arms.

'It's Jeremy,' Jill sobbed, and before Tansy was through the door Jill had pushed a note into her hand. Tansy was forced to stand where she was and read it.

'Dear Jill,' (it said) 'you are quite right. I am no good to you or anybody. I am a parasite and I have decided to free you. I have taken nothing that you say belongs to you, not even a spare suit of clothes. As you pointed out the other day everything I have belongs to you, so you may keep everything.

'I don't intend to harm myself, and I would rather you didn't try and find me. I am sorry that I have caused you so much anguish for so many years; that I was a failure in your eyes, because you did so much to help me.

'Please file for a divorce and, in due course, when I've regained my self-respect, I shall contact you again.'

Tansy walked into Jill's exquisite period drawing room, with its Regency furniture and Wilton carpet, still reading the letter, and when she'd finished she sat on the sofa and tried to collect her thoughts.

'Well,' she said at last, staring at Jill's anxious tear-stained face, 'he has been very honest.'

'But I didn't *want* him to *leave* me.'

'Nevertheless, you did taunt him a lot,' Tansy said

firmly. 'You made him *feel* inferior.'

'Did he tell you that?' Jill whispered, sitting opposite her sister-in-law on the edge of the chair.

'He didn't tell me very much, he had too much pride; but I knew. Jeremy is still a sick man, you know, Jill. He had part of his brain removed and I think it left him with a feeling of inadequacy. I don't think he'll ever completely recover. He wrote *A Shepherd in the Hills* in the flush of beginning to feel well again for the first time for many years, and then he realized he wasn't a superman and life had grown very comfortable. Too comfortable, perhaps.'

'Where do you think he's gone?'

Tansy knew, or guessed, where he had gone. In many ways they were alike, intuitive, and she knew where she would have gone had she been in his place: to rediscover his roots.

But she wouldn't tell on him. She wouldn't betray him, now or ever.

Jill, irked by her silence, got up and began to pace the room. She was smartly dressed in a striped suit with a plain white blouse underneath, and lots of fashionable chunky jewellery around her neck and on her wrists. She wore large earrings and her hair was scraped back into a chignon at the nape of her neck. Her eyebrows looked like wings, pencilled in on either side. She wore, as she always did, a lot of make-up and it had caked by the corners of her mouth, alongside her nose and under her eyes. She looked hard, brittle and successful, and Tansy wondered what it was about achievement that had made so many women like this? Maybe it had been too long coming; maybe future generations would let it sit more lightly on their shoulders.

Jill didn't look like a woman who would ever crack, ever allow herself for a moment to lose control yet, suddenly, to Tansy's astonishment, she threw herself against her once again and began to weep.

'It's so *unfair*,' she spluttered, clawing at Tansy's shoulder. 'I did everything I could for him to make him happy, help him to settle down. Of course I knew he was a sick man and what a long struggle he had to get away from that spiral of illness and become a success. I *was* ambitious for Jeremy and I thought he was ambitious too; but after *Shepherd* he never wrote anything else! Not a word! I don't believe he ever really *tried*. He had a study of his own with everything he needed. I was out all day and our daily had instructions not to disturb him. I did everything I could for him. Everything. And now he's left me.' She began frantically to bang on Tansy's chest with her fists and Tansy had to seize her hands and restrain her. '*Where* did I go wrong, Tansy? Tell me.'

'You did too much for him.' Tansy, surprised by her own strength, shook Jill hard to resist her almost manic onslaught on her. 'You should have left him to do some things for himself. You bought him everything and protected him. In fact you stifled him.'

'What a *horrible* thing to say!' It was Jill now who tried to push Tansy away, but she clung on hard to Jill's wrists.

'You didn't *mean* to, Jill; but did you ever ask Jeremy what *he* wanted?'

'He wanted a cottage in the country.' Jill flung back her head and gave a harsh, rather coarse laugh. 'Maybe it's because I wouldn't buy him that that he went off. Do you think he would have written there? No!' Jill's voice rose shrilly. 'Despite all I did for Jeremy, all the encouragement I gave him, he had but one book in him and that's written. I don't think, now, that he was capable of any more.'

Suddenly the heat and anger seemed to evaporate and Tansy, realizing it, let Jill go. She slumped on the sofa and, putting her head in her arms, began quite quietly to weep. Her immaculate couture clothes were now crumpled, and tears, little rivulets, ran delta-like through her make-up, smearing her mascara and blotting the rouge on her cheeks.

Tansy sat beside her and put an arm gently round her shoulder. 'Men aren't what we think they are. We expect too much.'

'I expected *nothing*.' Jill's voice was beginning to rise again.

'No, but I think Jeremy felt dependent on *you*. He didn't like that. I'm dependent on Michael, and *I* don't like that either.'

'It's different with a woman,' Jill sobbed, 'she expects to be dependent.'

'I still don't like it. In a way my situation is the same as Jeremy's. Michael supports me in every way. Without him I couldn't exist.'

'But that's the way most women are.' Jill took out a crumpled handkerchief and began to dry her eyes. 'And they accept it. When Tim and I split up I realized it was up to me to make a living, but when the girls were still small I accepted that he kept me. I worked because I had to in order to have the style of life I wanted.'

'But do you *like* it?' Tansy's air was one of mystification. 'Do you *enjoy* working so hard?'

'Yes I do,' Jill replied, gradually returning to normality. 'I do enjoy my career and the power it gives me; but I don't enjoy it so much if the price has been to lose Jeremy, to fail to understand him.'

'Do you really love him?'

Tansy saw that Jill looked surprised she'd even asked the question.

'Of course. I *adore* him,' she replied. 'I lived for him. Even the girls took second place. I would do anything in

the world I could to get Jeremy back.' She stared for a
moment at Tansy. 'Whatever makes you think I didn't
love him?'

'You had a habit of putting him down in public,' Tansy
said, biting her lip. 'It made him look rather foolish!'

'I didn't mean that,' Jill said. 'It's my barbed tongue. I
try to be amusing and it sometimes goes over the top.'

'With me too,' Tansy said. 'You often seemed to set
out to make me look small.'

'I didn't mean that either,' Jill whispered and, going
up to Tansy, looked searchingly into her eyes. 'Please
forgive me.'

'I forgive you,' Tansy said gently. 'But I can't answer
for Jeremy. He may never come back.'

Driving away in the taxi, after helping to pacify Jill,
leaving her to repair the ravages to her make-up and
change her clothes, Tansy thought how ironical it was
that what one had one didn't want, and what one lost
one continued to crave.

She knew now that more than ever she wanted to
leave London and live in the country; she wanted to
follow the same path to freedom that Jeremy had
attempted to take.

Coming out of the surgery Gilbert looked towards the
house and saw two figures sitting together beneath the
tree that was his father's favourite place in summer. At
first he thought it was his mother with his father but
then, with a surge of joy, he realized it was Eileen. He
bounded along the path towards them, noticing that her
Morris Minor was parked at the corner of the house, out
of sight of his surgery window.

As he drew near, both of them, who had appeared to
be deep in conversation, looked up.

'Hi!' Gilbert called.

'Hi!' Eileen replied, smiling at him.

'Are you all right?' He bent over to kiss her.

'Of *course* she's all right,' his father said. 'She came to have a talk with me. Your mother has just gone in to get us some coffee. You'd better call out to her if you want a cup.'

Gilbert consulted his watch. He had two calls to make before lunch and then his mother-and-baby clinic in the afternoon. Eileen was being looked after by the same gynaecologist who had supervised Tansy's first pregnancy; but still, the mother-and-baby clinic was his favourite work in general practice which, on the whole, continued to leave him feeling essentially unfulfilled.

'I can have a quick cup with you,' he said squatting on the grass at his wife's feet. 'It is a perfect summer's day for once.' He looked curiously up at Eileen. 'What made you come over and see Dad and Mum?'

'I just wanted to,' she said, and still there was that enigmatic smile, that look of tenderness on her face that, directed at him, could turn his heart over.

'We were hoping Eileen would stay the day with us,' his father said. 'We see so little of you both socially and when our grandchild is born we shall see even less.'

'That's fine,' Gilbert said, getting to his feet. 'I'll go in and ask Mum if that's all right and get myself a coffee as well.'

'Of course it will be all right,' Geoffrey said with an airy wave of his hand. 'You know your mother loves having you. We both wished you'd lived here. Still do.'

Not wanting to hear his father's litany repeated all over again, Gilbert strode briskly over the lawn towards the kitchen. The door was wide open and inside he could see his mother standing at the stove while, on the table, was a tray set with coffee pot, cups and a plate of biscuits.

Gilbert watched his mother for a moment, reflecting

that, if he were ever to look back and think of her, after she was gone, the thing he would remember most vividly would be the picture of her standing by the stove cooking something. She was, and always had been, primarily a domesticated being. It was in her role as a provider that he would always think of her but not, he fervently hoped, for a long time yet.

As she heard his footfall his mother turned and her eyes lit up immediately with pleasure. 'Gilbert,' she said, wiping her hands on her apron. 'Are you going to have coffee with us?'

'I'd love to, Mother, and lunch if that's possible.'

'Of course it's possible.' Catherine instinctively clapped her hands together with pleasure. 'We'll have it under the tree. It's just cold meat and salad.'

'Perfect for a hot day like this. In that case,' Gilbert perched against the table, 'I'll have my coffee here with you now, make my calls and be back in time for an early lunch.'

'Did you see your father and Eileen?' The kettle had boiled and Catherine turned to fill the coffee jug.

'I had a word with them. I was so surprised to see Eileen there. She was still asleep when I left this morning.'

Catherine poured the boiling water on the coffee grounds and stirred them in the pot; then, waiting for it to brew, she sat down and looked at her son.

'It's amazing the way your father has taken to Eileen. He really loves her.'

Gilbert smiled in agreement. 'That's because she is *really* loveable, Mother. I knew that when Father got to know what she was like he'd forget his prejudices.'

Catherine sighed and stirred the coffee grounds again. 'Your poor father,' she said. 'He has had so many disappointments in life that Eileen has brought a little sunshine into it. He was so upset about Jeremy leaving Jill and going back to Emily.' Wearily Catherine shook her head. 'I didn't think he'd get over it, but he has. In some things he's amazingly resilient.'

'Jeremy hasn't really gone back to Emily. She's just given him a room. He's a lodger,' Gilbert said.

'Whatever you call it, it's a funny arrangement. As for Tansy . . .' again she shook her head. 'I don't think all is well there with Michael. Your father was certainly right about that!'

Catherine rose, rather wearily, to pour his coffee and leaning across towards her Gilbert put a hand on her arm.

'Mum, why don't you have a break? Take a holiday without Dad? I don't remember a time when you weren't standing in this kitchen doing something or worrying yourself to death about us or Father. Because he doesn't like holidays you have never taken one yourself. Now you know you can go on package tours. Everything is done for you. The travel firm makes all the arrangements, looks after you from start to finish.'

'I should hate that,' Catherine said firmly, handing Gilbert his coffee. 'It's true your father won't go away. I think he's afraid he'll die away from home.'

'Try and persuade him to take a cruise.'

'Oh!' Catherine put her hands to her head as if in horror at the very idea. 'He'd *never* do that. He has a morbid fear of dying and being buried at sea.'

'Then *you* go.'

'No, no, no, Gilbert. Thank you, no.' His mother picked up the tray. 'You don't understand. I can't leave your father.'

'But we could look after him.'

'You mean you'd move in here?'

'Only temporarily,' Gilbert said hastily. 'But Eileen and

I would willingly do it just to give you a break.'

'I'll think about it then,' his mother said in an unconvincing tone as she went towards the door. 'Now don't be late for lunch.'

After lunch Gilbert took his mother-and-baby clinic while Eileen sat in the garden enjoying the sun with her in-laws. Everyone in fact was amazed at the way she and Geoffrey had taken to each other. Even Eileen herself was amazed. She had never been told the reason for his opposition to her; but she knew he hadn't liked her, or wanted Gilbert to marry her. In her simple way – because she always instinctively thought good of people – she thought it was because Gilbert was a doctor and she was a farmer's daughter. She suspected that her father-in-law thought Gilbert was marrying beneath him and, in a sense, she had supposed he was.

Eileen had been a lonely girl brought up in the shadow of her mother's death by a father who, although loving, had at times made her feel she was responsible for it. Occasionally, when his despair had been so great that he drank – which was not very often – he had actually suggested under the influence that, but for Eileen, his wife Jennifer would still be alive. It was in the dark days of depression after childbirth that she had killed herself.

Eileen had always felt different, apart from people and, growing up on an isolated farm without brothers or sisters, she had few close friends. Gilbert was the first and only man in her life and she loved him passionately. She would never have believed such happiness as she now enjoyed was possible and, from the moment of her marriage, the sun seemed to have shone not merely in the summer but every day.

Her happiness showed in her face as Gilbert drove them home after surgery that evening and, while she got the dinner, he sat in the kitchen chatting to her. He loved to watch her as she moved around, her dark hair casting a shadow on her grave, beautiful face; and he thought what happiness had come so unexpectedly to two rather lonely and withdrawn people like himself and Eileen, and how much they had to be thankful for. At six months' pregnant she still moved easily, and the baby hardly showed. Sometimes he was anxious because he thought she was too small, but the gynaecologist, a man he trusted, assured him that all was well. Eileen was a small woman and would probably have a small baby, but she was completely fit and the baby was normal.

'I tried to persuade Mother to take a holiday by herself today,' Gilbert said, as Eileen sliced the bread.

'Oh, what a good idea!' Eileen replied. 'What did she say?'

'She said no.'

Eileen smiled and shook her head as she daintily spread each thin piece of bread with butter and placed it carefully on a plate. 'That doesn't surprise me.'

'She's never had a holiday in her life that I can remember.'

'Didn't you go away when you were children?' Eileen looked surprised.

'Occasionally, but only as far as Southport or Scarborough and never for more than a few days. Mother had a sister in Scarborough and we stayed with her, and an old aunt of Father's who lived in Southport.'

'I never went away either,' Eileen said thoughtfully. 'But we could never leave the farm or the animals, so that's not surprising.'

'Well, *we're* going to have holidays and good ones,' Gilbert said firmly.

'What about the baby?'

'He or she will stay with Mum. She'd love that.'

'Well, I shan't want to leave my baby for long.' Eileen looked doubtful.

'Or babies,' Gilbert said softly.

'Or babies,' she corrected herself, looking up at him shyly.

'But I'm not going to let you be a house drudge as Mother has been.' He pointed a finger of warning at her.

'Your mother *likes* it, Gilbert.' Eileen put the plate of bread and butter on a tray. 'That's what you don't understand, *I* like it too.'

'It doesn't mean you can't go away.'

'But I *like* looking after you and I did Dad, and doing things around the house. Today I just felt lazy and it was so nice and sunny that, impulsively, I jumped into the car and went to see your mum and dad.'

'I'm glad you did,' Gilbert said. 'It was a lovely day. Dad is so fond of you. You make him happy.' As she turned he noticed a blush on her face. 'You do,' he went on, 'I think you've taken the place of us in his true affection. Dad now loves *you* better than me or Tansy.'

'Oh,' she protested, 'he loves your sister and he's *very* proud of you.' Eileen reached for some jam in the cupboard and turned back to the table.

'People always say he's proud of me, never that he loves me,' Gilbert said a little wistfully.

'But he does love you; being proud is a way of showing how much. You're the pride of the family, but it doesn't mean he doesn't love you too.'

'You're very wise,' Gilbert said, rising to his feet and kissing her cheek, holding her close to him for a moment. 'I can't think how I deserved to have someone like you.'

Chapter 21

Laura Page sat at her desk in the tall tower building that had risen in London's Docklands to become the home of an international chain of fashion magazines. They were ugly buildings in what had once been an ugly part of London; built in a hurry in a post-war boom on the ruins of the bombed-out sites.

Inside, the offices were unprepossessingly functional and untidy, mostly because of the calling of their occupants. Journalists were, as a rule, untidy people who kept things in piles; disorganized people who threw reference material on the floor, or jammed in cupboards, or scattered on their desks and could never find what they were looking for. By some miracle, like the deadline for copy, they invariably turned up just in time.

But Laura was a relatively well-organized member of this breed and her corner of the large open-plan office had a filing cabinet, a chair and pot plants on the window sill in a vain effort to give her few feet of territory a homely look.

These days Laura spent a lot of time gazing out of the window; it was quite a spectacular view looking over the outlines of many memorable London buildings such as the Tower, St Paul's or, on a clear day and in the far distance, the Houses of Parliament. Seen against a setting sun such a view could look very spectacular indeed.

Sighing, Laura turned her eyes from the window for about the tenth time in an hour and thumbed apathetically through a sheaf of articles, most of them uncommissioned, that had been presented for her inspection. On this particular day, however, nothing satisfied her and she rejected them all except one by a regular contributor whom she could always rely on. This one she didn't even bother to read.

Then she sighed again, lit a fresh cigarette and, once more, turned her face to the window.

It was now several years since she had begun her affair with Michael Garrett and, in that time, she had seen him change from rather an attractive man casually met at a dinner party to an international tycoon; a man who sat on the boards of many important companies, advised governments and would, one day, undoubtedly earn a knighthood.

But it was not merely Michael's achievements or prospects, or the chance of one day being Lady Garrett that attracted Laura. She loved him; she was obsessed by him, and she spent most of the time thinking not only about him but of how she could entice him away from his family.

For all these years Laura had been scrupulously correct in her behaviour or, rather, as correct as it was possible to be when having an affair with another woman's husband. She knew he had young children and she couldn't dislike his wife; but the years had gone by too quickly. The children were older and Jill knew that Tansy was restless. She and Michael had a lot of rows about the conflict between her yearning to live in the country and his desire to stay in town.

Laura knew that Michael liked her company, both in bed and out of it. She knew that he found her amusing, witty, articulate, brainy, entertaining and reasonably attractive. But she was no beauty – strictly speaking, she never had been – and she was nearly forty. She desperately wanted to have a child and she wanted that child's father to be Michael Garrett. But as a prerequisite she wanted them to be married, the child to be legitimate and everything correct, legal and above board. She thought it could be and that it should be because she was convinced that she and Michael were very well suited whereas he and Tansy, increasingly, were not.

But Michael was busy. He had plans for his empire, making it larger, greater, intercontinental, transatlantic, global. They saw each other twice a week if he was in London, but a lot of the time he was away.

At her age Laura would have given much to be Tansy, living in an elegant house in Knightsbridge with three children and a husband like Michael coming home to her at night.

But Laura was clever. Being a features editor she read so many articles about the way to behave with men that she knew all the cardinal rules, and the chief of these was: do not nag, do not pester a man or he will go off you and you will not get what you want, that being your heart's desire.

But Laura was by now sick of this game; sick of the sex sessions in her bedroom, where procreativity was barred; sick of the dinners scattered about London where Michael was so particular they should not be seen by anyone he knew. She was proud to show off Michael to her friends, but he kept their relationship a secret. Consequently Laura was sick of the isolation that their affair imposed and now she did not know what to do about it. It had been going on so long that it was almost impossible to break.

'Penny for them,' a voice said and, abruptly, Laura looked up to see the art editor, Laurence Hyde, standing over her desk with a sheaf of artwork under his arm.

'I'm just thinking of our next issue,' Laura replied with a professional nod of the head. 'What else?'

'That's what I *thought*.' Laurence put the drawing, the

painting and the photos on her desk and then he perched on it himself. 'However, it looks like love to me.'

'Oh *that*!' Laura said dismissively. 'I don't know the meaning of the word.'

'Well, to take your mind off whatever it is . . .' Laurence began to go through the ideas and material his department had come up with to illustrate the issue on which they were working, which would appear in about three months' time.

Of all the people in the group, which occupied several floors of the huge tower block, Laura enjoyed the company of Laurence the most. He was clever, easy going, popular, amusing, but he was also a homosexual forced to conceal his sexual preferences and live in that underground, forbidden, twilight world because of his sexual orientation.

In 1957 Sir John Wolfenden had come out in favour of liberalizing the laws on homosexuality and, although his report had been rejected by the government then in power, the movement towards more liberal laws, not only in this but in other matters considered taboo by society, such as divorce and abortion, was growing.

Very few people knew about Laurence, who had been married and had a child, but Laura was one.

After an hour's spirited discussion, accepting this, rejecting that, changing something else, they agreed on the illustrative material for the next issue and Laura found that she had enjoyed having her mind completely distracted for, in the whole sixty minutes, she had not once thought about Michael.

'Come and have lunch?' Laurence suggested, looking at his watch. 'How about a sandwich and a glass of wine at the pub?'

The pub was on the edge of the docklands, on a strip of the embankment close by London Bridge. This area had not yet fallen victim to the entrepreneurs and property speculators and contained much that was still peculiar to dockland, including the old spice warehouses, as well as the bombed, derelict sites strewn with weeds and overrun by wild cats.

They found a perch in the corner of the private bar and Laurence went over to order beef sandwiches, returning with a bottle of red wine, uncorked, and two glasses.

'This is nice,' he said, pouring a glass for each of them. Then he raised it to his lips and pointed it in Laura's direction. 'To you, my beauty.'

'And to you, Laurence,' Laura also raised her glass towards him. 'What a good idea. I was feeling miserable.'

'I could see you were miserable,' Laurence said sympathetically. 'I could see it a mile off.'

'Does it show that much?'

'It shows, my pet.'

The barmaid called from the bar and Laurence got up to collect the sandwiches and pay for them. He wore corduroy trousers and an open-necked check shirt, and Laura thought that, if one didn't know, he would really be quite a sexually attractive man. No wonder a woman had fallen badly enough for him to marry him.

'How's your daughter?' she enquired as Laurence returned and put the sandwiches and two plates in front of them.

'What made you think of her?' Laurence gave her a curious look as he put his change in his trouser pocket.

'I've got it on my mind, I guess.'

'Kids?'

'Yes.'

'Then what's the problem?'

'Well, *you* know about Michael.'

Laurence nodded because Laura brought him to all the office parties.

'Michael, I take it, is firmly married?' Laurence enquired, refilling their glasses with wine.

Laura nodded. 'I quite like her, actually. It would be silly to pretend I didn't. His wife is a very nice woman, and they have three nice children.'

'Awkward,' Laurence said, grimacing. 'Why don't you just go ahead?'

'And have a baby, you mean?' Laura looked rather shocked. 'Oh I couldn't *possibly*.'

'Why not? Lots of people do.'

'Well, *I* don't know many. Besides, my mother is a magistrate in Dorset. It would shock her to the core.'

'Yes, but it's you you've got think of, Laura, not your mother.'

'I would hate to upset Mummy, anyway. She has so many friends. I think she might even consider moving from the district if I did anything so bizarre. She couldn't help feeling it was a disgrace.'

'Oh, well, that's out, then.' Laurence shrugged his shoulders.

'Besides,' Laura continued, 'I simply couldn't cope.'

'I'm sure you could.' Laurence looked surprised.

'Well, I wouldn't want to,' she said firmly, hands readjusting the pair of large flamboyant spectacles on her nose. 'I'd definitely want a husband, I'm not that kind of woman.'

'Then what are you going to do, Laura?' Laurence looked regretfully at the bottle which was empty, but Laura shook her head.

'Not for me, thanks, Laurence. We have an editorial meeting this afternoon and I have to keep my head clear.'

She lit a cigarette as Laurence got up to settle the bill. He came back with a glass of wine for himself and a hunk of bread and some cheese on a plate.

'Got to look after my figure, too,' she said shaking her head as he offered some to her.

'You know, Laura,' Laurence said, studying her intently for a moment. 'You're a smashing girl. You're good-looking and clever. You must have had lots of opportunities, met many kinds of people. Why on earth do you throw yourself away on a married man?'

'Because I love him,' Laura replied with a catch in her voice. 'I've loved him for years. I couldn't give him up if I tried, and I *have* tried, lots of times. I always go back and he's there, waiting for me, as though nothing had happened.'

'He must be quite something, this Michael.'

'He *is*. He's the kind of man I've always wanted: strong, vigorous, dynamic, attractive. I think you'll agree he's all those things.'

'Sexy, too?' Laurence asked with a smile.

'Very, needless to say.'

'It's the wife then. The wife that's the real problem.'

'She and Mike don't actually get on very well. It's nothing to do with me. She's a country girl born and bred in a place called Netherwick.'

'Never heard of it.'

'Well, I hadn't until I met them. But she's crazy to get back there. I first met them together because a friend of mine called Jill was married to her half-brother. Jill nearly cracked up when he left her. They're now divorced.'

'Have you thought of divorce, Laura? Talked about it to Michael?'

'Of course I have! Hundreds of times. I've given him ultimatums galore. Threatened to leave him. I *have* left him for several months. It never works. As I said, I always go back.'

'Why don't *you* make him jealous?' Laurence spoke after a pause, as if half to himself.

'Jealous?' she echoed, looking at him. 'How do you mean?'

'Why don't *you* get another boyfriend? Did you ever try that? Tell him you're in love with someone else, and this time it's for good.'

'It never works,' Laura said, her voice faltering.

'Tell him you're engaged, then,' Laurence suggested smiling conspiratorially at her. 'To me.'

Tansy sat skimming through notices from the estate agents as Michael came down to breakfast. He looked rather pale. He had got home so late she didn't remember him coming to bed, and so she felt rather washed out herself.

'These late nights do you no good, Michael,' she said, glancing at him as he sat down and began to go through his mail. 'Or me,' she went on. 'I seriously do want to go and live in the country. There I shall at least have some peace.'

'Well, I shan't,' Michael said.

The daily woman always came in early these days to get breakfast as all the children now went to school. She brought Michael his toast and coffee, for which he thanked her.

'You can have a *pied à terre* in London,' Tansy went on after she'd closed the door. 'You should be able to afford it. They are going to build smart living accommodation in the City. You could have a flat there.'

'What a jolly good idea,' Michael said, his eyes visibly showing interest as he put down his mail and looked at her. 'It's certainly worth thinking about.'

'I'm really serious, Michael.' Tansy, lips pursed, sat back and folded her arms. 'I can't stand this kind of life. We never ever have an evening to ourselves. In fact I can't think when we last did.'

'Now that's true,' Michael said thoughtfully, pouring fresh coffee into his cup. 'I can't help it with the life I lead, Tansy. Some women would actually love it.' He looked speculatively at her over the rim of his cup. 'You've no idea how many.'

'In that case you married the wrong woman.' Tansy was fully aware of the meaning in his eyes.

'Seems like I did.' Michael shrugged and, flicking over the pages of the morning paper, ran his eyes down the share prices. 'Good, we've gone up five points since yesterday.'

'Michael, are you serious about that?' Tansy leaned across the table.

'Serious about what, dear?' His eyes still on the share prices.

'You just said you married the wrong woman.'

'Well next year is our tenth wedding anniversary. We've stuck it a long time, Tansy. Don't see why we shouldn't sit it out for good. Anyway you're joking, aren't you?'

'I wondered if *you* were, Michael?'

'You *are* a nag, darling. There is no doubt about that. I suppose it's because you don't have enough to do. This thing about living in the country seems to have been going on all our married life.'

'It has.'

'Well, then.'

'You promised me we could.' Tansy, still in her dressing gown, as though proof of the fact that she had insufficient to do, got up and began to pace the room. 'I don't *want* to nag. I *hate* nagging.'

From behind the paper came a deep sigh. This was what Laura always said. She had begun to nag too. In his experience all women were the same: never satisfied, no matter who they were or what they did.

'Actually I am very interested in a particular house, Michael.' Tansy stopped behind him. 'I have actually been to see it. It's only an hour from London by train.'

'Where is it?' Michael bit into another piece of toast and turned the page.

'Near Tunbridge Wells.'

'That's nice.'

'It has a stream flowing through the garden. It *is* beautiful.'

'Plenty of room for chickens, I hope?' Michael's voice was heavy with sarcasm.

'Oh *plenty*,' Tansy said with equal irony.

'There was a sudden rustle of the paper which shook violently as Michael brought it closer to his eyes. 'Good God,' he said peering closely at the page in front of him. 'Oh, my God!'

'What *is* it, Michael?' Tansy tried to peer over his shoulder at what he was reading as he jumped up, swallowing the remains of his coffee. 'Something to do with share prices?'

'Something like that,' Michael said. 'I must fly.'

'Can't you tell me what it is?' She noticed that his face, at first unnaturally pale, had turned puce.

'You wouldn't understand.' Michael thrust his letters in his pocket and, the paper under his arm, rushed to the door. As he opened it he turned to Tansy. 'Go and see that house,' he said. 'Sound nice.'

'I already have,' Tansy began, but stopped as Michael vanished through the door. Her words seemed to echo in the silent room.

*   *   *

Driving home through the lanes at sunset Gilbert felt infused with a sense of happiness such as he had seldom experienced, even when he had first made love to Eileen, or she had told him she was pregnant: the high moments so far of his married life.

Eileen was in fact the perfect wife for him, Gilbert thought, manoeuvring a sharp corner of the narrow lane that led out of the valley stretching for several miles between Netherwick and his home. She gave him a sense of security, even of continuity such as he had never felt, even at home with his mother and father. It was maybe because there he'd been prey for so many years to his father's moods and the vagaries of his temper. One never quite knew from day to day how it would be with Father, which was one of the reasons why Gilbert had from an early age become so introverted, shutting himself up in his bedroom with his books, and the world firmly outside him.

Only comparatively late in life had he blossomed into the contented, fulfilled man he was now. His ambition to be a consultant had evaporated as he and Eileen settled down to a lifetime of domestic bliss, now with the additional happy expectation of a first child to cement their bond.

Suddenly Gilbert, lost in thought, was forced to brake as, in front of him, a magpie flew across the road in the path of the car but landed safely on a dry stone wall at the other side. Gilbert was not superstitious – his scientific training had made him too sceptical for that – but the old proverb flashed unbidden across his mind: 'One for sorrow, two for joy', and he looked around for the magpie's companion. But the bird was apparently on a solo mission and, as Gilbert accelerated and passed it, it seemed to stare hard at him from its perch on the stone jutting out into the road. Irrationally, Gilbert felt a frisson of fear, a sense of impending doom, which he tried to banish from his mind as he came in sight of his home on the hillside.

The memory of that brief encounter, of childish taboos from the past, remained in his mind for a few seconds but, once he started the climb and entered the drive, the solitary magpie and his brief feeling of foreboding were instantly forgotten. This was home; this was joy.

As usual Eileen had been on the lookout for him and, as the car drew up by the door, she flung it wide open and stood waiting on the steps for him. Now she moved rather ponderously, but before she was so heavily pregnant she would run down the steps and into his arms. Instead Gilbert bounded out of the car and ran up the stairs to take her in his arms. He nuzzled his mouth against her ear and whispered: 'How I love you.'

'I love you too.' But Eileen seemed tense and, stepping back, she stood gazing at him, an expression of anxiety on her face. 'I was worried about you.'

'Why, darling?' Gilbert said tenderly, brushing back the hair from her forehead and looking deep into her frightened eyes. 'Why are you worried?'

'You're a bit late,' she said.

Gilbert tightened his arm round her waist and, as they walked into the house, he glanced at his watch. 'Not very. Just a few minutes.'

'It seemed like a long time,' Eileen said clutching him. 'I missed you.'

'Oh, *darling*.' Gilbert settled her on the sofa in the drawing room. 'I missed you too; but I haven't been away long.'

'Did you have lunch with your parents?'

'Only with Mother. Father had gone to the golf club for lunch with one of his cronies.'

'*That's* unusual isn't it?'

'Very.' Gilbert wasn't on call that night, so he poured himself a glass of sherry and sat next to Eileen on the sofa, taking her hand in his. 'Mother thinks he's better than he's ever been so she is considering that cruise I talked to her about.'

'It would do him *so* much good,' Eileen exclaimed with a sigh. 'Won't *he* go?'

'No.' Gilbert shook his head. 'Father hasn't left Netherwick for years. He has a fear of dying away from home. Don't ask me why, but you know Father. I think it's connected with his depressive tendencies. I told Mother that we will go and look after him while she's away. You'd like that, wouldn't you, darling?'

'Very much,' she said. 'I do like your father.'

'And he loves you, and he'll adore having us *and* his grandchild.'

'I can't really believe it, can you, Gilbert?' Eileen whispered, yet her eyes remained fearful.

'What, darling, can't you believe?'

'About the baby. It's like a miracle. I never thought it would happen to me.'

'Well, it will happen very soon now.' Gilbert got up and poured himself another sherry. It was still very exciting to be a prospective father, even for someone who was used to dealing with mothers and babies every day. To have one of one's own was quite special. Yet he couldn't quite understand what was the matter with Eileen this evening. Up to now she'd been so well.

'Gilbert,' she said suddenly, putting her hand in his once again as he sat down, 'I want to ask you something.'

'What *is* it, my darling?' He saw that the expression in her eyes remained one of apprehension.

'I want you to do something for me,' she said. 'It has worried me very much and I want you to promise.'

'What *is* it, Eileen?' He felt alarmed now, not only by

her expression but by her whole demeanour, which was taut and withdrawn. 'Are you afraid there's something wrong? I assure you, darling, nothing is. You're in the best possible hands.'

'Not with me, not with the *baby*,' she emphasized, 'but it's *you*. I want *you* to give up mountaineering, Gilbert. That does worry me and lately it has preyed on my mind. I think something awful is going to happen to you.'

'But, Eileen . . .' he said in dismay, 'it's my only recreation.'

'But still, it *is* dangerous. There was that avalanche in the Alps the other day.'

'Oh *that's* what you're worried about.' He smiled with relief. For a moment her irrational fears had reminded him of her mother, and also of her mother's fate; but there was a rational explanation after all.

'Well, that avalanche killed a lot of people.'

'But they weren't *climbing*, Eileen. They weren't even skiing. They were walking where they shouldn't have been.'

'Yes, but I've been worrying about it and thinking about it.'

'My darling.' He turned to her and began gently stroking her brow. 'It's just because you are *as* you are, because of your condition. You're emotional and sometimes expectant mothers do get strange, irrational fears.'

'It's *not* strange and it's *not* irrational,' she cried, angrily withdrawing her hand from his. 'I think it's *very* selfish of you to make excuses and, when we have our baby, how do *you* think I'll feel every time you go climbing?'

Gilbert got slowly to his feet, put his now empty glass on the tray by the drinks cabinet and walked to the window. They were exceptionally fortunate to have found this house in the position it was, at the time they wanted it. It was a gracious, double-fronted house set in two acres, with a drive and a copse at the back. Beneath them the road between Netherwick and Harrogate resembled a tiny snake slithering through the valley. Gilbert suddenly remembered the solitary magpie staring malevolently at him from the wall and shook himself with self-disgust at his own irrationality, his own absurd predisposition to primitive superstition.

He turned then and gazed at Eileen, who seemed so small, so fragile, crouched in the corner of the large settee which, now that it was autumn, faced the fire. In summer it was moved to the back of the large room from where one could see through the picture window right down the valley almost as far as Netherwick.

It was a gracious room, with a patterned carpet and a suite that had been given to them by Eileen's maternal Uncle Richard who was a mining engineer who lived abroad. He had no family of his own and had been very generous to Eileen, his only niece. Anthony and Richard Monk were brothers who remained close despite the fact they saw very little of each other.

From the centre of the ceiling hung a chandelier that Eileen had bought at a sale of antiques, and it was to be their policy, gradually, to acquire good items of furniture as, and when, they came up for sale.

Looking round Gilbert realized how solid, how important was this home; this nest which symbolized their strong, enduring love for each other.

'All right, I'll give up mountaineering,' he said, exhaling a long, slow breath. 'As you say it's not fair to worry you. I'm perfectly sure it's safe; but, if it worries you as much as it appears to, I'll give it up. I promise I'll never climb again.'

'Oh darling!' Eileen said, reaching for his hand as he came towards her. 'Oh thank you *so* much, Gilbert.' Then, as he sank on his knee beside her, she started to cry. He took her into his arms and stroked her head. The violence of her reactions began to worry him again.

'Eileen, *darling*,' he murmured anxiously. 'I think your time must be very near, my sweet. This isn't like you.'

'I've been worried all day,' she blurted out between sobs. 'Apprehensive – I don't know why. But every time the telephone rang I nearly jumped out of my skin thinking that something had happened to *you*. I was so fretful and anxious that when I saw your car coming up the drive I nearly broke down with relief and joy. You're *so* precious to me, Gilbert. I love you *so* much. I can't bear to think of *anything* happening to spoil our happiness. I can't bear it.'

'Nothing *will*, my darling. Nothing *will*,' Gilbert said kissing her cheeks, her brow, her wet eyes and, finally, her lips. 'Nothing will.'

The young Blairs ate early and, by ten, all was quiet in the house. They had watched a little television on their newly-acquired colour set, a present from Michael Garrett, who had given one to all the members of his family, as he was responsible for so many of the components and materials that had brought colour about; a hunch that had made his fortune.

There had been no more talk about Eileen's fears or apprehensions and, by the time they went to bed, she was much more composed, much more her usual serene self.

Now that Eileen was so heavy and moved so slowly she took a great deal of time getting to bed and when she finally lay down beside Gilbert she reached for his hand and, bringing it up to her mouth, kissed it.

'Thank you so much for agreeing not to go climbing again, Gilbert. I shall sleep much more peacefully now.'

And she gave him a smile of peculiar sweetness and, closing her eyes, was soon asleep.

But Gilbert did not feel peaceful. He felt strange, worried and anxious about her and her odd behaviour during the evening, her near panic when the telephone rang at about eight even though he was sitting by her side.

There was always this hidden worry about her mother; her breakdown at the time of Eileen's birth, and her subsequent suicide. The inheritance factor that had so disturbed his father. Gradually, the apprehension that Eileen had had overwhelmed him on her behalf, and he found it hard to sleep.

When at last he did he dreamed, and once he woke up with his heart pounding and his face drenched in sweat. He put the bedside lamp on to see what time it was and then he looked at Eileen but she seemed as peacefully asleep, even with the same smile on her face, as when they had put the light out. It was four o'clock.

Gilbert gave her a featherlight kiss on the cheek and put his arms around her, and then and only then, fell finally into a deep, quiet sleep.

At seven the alarm went as usual and Gilbert, feeling haggard with tiredness because he had had such a bad night, put his finger firmly on the button and pressed it hard until it stopped. Then, contrary to his usual practice, he fell asleep again and when he woke and looked at the clock it was after eight.

'God Almighty, Eileen,' he cried, jumping out of bed, 'why didn't you call me?'

He looked down and his heart turned over with shock. Eileen lay exactly as she had when they had gone to sleep eight hours earlier. It was as though her position had scarcely moved, and she had the same smile of contentment on her face.

'Eileen!' he cried bending over her. 'Eileen.'

But her eyes did not so much as flicker and as he knelt

by her side to look more closely at her he could swear she wasn't breathing.

He put a finger to her neck but could feel no pulse and then, beside himself with terror, visions of magpies mixed with coffins flitting madly through his brain, he ran down the stairs two at a time to his case which stood in the hall. Getting out his stethoscope he raced up the stairs, three at a time, already putting the ear-pieces into his ears. As he approached the bed he saw that she had still not moved.

A sob burst from Gilbert as he knelt on the floor and, with hands that shook, placed his stethoscope on her heart. Listening carefully he could just detect a very faint beat. She was alive, but clearly she was in a deep coma and the baby might already have died, or be in dire distress.

Chapter 22

The shock of Eileen Blair's death from a cerebral haemorrhage ravaged the entire community of Netherwick and the countryside around, many of whom stayed away from the funeral because they couldn't bear to see such sorrow on the part of the young husband she had left behind, and her immediate family. However, as the cortège passed through the street towards Netherwick Parish Church, the lace curtains at the windows concealed many a face that was tearful and sad, almost as grief-stricken as Gilbert's; but not quite.

Not quite because no one knew, or could possibly have known, the happiness Eileen had brought to her husband in the brief time of their marriage – a mere eighteen months. Thus it was impossible for even the most sympathetic or understanding person among them to comprehend the devastation he felt at the way she had been so cruelly taken from him.

However, their baby daughter, born by Caesarean section just before Eileen died, was her gift to him, her legacy just as she had been the gift that was left by her mother to her own sorrowing father, Anthony Monk.

Tansy, summoned from London on the morning of the tragedy, supported her brother during the terrible ordeal that he had faced: the knowledge that Eileen was brain dead and could not survive, and that the chances of such a thing ever happening to her, had been millions to one. But, occasionally, things like this did happen. One read about them in the papers; and such a terrible tragedy had happened to a man who had never harmed a soul, who wished nothing but good to his fellow creatures and had worked long and hard to serve them.

Gilbert called his baby daughter Kate, after his mother; not Catherine, just Kate. He couldn't bear to use the name Eileen, which some people urged him to do, because there would only ever be one Eileen for him. Because the baby was so frail she was baptized in the hospital on the day of her mother's funeral.

After the interment in the churchyard the vicar drove with Gilbert and the godparents to the hospital where, in the presence of her father and her two godparents, Tansy and Eileen's Uncle Richard, he baptized her Kate Blair with a hand that trembled and in a voice that shook.

For Tansy it was almost as much of a nightmare as it was for her twin, with whom she shared such a strong invisible bond. The call had come just as she was about to inspect the house in Kent with Michael. There had followed a rapid journey north in a car driven by one of Michael's chauffeurs, and then a desperate, vain, attempt to comfort Gilbert, who had yet to shed a tear; though he moved with the bewilderment and slowness of someone in deep shock.

Tansy was worried not only about Gilbert but about her father, who had retired to his bed, not even attending the funeral. He had loved Eileen so much that her loss seemed as cruel to him as it did to his son. He went into a deep depression and Tom Thackery was called.

Gilbert had not wanted to leave the house where Eileen had given him so much happiness, such love, so Tansy stayed there with him giving him the comfort and support that only such a close relation, a twin, could give.

Baby Kate had not been premature, but because of her mother's condition just before she was born, she remained for several days on the critical list at the hospital. Tom Thackery took over the whole of the practice for a short time, assisted by a locum, while Gilbert spent anxious hours at the hospital watching his new-born daughter hang on to the thread of life.

Gilbert had always been so strong and self-assured, as though his life were radiated by some inner serenity, but this bereavement had drained him. He said very little about his deepest thoughts but he seemed to reproach himself for what had happened to his wife as though he, as a doctor, and also as a husband sleeping by her side, should have been able to do something to have prevented her death. She was probably ill by the time he returned home the night before, the blood slowly seeping into her brain to cause such strange terrors and confusion.

Tansy drove Gilbert to the hospital each day and sometimes she joined him in his silent vigil; sometimes she sat outside in the autumn sunshine in the car waiting. Each evening she either drove him home, or over to their mother who was almost as worried about her husband as her son.

One day Tansy was sitting in the car park reading the paper when another car drew up beside her and a man with a familiar face got out. He had a large bunch of flowers in his hand and, as he turned to go into the hospital, he glanced into Tansy's car and saw her sitting in the driving seat looking at him. He removed his hat and smiled and Tansy wound down the window and called out:

'Hello again, Mr Monk,' she said recognizing her fellow godparent and extending her hand. 'Come to see the baby?'

'That's right.' Richard Monk shook her hand and looked almost apologetically at the flowers. 'I don't suppose she can appreciate them, but still. Are you with your brother?'

Tansy nodded and, folding the paper, put it on the seat beside her. 'Poor Gilbert. Naturally he's taken it so badly.'

'Naturally.' Richard Monk nodded sympathetically. 'Perhaps I'd better not go in.'

'Oh he won't mind,' Tansy said quickly. 'On the contrary, he'll be pleased. Would you like me to come too?'

'That would be nice,' Eileen's uncle said, his face brightening. 'Make it easier for me too. Would you like a cup of tea first?'

'Maybe we could have that after,' Tansy said as she got out of the car, closing and locking the door. 'The flowers first, a peep at the baby and, perhaps, a cup of tea if we can find one.'

Richard Monk nodded approvingly and stood back as she preceded him through the main doors.

'I think you'll be surprised by baby Kate,' Tansy said as they reached the hall. 'She is gaining a little every day and is almost out of the critical stage.'

'That *is* good news,' Richard Monk said as they made for the stairs. 'And what is Gilbert going to do? Will he . . .'

'I don't think Gilbert knows *what* to do,' Tansy said, smiling at one of the nurses she recognized on the way up. 'He is so confused and upset by the whole thing. It was so unexpected. Her pregnancy was so normal. They were so happy . . .' Tansy's eyes filled with tears – something that happened quite frequently because she too had to work out her grief – and, as she got out her handkerchief to dab at her eyes, Richard Monk put a hand on her arm.

'I'm sorry, I seem to have distressed you,' he said. 'Please forgive me. I'm afraid I really don't know very much about you. I only got home a short while ago. I've lived abroad many years, you know. Do you live in Netherwick?'

'I live in London, but I'm hoping to move to the country – Sussex or Kent.'

'You must be married, of course.'

'My husband is Michael Garrett. Do you know the Garretts? An old Netherwick family.'

'I know *of* the Garretts,' Richard Monk said, as they reached the top of the stairs. 'My brother wrote to me about that awful tragedy a few years ago. A fall from a horse.'

'That was my brother-in-law, Bob.' Tansy shook her head sadly. 'It ruined his life. My husband is his younger brother Michael, who is now in charge of the business.'

By now they had reached the corridor which contained the unit for the premature babies and, as they walked towards the ward, a sister came out and smiled at Tansy.

'Good news today, Mrs Garrett. Baby Kate is being moved out of the prem ward. Dr Blair will soon to able to take her home.'

'Oh that *is* good news,' Tansy said, turning to Richard Monk. 'Did you hear that? Kate will soon be able to go home.'

'Doctor Blair is with her now,' the sister said, handing them two masks which they tied round their faces before entering the ward where Gilbert, white coated and masked, could be seen sitting by the cot which contained his daughter.

Richard Monk left his hat and the flowers with the sister and, as Gilbert saw them, he stood up and shook hands.

'I hear she's a lot better?'

'She's over six pounds. Six pounds, one ounce. They

say I can take her home in a few days.'

'I was just going to offer your sister a cup of tea,' Richard Monk said after five minutes or so, during which they had chatted and cooed over the tiny baby. 'Or would you like me to sit here and you can both have tea?'

'No, *you* go,' Gilbert glanced at his watch. 'I have to leave in half an hour.'

'*Have*?' Tansy looked at him in surprise. There was so little compulsion in Gilbert's life these days except looking after Kate.

'I'm going to interview a nanny,' Gilbert said. 'She's coming to the house at seven.'

'I see. See you in twenty minutes or so then.' Tansy blew a kiss to baby Kate then walked out of the ward followed by Richard Monk. They both handed their masks to the sister in charge and Monk collected his hat.

'I thought I saw a tea bar in the hall,' he said. 'It might not be very good.'

'It's really all we've time for,' Tansy remarked and, as they walked down the stairs, she looked preoccupied.

'Is anything the matter?' Richard Monk asked her as they sat at a table with their cups of weak, institutional tea. 'I mean, anything more than what's been happening? You look very worried, yet Kate's much better.'

'I don't really think Gilbert should be at home on his own with the baby,' Tansy said in a confiding tone. 'I hoped he would let my mother look after her. She wants to.'

'Well, he seems to be engaging a nanny.' Richard sipped the hot tea.

'It will restrict his freedom very much.'

'I suppose he wants to behave as he would had she lived.'

'That's it,' Tansy nodded, looking searchingly at the

man on the other side of the table. Richard Monk had a kind face and she felt she liked him. He was the sort of apparently self-effacing person that one might not immediately notice. He was not at all handsome, and his hair was receding. He was about Michael's age, not very tall, but he was deeply tanned due to the years he'd spent in the tropics. He resembled his brother Anthony and his deep blue eyes, his most striking feature, were also very kind.

'I wish I could help more,' he said.

'Are you returning to – Africa, is it?'

'Rhodesia.' Monk shook his head. 'No, I'm packing it in. I'm coming back to live here.'

'Oh, really? That's nice.' Tansy felt unexpectedly pleased, but found it hard to say why. 'Will you live with your brother?'

'Oh no. I'm looking for a place of my own. I've always wanted to farm though by training I'm a mining engineer.'

'Have you any family?' Tansy couldn't help but be interested, but tried to hide it as she finished her tea.

'No, I'm divorced. I had no children.' He looked keenly at her. 'You've children, I expect?'

'Three,' Tansy replied, 'two at boarding-school, a boy called Roger and a girl called Julia. They're nine and ten respectively. Then the baby Frank, although he's not a baby any more, is still at home. He goes to a day school.'

'And when will you move to the country?'

'Very soon I hope.' Tansy glanced up at the clock to be sure she wouldn't be late. 'I hate London.'

'Doesn't everyone?' Richard Monk seemed to get up reluctantly as he saw her prepare to leave.

'Not my husband,' Tansy replied with a rueful smile. 'Would that he did.'

'What a pity you can't live here.' Richard Monk said,

but Tansy had moved on ahead and didn't appear to hear him.

A few days later Kate left hospital and was taken by her father to his home where a fully trained nanny awaited her. He also engaged a temporary nurse to sleep in at night. Tansy tried to persuade him to take Kate to their mother but he refused.

'Kate is *my* baby, Tansy, and I'm bringing her up,' he insisted on the first night the baby was home.

'It will be awfully difficult for you, Gilbert,' Tansy said as gently as she could. 'Have you thought of *all* the implications?'

'What implications?' Gilbert's tone was sharp. Tansy hadn't seen him so much as smile, even to the baby, since Eileen's death. His expression when he looked at his daughter was one of deep melancholy and Tansy was alarmed at the effect on such a young child of this bereaved father, still so obviously in mourning.

'Well, Gilbert,' she went on, 'when you resume your work Kate will hardly ever see you. Have you considered that?'

'I'm rearranging my schedule so that she will. Tom Thackery has agreed. I'm coming home for lunch every day, and he will take all evening surgeries so that I'll be back here just after four.' Gilbert paused and then looked away. They were in the lounge, before the wide picture window, having a drink before dinner which was being prepared by a housekeeper Tansy had engaged during her stay there. The pale evening sun came in through the window, seeming to cast a funereal pall over the furniture which Gilbert and Eileen had chosen between them with so much joy the year before. Tansy instinctively shivered almost as though she could sense Eileen's ghostly presence still in the house.

'I have to go back to London very soon,' she said. 'I miss Frank.'

'And Michael?' Gilbert looked at her.

'Michael too, of course.'

'You've hardly mentioned Michael's name since you came here. Do you realize that?' Gilbert studied her face intently for a moment or two. 'Frankly, I find it very surprising Michael didn't come up with you. At the very least he might have taken the trouble to attend the funeral, as a mark of respect if nothing else.'

Tansy stood up and walked slowly to the window. The setting sun was just beginning to dip over the hills in front, and soon the whole valley would lie in shade.

The valley of the shadow of death.

She shivered again and put her hands round her arms, rubbing them. 'I'm sorry Michael didn't come, too,' she said, walking back towards her brother. 'I can't really explain it or expect you to understand. But he *is* terribly busy.'

'Is life with him like this the whole time?' Gilbert raised his glass to his lips.

'Almost.'

'It must be hell. Obviously the family isn't all that important to him. Knowing you I should think you'd hate that.'

'Well, it's what I married,' she said stoically.

'*What* you married?' Gilbert repeated with surprise. 'You mean *who* you married?'

'No, I do mean *what* I married.' Tansy brought over the decanter to refill his sherry glass. Then she poured some into hers too and sat down next to him again, clasping her glass. 'I married an institution, oh not at the time; but Michael has become one. He has achieved so much in the years since he took over the company. To do that he had to forsake much that we had in our private life. We don't *have* a private life, in fact, any more. Only just before this happened – Eileen's death – I told him that we never spent a night quietly together. He never takes a family holiday; but sends us somewhere, joining us, maybe, for two or three days or a weekend. The kids don't know what a real father is. Even when he is with us he's always on the phone.'

'You don't *sound* very happy,' Gilbert murmured as he put out a hand and timidly touched hers. 'I'm sorry; I have been so absorbed in myself these last few days I haven't noticed anything else. I shouldn't have spoken about Michael as I did.'

'Understandably you've been absorbed,' Tansy said. 'I'm not as unhappy as you might think, because I have adjusted to the kind of life I share with Michael. The children don't really suffer, though Roger once said that he wished he had a daddy like everyone else, one who would take him to football matches or play ball in the park. Michael would never do that; never have time.'

'Is *he* happy?' Gilbert finished his sherry and glanced at his watch.

'I think he's very happy. Yes, he's doing what he likes. He sets the pace. Why shouldn't he be happy?'

'I think happiness is relative.' Gilbert sat back on the sofa and stretched his legs. 'I don't think I've been happier in my life than I was with Eileen. I never will be again. I didn't think such happiness was possible. Now, I'm paying for it.'

Suddenly Gilbert started to weep and Tansy, who had never seen him cry in her entire life, even when they were small, experienced a sense of shock. At first she didn't know what to do and then she realized that tears were cathartic, and that crying would be good for Gilbert. It was what he needed. Maybe he hadn't shed a tear since Eileen's death, even by himself, alone at night in the bed he once shared with her. Tansy got up and quietly refilled their glasses, but made no attempt to hand Gilbert his. It gave her something to do.

'I feel so wretched,' he sobbed kneading his fists in his eyes like a child. 'I feel so lost, Tansy, so deeply unhappy. I don't know what to do. I've no one I can turn to. Mother is too worried about Father for me to talk to her seriously, and you have your own problems.'

'Oh, but you *can* talk to me,' Tansy said, perching impulsively beside him and putting her hand on his knee. 'You can say *anything* you like to me.'

'I can't. You have your own problems. It's not fair.'

'I have *no* problems like yours,' she exclaimed. 'You can tell me *anything* you like. We're the same flesh, part of each other, Gilbert, and we have a special bond that only twins have.'

Gilbert got out his handkerchief and blew his nose hard. 'I don't know what to do about Kate,' he blurted out at last. 'I don't really want her. I've *tried* to love her but I can't. Isn't that an *awful*, shameful thing to admit?' He stared at Tansy, his features ravaged and distraught. 'I feel she killed my wife; *she* took her from me. How can I love someone like that?'

'Tom Thackery said that Eileen could have died anyway, whether she was pregnant or not,' Tansy replied. 'She had a fault in her brain. Sudden haemorrhages like that can happen to anyone. You can't blame yourself or the baby. *That's* not fair.'

'They can happen, but, usually, they don't,' Gilbert said bitterly. 'There's no doubt in *my* mind it was brought on by her pregnancy.'

'But you both wanted a baby, Gilbert. Wasn't it a decision you both made?'

'Yes,' Gilbert nodded. 'We both did badly want a child.'

'Well, then,' Tansy pressed his hand. 'Not fair to blame

the baby is it? Poor little mite. She does *need* you, Gilbert. She needs you, and you need her. Why don't you take her to Mother for a while? You've too much to do, to think about. Why don't you take a holiday climbing? Everyone will understand. They will know it's your way of recuperating. Mother would *love* to have little Kate and you would have something else to think about.'

Gilbert loudly blew his nose again; but his eyes were dry except that their rims were very red. 'The night before she died Eileen was very apprehensive about something,' he said in a calm, controlled voice, just like his former self. 'She was in a very nervous state and I realize now that it might have been because of the changes that were already beginning to occur in her brain. She said she had been worrying about me and thought something would happen to me. *Me!*' Gilbert gave a mirthless laugh. 'What she was in fact experiencing was an apprehension of her own death.'

'Gilbert, *don't* distress yourself needlessly,' Tansy said. 'Don't make it worse than you need.'

'Well, the point of telling you this,' his voice began to break once again, 'is that she made me promise that night to give up mountaineering. She said she was worried about it.'

'And did you?'

'To please her, I did. I said I would not climb ever again. I made that promise. It meant a lot to her and after that she was calmer.'

'Well,' Tansy said, a note of doubt in her voice, 'now that she is no longer here . . .'

'I can never break my word.' Gilbert shook his head wildly. 'Never. I would *never* break my word to Eileen and, who knows,' he looked sadly at Tansy, 'maybe she had foreknowledge of what was about to happen? Maybe *she* knew.'

He began to cry once more, softly to himself, and Tansy cradled him gently in her arms, his head on her breast as though, for a time at least, he had become a baby too.

The position of the house was quite spectacular. It was set on the brow of a sloping field at the bottom of which ran a stream, almost large enough to be called a river. The house had been built at the end of the nineteenth century by Sir Edward Lutyens for a wealthy family who had made their money in steel. The original owner had gone from poverty to riches in a very short time and become a millionaire. In a way Michael Garrett's life, to some extent, mirrored that of the nineteenth-century magnate, except that he had never been poor. But Michael had gone from relative prosperity to great riches in a very short time and, as he surveyed the house, its size and style, he had nothing but satisfaction that he could easily afford to buy such a place in which to keep his wife and family.

No one would be able to say of him that he had done less than the right thing, or let them down.

From the drawing room Tansy watched Michael walking on the terrace in a manner which suggested he already owned the place. Indeed it was a very fine house, the view was superb and, as well as twenty acres of land, it had tennis courts, a swimming pool and a paddock for horses. Her only regret was that, if they were to buy it now, they hadn't had it before; it was a marvellous kind of place for children to grow up in.

It was for sale completely furnished. The vendors, who were short of money, had refurbished it for a speedy sale. One could move in as it was. It was decorated and furnished with taste in a style Tansy liked, and there would be very little for her to do. That suited her too because, at last, she would be able to concentrate on the out-of-doors: the huge garden, the paddock *and* the chicken run that she proposed to erect alongside. That chicken run which seemed to have been for so long in her dreams.

As Michael walked towards the drawing room Tansy threw open the french windows and went to meet him.

'Like it?' he said, taking her by the arm and leading her indoors. However, involuntarily, he shivered and began to rub his hands. The central heating was not on and it was cold. Outside the estate agent waited in a car, having left them to inspect it at leisure on their own.

'It *is* very beautiful,' Tansy said. 'But it's awfully big.'

'Well, you said you wanted to live in style.' Michael turned to close the french windows and lock them.

'No I didn't,' she protested in surprise. 'I said I wanted to live in the country.'

'Well, you can't get much more countrified than this,' Michael said with a strained smile. 'Unless you go to Netherwick.'

'Netherwick isn't country,' Tansy said. 'It's a small town. Where Emily lives is country.'

'But is *this* what you want?' Michael seemed unusually edgy and exasperated by her remarks.

'Yes,' she said, also feeling tense because of his attitude, 'except that it *is* big.'

'You'll be able to entertain.'

'Why do you say "you"? Don't you mean "we"? You're the one who will want to entertain. I'm not keen on entertaining.'

'Tansy.' Michael sat on the arm of one of the deep comfortable chairs upholstered in a Liberty fabric that toned well with the room. He put his hand in the pocket of his trousers and gazed at the floor. A muscle in his face twitched. Tansy knew that Michael had something important to say and she waited with a patient air, trying to disguise her own unease. He would be correcting her on some point of detail, or making some arrangement or other to bring the whole deal together. Whatever it was it would be well and efficiently done.

'Yes, Michael?' Tansy prompted him again. 'What is it?'

'This is a very difficult thing for me to say, and don't think it isn't.' He raised his head at last and looked straight at her and she observed again that tiny twitch that invariably showed that he was under pressure. It was the price one paid for success; yet Michael took good physical care of himself: he swam, he played squash and he had regular check-ups with his private doctor in Harley Street.

'Well, obviously it is something very difficult if you can't get it out,' Tansy observed wryly and dropped into one of the chairs to be more comfortable. 'If it's going to take time I might as well sit down.'

Michael folded his arms, cleared his throat and threw back his head. He looked like the chairman of the board on the point of addressing shareholders. He wore a well-cut single-breasted suit in blue pinstripe barathea, a blue shirt and a dark blue tie which bore the crest of one of the many clubs he belonged to. But if he were addressing a board meeting, or shareholders, he would put on his glasses. Instead, his soft brown eyes seemed furtive. That, certainly, was an expression she had very seldom seen.

'This house is for you, Tansy,' he blurted out at last. 'It's for you and the children. It is what you wanted and it is my gift to you.'

'But, Michael . . .' She looked at him, still puzzled.

'Please don't say anything yet,' he interrupted her, 'before I've said my piece. I don't want you to misunderstand me, Tansy, or think me unduly generous because I feel *I* owe it to *you*, to make *you* comfortable and give *you* what you have always wanted. You see,' his voice appeared to falter for a moment, he coughed again and then went on, 'I am asking you for a divorce. I love someone else, and I want to marry her. You can guess how hard it is for me to tell you this, yet I think you will agree that you and I have not got on too well for some time. We have not seen eye to eye, wanted different things. Our marriage has been in the doldrums. Well, I have loved this woman for a number of years, but I had to think about you and the children. I am a man not without principle and I felt I owed it to you. But this woman,' Michael's voice seemed on the point of drying up again, 'would also like to have children. She is quite a bit older than you and it is very dear to her heart. I feel I owe it to her; indeed she has given me no alternative because she recently tried to break from me and become engaged to someone else. Actually engaged to another man! I'm afraid it was too much for me, Tansy. I realized then just how much she meant to me and I could not, cannot let her go.'

Michael finally paused and Tansy, mesmerized by the shifty look in his eyes, the apologetic tone of voice, kept her gaze riveted on him as if she wanted him to go on. But he seemed to expect *her* to say something and when she tried to speak she found that her throat, too, was dry.

Michael had robbed her of words. Seeing this, he said in an altogether different, even tender, tone of voice: 'I didn't expect you *not* to be upset, Tansy. Whatever you may or may not feel about me, I know it's a shock. It's bound to be. Some people jog along as we have done all their lives. We might have done too. I think, however, we should each have a chance of happiness with some-one else. You are still very young, just thirty. I know you have given me some of the best years of your life and I'm grateful, don't think I'm not; but you *can* start again. The woman I want to marry hasn't the time.'

'Who *is* this woman?' Tansy said at last, surprising herself by the control, even the polite note of interest, she managed to keep in her voice.

'Laura Page,' Michael murmured huskily. 'You've met her two or three times at Jill's.'

'Laura Page,' Tansy said slowly. 'Laura *Page*.' She remembered her quite well; a tall, rather striking woman with very short hair and spectacles with fashionably flamboyant frames. This was the very *last* person she could imagine Michael falling in love with. She imagined that confident, extrovert Michael went for fragile, vulnerable types such as she had been twelve years before when she had fallen so much in love with him and, if he was to be believed, he with her.

But obviously not. His tastes had changed. If the Laura was the Laura she was thinking of she must be Michael's age. Quite obviously in that case she *would* be in a hurry to have children.

'You remember Laura, of course,' Michael said diffidently.

'I think so,' Tansy replied. 'She's tall with short hair and glasses. We first met her when Jeremy and Jill were still married.'

'Yes.'

'But that was an *awfully* long time ago, Michael. You're not telling me you've been having an affair with her since *then*?'

Michael appeared again to lose some of his self-assurance and bowed his head. 'It's difficult to admit it, and I'm not exactly proud of it, but I have. I'm very sorry Tansy and I realize how hurtful it is for you; but you asked me and that's the truth.'

'But we'd only just moved to London.'

'I know.'

'Then you never loved me, Michael, at all,' she said in a voice that had suddenly broken, became very sad. Now it was her turn to break down.

'I did, Tansy. I did and I do. It *is* possible to love two people. I love you still; but I love Laura too. Unhappily, in this western civilization of ours, one cannot have two wives.'

'*Unhappily*.' Tansy's voice regained its strength and, with it, irony. 'What a perfectly *ridiculous* thing to say!'

'No, I'm perfectly serious.' Michael sounded as though it was important for her to believe him. 'They do in some societies, Muslims for instance; and I think that if one can afford it it is, in principle, a good idea. I don't think man *is* meant to be monogamous, Tansy. I have always liked women and I have always had affairs. I don't think it's in man's nature to be faithful. If I could marry Laura without hurting you I would.'

'Thank you *so* much.' Tansy's sense of indignation was such that she feared she might be unable to control her hysteria. The whole room took on the appearance of a dream, as though it had some kind of aura around it. It glowed as in a haze and she got up very slowly, and walked across to the window. Eyes that, only a few minutes before, had roamed over the fields with such anticipation now looked at the same scene as though it were dull and lifeless; a picture painted by an artist without any talent to bring it to life. It was as though the sun had gone in and, yet, it still shone. Maybe, for her, the world had ceased to have any colour in the dark cast by Michael's colossal deception. But there was the paddock, and there the swimming pool, there the field she had planned for the chickens, and there . . . well, she knew for sure that she would never live here now. That chapter was closed.

'Let's go,' she said abruptly turning to Michael. 'I feel I can't stand this place a moment longer.'

'But, Tansy, I want *you* to have it.' Michael stood up and came towards her, arms extended as though to placate her. 'I want you to live here, honestly I do. The children would love it.'

'What makes you think *I* want the children?' she asked abruptly, gratified to see Michael's shocked expression.

'But I assume you do.' His words stumbled. '*I* am the guilty party.'

'But if I didn't, if I wanted you to have them? They need a father too.'

'Well of course.' Michael looked extremely disconcerted and uncomfortable. 'I'd have to ask Laura, but it's normal for the mother . . .'

'You really *are* a swine, Michael Garrett,' Tansy burst out, control gone. 'I wish some of the people who admire you so much could see and hear you now. I wish our *children* could see and hear you now. As for this,' her arms swept round the room and seemed to encompass not only the house, but the outbuildings and country surrounding it, 'the only reason *I* ever wanted to live here was because I thought *you* wanted to be near London. Now that you are discarding me for another, albeit an older, model, there's only one place I want to go, one place I want to live: Netherwick.' And with that she swept out of the room, only just stifling an impulse to shut the door behind her in Michael's face.

The agent, sitting in the car, had almost fallen asleep by the time the front door opened and his wealthy clients, Mr and Mrs Garrett, emerged, having taken such a long time to view the house, she for the second or third time; a good sign that they were interested. He jumped out of the car and approached them, rubbing his hands in anticipation of an early and most lucrative sale.

'Well, Mr and Mrs Garrett, isn't it beautiful? Just up your street, I think.'

'Unfortunately we have had a sudden change of plan,' Tansy said with a composed, almost gracious smile and, preceding Michael, she got into the back of the car. 'Somehow it's not, now, quite what we wanted.'

Chapter 23

Emily turned the last sod on the vegetable garden, smoothed the soil on top with her fork and then, still with her foot resting on it, leaned over the handle, breathing hard. Emily loved gardening, but digging was the difficult part, turning over the soil in preparation for planting. Here it would be potatoes, in the next section cabbages and cauliflowers. It was very satisfying to grow your own produce, to become self-sufficient in food, as in everything else.

Emily straightened up and looked at the window of the room she rented to Jeremy. Somehow she had thought that when he returned to live at Cragbeck he would help with the household chores, the heavy work, the digging that needed to be done.

But Jeremy had stuck to their agreement. He paid her rent, he did his own cleaning and cooked his own food. Sometimes their paths scarcely crossed and they didn't talk all week except to exchange greetings. It was not an unfriendly atmosphere, but nor was it a close one; it was as though he really were the lodger and she the landlady, not as if they had ever been so passionately in love, married and had a child together. It was a strange relationship which, while it puzzled a lot of people, suited them.

Jeremy had a home, a shelter from the cold and his contribution helped to pay the rent. It also meant that when Fern made one of her occasional visits both her mother and father were there and that, at least, gave their daughter a great deal of pleasure.

But if only he'd *help* with the digging . . . She put a hand to her back and, rubbing it, walked across to the garden shed and put the fork away.

Jeremy had resumed his work as a shepherd. The farmer had been glad to have him back after a succession of unsatisfactory men, rejects from society, flotsam and jetsam thrown up by the war as Jeremy had been. Yet when he first worked as a shepherd Jeremy had a wife, a home and a future. Now that future seemed behind him. Or was it? Ever since he had returned to Cragbeck he spent every night in his room, working on the book that so many people had thought he had in him after the success of *A Shepherd in the Hills*.

Emily paused outside the kitchen door to remove her muddied wellington boots and then, entering the kitchen, she went over to the sink to wash her hands. It was Saturday and she started to prepare lunch. Jeremy had his day off on Saturday and, on an impulse, she decided to invite him to share the meal with her. Usually they ate separately. His irregular hours made that possible and also convenient.

She opened the kitchen door and, going to the bottom of the stairs, leaned on the newel post and shouted: 'Would you like some lunch, Jeremy?'

There was no reply. She shrugged her shoulders thinking that perhaps he had gone out, yet when she'd looked up from the garden his curtains had been drawn. On his day off he liked to sleep. Sometimes he stayed in bed all day.

Slowly she climbed the stairs and stood in front of his door listening. No sound. Quietly she tapped on it, 'Jeremy?'

Still no reply. Feeling a little apprehensive she tapped again.

'Jeremy,' she called more loudly, 'are you all right?'

She heard movement inside and then the sound of Jeremy's footsteps dragging across the floor. He opened the door a crack and peeped out at her.

'I wondered if you'd like some lunch?' Emily looked at him, perplexed.

Jeremy shook his head without saying anything and Emily firmly stuck her foot in the door as he was about to shut it.

'What's the matter?' she asked. 'Are you all right?'

Jeremy shrugged again and, without closing the door, crossed the room in the same slow, dragging way she had heard before, and flung himself on the bed, leaving Emily standing where she was. Fluttering on the floor beside him was an open letter, the envelope had been screwed up in a ball and lay in the middle of the floor.

'You've had bad news?' Emily asked, indicating the letter.

'You can read it if you like.'

Emily went into his room closing the door after her. She retrieved the letter from the floor and then said: 'I can't read it without my spectacles. Can I take it downstairs?'

'You can do what you like with it,' Jeremy said and then turned his back to her, his face to the wall.

In the kitchen Emily searched for and found her reading glasses which she placed on her nose as she shook the letter out in front of her. It was written on the notepaper of the publishing company Jill worked for and it went as follows:

Dear Squadron Leader Blair,

Back to the Hills: A Countryman's Return

We have now had a chance to read the above manuscript and I very much regret to tell you that the decision of the editorial board has gone against it. As we published your first book so successfully this was a hard decision to take. However, we felt it lacked the quality that made *A Shepherd in the Hills* so memorable, and we felt that it needs too much work doing on it to bring it up to the same standard.

This does not mean, however, that another publisher may not have other ideas and we do wish you every success in placing it. Have you thought of an agent?

With kind regards,
Yours sincerely,
Marilyn Mortimer,
Editorial Assistant.

Emily read the letter through twice, then she folded it carefully and tucked it behind the clock on the mantel-piece. She removed her reading glasses and put them in their case, and then she went on with her preparation of the lunch which entailed mashing the potatoes and reheating a stew she'd made the day before. When it was ready she returned to Jeremy's room. The door was still open and he lay where she had left him as if he'd fallen asleep again.

She went in once more, crossed the room and put a hand on his shoulder. 'Put your dressing-gown on and come and have a bit of lunch. It will do you good.'

For a moment there was no reply and then Jeremy murmured in a scarcely audible voice, 'Did you read the letter?'

'Yes.'

'What did you think of it?'

'I thought, what can you expect from Jill? She's getting her own back.'

'That's what I thought too!'

Jeremy turned and she saw that, although his unshaven face was pale, he had not been crying; maybe he had just been thinking about the irony of fate, feeling sorry for himself. Emily had not read the book and had no idea as to its merits or demerits; but she did know revenge when she saw evidence of it. She could even smell it.

'It was a very bitchy thing to do,' Emily said, gently shaking his shoulder. 'Try and put it out of your mind and come and have lunch.'

He was not a baby. He was no longer her lover. She wasn't going to mollycoddle him so she left the bedroom and, returning to the kitchen, put sufficient lunch on a plate for herself and, sitting down at the table, started to eat.

She felt sorry for Jeremy. It must have seemed just then as if his whole world had collapsed. Night after night, month after month he had worked on his book in manuscript form and then, to save money, bought a second-hand typewriter and typed every single word himself. The day he'd sent the manuscript off to Jill he'd bought Emily a beer. That had been about two months ago, and this was the first word he'd had. What he'd thought in the meantime she didn't know.

She was halfway through her lunch when the kitchen door opened and Jeremy came in. He hadn't shaved but he had on trousers and a clean shirt.

'It's in the oven,' Emily said, looking up at him.

'Thanks.'

He got a plate, lifted the stew pot from the oven, took two spoonfuls of mashed potato and joined Emily at the table.

'This looks good,' he said smiling at her. 'Thanks.'

'I'm glad. I thought of it before I saw that letter,' Emily said, with a trace of sarcasm in her voice. 'You might have thought I was being kind.

'You *are* being kind,' Jeremy said, breaking a piece of bread and dipping it in his gravy. 'Everything about you is kind. My mistake was in not realizing what a valuable, irreplaceable commodity *real* kindness is, and doing what I did. When I left you I cut myself off from the true, decent things in life.'

'Well, that's a long time ago now,' Emily said practically. 'I think we've found a way of living that suits us both; but I'm sorry about your book. I really am. I know what pleasure it would have given you to have it published.'

'It's just as good as the first, if not better,' Jeremy said. 'I know. I can tell.'

'I'm quite sure it is.' Emily too broke a piece of bread and wiped the gravy from her plate. 'It's just Jill. She has the power and you don't.'

'I never thought she'd be so bitter, so small-minded. That's women for you.'

'Not every woman.' Emily looked at him defensively. 'I don't think I'd have been capable of a thing like that, at least I hope not.'

'I'm sure you wouldn't.' Jeremy shook his head. 'Anyway, if it makes Jill happy maybe revenge is sweet, after all.'

'*Have* you thought of an agent?' Emily looked at him. 'How does one begin to find an agent?'

'It will be very difficult to place a book that someone has rejected,' Jeremy replied. 'Especially a publisher with an option to buy. I know enough about the publishing world to know that.'

'You must give it a try, Jeremy. Don't despair. You try and find an agent. There's sure to be a book in the library that tells you where to go. There *are* other publishers. You mustn't give up. Never. If you do Jill will have got just what she wants. You don't want that, do you?'

Impulsively Emily reached across the table for his hand and held it in her own for quite some time.

* * *

'I never did think that man was any good,' Geoffrey Blair said mournfully, having read the letter from Tansy twice. 'If she'd taken my advice she would never have married him.'

'Too late for that now, dear,' Catherine briskly removed his coffee cup from beside his chair. 'Anyway, if you didn't like him you should be relieved they're splitting up.'

'Really, Catherine,' Geoffrey said irritably. 'This is no occasion for levity. That man is abandoning my daughter and his three children after eleven years of marriage and *you* expect me to be glad? Shame on you.'

'Geoffrey Blair,' Catherine sat down opposite him, cup still in her hand, 'Michael is *not* abandoning Tansy. He wants to marry someone else and he is setting her up very handsomely, making ample provision for her and the children. Even she admits that. He wanted to buy her a large house in Kent. She says she prefers to live here.' Catherine shook her head. 'Even Tansy admits that she and Michael are not in love any more. I think she feels that their last years together have been a strain, and she's relieved.'

'Her letter *does* sound quite cheerful,' Geoffrey admitted, rubbing his chin reflectively. 'I wish she'd come and live with us. This house is so empty with just the two of us.'

'Well, would you like to leave it, Geoffrey?' Catherine rose and looked quizically down at him.

'Leave? I've lived here since 1912! Are you taking leave of your senses, Catherine?'

'No, I'm not, and there's no need to be rude,' she replied brusquely. 'But it *is* a very large house. It's a family house and our family is now dispersed.'

'I still dream that Gilbert may want to come back to us one day and let us help him with Kate. You'd love that, wouldn't you, dear? I can't think why he stays where he is, cut off from everybody. Here the surgery is right next door.'

'Gilbert wants to be independent,' Catherine said a little wistfully. 'That's the reason he stays where he is; he can't accept the fact that Eileen's dead.'

Geoffrey looked thoughtfully into the fire. 'He'll have to give up sooner or later. He can't manage by himself. Or marry again maybe.'

It was a bleak February day and they had just received the news that Michael and Tansy were to split up. Amicably, it seemed. It had been, indeed, quite a long optimistic letter in the circumstances and, after some discussion, her parents had agreed that someone of Tansy's practical temperament would stoically accept the inevitable rather than start to whine and then go under. Her only bitterness, and this she did not put in her letter, was that Michael had deceived her for so long. That made her feel bitter, and foolish too. She felt he had demeaned her in the eyes of other people who must have known about Michael and Laura.

Catherine went to the door, both cups in her hand. 'I can't see Gilbert marrying again for a very long time, if ever, to be honest with you. I never saw a man so devoted and it isn't as though he had a number of girlfriends. He never had any. I thought he was only interested in medicine and had no time for women. That's why it's so cruel that something like Eileen's death should happen to a person like Gilbert, when you think of people like Michael, or even Jeremy in the old days, who never seemed to be without.'

Geoffrey shook his head, biting on his cold pipe which now had to be renewed every few months because he nearly bit through the stem. 'I can't get over Jeremy. Going back to Emily! I simply can't believe it. I can't get over it. I was so fond of Jill, so fond. She had such life, such vivacity . . .'

'*And* such a mean streak,' Catherine retorted, 'turning down Jeremy's book. I can't get over *that*.'

'Maybe it wasn't any good.' Geoffrey shrugged. 'She'd know from a professional point of view.'

'Of *course* it was good! It's just that you have a different angle on people, Geoffrey Blair, from anyone I have ever known. For a physician, someone used to observing people, you've made an awful lot of errors. You didn't like Eileen to begin with and then you adored her.'

'I didn't like her history,' Geoffrey began stubbornly to defend himself, but Catherine hurried on:

'You never *liked* Emily and she has been a very good mother, a long-suffering wife who has taken her husband back.'

'As a *lodger*.'

'Well, even as a lodger. She is very kind. Some ex-wives wouldn't have taken a husband who treated them so badly back at all. You have never invited her here, or shown any kindness towards her. As for Jill! You were taken in by her charm, her good looks and then she goes and does this to Jeremy. An act of sheer spite. How you can still like her, I don't know.'

For a few moments Geoffrey stared malevolently at his wife. 'I was right about Michael,' he said. 'I was right about him from the beginning. If Tansy had married anyone else *but* Michael she wouldn't be in this predicament at the early age of thirty-one. I don't care if he has been generous to her or not. He should be; he has the means. He is just buying his freedom by opting out of his responsibilities. Tansy could have married any number of young men with good jobs or prospects and who would have happily settled in Netherwick.'

'They don't always remain faithful; even in

Netherwick.' Catherine said wryly. 'Now read your
paper. Lunch at one.'

Lunch was always at one; coffee at eleven, afternoon
tea at four. In his seventy-sixth year Geoffrey Blair had
scarcely varied his routine for as long as anyone could
remember; even when he was in full-time practice his
habits had been the same.

Sitting in the sun lounge, well wrapped up against the
cold, he could look back on those years whose only
variety seemed to be the seasons, and the activities of his
children. These had been anything but routine. He loved
them all; yet the only one who had really pleased him,
who had done exactly as he wanted had been Gilbert.
Yet, just as Gilbert had found the happiness, the reward
he deserved for being a dutiful son, what had happened?
What a cruel, cruel fate to deprive someone as good as
Gilbert of the wife whom he had so loved.

Geoffrey shook his head a little wearily, picked up the
paper left folded by his side and opened the front page.
Then he put on his reading glasses and attempted to get
on with the daily routine.

But the print blurred before his eyes with tears for the
woman who had died too young, and whom he had
loved too.

If asked about herself by a frank interviewer Tansy might
have said that, in all honesty, she didn't consider herself
a woman of much strength of character, or of purpose.
She was completely without ambition and had always
wanted merely to be a wife and mother, content with
the simple domestic joys.

It was true that she loved her home town, her parents
and would have preferred to live somewhere within easy
reach of both. But when her husband's work had taken
him elsewhere she had followed, despite her own

instincts, and had done her best to mould her life, as he wished, to his.

Was it she who had failed? Had she failed Michael and made his adultery with another woman inevitable? Had she flung him into someone else's arms because she was inadequate as a wife, as a lover? She would never know that until she was able to compare Michael with someone else. Up to now he was her one and only man.

Tansy might have gone on to tell this mythical interviewer that Michael's revelations, his request for a divorce, surprised in her instincts for survival she didn't know she had; toughness and a resolution that seemed to come out of nowhere, that made her strong enough to plan and take the decisions she had to make not only for herself but also the children and, surprisingly, Michael too.

For some time chaos threatened their domestic lives; but Tansy consulted solicitors, put the Knightsbridge house on the market and made plans for the future without breaking down or finding the need for comfort, other than from the few, the very few, close friends she had.

Very, very few to show from all those years in London. Friends, yet, in their eyes she saw not compassion but fear that the same thing might happen to them. In the end there was no one but herself and, afterwards, she was to reflect how amazing it was that she had the time, the patience and the knowledge to do what she did: quietly arrange the dissolution of her marriage while everyone around her panicked.

It was true Michael did help to make it easy. He was willing, helpful and grateful. There were no financial worries. It was so civilized that it was almost unbelievable. Even the children seemed to be persuaded that something exciting was going on, rather than the disaster it might have appeared to others.

There was even an element of enjoyment for Tansy in everything she did. She enjoyed seeing the *For Sale* notice go up outside the Knightsbridge home. She enjoyed giving notice to Frank's daytime school and saying good-bye to the friends, who were not quite friends, she had made through the children. None of them had been close enough to be more than superficially helpful; none of them could have taken her in their arms if she needed to have a good cry.

When she eventully did go home to Netherwick Tansy realized that, except for the children, the last eleven years had been relatively wasted, and that she was now returning to a place that she should never have left. Not only her parents but the whole of Netherwick seemed to welcome her when she returned home. Her mother had had her bedroom redecorated; the children's rooms had all been put on the same floor as hers, and they had not only been redecorated but had new furniture as well, so that when they came back for the holidays it would seem like home. But, more welcoming even than that, were the various reactions of the townsfolk who greeted her in the street without pity or recrimination, as though she had never left, as though there were nothing scandalous or shameful in being abandoned; and that the shameful and scandalous one was the person who had done the abandoning – Michael Garrett.

Michael's mother had died in a nursing home two years before and his brother Bob lived in the institution which would be his home for life. The Garrett Great Engineering Company had long been absorbed by its much more powerful parent, and nothing remained of the family that had once been among the most important in Netherwick except, of course, for Michael's wife and children who still bore the Garrett name.

Tansy found she had plenty to do at home. Her return coincided with the school holidays and she personally fetched the children and drove them to Netherwick because for them, inevitably, it was a time of great difficulty and readjustment. Frank had remained with his mother throughout and had settled in happily as his grandfather's pet.

Both Roger and Julia were at schools where parents living separately was no phenomenon, and Julia, especially, seemed quite excited at being like everyone else: her friends Margaret, Jenny and Melissa. Their parents were *all* divorced, some even more than once. Roger was more circumspect and needed a great deal of reassurance that his mother still loved him and that nothing much would change.

But Roger knew that everything would in fact change; that he would have two homes to go to in the holidays instead of one; that he would have two lots of allegiances and, if the experience of his friends was anything to go by, one parent would try to play him off against the other.

Tansy had half-expected some sort of reaction in herself when she finally arrived back in Netherwick with all her luggage but minus a home of her own; but all she felt was a sense of relief. A game of charades, of pretending to be something one was not, was over.

Tansy did nothing that spring and summer except recover in the loving bosom of her family. Her father was especially happy to see her, and the two sat a great deal in the garden together talking. Her father was suspiciously and uncharacteristically tactful about not raking over the past. Gilbert was on his mind a lot so he talked about him instead, and about Gilbert's future and that of Kate.

Tansy had thought a lot about it too. At one time she

had wondered if Gilbert would like her to move in with him so that she could help look after the baby, who was by this time nearly a year old. But as Gilbert didn't suggest it neither did she; though she and her father often talked about the problem as they sat on the lawn watching the children at play.

'I'm so happy to have you all here,' Geoffrey said one day, reaching for her hand. 'It's like old times.'

'Isn't it, Dad?' She took his hand and pressed it.

'Do you remember before you went to Australia?'

'I do. Roger was a tiny baby. Only I never went to Australia, Daddy. Michael came back here instead because of Bob's accident.'

'Very tragic that was.' Geoffrey shook his head and then paused as Catherine started signalling from the other door. 'Your mother wants something.'

Tansy was about to get out of her chair but Catherine started walking towards her. 'Don't get up,' she called when she was within earshot. Her face was red and her hands and arms were, as usual, covered with flour. Now that she had four additional people in the household she was in her element, forever baking and preparing meals.

'Gilbert is coming over with baby and Richard Monk. I said they should all stay for lunch.'

'Have you *enough* for everyone, Mother?' Tansy asked.

'More than enough. We have a large piece of beef and plenty of vegetables. It's like old times,' she said happily, 'all these people here.'

As she returned to the kitchen Geoffrey smiled after her. 'Your mother loves all this.'

'I don't know how she does it.'

'She loves it. She loves to work and to keep busy. This reminds *her* of old times too. She likes that, the family, and so do I.'

'But we never had as many people as we have now,' Tansy remarked.

'We have.' Her father began to count on his fingers. 'We had Edward and Emily, Jeremy, you, Gilbert . . .' Geoffrey paused. 'No, we never had Edward *and* Emily here did we? I'm getting confused. I'm too old. Do you know, Tansy,' he pressed her hand again, 'I hardly ever think of poor Edward. He has been dead twenty years. I can't believe it. I don't suppose you remember him at all, do you?'

'Only hazily,' Tansy said guiltily. 'I confuse him in my mind with Jeremy.'

'One should never forget the dead.' Geoffrey sighed deeply. 'If Edward had been buried here we would have his grave somewhere to visit and remind us. We forget the dead too quickly if there are no visible signs.'

Tansy gently stroked his hand because she knew that he was also thinking of Eileen.

'Who's Richard Monk?' her father said after a pause during which he wiped a tear from his eye.

'Eileen's uncle. Her father's brother. He was one of the godparents at Kate's baptism.'

'Does he live locally?'

'I think he's looking for somewhere. I'm not too sure.'

'What does he do?'

'He was a mining engineer in Africa. He decided to retire and farm in the Dales. That's what he told me, but I haven't seen him since the christening.'

'Is he married?'

'I think he was married. I really don't know much about him,' Tansy replied rather irritably. 'I don't know why *you* should be so interested.'

'I just wondered why he was coming over with Gilbert.' Her father was surprised by her reaction, a little taken aback.

'Because he's the baby's great-uncle,' Tansy said. 'Obviously he has an interest in her.'

'Oh, I see.'

About half an hour later Gilbert drove up with Kate in a carrycot which was brought onto the lawn by her great-uncle, Richard. He seemed surprised to see Tansy and held out his hand.

'How are you?'

'Fine,' Tansy said shaking his hand. 'How have you been?'

'I've been very well. And you?' Richard put down the carrycot while Gilbert, who was carrying a rug and various toys and bits and pieces to keep the baby happy, knelt on the grass.

'I've been very well, thank you.' Tansy moved up to make room for the chairs which Roger had been asked by his grandmother to bring over.

'Just visiting, are you?' Richard looked curiously at her.

'Well, I'm staying for a bit.'

'Oh, that's nice.'

'Tansy and Michael have separated,' Gilbert said, taking Kate from her cot. 'I don't know why you don't say so.'

'Not *everyone* is interested in my marital affairs, Gilbert.' Tansy in her turn was surprised by her brother's uncharacteristic sharpness.

'I'm very sorry to hear that.' Richard seemed embarrassed. 'I would never have brought it up if I'd known.'

'You didn't. Gilbert did.' Tansy gave him a reassuring smile. 'Now can we talk about something else?'

Despite the awkward beginning it was a happy occasion. The children were given their lunch out of doors because it was so fine, and the adults had plenty of room in the dining room. Catherine happily bustled back and forth assisted by Tansy who had introduced Richard to her children and found him quite agreeably relaxed.

'How are you getting on with your hunt for a farm?' she asked him.

'I think I've found one,' Richard replied. 'It's not too far from my brother, so he can help me to get started. I was toying with the idea of going in with him, but I think being a neighbour is better.'

'How *is* he?' Catherine stood at the head of the table carving while Tansy passed round the plates and the vegetables. 'I think we really should ask him over more often.'

'He is very well,' Richard said. 'He's very independent. He has accepted that his daughter died from a medical condition that no one could be blamed for. He was always a solitary man. He enjoys solitude. That's why both he and Eileen were so quiet.'

Tansy looked over at Gilbert who had Kate on a high chair next to him and was feeding her mashed-up food. She was now a beautiful, healthy baby who was clearly of a happy and equable disposition. It was difficult to say quite who she resembled. It was nearly a year now since Eileen had died and Tansy thought that, at last, Gilbert seemed to have come to terms with her death too; but what was his future alone in that large house he had bought to share with her and, perhaps, fill with more children?

At the end of the meal Geoffrey, who had been sitting at the top of the table, called for silence and slowly got to his feet. In his right hand he clasped a glass of wine which he held aloft.

'I want to say just before we disperse,' he began with a look at his wife, 'how happy Catherine and I are to have our family with us again: Tansy, Gilbert and their children. It is a long, long time since we sat at this table together and the sight of dear little Kate with her father, and the sound of Tansy's children running about outside gives me, as their grandfather, a deep feeling of pleasure. There is *plenty* of room in this house for you all; and if Gilbert ever decides he wants to live here, or Tansy that she will stay, we shall be overjoyed. Thank you for being here.'

'Thank you, Dad,' Gilbert said. 'That was very nicely put.'

'I want you to think about it seriously, my son,' Geoffrey replied, from the far end of the table. 'I'm making a suggestion you should consider.'

After lunch Tansy helped her mother clear away and then she and Julia helped with the dishes. Geoffrey went up to his room for his usual afternoon nap and Gilbert took Kate for a walk round the garden. Richard also offered to help with the dishes and Tansy said to him:

'I can see you are a very useful man.'

'I am,' he laughingly caught the tea towel she threw him. 'Wasn't Michael?'

'No, he was not,' Tansy winked at her mother who had her arms in the sink. 'And neither was my father. Gilbert is good with the baby but not in the house.'

'Things are changing,' Richard carefully dried a plate he had taken from the draining board. 'I can look after myself quite well. Women are beginning to assert themselves. I think that's right. I don't think a woman's place *is* in the home or by the sink.'

'I do.' Catherine leaned for a moment with her arms in the suds to her elbows. 'I think women are meant to be domesticated. I brought Tansy up to be a good cook, to know what to do in the house.'

'And look where that got me,' Tansy replied with a rueful smile. She had left Richard to continue drying while she began to put away the cutlery, the plates and the glasses. Julia had been allowed to go back to her games on the lawn.

'That wasn't your fault,' her mother said. 'That was Michael's. He had a wonderful wife and he didn't appreciate her.'

'Mother, I really don't want to talk about it.' Tansy looked over at Richard who appeared not to be listening but, later, when they were sitting under the elm in the garden drinking coffee, he said:

'I *am* very sorry about your domestic troubles. You needn't be embarrassed with me. I feel part of the family. Besides, something similar happened to me. My wife went off with another man. It affected me very much and, at the time, made me very bitter. That's why I travelled so much to try and get over it.'

'And did you?' Tansy asked.

'Eventually. It is inevitable one feels bitterness, sadness and humiliation. I imagine there's a lot you're hiding under that calm exterior.'

Richard looked at her shrewdly and Tansy decided she really liked him very much. At first she had thought his personality too subdued, too negative but, maybe, that's because she was used to the exuberance of Michael. Richard was a quiet, thoughtful man. He was different from Michael in every way. Michael was a strong character; but Richard's strength came from an inner certainty, how she didn't quite know. She could see him as a good friend, someone one could turn to. She couldn't see him as a husband, but she wasn't looking for one. That kind of relationship wouldn't figure in her mind for a long, long time to come.

Tansy said, after a few moments' thought; 'If you mean I'm bottling a lot up, you're wrong. I went through it all with Michael years ago. We drifted apart. Of course

I was shocked he had another woman in mind, but I don't know why I should have been. We lived in that kind of society where it was happening to people all the time. No one was really faithful for long to anyone else. Why shouldn't it happen to me? I didn't even think about it. I was too naïve. A country girl. I should never have left Netherwick, where I belonged.'

Richard, listening carefully, threw his cigarette on the ground and put his foot on it. Tansy saw him lean his head against his hands and look at the sky as though, for the first time for a long while, he felt really relaxed.

'Would you like to drive out and see the property I have in mind one day?' he said, continuing to look not at her but at the sky. 'I'd appreciate your honest opinion.'

Chapter 24

'I don't know why you don't start asking her out, courting her properly,' Anthony Monk sternly addressed his brother who was sitting in an embrasure by the kitchen window going through notices from estate agents. 'She seems to be on your mind.'

The farmer sat at the wide deal table doing the weekly accounts for the farm, a job that had once been done by Eileen. But in the last two years he had got used to doing almost everything for himself: he was a self-contained, self-controlled, very lonely man.

He enjoyed having the company of his brother, but he knew he was restless. He didn't seem to know what he wanted to do and, in Anthony's opinion, Richard was in love with Tansy Garrett; but could not, or would not, admit it to himself.

Richard's failure to reply now to his question was typical. Yet it didn't surprise him; they were alike as brothers, taciturn, reluctant to share their most intimate thoughts even with a blood relation, just as he, Anthony, had never told a soul how much he still grieved for Eileen, and always would.

Richard finished looking through the material that arrived every day from estate agencies scattered throughout the county, and then tossed it in a heap on the window seat.

'Any good?' Anthony asked, looking up from his neat columns of figures.

'There's a farm for sale near Barden. That might be worth looking at.'

'That's not far from where Tansy's brother lives, Jeremy, I mean,' Anthony remarked, glancing down at his papers again. 'The one that's a bit daft in the head.'

Richard, smiling to himself, got out a cigarette. Anyone who did anything the least out of the ordinary was, to someone like his brother, sure to be a bit 'daft'. Writing books was definitely on a par with madness.

'To answer your first question,' Richard said ponderously, as though he had carefully weighed it up, 'Tansy's a married woman. I don't think it right to start asking her out until she's free.'

'But when will that be?' Anthony grunted without raising his head.

'She's getting a divorce. She knows how I feel about her; but she's not sure in her own mind. She say's she's not ready to have a relationship with anyone else and I respect that. I can wait.' Richard put a match to his cigarette and puffed away at it happily. He could wait, and it was with Tansy in mind that he was looking for just the right property; somewhere with a view, and where she had plenty of room for her horse paddock and chickens. He'd see to that all right.

In fact Tansy and Richard regularly saw each other because of their mutual interest in baby Kate; but there were always people about and they were seldom, if ever, alone. There was between them, however, a sense of camaraderie that those around them could not but be aware of and, secretly, rejoice in. Catherine thought they were very well suited; Gilbert liked him, and even Geoffrey thought he was a man who was out of the ordinary: a well-educated man who had travelled abroad and was, above all, sound. 'Sound' to Geoffrey meant having both financial and moral integrity; and he approved of the subtle, undemonstrative way that

Richard made known his interest in Tansy. They mainly met in groups on family occasions: dinner parties, Sunday lunch and so on, so that there was no talk in the town, no breath of scandal.

After all that had happened in his family Geoffrey was, at least, thankful for that.

As for Tansy, she went about her business as though there was no such person in her life as Richard Monk. As, in fact, was the case. She liked him but she didn't think she loved him. She could see that he would make an admirable husband and stepfather for her children; but, in a marriage, one needed more than that. She felt that she was still suspended in some spot midway between loving Michael, and liking, even being attracted by, Richard. Both men were different; but there was a certain sterling quality about Richard that Michael lacked. Michael was brilliant, mercurial, whereas Richard was what one would call stolid, not because he was dull or boring; but in the sense of being dependable, a man of the country with deep roots. She was quite sure that Richard would be faithful and would never dream of deceiving his wife with another woman.

But all this was a long time off, in Tansy's view. It might be years before she could make up her mind and, by that time, Richard might have found someone else to marry. He was looking for a farm and wanted to settle. Tansy had no claim on him and would never stand in his way. As she was not free to commit herself she didn't expect him to wait for her, just in case, just in the hope . . .

So her life went on as usual, the welfare of the children taking up a lot of her time. Frank, particularly, missed his father in a way she had not expected him to. In fact, all three children felt the effects of the break, in spite of the solidarity and support of their friends in similar situations. The reality of separated families wasn't half the fun they had supposed.

Tansy knew they would hate to think there might possibly be another man in her life; so she was very circumspect in her attitude to Richard, taking special care not to appear too intimate, too friendly with him when the children were around. But it wasn't difficult. They seemed to regard him as a kind of uncle to them as well as Kate, and happily accepted him as a member of their extended family now that they were living in Netherwick.

Tansy still felt it important to a acquire her own home, and while Richard continued his search, so did she. They followed separate paths in their quest but often converged by chance, encountering each other in the offices of estate agents particularly. But as they were each looking for different types of property there was no rivalry or sense of competition, although there might have been an unspoken hope on Richard's part that he would find what he wanted before Tansy.

However, he was wrong. By Christmas Tansy found a house which she considered suitable for her and her children. It was situated just outside Netherwick on the Skipton road, perched on a hill with an attractive view both of the town and the surrounding Dales. She was five minutes from her parents and about a quarter of an hour away from Gilbert by car. Not too far away were Jeremy and Emily living their chaste, celibate life together; yet finding increasing happiness and peace in each other's proximity.

The house, appropriately named Crossways, had been built towards the end of the nineteenth century and was made of grey Yorkshire stone. It was a good-sized, double-fronted house, and, although it did not have a stream at the bottom of the garden, or a swimming pool or tennis courts like the house in Kent, it had enough room in its two acres of land for a paddock and a chicken run.

Tansy felt that at last she had a place she could call home. Michael and Laura had been married the moment the decree *nisi* became absolute. It had been a quiet register office wedding at which none of the children had been present. They were not invited. It was as though Michael wished to put that part of his life behind him and begin again with his new wife; but he also had in mind the children's welfare and the possible effect of their jealousy on Laura.

Tansy was beginning life again too. She had a final look round the house before driving down to the estate agents to make the arrangements to purchase it. Michael had told her that all the funds she wanted would be available. He had not placed any limit as to how much she could pay for the house. One had to hand it to Michael; there had been no meanness in him at all. But people also complimented her on the dignified way she had handled their separation. In the interests of both parties, and of their mutual children, compromise and conciliation were the best policy. There was no doubt about that.

Tansy, feeling curiously happy and at ease, did a little shopping in the town before going home to tell her parents that she had made an offer for the new house. This was the part she was dreading because she knew it would make them both unhappy. They very much hoped that she would make her home with them, and had done everything to facilitate this. It was really painful to see the efforts they had gone to and, in a way, it had strengthened her resolution to have a place of her own. Surely they must understand that at her age, and with her responsibilities, she would want her freedom? But, according to her father, she had all the freedom with them that she wanted. They had even suggested dividing the house so that she could be completely self-contained.

All her life Tansy had felt that she had to please other people: her parents, particularly her father, her husband, her children and, now the wheel had gone full circle, it was her parents again. Although in recent years her father's depressions had been much milder — he had gloomy days rather than periods when he withdrew altogether, sometimes for weeks — she knew he would use his health as well as his age to try and blackmail her into doing what he wanted. Accordingly, after she had put her car in the garage, she took a deep breath before opening the front door.

The first thing that struck her about the house was its silence. Usually there was the noise of chatter in the kitchen between her mother and the daily woman, or the sound of a hoover upstairs. Often an old friend or patient of her father would pop in for a chat but just now — it was about noon — the silence was so total, so oppressive it was almost uncanny. For a moment she stood listening, trying to detect any sound at all and then, swiftly, she took off her coat and was about to enter the kitchen when the door of her father's study, where he still spent his mornings, opened and her mother appeared ashen-faced, her hands on both cheeks. After closing the door she stood outside for a moment as if she had not even seen Tansy. Then when Tansy cried: 'Mother! Whatever is the matter?' she raised her finger to her lips. 'Ssshh,' she said.

Catherine drew Tansy along the hall and into the kitchen shutting the door carefully on them both.

'What *is* it mother?' Tansy whispered but already she knew it must have something to do with her father. 'Is Daddy ill?'

'Something absolutely terrible has happened,' her mother said, sitting down, one hand still clasping Tansy's. 'Your father's had the most awful shock.'

'But *what*?' Tansy urged, sitting opposite her.

'It's Gilbert. He wants to give up the practice.'

'What?'

'He came and saw your father this morning after surgery.'

'But what does he want to do?'

'It's not what he *wants* to do. It's what he is *going* to do. His mind is made up. He has even discussed the whole thing with Tom Thackery without so much as a *word* to your father.'

'Well, that doesn't surprise me,' Tansy said, knowing how her father would react. 'What disturbs me is that he didn't discuss it with *me*. What is he going to do?'

'He's going to specialize as he's always wanted to, only in medical research. He's going back to university to take a higher degree. It's all arranged. He's applied and been accepted. By Cambridge.' Her mother's expression suggested that, despite everything, she was still proud of him. 'He must have had it in his mind for months. Perhaps since Eileen died.'

'But he can't take the baby to Cambridge!'

'He wants *me* to look after her until he's found somewhere to live. Of course he won't have the money he has now, being a student again.' Catherine finally let Tansy's hand fall and then shrugged. 'It's all quite settled. Yet still I can't believe it. You think he might at least have *discussed* it with *me*.'

'He knew if he did you would try and put him off,' Tansy said, 'just as you have tried to put me off buying a house. You see, Mother, if one discusses anything in this family that does not please Father – and it *is* Father, after all, whom we're always considering, always *have* considered – he tries to dissuade us. You both always attempt to put us off.'

Tansy was on the verge of telling her mother that she was actually on the point of buying a house, but thought that it would be too much. That, for the moment, would have to wait. She got up and, straightening her skirt, looked at the clock.

'I'd better go and see Father.'

'I wish you would,' her mother said. 'He's in a terrible state. I had to give him one of those strong sedatives Tom prescribed for him. Oh dear,' she continued, shaking her head as she turned to the stove, 'I do wish Gilbert hadn't done it.'

Tansy quietly opened the door to her father's study and found that, as expected, he was slumped in his chair in an attitude of complete dejection.

'Father,' she called, but he didn't even raise his head. When she approached him she saw that his eyes were half-closed, and yet he appeared to be staring out of the window.

'Father,' she called again, kneeling in front of him and taking his limp hand. 'Mother just told me about Gilbert.'

From the tone of her voice one would have thought Gilbert was dead. Swifltly it passed through Tansy's mind how ridiculous it was that one still had to behave like this, even though she was over thirty and the mother of three children. Gilbert would have had much the same kind of trauma when he broke the news of a decision he had, no doubt, correctly made to his father.

'I just don't know how Gilbert could do it,' her father said in a sleepwalker's voice, shaking his head. 'He *promised*.'

'Father,' Tansy said again, shaking his hand, 'he *kept* his promise. He has been in practice here for seven years. If Eileen had lived I have no doubt that that would have been where he would have stayed for the rest of his life.'

'He had no *right* to do it,' Geoffrey went on as if talking to himself.

'Father,' Tansy's voice rose a little, 'he *has* a right. It *is* his life. He has never really been very happy in general practice and yet he kept at it, first for your sake and then for Eileen's.'

'Did you *know* he wasn't happy?' her father looked accusingly at her. 'I didn't. I thought he *was* happy. I knew, of course, how he felt after the death of that dear girl, but I've felt lately he was getting over that; it's nearly two years.'

'He probably seems happier, Father, because he has made up his mind to do what he always wanted to do. It must have taken some time to apply to Cambridge and get the acceptance and so on.'

'That's what I don't like,' her father's anger flared briefly, 'the deceit.'

'But, Father, Gilbert has a right to do as he wants. You can't begrudge him the chance to make something of his life after the terrible disappointment he has had.'

'He could have been happy here, married again. He's still a young man. I wanted to think of him carrying on my practice and after him a son, or daughter, maybe little Kate . . .'

'But, Father, you can't govern people's lives in that way any more and, let's face it, you have always tried to tell us what to do.'

'And I've been *right*,' her father said aggressively. 'I *was* right to tell you not to marry Michael. I *was* right about Emily, and I'm right now about Gilbert. How can he look after a little child on the kind of money he will be getting as a student? He'll be on some kind of grant I expect.'

'If he sells his house he will get quite a lot of money

and, no doubt, he has savings. I think he will have to live carefully, but Gilbert has never been very concerned about material possessions. He wants to fulfil himself as a person, and medical research is the way he thinks he can do that.'

'But he wanted to be a specialist,' her father said peevishly. 'Now it's medical research.'

'Father,' Tansy began to feel angry herself, and let his hand drop abruptly as she got to her feet, 'it is too late to become a consultant. He would have to start at the bottom of the ladder, as a junior registrar. He's out of the race. As it is, it will take him long enough to get a higher degree, and I think that, for *once* in your life, it would be very nice if, instead of being so negative, you supported one of your children in what they wanted to do.'

And suddenly, without even knowing she was going to do it, Tansy left the room feeling that the presence of her selfish father had become intolerable.

She didn't see her brother until much later in the day when, after a meal with her parents, eaten in silence, she drove over to Gilbert's house hoping he would be home. From the lower road she saw that the house lights were on and, as soon as she parked in the drive, the front door opened and Gilbert switched on the light in the porch.

'Tansy,' he cried running down to greet her, hands outstretched. 'I *knew* it would be you.'

He kissed her on the cheek, and drew her into the house. It was very cold outside and she was glad of the warmth indoors. Gilbert helped her off with her coat in the hall and then, together, they went into the drawing room where the curtains were closed and a fire roared in the grate. For a moment or two she stood in front of it, warming her hands.

'So you know,' he said from behind her.

'I wish you'd told me.' She turned to look at him reproachfully. 'I might have helped.'

'Yes, I wish I had now.' Gilbert wearily passed his hand over his eyes. He looked very tired. 'I just wanted to have everything tied up before I told *anyone*. It only came out with Father because he was busy discussing plans for rebuilding the surgery so, on the spur of the moment, I told him.'

'You knew, of course, he'd be terribly upset.'

'Of course. But . . .' Gilbert paused as if at a loss for words.

'I know.' Tansy nodded her head. 'We can't go on letting our lives be dominated by father.'

'Exactly. Father could live until he's ninety still ordering the way we live. It really is time we put a stop to it.'

'I'm just buying a house.' Tansy sat down in a chair close to the fire. 'I went to the estate agent today and made an offer. You can imagine how I felt about that, so I know how you feel. I've been so secretive about it all because Father has plans for me to live with him and Mum permanently. I don't want to do that. I want my own home. And you, Gilbert,' she looked at him and put out her hand, 'I know you've never been happy in general practice.'

'I was happy for a while.' Gilbert took a seat beside her. 'It seemed just the right thing to do when I was married to Eileen. She wasn't very interested in medicine or ambitious, so being the wife of a country doctor suited her. I felt it suited me then, that we would have a large family and live here,' he looked sadly round the room as though it held nothing for him now but memories, 'possibly for the rest of our lives.' He got up suddenly and walked over to the fire, bending to the flames to warm his hands. 'I *can't* go on living here with the ghost of Eileen, however precious it is to me. I simply can't. I see her everywhere. Sometimes I imagine I hear her voice. This house seems to contain the seeds of everything we hoped for, but can now never have. Father says I'll marry again, but I know I shan't. I only ever loved one woman and she is dead. I shall never ever love another.'

Gilbert's voice finally broke and he turned his face away from Tansy. Quickly she rose and put an arm around him, leaning her head against his shoulder.

'I'm with you,' she whispered. 'I'm supporting you. I know you're doing the right thing. When I have my own house I can help Mum look after Kate.'

'As soon as I can I shall have her with me in Cambridge,' Gilbert replied, 'but for the first year I'll be living in college. It was one of the conditions of my acceptance as a research fellow. But I shall come often to see her.'

'I know; but Mum will love having her, and so shall I. In a way you're leaving something of yourself behind.'

Just then the telephone rang and Gilbert checked his watch and said: 'Hell, I'd forgotten I was on call.'

He went into the hall and Tansy could hear his voice raised, she thought, in alarm. She had just reached the door as he put the telephone down and looked at her.

'It's Dad. He's been taken straight to the General.'

Geoffrey Blair died in the small hours of the morning following the heart attack he'd sustained the evening of the day he received Gilbert's news. With him were his three children – Jeremy, Gilbert and Tansy – and his wife Catherine.

He was in his seventy-sixth year and, during his life, he had achieved many things. Yet it was undeniable that, in a curious way, he had used his health throughout his long life to get what he wanted. He had dominated the lives of his family, all of whom still felt a sense of guilt as they saw his coffin lowered into the earth of his beloved Netherwick, the town to which he had first come as a young man over fifty years before.

Jeremy, watching the coffin sink into the earth, felt guilty because he had so often opposed his father, because he had moved out and left him when he went off with Emily. Tansy felt guilty because the very last words to a father she adored had been uttered in tones of anger. But Gilbert felt the most guilty because there was no doubt that, had he stayed on in Netherwick as a country doctor, his father would still be alive. His was the greater guilt; his thoughtlessness the greater crime.

Yet death is never a very tidy thing. As the proverb says: *We know not the day nor the hour*, and it is given to few people to say that they have no guilt at all, no regrets whatever. No memory of injuries, of things done or not done, because the moment of death is always a secret. For everyone there is more than grief; there is anger, pain, remorse, perhaps even a sense of revenge, when laying a loved one to rest.

A month after their father's death Gilbert and Tansy persuaded Catherine to take the cruise around the world they had so often discussed. She had not had a holiday or any time on her own for most of her married life. Gilbert would not be leaving the practice until the autumn when he went to Cambridge; but he did sell his house and move into the family home to be with his mother, his daughter and Tansy, who had given up any idea, for the time being, of purchasing a place of her own.

In an odd sort of way Geoffrey Blair had got his own way, even in death.

Epilogue

1965–1966

In due course Gilbert did as he had always wanted, and left general practice to read for a doctorate in biochemistry at Cambridge. He lived there during term time but made his permanent home with his mother and sister, just as his father had always wanted. His daughter Kate and Tansy's children came to accept the idea of a large extended family as the norm. Roger, Julia and Frank frequently visited their father at his flat on the thirty-fifth floor of one of the towers in the new Barbican building in London. Laura had not realized her dream of having children. Maybe she had, after all, left it too late.

On the anniversary of Geoffrey Blair's death the family gathered at his gravestone to lay flowers and a wreath. The one member missing was Emily who had never forgiven her father-in-law, in the way that he had never forgiven her.

Tansy frequently visited her half-brother and his ex-wife. Jeremy had not succeeded in getting his book published, but he kept on trying. He was cheered up by the many stories he read about other authors who succeeded when they thought all hope had faded.

Jeremy enjoyed his life on the hills among the sheep. His return to the Dales had enhanced his life. He looked well and felt better than he ever had since before the war. He spent his evenings in tranquil contentment sitting on the other side of the fire across from Emily, whom he regarded with gratitude and affection rather than love. Their curious life style seemed to bother everyone else but themselves.

One day, about two years after the death of her father, Tansy was driving home from visiting Emily, after which she'd gone up the Fell to talk to Jeremy. It was a warm spring day, rather unusual for the Dales because the month of April could be bitterly cold. It was nearly Easter time and the lambs were nestling against the sides of their mothers. The children were home from school, but they'd gone with their grandmother on an educational tour of York and so Tansy had something that these days was very unusual: a precious day all to herself.

She left Emily at about four so as to be home in time to get tea and, driving along the familiar Dales road that wound between the hills that she had known all her life, she felt an unusual feeling of contentment, of hope, almost of exhilaration as though there were something special in the air. The grief and guilt occasioned by their father's death had gone, and she and Gilbert had grown used to the fact that they now had their own lives to lead, and could do as they pleased. Once Gilbert had his higher degree he would make a home for his daughter and Tansy was again thinking that, maybe, it was time she began looking for a home of her own, or else she would become as submissive to the needs and wishes of her mother as she had to her father and her husband.

She came to a fork in the road and was about to go left when she saw a figure waving to her from a nearby field. She stopped and, recognizing Richard Monk, backed her car off the main road and drove down a narrow lane by the side of the field. Then she got out and went up to the wall over which Richard was leaning, a grin on his face.

'Come to see me?'

'I'm afraid not,' Tansy said with a teasing smile. 'Have you moved in yet?'

'Not yet. Like to come and see?' Richard gestured towards the farmhouse in the distance.

'I really haven't time . . .' Tansy glanced at her watch. 'The childen have gone with Mother to York . . .'

'Come on. I want *someone* to see my new house.'

Richard vaulted over the wall and Tansy, admiring his athleticism, realized he was still quite young. Well, he was about the same age as Michael, somewhere in his mid-forties. She saw a lot of Richard; she regarded him now as a great friend. He was a frequent guest at the Blair house to visit his great-niece and, some suggested, Tansy herself. Occasionally he invited her for dinner or took her and the family to Sunday lunch at some country restaurant.

Tansy now had her divorce; but the death of her father had concentrated her thoughts elsewhere. It seemed selfish to think about herself when her mother and the children had to be considered. It was a long time since she'd given Richard Monk a serious thought, and he had now bought a smallholding, about five miles from Cragbeck, without consulting her.

Yet one couldn't help liking Richard. He was a good man and a kind and understanding friend. But love? Like Gilbert, she thought she would never fall in love or marry again.

'Give us a lift to the house,' Richard said pointing to her car. 'That way I can compel you to come in.'

'All right,' Tansy laughed, his sense of fun and gaiety was infectious. She thought he was much happier than he used to be. 'But I can't stay long.'

It had taken Richard some time to find the right place. He kept on haring off and then being disappointed. But he had taken his time. He had continued to live with his brother because Eileen's death had shaken him so much, and Anthony needed as many years to recover from his bereavement as his son-in-law.

'I've been dying to see your place, actually,' Tansy

murmured as they came to the turning off the lane that
led to the yard.

'I hope you like it,' Richard said, glancing sideways at
her.

'Oh?' Tansy's heart gave a sudden lurch. 'Why?'

'Because I hope you'll come here a lot with Kate and
your children. It's a big old family house and it would be
nice to have a family in and out of it again.' She could
tell he was putting his words very carefully.

As they got out of the car and she saw the house
clearly for the first time, Tansy instinctively gave a loud
whistle.

'It's *lovely*!' she said. 'Have you exchanged contracts on
it yet?'

'Yesterday,' Richard replied, smiling, his eyes on the
house. 'That's why I'm here today. A few more weeks
and it's mine.'

'It's a beautiful place, I'd no idea it was so big. I see
what you mean about being a family house.'

Tansy felt a little odd, rather peculiar, as she walked
through the front door into the large stone-flagged
hallway. The sunlight flooded in on the white walls, the
old oak beams blackened with age. The house had a
smell that was almost familiar; it gave an impression of
friendliness and charm – a much lived in, happy place.

As Richard took her through the empty rooms she
liked it more and more.

'I wish I'd seen it first,' she announced.

'Why, are you getting ready to move again?'

'I think so, or Mum will keep me there for ever.' As
Tansy looked out of the window she saw at the end of
the field a broad stream that trickled directly into the
Wharfe some two miles down the valley. Above her on
all sides rose the wooded slopes, the green fields of her
native land: Yorkshire. There were already chickens in

the run and cows in the field because she knew that Richard had bought the stock and would run the farm as a going concern. Behind her Richard continued talking, but his voice seemed muted, far away.

Just then, in front of her, a magpie swooped low and poised itself a little unsteadily on the stone wall a few feet away from the house. She shivered instinctively, glancing back into the room at Richard.

'Pardon?' she said apologetically, realizing that while she had been studying the magpie, considering it as a portent, an omen, Richard had been speaking. 'I'm sorry I wasn't listening.'

'I was saying,' Richard said with exaggerated patience, 'that if you like this place, it's yours.'

'Mine?' Tansy gasped with surprise, realizing that, at the same time, he had moved imperceptibly closer to her.

'I'd like you to have it, Tansy, but there is a condition.' He looked nervous and put out a hand towards her. 'I want you to live here, with me. There's plenty of room for a paddock too. The chickens you see, I have already.'

Richard put an arm casually round her waist and gestured towards the countryside that lay within view from the window. 'I had you in mind when I bought it, but I knew that if I asked you first you'd never say "yes".'

'"Yes?"' Tansy's feelings and emotions were confused. 'You mean . . .'

She looked out of the window again and there was the magpie still solo on the wall. It seemed to look at her and, for a few seconds, she looked anxiously at it.

She was a country woman, yes, and she *was* superstitious; most country people were. Just then there was a flapping of wings in front of the window and another magpie, sweeping low, settled on the wall with its mate.

Tansy smiled, her heart filling with sudden joy, and she put one of her hands tightly over Richard's. As he turned her gently to kiss her she saw, or imagined she saw, from the corner of her eye, the magpies on the wall exchange knowing glances. Then they took off from the wall to resume their flight, swooping down towards the river.